Life is sweet with

Jenny
COLGAN

Praise for Jenny Colgan

'This funny, sweet story is Jenny Colgan
at her absolute best'
Heat

'She is very, very funny'
Express

'A delicious comedy'
Red

'Fast-paced, funny, poignant and well observed'
Daily Mail

'Sweeter than a bag of jelly beans …
had us eating up every page'
Cosmopolitan

'A smart, funny story laced with irresistible charm'
Closer

'Chick-lit with an ethical kick'
Mirror

'A quirky tale of love, work and the
meaning of life'
Company

Jenny COLGAN

the Loveliest Chocolate Shop in Paris

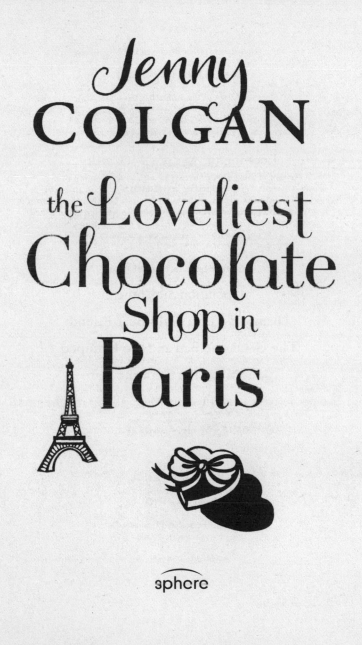

sphere

SPHERE

First published in Great Britain in 2013 by Sphere

A CIP catalogue record for this book
is available from the British Library.

ISBN 978-0-7515-4920-1

Typeset in Caslon by M Rules
Printed and bound in Great Britain by
Clays Ltd, St Ives plc

Papers used by Sphere are from well-managed forests
and other responsible sources.

MIX
Paper from
responsible sources
FSC® C104740

Sphere
An imprint of
Little, Brown Book Group
100 Victoria Embankment
London EC4Y 0DY

An Hachette UK Company
www.hachette.co.uk

www.littlebrown.co.uk

The clue is definitely in the title! If you love chocolate and love Paris (or think you might one day – don't worry, you'll get there. She doesn't change much), then this book was written just for you.

JC xx

A Word From Jenny

There are lots of marvellous artisan chocolate shops in Paris. My favourite is called Patrick Roger, on the rue du Faubourg Saint-Honoré. I would strongly recommend a visit there, and to taste their hot chocolate, whichever season you go. It's run by the eponymous Patrick, who is a curly-haired, twinkly-eyed, roguish-looking chap.

This book is not based on any of those shops in particular, but instead on the principle that when people dedicate their lives to one thing that they really love and have learned a lot about, amazing things can happen.

Somebody once said that the reason we love chocolate so much is that it melts at the same temperature as the inside of our mouths. Scientists also talk about releasing endorphins and so on, which may be the chemical reason for it, but whatever the explanation, it is a wonderful thing.

It's not just women either. I can't even smuggle a packet

of chocolate digestives into my house without my husband sniffing them out and guzzling them. So I've put some really lovely recipes in the book. I like to think that as I get older I can actually cook with chocolate instead of just, you know, accidentally eating it as soon as it gets in the house or sometimes in the car.

When we moved to France a while back (for my husband's work), I was surprised to find that they took chocolate there as seriously as they take any kind of food. La Maison du Chocolat is a really high-end chain and you'll find one in most towns, where you can chat with the chocolatier about what you want and what else you're going to be eating, like discussing wine with a sommelier. Personally I am just as happy with a great big slab of Dairy Milk, or Toblerone, or my absolute fave, Fry's Chocolate Cream (plain). Not everything has to be luxury to be enjoyed. Alas, my children have now reached the age where it's becoming obvious who keeps stealing the Kinder bars out of their party bags. Kids, hum, look, I hate to have to tell you this. It was definitely your dad.

Before we start, I wanted to say a word about language. In my experience, learning another language is really bloody difficult, unless you're one of those people who pick things up in two seconds flat, in which case I would say *bleurgh* (that's me poking my tongue out) to you because I am extremely jealous.

Traditionally, too, when people in books are speaking a foreign language, it's indicated in *italics*. I've chosen not to do that here. Basically, anyone Anna speaks to in Paris is speaking French back to her unless I've mentioned otherwise. To which you and I would think, cor, that's AMAZING, she's learned so fast. Obviously she has lots of lessons with Claire, but if you've ever learnt another language you'll know that you can be totally confident in a classroom, then turn up in the country and everybody goes 'wabbawabbawabbawabbaWAH?' to you at a million miles an hour, and you panic because you can't understand a single bloody word of it. That's certainly what happened to me.

So, anyway, you need to take it on trust that it's exactly the same for Anna, but for the purposes of not repeating myself endlessly and slowing down the story, I've taken out the millions and millions of times she says 'What?' or 'Can you say that again, please?' or needs to check her dictionary.

I do hope you enjoy it, and let me know how you get on with the recipes. And bon appetit!

Jenny x

Chapter One

The really weird thing about it was that although I knew, instantly, that something was wrong – very, very wrong, something sharp, something very serious; an insult to my entire body – I couldn't stop laughing. Laughing hysterically.

I was lying there, covered – drenched – in spilled melted chocolate and I couldn't stop giggling. There were other faces now, looking down at me, some I was sure I recognised. They weren't laughing. In fact they all looked very serious. This somehow struck me as even funnier and set me off again.

From the periphery I heard someone say, 'Pick them up!' and someone else say, 'No way! You pick them up! Gross!' and then I heard someone else, who I thought was Flynn, the new stock boy, say, 'I'll dial 911,' and someone else say, 'Flynn, don't be stupid, it's 999, you're not American,' and someone else say, 'I think you can dial 911 now because there are so many idiots who keep dialling it,' and someone else taking out their phone and saying something about needing an ambulance, which I thought was hilarious as well, and then someone, who was definitely Del, our grumpy old janitor, saying, 'Well, they're probably going to want to throw this batch away then,' and the idea that they might not throw away the enormous vat of chocolate but try and sell it instead when it had landed all over me actually was funny.

After that, thank God, I don't remember anything, although later, in hospital, an ambulance man came over and said I'd been a total bloody nutter in the ambulance, and that he'd always been told that shock affected people in different ways, but mine was just about the differentest he'd ever seen. Then he saw my face and said, 'Cheer up, love, you'll laugh again.' But at that point I wasn't exactly sure I ever would.

♥

'Oh come off it, Debs, love, it's only her foot. It could have been a lot worse. What if it had been her nose?'

That was my dad, talking to my mum. He liked to look on the bright side.

'Well, they could have given her a new nose. She hates her nose anyway.'

That was definitely my mum. She's not quite as good as my dad at looking on the bright side. In fact, I could hear her sobbing. But somehow my body shied away from the light; I couldn't open my eyes. I didn't think it was just a light; it felt like the sun or something. Maybe I was on holiday. I couldn't

'You ought to be able to,' she said. 'You had me.'

'Yeah, kind of,' I muttered.

'You were a good student,' said Claire. 'You showed a real aptitude, I remember.'

Suddenly I flashed back on my first-year report card. In amidst the 'doesn't apply herself' and 'could do better' I suddenly remembered that my French mark had been good. Why hadn't I applied myself?

'I thought school was stupid,' I said.

Claire shook her head. 'But I've met your parents, they're lovely. You're from such a nice family.'

'You don't have to live with them,' I said, then felt guilty that I'd been mean about them. They'd been in to see me every single day, even though, as Dad complained almost constantly, the parking charges were appalling.

'You still live at home?' she asked, surprised, and I felt a bit defensive.

'Neh. I lived with my boyfriend for a bit, but he turned out to be a pillock, so I moved back in, that's all.'

'I see,' said Claire. She looked at her watch. It was only nine thirty in the morning. We'd already been up for three hours and lunch wasn't till twelve.

'If you like . . .' she said. 'I'm bored too. If I taught you some French, you could read to me. And I would feel less like a big sick bald plum who does nothing but dwell on the past and feel old and stupid and useless. Would you like that?'

I looked down at the magazine I was holding, which had

15

an enormous picture of Kim Kardashian's arse on it. And she had ten toes.

'Yeah, all right,' I said.

♥

1972

'It's nothing,' the man was saying, raising his voice to be heard over the stiff sea breeze and the honking of the ferries and the rattle of the trains. 'It is tiny ... look, La Manche. You can swim it.'

This did nothing to stem the tide of tears rolling down the girl's cheeks.

'I would,' she said. 'I will swim it for you.'

'You,' he said, 'will go back and finish school and do wonderful things and be happy.'

'I don't want to,' she groaned. 'I want to stay here with you.'

The man grimaced and attempted to stop her tears with kisses. They were dripping on his new, oddly shiny uniform.

'Well, they will make me march up and down like an ape, you see. And I will be an idiot with nothing else to do and nothing else to think about except you. Ssh, bout de chou. Ssssh. We will be together again, you'll see.'

'I love you,' said the girl. 'I will never love anyone so much in my entire life.'

'I love you too,' said the man. 'I care for you and I love you and I will see you again. I shall write you letters and you shall finish school and you will see, all will be well.'

The girl's sobs started to quieten.

'I can't ... I can't bear it,' she said.

'Ah, love,' said the man. 'That is what it is; the need to bear things.'

He buried his face in her hair.

'Alors, my love. Come back, soon.'

'I will,' said the girl. 'Of course I will come back soon.'

Chapter Two

My two brothers stopped coming to visit me the instant it was clear I wasn't actually going to snuff it. I loved them, but at twenty-two and twenty you have a lot of other things to do that don't involve talking to your weird big sister about her weird accident in hospital. Cath, bless her, of course she was brilliant, I couldn't do without her, but she worked really long hours at the hair salon and it was a forty-five-minute bus ride from the hospital so she couldn't come that often, though I so appreciated it when she did. She liked to tell me who'd won hideous hairstyle of the week and how she'd tried to convince them to go for something different but they'd fought on regardless, desperate to emulate Cheryl Cole or someone from *TOWIE* even though they had short greasy brown wisps that wouldn't take an extension so they'd be back in a week shouting and screaming and threatening to sue because what was left of their hair was falling out.

'I tell 'em,' said Cath. 'They don't listen. Nobody listens to me.'

She made me look in the bathroom mirror and tell myself I'd be all right. I looked absolutely hellish. My eyes were bloodshot all the time from the antibiotics and looked a bit yellow; my curly hair – normally blonde, with the help of Cath, but now all growing out – was frizzy and all over the place, like a crazy person, and my pale skin was the same colour and texture as hospital porridge. Cath tried to say encouraging things, mostly because she's like that, and also because she has to say those sort of things in the salon to sixty-year-old women who are fourteen stone overweight and come in asking to look like Coleen Rooney, but we both knew it was a vain effort.

So a lot of the time it was just me and Claire. It was a weird situation, in that we got to know each other a lot faster than I suppose we would have otherwise. But I also realised, with a bit of a shock, that I was kind of glad, really, that I wasn't with Darr any more. He was a nice bloke and everything, but not much of a one for conversation. If he'd had to come and see me every day it would have been a disaster; by day three we'd have been talking about nothing but chips and Man City. Without the possibility of a snog (I still had a tube in my arm and a tube up my pee hole – sorry – and even if I hadn't, there was something about only having eight toes that made the idea of ever feeling sexy again rather unlikely), I don't know how we'd have carried on, exactly. Being sick gave me a lot of perspective. I'd been gutted when we broke up (he kept trying to

19

be unfaithful, and in a town the size of Kidinsborough, that didn't stay secret for long. His defense – that he'd been serially unsuccessful – didn't help him), but the only thing I missed now was the little flat we'd rented together.

But he gave my brother Joe a box of chocolates to pass on to me (which Joe promptly ate, being twenty), and texted me to see if I was okay. I think he might even have taken me back, toes or no toes. I had heard his pulling had been about as successful single as it had been with me, though that might just have been Cath trying to make me feel better.

Without Claire I think I would have gone mad with boredom. I'd bought a cheap smartphone six months before and now cursed my luck for not having something to play with that had anything better than, basically, Snake on it. I read lots of books, but there's a difference between reading a book when you're tired after working all day and desperate to get into the bath and enjoy a few pages with a cup of tea even when your twenty-year-old brother is banging on the door shouting about hair gel, and reading a book because there's nothing else to do.

Plus I was on lots of medication and it was a bit tricky to concentrate. There was a telly in the far corner blaring away, but it was set to the same channel all day and I got really tired of watching loud fat people shouting at each other, so I kept my headphones on. It was kind of great to see people who came to visit, except I had nothing to say to them except how much fluid my wound was draining and other fricking disgusting things, so I didn't really enjoy chatting.

The nurses were a great laugh, but they were always in a rush, and the doctors were always knackered-looking and most of them not really interested – they were all interested in my foot, but it might as well have been connected to a cat for all the attention they gave me above the ankle. And the other ladies on the ward were old. Really, really old. 'Where am I? Is this the war?' old. I felt sorry for them and their anxious, exhausted-looking families coming in every day to hear 'no change', but I couldn't really communicate with them. I hadn't realised that young people – youngish – didn't often get that sick. Or if they did, they were over in surgery, having glamorous bits chopped off, or in accident and emergency recovering from a fabulous night out that got a bit out of hand, not here in medicine, which was ageing patients with a million things wrong with them and nowhere else to go.

So it was an absolute relief to sit calmly with Claire and repeat, steadily, avoir and être and remember the difference between the recent past and the ongoing past and learn how to roll my r's properly. ('You must,' she said, over and over again, 'work so hard on your accent. Be French. Have the Frenchiest French accent of everyone. Do a massive Inspector Clouseau and wave your arms about.' 'I feel like an idiot.' I said. 'You will,' agreed Claire. 'Until you speak some French and a French person understands you.')

We puzzled our way through children's books and flash cards and test extracts. It was good for me to realise that Claire was enjoying it too, much more than her short, slightly awkward conversations with her sons – she had been divorced for a long time, I found out.

Finally, eventually, like a musician tentatively picking up an instrument, we started to speak a little – haltingly, painfully – in French. I found it easier to listen than to speak, but Claire was endlessly patient, and so gentle when she corrected me that I couldn't believe what an idiot I had been not to pay closer attention to this wonderful teacher when I'd had the chance.

'Did you live in France – est-ce que tu habitait en France?' I asked slowly one damp spring morning. The green buds on the trees outside seemed to be enjoying the rain, but nobody else was. It was always the same temperature inside the hospital anyway, a hermetically sealed ship disconnected from the outside world.

'A long time ago,' she replied, not quite meeting my eye. 'And not for very long.'

♡

1971–2

It was, Claire knew, the daftest form of rebellion. Hardly rebellion at all really. Still. She sat at the breakfast table, staring fixedly at her Ready Brek. She was too old, at seventeen, for Ready Brek, she knew. She'd rather just have coffee, but it wasn't a fight she was prepared to take on. On this other matter, however ...

'You're not wearing those things to my church.'

'Those things' referred to a new pair of flares Claire had saved up for. She'd had a Christmas holiday job in Chelsea Girl.

Her father had had a very difficult time reconciling himself to the fact that although she was willing to take on the mantle of hard work (which he did believe in, very much), it was clearly taking place in a den of iniquity that sold harlots' clothing. Her mother, as so often, must have had a word behind the scenes; she had never, and never would, dared contradict the Reverend Marcus Forest in public. Few would.

Claire glanced down at her denim-clad legs. She had spent her entire life being relentlessly unfashionable. Her father thought fashion was a fast track to eternal torment. Her mother instead had made her pinafores and long school skirts and dirndls for Sundays.

But working had opened her eyes; made her feel more grown-up. The other girls in the shop were twenty, older even, worldly-wise. They discussed nightclubs and boys and make-up (strictly banned at Claire's house), and they found Claire's life (everyone knew the Reverend) hilarious. The older, sophisticated girls took her under their wing, made her dress in the latest clothes, cooing over her slender figure and undyed pale blonde hair, which she always thought made her look washed out (although there weren't many mirrors in the house for her to check in). No boy had ever asked her out at school. She had told herself that it was because of her father, but inside she feared that it was something else; that she was too quiet and uninteresting, and her pale hair and eyebrows meant she sometimes felt she was barely there at all.

As the days passed, she grew steadily bolder. It finished nastily one weekend, when her father was trying to write his Christmas sermon and she arrived back from the shop with her eyes heavily made up; dramatically kohled in a shimmering emerald green with brown shading all the way round the socket and – most shocking of all – her eyebrows coloured in dark brown with a pencil one of the girls had produced. She had stared and stared at the reflection in the mirror of the strange, mysterious creature she had become; no longer pale and colourless. She did not look skinny and gaunt; instead she was slender and glamorous. Cassie had pulled her pale hair off her face and pinned back her childish fringe, and it added years to her. All the girls had laughed, and insisted she come out with them that Saturday.

Claire didn't think so.

Her father stood up, furious.

'Take it off,' he said, resignedly. 'Not under my roof.'

He didn't get angry, or shout. He never did, that wasn't his way. He just told her exactly how it would be. In Claire's mind, the voice of her father and the voice of God, in whom she believed completely, were very much the same. There was no doubt.

Her mother followed her to the avocado-coloured bathroom and gave her a consoling cuddle.

'You do look lovely,' she said, as Claire furiously wiped her face with a brown flannel. 'You know,' she added, 'in a year or two you can go off to secretarial school, or teacher training, and then you can do whatever you like. It's not long to wait, my darling.'

But to Claire it felt like a million years away. All the other girls got to dress up and go out and have boyfriends with tinny old cars or terrifying motorbikes.

'That job . . . I thought it was a good idea, but . . .' Her mother shook her head. 'You know what he's like. It's driving him crazy. I just thought you needed a bit of independence . . .'

Later that night, Claire heard a whispered conversation going on *downstairs. She could tell by the tone that it was about her. It was difficult being an only child sometimes. Her father seemed to treat her as someone who wanted nothing more than to get into terrible trouble, which drove her mad. Her mother did what she could, but when the Reverend went into one of his glowering sulks, it could last for days, and it made the atmosphere in the house very unpleasant. He was used to the two women in his life doing his bidding without question. But Claire yearned, more than anything else, for a bit of freedom.*

The job finished at the beginning of January. The shop had offered to keep her on as a Saturday girl, and she was desperate to do it, but it wasn't worth the grief. So she carried on working hard at school, even though she knew she wouldn't be going to university; Marcus wasn't a huge fan of it for women and wanted to keep her close to home instead of going off to York or Liverpool. Sometimes, late at night, after her parents had gone to bed, she'd stay up late watching the movie on BBC2 and feeling a tiny clutch of panic around her heart that she would have to stay in Kidinsborough for ever, watching her parents get older and older.

Two months later, in early March, her mother came to breakfast with a sly expression on her face and an airmail envelope in her hand. It had red and blue stripes round the edges of the pale blue paper, and looping, exotic-looking handwriting on the front.

'Well, it's all decided,' she said, as the Reverend looked up from his grapefruit half.

'What?' he growled.

'For the summer. Claire has been invited to go and au pair.'
Claire had never even heard the expression.

'You're going to be a nanny,' her mother explained. 'For my penpal.'

'That Frenchwoman?' said Marcus, folding his Daily Telegraph. 'I thought you'd never met.'

'We haven't,' said Ellen, proudly.

Claire looked from one to the other. She didn't know anything about this.

'Who is she?'

'Her name is Marie-Noelle and we've been penpals since school,' said Ellen, and Claire suddenly remembered the Christmas cards that arrived each year with 'Meilleurs Voeux' on them. 'We've kept writing to each other . . . here and there of course, not very often. But I know she has two children now, and I wrote and asked if she would like to take you for the summer. And she said yes! You will look after the children; she has a cleaner, she says here . . . goodness.'

Her mother's face went a little strained.

'I hope they're not terribly posh,' she went on, looking around at the nice but plainly furnished vicarage. A churchman's stipend didn't go far, and Claire had always known better than to expect new things.

'I don't care if they're posh. Are they decent people?' said Marcus.

'Oh yes,' said Ellen, cheerfully. 'There's a little boy and a little girl; Arnaud and Claudette. Aren't those the loveliest names?'

Claire's heart was starting to race.

'Where . . . whereabouts in France?'

'Oh, sorry, where's my head?' said Ellen. 'Paris, of course.'

Chapter Three

The settlement from the chocolate factory, which was really a tiny goodwill gesture, was not at all life-changing. It was barely changing anything once I'd paid off my credit card. I wondered if we should have maybe got more, seeing as I now walked with a pronounced limp and had nearly died and everything, but the factory said that bit was the hospital's fault and the hospital said I was getting better now and getting me better was technically all they had to do really. I did mention to Dr Ed that actually if the hospital hadn't let me get so sick they would have been able to reattach my toes, and he smiled and patted my hand in the manner of doctors he'd seen on television and told me that if I ever had any questions to go right ahead, which completely bamboozled me as I thought I'd just asked one, then gave me a smile and a wink and floated on to sit on Claire's bed.

It was time to go home. After dreaming for so long of

being set free, I suddenly realised I didn't actually want to go. Or rather, that it would be weird to lose the institutionalised days of drugs and meals and physio and not having to focus on anything else but getting better.

Now I had to face the world again and find a new job (it was a feature of the settlement that I didn't go back to Braders, presumably in case I had another one-in-a-million freak accident. If anything, I would have thought I'd have been a safer bet than other people, statistically speaking).

And I was going to miss Claire. We'd been chatting more and more in French, to the annoyance of almost everyone, and it was truly the one good thing in my life, demonstrating that I could learn something, that I had a new skill. Everything else was just dread. There weren't any jobs, I knew that much. Cath said I could come and sweep up in the hairdressing salon, but that paid about absolutely nothing, and I wasn't that good at bending down without falling over yet. On the up side, I'd lost a stone. That was the only up side. I wouldn't recommend my method of losing a stone.

I told Claire about my worries, and she looked pensive.

'I've been thinking,' she said.

'What?'

'Well,' she said. 'I knew . . . I knew someone in Paris who worked in chocolate. It was a long time ago, though. I don't know what he's doing now.'

'Ooh,' I said. 'A young flirtation?'

Her thin face took on a little colour.

'I don't think that's any of your business.'

'Were you madly in lurve?'

We'd got to know each other well enough that I could tease her, but she could still get a teacherly glint in her eye. She did so now.

'He is not,' she mused, glancing out of the window, 'very good at writing letters. But I will try. I shall ask Ricky to use that email thingy when he comes. You can find anyone these days, can't you?'

'You can,' I said. 'But if he's a friend of yours, why haven't you been back to Paris for so long?'

Claire's lips pursed. 'Well, I was busy raising a family. I had a job. I couldn't just jump on a plane whenever I felt like it.'

'Hmm,' I said, suspicious. She was very touchy all of a sudden.

'You could, though,' said Claire. 'You can do whatever you like.'

I laughed. 'I don't think so. Hopalong Cassidy, that's me.'

♡

The impact – the emotional impact – of the accident didn't really hit until I went back home to Mum and Dad's. In hospital I'd been – well, special, I suppose. I'd got flowers and gifts and was the centre of everyone's attention; people brought me drugs and asked after me, and even though it was kind of horrible, I was being taken care of.

Home, though – it was just home. The boys clattering in late at night, grumbling because they had to share a room again; Mum fussing around predicting doom for my chances of finding another job, and worrying that they would cut disability living allowance, to which I said, don't be stupid, I'm not disabled, and we both looked at my crutches and then she would sigh again. My face in the mirror: my pale blue eyes looked so tired; my fair-ish hair, without its usual highlights by Cath, just looked colourless; I had lost weight, but because I hadn't moved around at all I just looked slack and saggy. I used to love putting on make-up to get ready for a night out, but it had been so long I'd kind of forgotten how, and the drugs had made my skin so dry.

That's when I really got sad. I cried in my little childhood bed, I slept later and later in the morning, I became less and less interested in doing my exercises, and my friends' stories about new boyfriends and fall-outs and all those sorts of things sounded completely inconsequential to me now. I knew my parents were worried about me but I just didn't know what to do about it. My foot was slowly healing, apparently, but I could feel my toes, feel them all the time. They itched, they twitched, they hurt and I lay awake at night staring at the ceiling and listening to the boiler make the same noises it had made since my childhood and thinking, what now? What now?

♡

1972

*Her mother had wanted to accompany her, have a 'girls' day out'
in London, but the Reverend had looked very suspicious indeed
and hummed and hawed about it. Seemingly the fleshpots of Paris
wouldn't be quite as wicked as the den of iniquity that was
London – he hadn't, thought Claire, quite got the idea of 1972. He
had demanded numerous and repeated reassurances, from both her
mother and from Mme Lagarde on the telephone, that the house
was extremely traditional and strict and that it would be nothing
but childcare and learning another language, a refinement in young
ladies the Reverend did approve of. So after endless lists and
imprecations about how she was expected to behave – Claire was
already absolutely terrified of Mme Lagarde, imagining her as
posh, rich and demanding, and didn't know how she was going to
cope with small children she could barely talk to – he had driven
her to the railway station under a sky threatening large amounts
of rain.*

*Rainie Collender, the school bully, had cornered her before school
broke up.*

'Off to get even more stuck-up?' she sniffed.

*Claire did what she always did. She kept her head down as
Rainie's cronies burst out laughing and moved away as quickly as
possible to try and escape their gaze. It rarely succeeded. She couldn't
wait for the holidays. However much she was dreading looking after
the French brats, it had to be better than being stuck here in
Kidinsborough.*

*As the train pulled out of Crewe, she opened her Tupperware
sandwich box, nervous and jittery and filled with the sense that she*

was leaving, going on a journey by herself, and that it was going to be vastly important.

Inside the box was a little note from her mother.

'Have a wonderful time', it said. Not 'behave yourself' or 'don't forget to clean up after yourself' or 'don't go out alone'. Just 'Have a wonderful time.'

Claire was quite a young seventeen. She'd never really thought about her mother's life in any terms apart from the fact that she was just there, providing meals, washing their clothes, agreeing with the Reverend whenever he had something new to say about the long-haired youths with hippy values who had reached even Kidinsborough. It didn't cross her mind that her mother might have been jealous.

♥

Claire was nervous getting on the ferry, terrified she wouldn't know what to do. It was absolutely huge. The only boat she'd ever been on was a pedalo at Scarborough. The great white ship seemed to her romantic, the smell of the diesel, the blast of the horn as it moved slowly away from the huge terminal at Dover, lined with adventurous-looking people with estate cars piled high with tents and sleeping bags, and, even more exotically, Citroën 2CVs with real live French people opening their picnics (a lot more exotic than Claire's meat paste sandwiches) with actual bottles of wine and glasses and long sticks of bread. She gazed around, drinking it all in, then went up to the very front of the boat – it was a blowy day, white clouds flicking across the sky – and looked hungrily back towards England – her very first time of leaving it –

then forwards towards France. She thought she had rarely felt more alive.

♥

Claire had left a message on my phone. 'Come and have a coffee.' She'd been discharged, temporarily, and she sounded a little breathy, a little tentative. I called her back – this was one thing I could manage – and arranged to meet up in the cosy bookshop coffee shop, where I thought she'd be more comfortable.

Her nice daughter-in-law Patsy dropped her off and made her promise not to buy too many books, and Claire rolled her eyes when she left and said she loved Patsy, but everyone seemed to equate being sick with being four, and then she remembered she didn't have to tell me that and we cheered ourselves up with imitations of Dr Ed sitting on the bed doing his empathising.

Then there was a pause during which in a normal conversation someone would have said, 'Hey, you look well' or, 'You've cut your hair' or 'You look healthy' (code for 'cor, you've got fat', as everybody knows), but neither of us could say anything. In the hospital, with its crisp white sheets, and Claire's spotless cream pyjamas, she didn't look well but she seemed to belong. Out here in public she looked terrifying. So thin that she might break, a scarf tied artfully around her head that served only to announce: 'I've had cancer for so long I've got really good at tying scarves' and a smart dress that would have looked rather nice if it had fitted her. She looked ... wow, she looked sick.

I got up to go and fetch us some coffee and chocolate brownie cake, even though she had said she didn't want any and I said she would when she tasted the home-made stuff they did in here and she smiled thinly and said of course, that would be great, in a way that wouldn't have fooled a horse. I was conscious of her eyes on me as I limped across the floor. I still wasn't at all confident with my stick, and had basically decided to get rid of it. Cath kept trying to get me to come out, saying that everyone was dying to hear all about it, but that thought filled me with total horror. I did, though, desperately need to get my hair done. And some new clothes. I was in my daggiest old jeans and a striped top that had taken absolutely no effort whatsoever, and it showed.

'So,' said Claire when I got back. The lady behind the counter had agreed to bring the tray over, thank goodness. We shared a look.

'Crocks' corner,' I said, and Claire smiled. The lady didn't. I think she was concerned that we were about to throw up or fall over in her lovely café. The chocolate brownie cake was exceptionally good, though, and worth all the weird looks we were getting.

'So,' said Claire again. She suddenly flushed a little and looked excited. 'I got a letter.'

'An actual letter?' I said, impressed. I never got letters, just instant messages from Cath about the latest bloke she'd got her eye on.

She nodded. 'Well, more of a postcard ... Anyway, he said he does need a new factory worker. And there's an apartment where you can stay.'

I looked at her, totally taken aback.

'What?'

'Well, I didn't ... I didn't think you'd actually do it,' I said, stunned and touched. 'I mean, go to all that trouble.'

'It was two letters,' said Claire. 'I hope that's not your idea of hard work. I've talked you up quite dramatically.'

'Uh-oh,' I said.

She smiled. 'It was ... it was nice to hear back after all this time.'

'This was definitely a romance,' I said.

'It was definitely a long time ago,' she said crisply, in her teacher's voice again.

'Don't you want to go?' I said.

'Oh no,' she said quickly. 'That time of my life is well over with, quite done and dusted. And I have more than enough on my plate. But you're still young ...'

'I'm thirty,' I said, moaning.

'That's young,' she said, sharply. 'That's very young.'

'So, what's it like, this factory?' I said, changing the subject. Her own kids weren't much older than me and were both married and settled with good jobs. I didn't think I could handle the comparison.

'Oh, it's probably changed a bit,' she said, looking dreamy. Then she came back to herself. 'Anyway, it's not a factory, more an atelier – a workshop. Le Chapeau Chocolat.'

35

'The Chocolate Hat?' I said. 'That sounds ... I mean, do they actually make hats out of chocolate?'

Claire ignored me.

'They'll take you on as a general factotum, normal hours. I've arranged a room that you can stay in. It's extremely expensive that area of Paris, incredibly, so it's very helpful. He says they're busy till about October, so you could stay until then. By the time you come back the UK shops will be gearing up for Christmas. I'm sure you'll get a job then.'

'Don't they have Christmas in France?'

Claire smiled at me. 'Yes, but it isn't the crazy obsession it is here. A few oysters and some time with your family, that's about the size of it.'

'That sounds rubbish,' I said, suddenly a bit cross. I felt as if I were being railroaded, rather than worried about and cosseted.

'It's lovely,' said Claire, her thin face going dreamy again. 'The rain hits the pavement and the lights go all misty over the bridges, and you huddle up in front of the fire ...'

'And eat oysters,' I said. 'Bleurgh.'

Claire took her glasses off and rubbed her sore-looking eyes.

'Well,' she said, hopefully, 'I think it's a very generous offer, considering he's never met you.'

'What about speaking French?' I said, sounding slightly panicky. 'I won't be able to understand anything.'

'Don't be silly, you're coming along brilliantly.'

'Yes, but that's talking to you. Real French people will talk like this ... zubba zubba zubba zubba zuBBAH at like one hundred miles an hour. One hundred kilometres an hour,' I corrected, gloomily.

Claire laughed. 'The trick is not to panic. Trust your brain to know what people are saying. Also, people talk just as much rubbish in French as they do in English. They repeat themselves all the time, just like people do here. Don't worry about it.'

I blinked.

'Does he speak English?'

Claire smiled, shyly.

'Not a word, as far as I remember.'

♡

1972

His moustache had been the first thing she'd noticed about him, not because it was unusual – lots of men had them at that time, along with long, unruly sideburns, which he also had – but because it had chocolate on the ends. She had blinked at it.

'What?' he had said instantly, waggling his eyebrows at her. 'What? Tell me – you cannot believe such a devastatingly handsome man has just walked through the door?'

She had smiled involuntarily. With his thick mop of dark brown curly hair, mischievous brown eyes and burly body, he was undeniably attractive – but handsome, no. Especially not in the traditional French style, where the men were neat and well-groomed, slim and rather refined. There was nothing refined about this man; he looked a bit like a lost bear.

'You are laughing? It's funny that I am not handsome? Hmm? How is that funny?' He mimed a position of extreme woundedness.

Claire had been wallflowering near the elaborately corniced door for nearly an hour, waiting for Mme Lagarde to want to go. Her hosts were terribly polite and not the tyrants she had been dreading and her father had been hoping for, but they also considered it quite a privilege for her to be allowed to take part in their social lives.

Claire, however, found it all incomprehensibly sophisticated, and suffered from dreadful nerves. She had no idea what to say. There were young men in berets arguing furiously about communism; stunning slender women smoking and occasionally raising an eyebrow at the men, or mentioning how boring such and such an exhibition was. She wasn't a party person, even amongst people she knew. Paris itself was knocking her out daily with its astonishing beauty, but the people absolutely terrified her.

She treated it as an extension of her language classes, and tried to listen in as much as she could, but in her mind these people were undoubtedly grown-ups. And she, equally undoubtedly, was not. At seventeen, she felt neither one thing nor the other, and the fun and glamour made her feel more and more like an uneducated country hick. She found it hard enough to follow what people were saying, they spoke so fast; she was constantly dazzled by how beautifully everybody dressed, so different from her mother's homely style; and on top of that, they all talked about exhibitions they'd seen and writers they'd met and everyone talked about food absolutely without stopping. It was exhausting. People took an interest in the Lagardes' English girl – she was pretty and endearing-looking – but she found herself clamming up like the worst kind of wallflower. She could see *that Mme Lagarde, who was extremely beautiful and well-groomed, wasn't particularly impressed by this, but after Kidinsborough and the rectory, Paris was completely overwhelming.*

This chap, on the other hand, was different. He had a spark of mischief in his eyes that he couldn't hide.

'I didn't mean it,' she said, hiding her mouth with her hand so he wouldn't see her smirking.

'OH! An Englishwoman!' he said immediately, standing back as if in amazement. 'Enchanté, mademoiselle! Thank you so much for bestowing a visit on our little backwater town here.'

'You are teasing me,' said Claire, trying to match his humorous tone.

'That is not possible, mademoiselle! I am French and therefore of course have no sense of humour.'

'What have you got on your moustache?' she said.

He made a comical face trying to see it.

'I don't know. Is it a sense of humour?'

'It's brown.'

'Ah, well of course . . . that is my job.'

This made no sense to Claire, but just then the host of the party turned round and noticed the newcomer standing there. Delighted, he marched up and bustled him away, introducing him to everyone. They seemed far more delighted to make his acquaintance than they had been to meet the Lagardes' new au pair.

'Who is that?' Claire asked Mme Lagarde in a whisper.

'Oh, that is Thierry Girard, the talk of the town,' said Mme Lagarde, eyeing him affectionately. 'They say he is the most gifted chocolatier since Persion.'

Claire was amazed that this was news of any kind, or that it was so important. On the other hand, it explained what was on his moustache, which was a good thing at least.

'Is he going to be a big success?' she asked casually.

Mme Lagarde watched as Thierry Girard spoke to a top food critic, charming him effortlessly by insisting on drawing out his latest recipe.

'Oh, I think so,' she said. 'He studied in Switzerland and Bruges. I think he's going to be really terribly good.'

After touring the room, and accepting a second glass of the delicious champagne, Claire, back in observational mode, realised that Thierry was the focus of attention and laughter in the room. People just seemed to flock to him. As someone who people tended simply not to notice – the curse of being quiet – she was transfixed. His shaggy bear face was not at all handsome, but it was so cheerful and animated it was hard not to enjoy looking at it, or wish that its sunshiny beam of attention might come near you. She spotted several of the beautiful women, who had been so sulky and superior before, suddenly start laughing and fluttering about in front of him.

Claire bit her lip. She would have liked another glass of the amazing icy champagne – she'd never had it before – but suspected, rightly, that Mme Lagarde would disapprove. In fact, even now they looked like they were getting ready to leave. She glanced around for her coat, before remembering that it had been taken by a maid at the door.

'You are not leaving,' came a growly voice. She turned round, her heart suddenly jumping. Thierry was standing there, his face crestfallen.

'Where are you going?'

'I have to work tomorrow,' she stuttered. 'And Mme Lagarde ... she is taking me home. I have to go with her.'

He waggled his eyebrows. 'Ah, mam'zelle, I did not realise you were a child.'

'I'm not a child,' she said emphatically, hearing immediately as she did so what a child she sounded.

'Alors, then I will take you home.'

'You shall not,' said Mme Lagarde, who had suddenly materialised out of nowhere and was giving him a freezing stare.

'Enchanté,' said Thierry, not in the least perturbed. He bent and kissed her hand. 'This is your sister?'

Mme Lagarde rolled her eyes.

'This is my au pair, and whilst she is here, my ward,' she said crisply. 'Claire, it is time to go.'

'Claire,' said Thierry, rolling the name round his mouth as if he were savouring it. 'Of course you will visit my new shop?'

Claire realised immediately that this was difficult for Madame. Obviously all of Paris would have to try the new shop, otherwise how to admit it at the next soirée? The older woman cast a sideways glance at her. Claire imagined that she was trying to think of ways to keep her apart from this fascinating person.

In fact, she couldn't have been further from the truth.

Marie-Noelle Lagarde was a woman of the world who thought Claire had been ridiculously protected and cosseted at home, completely stifled in the English bourgeois fashion. If she didn't open her eyes soon, she'd end up buried in some ghastly English tomb like her mother and never experience any fun in her life. Marie-

41

Noelle had just rather hoped it would be one of the charming, well-educated sons of her friends who would take her in hand, teach her to live a little and send her home with wonderful memories of Paris and a horizon broader than the church flower-arranging society. She sensed a hidden spirit in the young girl, and felt it her responsibility, as a woman of the world, to give it wings – for her, and for her wonderful spirited mother, who had married the charismatic young churchman and lived to rue the day. But it had to be someone suitable, and careful. She didn't want to send her back to England knocked up by a fat cook.

'Bien sur – of course,' she said swiftly to Thierry, simultaneously signalling to the maid to bring their coats.

As they drove away into the still warm summer evening, Claire, looking behind her from the back window of the taxi cab, glimpsed the huge French windows of the apartment flung open to the night, exuding the noise of music and chatter and cigar smoke drifting upwards into the hazy night.

Chapter Four

Dad never came up to my room, not since I was about twelve or so. It was my sanctum, my escape from the boys. Also, he just isn't the kind of dad that goes in for long chats. He's the kind that cracks really awful jokes to your friends, and makes sure your bike chain is oiled up, and gets a bit pink in the face at Christmas and doesn't remove his party hat all day. I doubt he's said 'I love you' in his entire life, not even to Mum. I know he does, though, so it totally doesn't matter. He also spends his life calling the boys buggers, but I knew he was proud of me when I got promoted at Braders.

Anyway, my mum had been rabbiting on about what I was going to do and what I was up to and what my future was going to be, and just listening to it was exhausting. I'd lost two toes, I wasn't paralysed or in a wheelchair; I didn't even qualify for a blue parking badge for my dad's car (much to Mum's evident disappointment, seriously). Then she read something in one of her magazines and decided I was depressed and started muttering about seeing someone, and that was annoying too, because depression is a horrid illness and not a way to describe feeling a bit sad when you've lost a bit of you off the end, which in my opinion is a totally natural reaction and doesn't need talking through. Then again, I couldn't deny that I didn't feel myself. Have you ever had a really bad hangover that's gone into a second day? Well, like that second day, I just couldn't summon up the energy to do the million and one things I knew I needed to do. There were just so many of them.

He knocked quietly, which was interesting, as Mum never knocks and the boys never drop by, just holler from the bottom of the stairs.

'Hello, love,' he said, proffering a cup of tea. I wouldn't say we were a really old-fashioned family, but one thing was for sure: Dad never made the tea.

'Did you make this?' I said, eyeing it suspiciously.

'Yes,' said Dad quickly. 'Two sugars?'

He must have asked Mum.

'Can I come in?'

'It's your house,' I said, surprised. He looked nervous. Worse than that, before he sat down, he carefully removed two wrapped chocolate biscuits from his pocket. I looked up at him.

'What's wrong?'

'Nothing's wrong.'

'It is if it needs a chocolate biscuit. Tell me, quickly.'

44

My dad shook his head. 'I just thought you'd like a chocolate biscuit.'

I just stared at him, unconvinced.

'Listen,' he said. 'I got a call from your teacher friend ...'

'She's not my teacher any more,' I said.

'Sounds like she's been teaching you a few things,' he said, sitting at my white vanity unit. He looked strange there. The back of his head was reflected in the mirror; he was going really bald back there.

I shrugged. 'Just something to do, you know.'

He glanced at my bed, where there were several French books Claire had lent me that I'd been puzzling through with the help of a massive dictionary. It was a slow, boring business, but light was beginning to dawn.

'Well,' he said, 'she says she's found you a job.'

I shook my head. 'She hasn't really. She just knows someone ... or she used to know them. It was ages ago. She reckons I might be able to help out in the summer.'

'She says it's in your line of work.'

'Yes – in another country. Sweeping floors, probably.'

Dad shrugged. 'What's wrong with working in another country?'

'What, you want me out of the house now?'

'No,' he said carefully. 'All I mean is, you're thirty, you've got no ties, you're still young ... Don't you want to travel a bit? See the world?'

It was my turn to shrug. I hadn't really thought of it like that. In fact I'd only really thought about what a gigantic pain in the arse this was for me and how people should be feeling more sorry for me, not what I was going to do next. I'd lost two bits of myself. That was enough for one year, surely.

The way Dad had put it, though, I did think for a second that it would be quite nice to go somewhere where nobody knew what had happened to me, and people didn't eye me with looks of concern and slightly prurient interest. The kids on the estate definitely talked about me when I went by. The one time I'd gone out with Cath so far, Mark Farmer had cornered me, drunk at about one a.m. and begged to take a look at my foot. I hadn't much fancied going out again after that. I didn't want to be the local freak show. And I knew what it was like here in Kidinsborough. Sandy Verden had pooed her pants once in Year Four and no one had let her forget it yet.

Dad looked at me kindly.

'Love, you know I don't like to give advice.'

'I know,' I said. 'And I appreciate it. Mum gives me enough for two.'

He smiled, a little sadly.

'Honestly, love, at your age, the chance to go see somewhere new, live somewhere different, even if it's just for a little while . . . I'd jump at it. I think you'd be mad not to.'

I'd never seen my dad so passionate about anything, not even when Kidinsborough Wanderers won the league in 1994 and everyone went demented for about a month and a half (the next season they got relegated, so it was a short-lived thing).

'Please,' he said, and then he sighed. 'The boys, you

46

know, good for nothing half the time ... They'd have been down a pit in the old days, or doing something useful, but now there's nothing for them but to hang around, wait on building work ... It's a damn shame is what it is. But you ...'

He looked at me, his tired, kind face full of something so emotional I found it quite difficult to look at. 'You were so good at school, Anna; we couldn't believe it when you wanted to leave. Mrs Shawcourt rang us then too, you know.'

I did know. She had told my parents I should stay on, go to college, but I really didn't see the point of it. I already knew I wanted to work in food and I wanted to earn some money. I didn't really understand that I could have gone to college to specialise, to spend a couple of years really learning stuff rather than picking it up here and there in industrial kitchens ... Well, after that, my pride wouldn't let me go. My dad kept saying it wasn't too late, but I was used to a wage by then, and didn't want to go back to being a student. Students were supposed to be spotty losers anyway, that was what people said around the factory. I always thought it looked like fun, watching them heading up to the big agricultural college nearby, laughing and looking carefree with their folders and laptop bags, whilst we slouched into work every morning. Anyway.

Mrs Shawcourt had told my parents I had a real gift for languages and I should stay and do more exams. I'd snorted and wondered what the point of that was. Wasted on teenagers, education. Well, teenagers like I had been.

Dad was still talking.

47

'You know,' he said mildly. 'I really believe you could. I totally believe you could do it.'

I half smiled at him. 'But you also told me that I could grow up to become Spiderman.'

'I believe that too,' he said, getting up, more slowly than he used to, I noticed (I always noticed people's walks these days), and kissing me gently on the head.

Chapter Five

Two months later

If one other person told me how lucky I was, I was going to scream. I didn't feel lucky at all. At the huge, mobbed railway station in Paris where the Eurostar stopped, everyone had literally charged off in every direction as if holding a Look How Well I Know Paris competition and left me standing there feeling totally exposed, so then of course I figured I would *look* like someone totally exposed and become a massive target for pickpockets. This was why my mum and my dad had been to Scarborough every single year for a hundred and seventy years, I swear to God. At least in Scarborough you knew which end of the pier to avoid and you could tell if someone was wearing a real police uniform or a novelty hat for fun. Here I couldn't even read the signs, and I didn't dare take a cab. As I limped down an escalator pulling my wheelie bag and remembering all the people who'd swooned and said I was so lucky to be going to Paris and how amazing it was going to be, all I could think was, well, yes, I'll probably sit by myself in a room for six weeks watching it all go on around me and not notice a thing. That was entirely within the realms of possibility. And I wouldn't like the food.

I looked up at the Métro map. It made totally no sense to me, none of it. I gazed at it, hand tightly clutching my wallet and passport. It could have been upside down as far as I could tell. None of the lines had names, just numbers, but the signs in the station all had names. Eventually I figured out that they were the names of the places at the end of each line.

I boldly strode forward and requested a ticket from the man behind the counter, who I then asked in my best French for the way to my platform. He gave me a gigantically long stream of hugely complicated directions. I didn't understand any of them, but I said thank you and went to walk away. He shouted at me loudly and I turned round, panicked, as he indicated that I had already started heading off in the wrong direction. I thanked him, tears pricking my eyes with embarrassment.

The platform was packed with every conceivable type of person, most of them speaking French loudly at a billion miles an hour as if showing off, and a few of them looking like horribly lost tourists, just like me. We avoided each other like plague victims, too scared to reveal our vulnerability and ignorance. If I could have turned around and got back on the nice cosy Eurostar, I would have done it in a heartbeat. I glanced at my watch. It was four o'clock here, which meant three o'clock in Kidinsborough. Tea break time. At Braders I'd have been sitting down with a cuppa and a packet of salt'n'vinegar. Even thinking of that stupid factory, which I hated and detested and slagged off almost continuously, was making me homesick. In hospital they served custard creams around about now.

I stared nervously through the dirty graffitied window of the loud silver train as it rattled past stops including, I thought, the one I should have got off at. Within another few minutes we were practically out in open fields. Wherever it was I was meant to be going, it wasn't out here. My heart racing, I jumped out at the first station the train stopped at. Several people in the carriage watched me with amused eyes, which made me hot and cross and anxious. I took the first train going the other way. This one, thank goodness, turned out to be a slow stopping train. I perched on a tiny orange plastic seat near the door and strained my eyes at the passing signs, trying to stop the train by will power alone.

When we finally reached Châtelet-Les Halles, I got my suitcase shut in the ticket barrier and had to be freed by a very well-dressed man who was rushing past. I turned to thank him, but he gave me a look that indicated a very stern telling-off for getting in his well-shod way. Above ground again at last, dirty, hot and grumpy, I tried to orientate myself by my tiny map. Stupid bloody Paris and its stupid bloody hard-to-get-about-on Métro and its grumpy people and its shouting railway staff and stupid well-dressed men … I was very close to tears. My toes were killing me.

Next to the Métro station was a little café with tables and chairs pushed out on to the pavement, despite the fact that there were cars close by and exhaust fumes in the air and a florist whose blooms spilled over on to and under the chairs. I felt for my wallet for the thousandth time that afternoon, and then collapsed into a chair. A little man in trousers and a white shirt came running out importantly.

'Madame?' he said fussily. I didn't know what I wanted really. Just a sit-down. And given the perilous state of my finances, I would really just have liked a glass of water, but that wasn't going to go down well, I could tell already. I glanced at the next table. An old man with an equally old dog dozing under his chair raised an eyebrow at me. In front of him was a tall glass brimming with icy-cold lager. The waiter followed my eyes.

'Comme ça?' he barked. Like that one? I nodded my head gratefully. Yes. Fine. Bit naughty at four o'clock in the afternoon, but then I'd been up since five, and I was hot and tired and cross. It was nice, for two seconds, to stop panicking about everything I had to do and whether I was going to lose my ticket on the train or drop my passport or leave my bag unattended and have it blown up.

I sat back in the chair, and turned my face to the sun. Having left England in a light drizzle, I hadn't expected sunshine. Blinking and wondering where I'd packed my sunglasses, I took a deep breath as my beer arrived fast as lightning, took a sip – it was freezing and delicious – and glanced around me.

I couldn't help smiling. Forget the dirty Métro with its hard-to-negotiate ticket barriers. Instead, here I was on a corner of a crossroads of cobbled streets leading towards, on my right, a great humpbacked bridge over the Seine from which I could just make out the back of a huge church. My heart leapt. It was Notre-Dame, it had to be. On my other side were long rows of huge white buildings, seven or eight storeys high, one leading down to the embankment of the river, one in the other direction filled with shops. The road was several lanes wide, striped awnings poking out over the pavements as far as the eye could see.

Despite my tiredness and anxiety (I know, I know there are people who travel without ever worrying about it; who turn up and bounce on to trains and planes and enjoy it and wake up in a new city without even batting an eyelid. I am not like that. I worry all the time), slowly my shoulders began to lower themselves, and my heart rose a little as I took another sip of beer. A handsome young man with slicked-back hair came out of the flower shop next door looking slightly furtive and carrying a large bunch of white lilies. I wondered who they were for. As I wondered, he caught my eye and winked. Heh. I grinned at that too.

People were starting to leave their offices for the day – early by my standards for rush hour, but they were leaving nonetheless. The women all looked like they'd just been in the hairdresser's. Their make-up was subtle, their hair was dark and lovely and didn't even look dyed – I thought regretfully of the highlights Cath put in, which cost me a fortune once every six weeks, even at mate's rates – and they wore really understated clothes in black or navy or grey; not many trousers, I noticed. The female managers at Braders wore trouser suits, mostly, too tight trousers over fat bottoms with little short jackets perched on the top. It was not a look, I felt, that suited them. Here if the women did wear trousers they were over non-existent bottoms and were flowingly cut and looked rather chic and boyish. Of course, I thought. This was how Mrs Shawcourt – Claire – dressed. This was obviously where she had learned. I wondered how she had done it.

The old man at the next table leant over.

'Anglaise?' he said.

Well, yes. Although I wished it wasn't quite so obvious. I nodded, smiling.

'You 'ave been to Paris before?' I shook my head.

'Oh,' he said, his face completely creased with wrinkles. 'Oh, you will adore it. To be young, and in Paris for the first time ... Mademoiselle, I envy you.'

I tried to smile back as if I wasn't desperate for a bath, and feeling positively ancient really compared to the beautiful young French girls rushing back and forth, and for a second let myself believe that he was right; that a whole new world of adventure and excitement could open up for me, Anna Trent from Kidinsborough, here in Paris. The idea was ridiculous and absurd. The most exciting thing that had happened to me was finding those boots I loved with seventy per cent off in the Debenhams sale. But as I drained the rest of my golden beer and looked around at the warm-tinged early Parisian evening, I wondered, just for a moment, if it might be true.

Chapter Six

The Île de la Cité was indeed an island; there were two, right in the middle of Paris, connected by a series of bridges. It was mostly large buildings – a huge hospital and the law courts and police stations in proud, imposing stone, with Notre-Dame cathedral marking the west side – but round the back of the smart edifices were little streets too, cobbled and twisted, marking out an older city, and it was in one of these that I finally found myself, on a road called the rue des Ursins, which was down some steps from the pavement, near a bridge, and across from a cobbled area surrounding a tiny triangle of garden.

The street numbers didn't seem to make any sense; they jumped hither and thither, and areas called arrondissements just seemed to pop up out of nowhere. There's something about the first time you go to a place; it takes far too long, and you notice little details that you remember forever, like the wrought-iron lamps that lit the way as night started to fall. But finally I tracked it down. It was on the sixth floor of an old building made of golden stone, with balconies lined with flowerpots full of pansies and large floor-length windows.

When I first saw it, my heart leapt. As I drew closer, I noticed that the stone was a little shabby; that the pansies were dead or plastic; that the beautiful windows had rattling frames and were single-glazed; it was not a set of smart apartments, but rather a subdivided old house, somewhat neglected. I sighed. Our house at home was small and smelled of boy and Lynx aftershave and fish fingers and sometimes our farty old dog, but my little room was warm and cosy – Mum liked to whack the heating up, and Dad would chide her that it was getting too expensive – and it was double-glazed and nice and modern. I'd never lived in an old building before. It was almost impossible to work out what colour the huge old door had once been; a sort of sandy red seemed to cover it, just about. There was a jumble of bells with writing all over them, and the steps were worn smooth. I couldn't see the name that I was looking for, so I tentatively pushed at the door. It creaked open ominously and I stepped in.

'Bonjour?' I called. There was no response. 'Bonjour?'

Nothing. There was a glassed door at the end of the hallway which let in just enough light to let me see the dusty piles of old mail over the broken parquet floor and a tired-looking pot plant by the stairwell. The stairs led up into the dark. I fumbled a bit and found a light switch, flicked it on and moved upwards, but before I'd even reached the next landing, the light went out. I cursed crossly under my breath and trailed my hand till I found another switch. This wasn't, it turned out, a light switch, but instead a loud doorbell that went off like a gun.

'ALLO?' shouted an old lady's voice. I knew I was meant to be on the top floor, so I cried out a quick 'Pardon, madame,' and continued on my way.

What was with these accursed lights that couldn't stay on? One had to dart between them. The staircase was incredibly twisting and narrow, and by the time I finally made it to the top, hauling my heavy bag, I was sweating and out of breath. Down below, the lady whose bell I had rung by accident was shouting her head off, saying things I couldn't make out, but I think one of them was 'Police!' I cursed under my breath, some proper Anglo-Saxon words.

I had emerged on to a small landing with – thank goodness – its own light coming through a dirty skylight above me. It was a tiny space, like being inside a turret. Someone had put a little white bookshelf crammed full of books at the top of the steps, so I couldn't get my bag past it. On the other levels there had been two apartments, but here there was only one. I stepped forward. On the low white door in front of me was a little brass plaque, which had 'Sami' written on it in minute letters. I blew out a breath of relief. I didn't fancy reliving the stairway of death. It then occurred to me that if I was going to stay here, I would have to negotiate the stairway of death on eight toes every day. I put that thought out of my mind for the time being and knocked sharply on the door.

'Hello?'

Inside I heard the sound of someone moving about. Thank goodness. I didn't know what I would do if I had to turn around again. Probably just get back on the train, I thought. No. No I wouldn't do that. Definitely not.

'J'ARRIVE!' called a voice, sounding slightly panicked. There was a clattering noise inside. I wondered what was going on.

Finally the door was flung open. A gigantically tall man stood there. His skin was a dark olive colour, his eyebrows black and bushy, his jaw bristly and jutting. He was wearing a patterned robe which didn't appear to have much underneath it. He glanced at me without the slightest flicker of recognition or awareness whatsoever.

'Bonjour,' I said. 'Anna Trent? From England?'

I worried suddenly that Claire hadn't managed to set it up, or there'd been some misunderstanding, or he'd changed his mind, or . . .

He squinted. 'ATTENDS!' he commanded. I waited.

He returned two seconds later wearing a huge pair of black-rimmed glasses. I sniffed. He smelled of sandalwood. With the glasses on, he looked at me once more.

'La petite Anglaise!' he said, a sudden smile splitting his face. He switched to English. 'Welcome! Welcome! Come in! Come in! I will say, I did forget. You will say, 'ow could you forget, and I will say . . . I will say . . . welcome à Paris!'

The second I stepped into the room, I could see there was absolutely no doubt that he had indeed forgotten. There was almost no hallway, just room for a hat stand with a collection of esoteric hats on it – I counted a fez, a trilby and the head of a gorilla costume – then it opened out into a room. It wasn't a large room, but it was stuffed incredibly full. There were capes and material, feathers, scissors, fur stoles and pillow-cases; ashtrays, empty champagne bottles and an enormous red sofa with huge cushions strewn about it and over the floor. In the corner was a kitchenette that had blatantly never been used. The peculiar man straightened up, even though the ceilings were much lower than I'd been expecting and he could hardly stand upright; he must have been six foot five.

'Oui,' he said, looking sadly around at the mess. 'I did forget.'

He turned to face me happily.

'But what if I said, yes, welcome, Anna Trent' – he pronounced it 'An-NA Tron' – 'thees is always my house prepared at its best for visitor? You would not like that?'

I shook my head to indicate that I wouldn't.

'You are cross with me,' he said. 'You are sad.'

I shook my head again. I was neither of those things; I was just a bit overwhelmed and tearful and exhausted from trav-elling and as far away from home as I'd been in my whole life really, and I kind of just wanted a table and a chair and a cup of tea, not some crazy bohemian workshop super-mess if that was all right with everyone.

'What is all this stuff?' I said, gesticulating.

'Oh, I bring my work home,' he said.' I work too hard, it is my problem.'

This, I was to discover, was nothing like Sami's worst problem, but that first evening I took him at his word.

It turned out Sami worked in the costume department at the Paris Opera House, earning next to nothing at all making clothes for the opera productions with dozens of tiny seamstresses. He'd come to Paris originally to work in one of the big couture houses, but had had no luck, and was practising his trade letting out stays for singers and complaining about fat tenors and sullen sopranos who insisted they needed space in their costumes to sing but who were, he confided, actually just greedy.

But that came later. Now it just all seemed a big mess.

'I have a room for you!' he said. 'It is nothing like this.'

His face looked briefly panicked.

'Wait here,' he said, and vanished through a door at the back. From a quick count of the doors I ascertained, with some relief, that there must be another bedroom and a bathroom. For a hideous second, I'd thought that might be it, and that I would be stuck in one hideously messy room with a distracted giant.

Within a few moments, and looking rather as if he were concealing something about his person, Sami returned rather sheepishly.

'It is prêt, ready for you,' he said, bowing from the waist. I picked up my clumpy bag, and followed where he was pointing.

My bedroom in Kidinsborough was very small, so it wasn't like I wasn't expecting it. But there's something about being

thirty and walking into somewhere tinier than a prison cell …
It was absolutely minuscule. They'd squeezed a single bed in
there – who knows how – and a tiny chest of drawers
crammed up against it, and apart from that there was nothing
else at all; there just wasn't the space. I blinked once, twice.
I wasn't going to start crying. For starters, there was nowhere
private to do it. I must admit, I'd fantasised, maybe a tiny bit,
about a little en suite, maybe, or some grand space like I'd
seen in magazines; Paris had all those vast apartments with
posh rooms and marble fireplaces and high ceilings and … this
was basically a coffin. Probably where the maids used to sleep
or something. It was painted totally white, with dark brown
scuffed parquet on the floor.

'What do you think?' said Sami. 'Isn't it AMAZING?'

I put my head back out of the doorway.

'Amazing?' I wondered. What on earth must his be like?

'AMAZING!' he said.

I blinked at him.

'Oh, AnNA Tron, she is very cross with me,' he said,
making his face go sad. 'Can I get you something?'

'Tea?' I ventured.

'I 'ave no tea.'

'Coffee?'

'Mais bien sur!'

He clattered happily over to the tiny kitchenette whilst I
advanced inside my little monk's cell with my large purple
bag. I put it down on the bed – there was literally nowhere
else it could possibly go – and clambered past the chest of

drawers over to the window. And that's when I saw it. I gasped.

The window opened sideways and was full length. I thought briefly of how many children must have fallen out of it. But I didn't think about it for long, because lifting the net curtain and opening the catch, I found two extraordinary things: the tiniest balcony, only just big enough to fit a small wrought-iron table and two chairs, but directly in the path of the sun; and, from six floors up on the Île de la Cité – Paris. The rooftops of the other buildings across the water, with tables out on their south-facing side. The bridges all the way down the Seine. To my left, to the north-west, I could just make out the sinister black tip of La Defens, the great centre of the financial district. And everywhere the teeming, pulsating life of the city, the noise insulated from six storeys up: the little fruit van parping its way furiously down the street; a collection of stunningly attractive people emerging from a sleek black car to a chic bar down the road; two little lines of schoolchildren walking politely down the next street hand in hand. And if I craned my neck really, really far to the left, to the far east, I could see it. The one and only, unmistakable Eiffel Tower.

I gazed and gazed and gazed at the pinkening skyline, as if I was thirsty and this was water. I could no longer feel the pain in my foot, or my longing for a shower, or my general exhaustion.

'Your café,' said Sami, coming into my room without bothering to knock. 'You really not like?'

I smiled. 'I didn't see the balcony. It's amazing. Amazing.'

He had made me a tiny cup of black stuff with a sugar lump sitting next to it. I normally just like lattes or Nescafé. I looked at him.

'Have you got any milk for the coffee?' I asked apologetically.

'Milk? No. Milk is a feelthy thing. You suck the teats of a cow? No. Milk? No.'

'Okay,' I said.

'Brandy? I have a leetle brandy.'

And as it was such a gorgeous evening, I said yes, why not, and we sat out on my little 'balcon' (he had one too, on the opposite side of the sitting room; we could wave to each other in the morning) and drank coffee with brandy in it and gazed out over Paris, and if anyone had looked up and seen me (which they couldn't, because we were up in the eaves, where pigeons flew by and the sky turned pink and yellow and lavender and there was no one else there but the birds), they would have thought that I was as much a part of Paris as anybody else, and I looked out on the strange and extraordinary foreign landscape and I wondered. I wondered.

♡

1972

Claire was totally charmed by Arnaud and Claudette, her charges. They were incredibly polite, thought her accent was hilarious, and tested her endlessly on words she did and didn't know, marvelling at the way she said 'Mickey Mouse'.

In return she let them dictate the pace of the lazy summer days; normally a stroll around the play park of the Tuileries, in the shadow of the Eiffel Tower; a gouter, or snack, of warm croissants, torn apart and guzzled on a bench, followed by home for lunch. The two children still took naps in the afternoon, leaving Claire free to read or do her French grammar (Madame was very strict on the matter), and on Fridays Madame liked to take the children to their swimming lessons, so Claire had the afternoon off.

At first, unsure what to do with her free time, she took herself off to the exhibitions and museums she felt she ought to see, as if ticking things off in a guidebook. Madame would ask her questions about them when she returned, and occasionally ask her to take the children. But it was hard for Claire to enjoy sightseeing; she felt lonely amongst large families and young lovers and crocodiles of schoolchildren nattering away without a care in the language she found so difficult to master. She didn't know a soul here, and Kidinsborough felt a long way away.

But as she grew more confident, she began to stride further afield, and she found her fear gradually falling away as she saw and visited more. Montmartre, with its winding streets, odd, highly perched church and candy-coloured steps, stole her heart almost immediately, and she spent many days there watching the young women with their scooters, helmetless, scarves tied around their thick hair, chatting and laughing with the young men on the steps, their cigarettes drooping from their mouths. Other afternoons she took a book to the Luxembourg gardens, and lay on the grass watching her legs go brown. Everywhere, it seemed, were couples kissing, chatting, gesticulating in the air, sharing a picnic with wine in unmarked bottles. To feel alone at seventeen is to feel very lonely indeed, and even as she looked forward all week to her free time, she found the Friday afternoons sometimes very long. It was a relief, as her French improved, to be able to slip into a cinema on the Montparnasse Boulevard, where it didn't matter that she was by herself, or at least not so much. There were, she had heard, places for young English people to meet, but Mme Lagarde had made it clear that she didn't think they were a good idea if she was to have a proper French experience, and Claire always wanted to please.

She wanted to see Thierry again – partly because she had liked him, she thought, but mostly because he had shown some interest in her; and at the moment nobody was showing the least bit of interest in her; they were too busy being glamorous and busy and having stuff to do that she simply didn't have. Two Fridays after the party, she found herself straying closer and closer to the part of the Île de la Cité where she'd heard, from fervent eavesdropping at one of Madame's lunches (lunch when Claire's mum's friends came round was a large tray of home-made ham sandwiches on white bread with margarine and a packet of chocolate digestives for after, dished up with pints of dark brown tea; lunch for Madame's friends involved much planning, four courses, an ice bucket full of champagne and lots of running back and forth to the fishmonger's early in the morning), that the new shop was to open, the first of its kind in Paris. There was Persion's, which had been in situ since 1794 and was respected for that, but there was a rumour that its products had grown as dusty as its upper storeys, and its offerings hadn't changed in centuries.

Friday afternoon in July on the Île de la Cité was hot and sticky and bustling with tourists. Away from the formal placement of the organised streets and wide boulevards, this district betrayed its twisty, *hugger-mugger medieval origins: little alleyways springing hither and thither; roads narrowing to nearly nothing or ending abruptly at the wall of one of the great churches. The previous weekend Claire was to accompany the family to a wedding, and had taken out a summer dress that she'd brought from home. Mme Lagarde had immediately shaken her head, pointed out to Claire that it didn't actually fit very well, and disappeared. When she returned, it was with a soft brown and green silk dress, very loose and almost weightless.*

'This was mine,' she said. 'After the children, pfft. I cannot wear.'

Claire pointed out that she was very slim still, but Mme Lagarde waved dismissively.

'It does not matter, my shape,' she said. 'It is my age, my outlook that cannot wear it.'

For a moment she looked sad.

'Oh, these days come and go,' she said.

Claire had barely met Madame's husband, Bernard; he travelled almost constantly for work and seemed tired and distracted when he did appear. But the Lagardes were, to her, so grown-up; far more so than her own warm family. They were sophisticated, worldly, socialites who dressed for dinner and drank cocktails. Claire simply assumed that anything they did was correct.

The dress was totally out of style – fashionable women in Paris were wearing flared denims on their long skinny legs, big hair, huge sunglasses and large felt hats tied round with Hermès scarves. But the soft leaf pattern and the pulled-in waist suited Claire's shape; made a virtue out of her slenderness and by making her look petite and delicate turned her short stature into a positive attribute; in her jeans, she was often overshadowed.

'There,' said Madame. 'Much better.'

Several men were actively appreciative as she walked past now, with an approving smile or a murmured 'Très jolie, mam'zelle', which made a change from the shouts and wolf whistles girls were subjected to at home, and put a bounce in her step. Her nerves added a pinkness to her face and a sparkle to her eyes.

Of course, she told herself, he was hardly likely to remember someone he'd met for two seconds at a party. And he would doubtless be far too busy; the shop would be a huge success, and he wouldn't have a moment to spend on her. Still, what would she even say to him if he did? Maybe he wouldn't be there at all, too busy off being creative somewhere else.

She decided to pretend to herself that she was only going to find some lovely chocolate, nothing more, and tried to concentrate on how excited Arnaud and Claudette would be when she brought it home. Yes. That was all.

There was a bustle of people outside the shop as she arrived; already the buzz around town was growing. Claire couldn't help smiling; she was so pleased. It seemed such a bold thing to do, to announce to the world that you had made something wonderful, and everyone was welcome to come and pay you money to have it. She couldn't imagine anything she could do possibly being worth that amount of attention.

She advanced a little closer, drawn by the window. The crowd stood, just looking at it, and as she came closer, Claire realised why: it was an entire, beautiful scene, a fairy-tale castle with a carriage arriving at the door and a princess emerging. In the sky above was a hot air balloon. Every single bit was sculpted from chocolate. There was white piping on the princess's lacy gown, and the castle windows were of dark chocolate, cut into shapes. The trees had chocolate leaves and the balloon white chocolate designs inlaid on it. In the middle of the castle courtyard stood a fountain, chocolate bubbling through it merrily.

It was so childlike and adorable and witty, Claire couldn't help it; she burst into a huge smile and clapped her hands together. As she did so, she suddenly felt someone's eyes upon her and glanced up. On the other side of the glass, clearly in the middle of talking to somebody else, was Thierry, suddenly stock still, and gazing at her like he couldn't tear his eyes away. Claire felt her smile fade from her face and she bit her lip anxiously. It was as if all the crowds, the customers, the noise and bustle of the summer in the city had completely vanished. Tentatively she raised her hand in a gesture of hello, and pressed it against the shop window. Ignoring his customer, Thierry raised his own great bear-like paw. Claire noticed what she hadn't seen before: his thick black eyelashes were ridiculously long, protruding over the lively dark brown eyes and the hooded lids. She felt, even through the window, as if she could make out every hair, every cell.

Suddenly, someone trying to get a better look jostled her out of the way. Instantly it was as if the spell was broken. She staggered slightly to the side, and in an instant Thierry was out of the door, pushing his way through the crowd.

'Are you all right? Are you hurt? Who did that?' he barked.

The crowd sidled away from one small slightly awkward-looking man.

'You!' said Thierry, waggling his finger directly in the man's face. 'You are banned from this shop for ever. Go!'

The man blushed violently, muttered some words of apology in Claire's direction and disappeared.

'BON!' said Thierry. 'Everyone else, come in. Well, only if you wish to experience the best chocolate in the world. Otherwise, it is unimportant to me what you would like to do.'

People started flooding into the shop, Thierry leading from the front, a huge arm round Claire's shoulders. Next to him, she thought, all the other men looked puny.

He led her straight through the selling area, with its original thirties golden lettering and polished glass cases. The walls were lined, Claire saw, with great old jars full of different kinds of sugar – vanilla, demerara, violet, lemon, icing. In the back of the shop, a grumpy old man with a monobrow was tending a large copper vat. Thierry nodded him through to the front, and the man went, looking sullen.

Claire hardly noticed. She was too busy gazing around the room. To her, the back wall was a flower garden. Many of the herbs and plants she didn't even recognise; her family's meals at home were plain affairs. Her mother had attempted spaghetti bolognese once and everyone had felt it dangerously daring. Mme Lagarde believed in eating lightly and cleanly, so there was much plain steamed fish and vast amounts of salad and vegetables. But this was something else. The assorted greenery sent its competing perfumes into the air, set against the warm, comforting utterly solid scent of chocolate every-where; the scent, Claire realised later, of Thierry himself.

'You like it?' he said.

She beamed, her face and heart full.

'I . . . I love it!' she said, completely sincerely. She saw how much this pleased him; he couldn't hide anything he felt.

'Here, here,' he said, beckoning her to the vat. He dropped in the long ladle, then drew it up to her. Then he stopped.

'Non,' he said. 'Close your eyes.'

Claire looked at him quizzically. Inside her chest she could feel her heart beating. 'Why?' she asked.

'Oh! Coquette!' he said, smiling. 'So I can kidnap you and sell you to white traders. Then, so I can chop up your body and disguise it in the chocolate.'

He took a handkerchief from his pocket – 'Clean, I most solemnly vow' – and tied it round her eyes.

'It is so,' he said, his voice suddenly disturbingly close to her ear, 'that you can truly taste it. So you shut out distractions.'

Claire, her eyes tight shut against the handkerchief, which smelled exactly as Thierry did – of chocolate, and tobacco – felt as distracted as she had ever been in her entire life.

'Only then can you truly appreciate it.'

She felt his breath briefly on her neck, then the next second the ladle was prodding at her lips, pushing them apart.

'Take it,' said Thierry, and she opened her mouth a little wider as he tipped in a large mouthful of just-melted chocolate; warm to creaminess, the same temperature as her body. It was absolutely extraordinarily sensual and good. She was conscious, even as she tasted it, that he was, for once, silent, his eyes on her, watching her.

At last it was gone, and she felt her tongue round her lips, looking for more. Now his voice was lower, all mischief gone.

'You like?'

'Oh yes,' she said.

Chapter Seven

Sami had come over from Algeria, I learned, at the age of six, on a scholarship from a kindly great-uncle who had done well in France. He had been sent to good schools, and was expected to go on to a good university. Instead he had spent all his time poring over fashion magazines and choosing clothes. It had been, he said, with commendable under-statement for someone so flamboyant, a difficult time for everyone.

He had worked his own way through fashion college, and had made it alone ever since, poorer, he said, than Job, rent-ing this tiny eyrie so he didn't have to commute too far, and taking all his exercise, he explained, getting up and down the six flights of stairs, something I was to learn about myself only too quickly. He worked late in the evenings, but I was not to worry as he was very difficult to wake in the mornings.

That first morning was freezing. When my alarm woke

me in my little white cell, I was completely disorientated at first. Then I felt a sudden jolt of excitement. I was here! In Paris! Alone! From the other side of the sitting room came a deep and resonant snoring, which wouldn't have allowed me to fall asleep again even if I'd wanted to. I jumped up, had a bath (there wasn't much hot water in the tiny half-tub; I hoped it would heat up again before Sami woke up), then looked at my map of Paris. I had been ordered to present myself at 5.30 a.m., which was clearly ridiculous and possibly just a first-day test, I told myself. It was still dark outside. I didn't know how to work the odd stove-top coffeepot Sami had left on top of the cooker, and didn't want to start making noise before I'd been there five minutes, so I cleaned my teeth quickly, added an extra jumper and picked my way down the pitch-black stairwell, trying to make it from light switch to light switch. To my utter horror, I accidentally pressed the first floor bell again, and ran out like a wet cat before the voice started up.

♡

The address of the shop was 63 rue de Chanoinesse. It was a large building of golden stone, similar to the one I was staying in, though nothing like as scruffy. Within two streets, the boulevards had widened slightly. There was a beautiful square leading to a church, and smart shops and cafés under striped awnings. The sun was just starting to creep up over the horizon, and people were up and about: little trucks going to markets and restaurants full of leeks and flower bulbs and lobsters; bundled-up people making their way quietly to cleaning jobs; bus drivers, yawning and stretching in their warmly lit cabs. Silent bicycles squeaked past me. On every corner was a bakery, casting a pool of light; the smell of warm bread was intoxicating, but alas, even they weren't open yet. I felt like a child with my nose pressed against the window, my stomach completely hollow; I hadn't had the energy to sort out dinner the night before and had ended up foraging for old sandwiches in my luggage.

After a couple of wrong turns, suddenly there it was in front of me. I saw it right away, then smelled it a moment later. 'Le Chapeau Chocolat de Thierry Girard' was written on the brown-painted wall in pale rose-coloured script. It wasn't blaring, shouting out about the shop; it was a gentle note that they were there, almost easy to overlook and all the more impressive for that in its confidence. Outside stood a young man smoking a cigarette. As I watched, another, larger man came up to him and gesticulated, and as if in response, the younger man threw his cigarette into the gutter. I wasn't fluent enough to divine whether the older man was telling him off about his smoking or just moved his arms a lot. They had turned to go inside when I stepped tentatively on to the cobbles and caught their attention.

'Uh, bonjour?' I said. I wondered which of them was the famous Thierry Girard. It couldn't be the young one, surely.

The two men stared at me. Then they looked at each other, and the younger one clasped his hand to his forehead. I didn't need much French to know that that meant 'I have completely forgotten that you were coming today'. It was the same in every language in the world.

'J'arrive ... d'Angleterre,' I stuttered.

'Oui, oui, oui, oui,' said the younger man, looking furious with himself. The larger one let loose a stream of invective, which the younger man totally ignored. He had wild curly black gypsy hair, a huge nose and an intense expression, and was looking longingly at his discarded cigarette.

Finally, his expressive face seemed to decide something.

'WELCOME ...' he said loudly in English, then waved his arm towards me, clearly without a clue as to what I was called. This was beginning to feel like something of a theme.

'I'm Anna ... Anna Trent,' I said.

The larger man looked mutinous. He had the build of a rugby player, solid and wide.

'AnNA Tron,' he said crossly. 'Bonjour, madame.'

And he turned and stomped into the shop. The younger man didn't seem to see anything strange or rude about this at all. In fact he smiled cheerfully.

'He doesn't say much,' he said. He glanced back towards the shop. 'I believe that may be it for today.'

'Vous êtes ... Thierry?' I asked tentatively. At this he laughed, revealing very white teeth.

'Non ... non. Je ne suis pas Thierry. I am Frédéric. MUCH more handsome.' He looked at the pavement. 'So, AnNA Tron, shall we see if we have some things for you to do?'

'Did you forget I was coming?'

'Non, non, non. Yes. Yes, I did do that.' He looked up at me with a charming smile. 'You understand ... many things happen ... many nights ... I cannot remember all lovely girls.'

Even though it wasn't even six o'clock and I knew for a fact that I looked like death, and he looked a little peaky himself and had no clue what I was doing there, clearly he still felt duty-bound to chat me up. Not seriously or intently, just as if he was passing by. I wasn't tempted, but I was quite impressed.

From the outside, the shop looked like nothing at all: a tiny, discreet store front leading to a selling space the size of somebody's front room. At the moment it was empty, just glass display cases polished clear, standing to attention. The street lights outside cast an orange glow from their wrought-iron posts through the front windows, and I could make out a polished wooden floor and shelving filled with boxes behind the counter. Over everything lay a layer of scent; a heavy, deep smell of dark, dense chocolate, thick as tobacco smoke. It was as if it were rubbed into the wood; used as varnish on the floor; as if the whole building were steeped in it. I wondered how long I would notice it for; it was almost intoxicating, even in the empty room.

Frédéric had already threaded past to a small door set in the back wall. It was a swing door with a semicircular window, like an old-fashioned restaurant kitchen. I tried not to let it hit me on the rebound.

''Ere we are!' said Frédéric. 'Willy Wonka exist!'

I smiled at him, but it was true, I had never seen such an

odd room in my entire life. It wasn't a room at all, in fact. Back at Braders, everything was done in large industrial stainless-steel vats, something that never failed to disappoint every child I had ever met. (Well, either that or they refused to believe me.) But here, the tiny front room of the shop widened out considerably to form a large glassed-in warehouse, not unlike a huge greenhouse. It was peeling and very old and must have been built in what at one time would have been the garden. It was wood-framed and rickety, but I could feel a humming in the air of an ioniser; the space was perfectly controlled for temperature and humidity. Frédéric nodded towards a large industrial sink by the door and I quickly washed my hands with antibacterial gel.

The room was lit warmly with lamps, not fluorescent lights. At the back, window boxes of fresh herbs lined the sill: rosemary, lavender, mint and a small chilli pepper tree. It made the room feel even more like a greenhouse. Three large copper pots – dark, milk and white, I assumed – stood in the middle of the room, and there were a whole load of burners, test tubes, ovens, pipes and utensils that I had simply never seen before in my life. It smelled like heaven but looked like a mad gardener's shed.

There was no chocolate to be seen. Not a drop anywhere. The copper pots were empty, the arms unturning. The smell hung heavy in the air, but apart from that the place could have been a museum. Frédéric approached holding a tiny cup filled with sticky black coffee, which I accepted gratefully, choking it down.

'The elves come,' he said, smiling at my obvious shock.
'Oh yes. For Thierry Girard, we start anew every day.'

An unpleasant thought struck me suddenly.

'You scrub everything out? Every day?'

Frédéric nodded solemnly.

'. . . And now I'm here.'

Frédéric's impish face turned solemn all of a sudden. I
realised then that I hadn't thought too much about the actual
'work' part of the plan, just the 'getting away' part. In my old
job I'd advised on flavourings, worked on quality control, carried a clipboard. And I suppose I had allowed myself a little
fantasy of aiding and perhaps even inspiring the greatest
chocolatier of his generation; of fluently swapping tips and
ideas with his customers; of perhaps even coming up with my
own brilliant new recipes, capturing the heart of the famous
store . . .

I wondered gloomily what the French was for 'rubber
gloves'.

'Eet is a great experience and privilege,' said Frédéric
gravely.

'Is that what they told you when you started?' I said.

'Oui,' said Frédéric, clearly not in the least sorry. He
looked like a freed spirit. He glanced at my hands. 'I would
not spend too much money on le mani, non?'

It was true; I had had my nails done specially for coming.
A French polish, on purpose. Seeing it now made me want to
bite them off.

'But that is just one of many, many interesting things you

will be doing through the day,' said Frédéric, raising his eyebrows. 'Come, I will show you.'

And I couldn't deny it; it was interesting. It had never even occurred to me that chocolate was something that needed to be eaten fresh. Indeed, one of its great benefits was that it could be stored, could travel. It wasn't like milk or eggs.

'Thierry would describe it to you,' said Frédéric, 'but he does not like to talk to us leetle people so much. He likes everybody to think he is a genius inventor like the Wizard of Oz who does not need us leetle ants who scurry in his house. SO. I, Frédéric, shall tell you.'

'Fresh chocolate is of the utmost importance,' he said, as if reciting from a script. 'For with the freshness you get lightness, and churn, and a delicacy that does not come from a huge slab which sits on the shelf for three months getting heavier and heavier and sinking into itself. NON! This is not good. Chocolate should be treated as a delicacy; something to be plucked fresh from the trees.'

The large man, who was introduced to me as Benoît, had laid down a large box of raw cacoa beans, and now fired up a huge industrial oven.

'From first principles,' said Frédéric. The beans smelled dark and wonderful. Benoît poured them into a huge rotating sorting drum that looked like the inside of a washing machine. The noise was phenomenal.

'Okay now,' said Frédéric after about fifteen minutes, during which I had wandered around smelling the delicious herbs lined up in rows along the back of the greenhouse. Then he said something I didn't understand, and motioned me to copy him as, ferociously quickly, he started cracking the beans with a hammer and unleashing their warm chocolatey insides. Every fourth one he threw away.

'I thought you made chocolate?' he said, puzzled, as I stared at him in disbelief.

'Machine-made chocolate,' I said. 'I kind of switched it on and off.'

He made a very Gallic pouting face at me. Benoît barely glanced up before continuing with his own hammer. This seemed extraordinary, like we were making chocolate in the Middle Ages.

'Hand-made is how we do things,' said Frédéric patiently. He'd lost his flirtatious edge, I noticed. Perhaps he only liked girls who knew how to hand-make chocolate. That must cut his prospective pool down quite substantially.

Frédéric nodded towards a spare hammer. I took it and tentatively hit a bean. Nothing. I hit it harder. *Splat*. I'd flattened it. Benoît took it wordlessly and threw it in the bin. I gulped. I wasn't entirely sure how much help I was going to be here.

'Perhaps you just watch for now,' said Frédéric. As I did, I noticed a quick little flick of the wrists they made as they assaulted the beans. It was a bit like a very good game of Whack-a-Mole.

When they had finished, Frédéric took out a surprisingly dainty minivac and blew away all the husks. I gulped my scalding little coffee, which tasted less like coffee and more like a very strong cleaning solution. There was absolutely no way I could drink the filthy stuff. I would never get used to it.

'Now, we feed the beans,' he said, indicating a large industrial grinder.

'So you do use a machine,' I said, as if I'd scored a point. I got a look.

Benoît came back in, lugging huge crates of milk, butter and cream from outside. It was all in rough, reused glass. I hadn't seen milk delivered in a glass bottle for a long time. Benoît was calling a farewell to someone out of the back door. It still wasn't light, but the sky wasn't as pitch black as it had been.

'We use only one dairy,' said Frédéric. 'The Oise. It delivers every morning. Swiss would be better, alas, but time is of the urgency to us.'

He started up the grinding machine and little by little fed in the precious beans, gently and carefully. Gradually a thick, dark liquid started to gather at the bottom, strained through a net in the collection bottle. Frédéric stared at it happily. When it finally stopped, I straightened up.

'Now what?' I said. At Braders we'd just started with the liquid and hurled stuff at it, but I didn't want to admit that.

'You conch,' said Frédéric.

The word was the same in English. Conching was mixing up the various ingredients, the levels, to make the chocolate dark, light, milk, flavoured. A tiny mistake one way or the other would make it disgusting, too sweet, grainy or crystalline. The machines at Braders were calibrated to make everything the same every time; they used cheap milk powder and life-prolongers and additives.

'Of course, that is for Thierry,' said Frédéric, lowering his head. 'It is the most important, the most sacred part.'

To conch by hand was very difficult. And then it would need refining and tempering, so it held together. I raised an eyebrow.

'This is for tomorrow,' explained Frédéric, and indeed, Benoît had now moved on to pouring a thick gooey mass from a pot, tempering it by working it back and forth with a spatula whilst he stirred another pot on the stove gently. Normally people would use a thermometer for this, but Benoît had been practically raised in the shop, as I learned later, and knew the consistency as instinctively as a musician knows when their instrument is out of tune. If he was happy, he would hum tunelessly. If he was not, he would dump everything back in the huge pot and start all over again until it was perfect.

Finally, he was ready.

'Rien plus!' shouted Frédéric, only just audible above the din of the grinder. 'No more. Nothing but the finest of dark beans from Costa Rica, the finest of fresh cream milk from the best-fed cows this side of Normandy, the finest cane sugar from Jamaica, all churned to perfection in the traditional way, not by huge machines full of fat and preservative and old bits of truc and the Band-Aids of the paysans, non?'

The colours blending together and being poured into moulds were absolutely beautiful; in fact, looking at them, you'd be hard pressed to disagree with Thierry's philosophy that chocolate was something meant to be made fresh and consumed fresh, no less than coffee or a croissant. And the smell was warmer, richer, purer than anything back in the UK, where we'd used a hefty dose of vegetable fats to bolster up the mix (which was why so many people who loved British chocolate found the posh stuff so hard to take to – it was the comforting fats they really liked).

'Do not dip the fingers,' ordered Frédéric, but I would never, ever touch food being prepared; I'd been on enough tedious health and safety courses to have got that one through my head, I wasn't an idiot. Frédéric, however, was passing me a long ladle, which looked to be one solid piece of curved metal with a tiny tasting spoon at the end. Benoît stood out of my way.

'Attention,' he warned. 'Be careful.'

Frédéric shook his head, but declined to say any more, simply watching my face curiously and intently. He was staring very closely at my lips. I found it oddly off-putting, but in a nice way. I carefully let down the ladle and scooped up a mouthful of the pale brown liquid.

Blowing on it to cool it, Frédéric staring at me all the while, I raised it to my lips.

Heroin addicts often say that all they are ever doing is chasing that first hit; the first time they felt wrapped in cotton wool, all the worries of the world behind them. I wouldn't say it was quite as dramatic as that. Nonetheless, the moment the still-warm, gently thickening substance hit my tongue, I really did think, for an instant, that I was going to fall into the pot – no, worse, that I was going to DIVE in, to drink in every morsel of that sweet – but not too sweet – creamy but not sickly, dense, deeply flavoured, rich, smooth, all-enveloping chocolatey goodness. It felt like someone giving me a warm hug. As soon as I had swallowed it, I wanted the taste back in my mouth again; wanted to cram myself full of it. I found myself embarrassed suddenly, blushing, as I noticed Frédéric's eyes still on my lips, watching me intently. My hand went automatically to dip the spoon again, then at the last minute I realised this would look desperate; unprofessional, greedy, hungry. Instead, I lifted it out empty. Frédéric raised an eyebrow.

'It's . . .' What could I say? That it pissed on almost anything else I'd ever eaten anywhere? That it was so good I felt like I wanted to cry? That I would never eat anything else as long as I lived? And it was still not even set.

'It's very good,' I said finally. Frédéric glanced at Benoît, who shrugged. Just as the room was heating up uncomfortably, the aircon clicked on and a cooling hum began. Everything here was rickety, antiquated and held together with tape. But there was absolutely no doubt that it worked. It worked beyond the wildest dreams of Braders; beyond the wildest dreams of every chocolate I'd ever eaten in my entire life.

'Eet ees better than very good, non?' Frédéric asked. He seemed insulted.

'I'm sorry,' I said. 'It's . . . le style Anglais.'

He seemed happier about this. Typical British stiff upper lip couldn't be passionate about anything, I suspected as far as he was concerned. In truth, I didn't want to tell him how impressed I was. It would make me sound like a rube; like I knew nothing about chocolate when in fact I'd been sent here to help. The gap between what I'd been making and what they were doing here was like the difference between a Fairy Liquid bottle rocket and the NASA Mars mission. So I decided it was best to keep my mouth shut. At least until I could fill it with more of that unbelievable chocolate. In secret.

Frédéric, with some relish, set about showing me where the cleaning equipment was kept, and what my duties were, then got me to hammer pounds of cacao beans until I stopped ruining their stock, showed me how to winnow for husks, and took me through the schedule of the shop. By the time we were finished, it was nearly ten o'clock and the sun was shining strongly through the long planters of herbs, making it look more like a greenhouse than ever. I wondered if we were about to open, as Frédéric and Benoît glanced nervously at their watches, but as it turned out, they were waiting for something else. Five minutes later, the shop door was thrown open with a spectacular clang. Benoît suddenly made himself completely invisible, while the jolly, puckish look on Frédéric's features was replaced with a kind of servile watchfulness. I looked behind me as the door into the little factory swung open heavily.

'ALLONS-Y! LET'S GO!' came a huge, booming voice.

Of all the surprises Claire had vouchsafed me, all the confusions, this was by far the weirdest.

The way she had spoken, the way she had gone pink when she mentioned him, it was clear to me that this had been someone serious in her life, whereas whenever she mentioned her ex-husband, Richard, it was with pained courtesy.

You could still see in her the traces of the younger woman she had been; she'd been beautiful. She still was, in a certain light, when the years of pain weren't so strongly etched on her brow.

I had fantasised, perhaps, of a suave, grey-haired type, perhaps with jet-black eyebrows, wearing chef's whites, or maybe a very well-cut suit. Smart and stylish, just like her; chic and a little bit distant. Perhaps we would smile wryly when Claire's name came up; or perhaps, sadly, he would barely remember her at all, just a girl from a very long time ago who had had a wild crush on him; a summer of his youth, but nothing to do with his real life at all. Romantic and handsome, obviously, perhaps a little sad …

None of these described Thierry Girard.

I don't know if Thierry spoke any English. I couldn't imagine how he made his trips to Australia and America, where he was feted and famous, if he couldn't. But I never heard him speak a single word. He was huge; he never spent any time in the shop without making it look as if there wasn't any room for anybody else. His belly, normally enswathed in a huge white apron, seemed to be a separate entity from himself, entering the room before he did.

'Who is this?' he boomed as he looked round the kitchen. 'Frédéric, have you been bringing night girls home with you again?'

At this stage my French was a beat behind what was actually being said, so I didn't realise till a moment or so later that I was being horribly insulted. Which was lucky, because if I'd shot my mouth off, I'd have been out of a job about two milliseconds later.

'This is AnNA Tron,' said Frédéric. 'The new kitchen assistant.'

Thierry lowered his enormous face towards mine. He had a flamboyant moustache; without it, his face was so sunk in fat that it would have been borderline featureless. His little black eyes were like raisins stuck in a huge muffin. His skin was doughy, and hair came out of his flat nostrils. He gazed at me.

'Women in amongst my chocolate,' he said. 'I'm not sure.'

I was taken aback. You would never hear this type of thing in the UK. Just as I was about to get annoyed about it, his enormous meaty shoulders shook with a huge belly laugh.

'I am joking! I joke! I joke!'

He looked at me again, then suddenly snapped his fingers.

'I know who you are!'

I wasn't at all sure he did.

'You are Claire's friend.'

I nodded.

'Her friend?'

'Yes. Well. She was my teacher.'

'Your French teacher?'

I nodded again.

'Ha! She spoke French like a dog eats salad.'

I bristled. 'She was a wonderful teacher.'

His eyes blinked rapidly, twice.

'Ah yes. I'm sure she was. I can imagine she was. Mind you, she was a terrible nanny . . . although alors perhaps that was my fault . . .'

He drifted off then, and I shifted uncomfortably. I wasn't at all sure how much he knew about Claire's illness, nor how serious it was.

'And you were ill?'

'I'm fine,' I said stoutly. I wasn't really in the mood for volunteering exactly what was wrong with me unless somebody absolutely had to know.

'You are fine for working hard, yes?'

'Without a doubt,' I said, smiling as convincingly as I could.

'Bon. Bon.'

His expression was far away again.

'And Claire . . . she is also ill.'

I nodded, not quite trusting myself to speak. He looked as if he were about to ask more, then stopped himself.

'Alors. Welcome, welcome. Do you know your chocolate?'

I looked into his big friendly giant's face sincerely. This I could answer.

'I do, sir. I've worked in chocolate for ten years.'

He looked at me expectantly.

'Yours is the best,' I said simply, not sure I could trust my French to elaborate. He paused, then the huge laugh was back.

'Listen to her!' he yelled. 'Alice! ALICE! Come, you must hear this. A countryman of yours.'

A languid, incredibly scrawny woman who must have been about fifty, but a really, really well-preserved fifty – her lipstick red on her wide mouth, her hair a perfect black helmet with an elegant swoop of pure white at the front – emerged into the back room. She was wearing cigarette trousers and a man's jacket and looked (there were no two ways about it) absolutely amazing. She was originally English, but, I would discover, kept insisting that she had lived in Paris for so long she had forgotten how to speak it, when what she actually meant was that she didn't want to waste her time on a guttersnipe like me, or any of the English newspaper-reading expats who gathered by the Shakespeare bookshop or the Frog or the Smiths on the rue de Rivoli. The best way to annoy Alice was to guess she was British before she opened her mouth, something I often prompted people to do. Which was childish, but she really was very rude to me.

She raised an eyebrow at Thierry.

'Chéri?'

'We have an English girl!'

Alice looked at me and I was suddenly very conscious of my plain skirt, my flat shoes, my Gap bag, my morning hair.

'Evidently,' she said. I couldn't believe this snotty cow was English. Well, I could, but she couldn't have looked more French had she been wearing a beret, a small twirled moustache and a Breton shirt and been carrying a chain of onions round her neck whilst riding a bicycle and surrendering a war.

'Hello,' I said in English.

'Bonjour,' she replied, then immediately glanced elsewhere in the room as if bored to death. I don't know exactly what had made Thierry go from lovely Claire to this, but no wonder he ate all the time.

Thierry beckoned me over. First he turned his attention to the fresh cacao. Frédéric added it to a large vat, and Thierry, with a deftness unexpected in such a large man, flicked a tap. Suddenly the vat filled up with warm, gently steaming thick chocolate liquid, followed by the milk, then added a fresh powder snowfall of sugar, stopping, tasting, stopping, tasting so quickly he looked like a blur. 'Yes, no, yes, no, more, quick!' he yelled as the men rushed to follow his bidding. Finally he declared himself satisfied.

'Now we really start,' he pronounced.

'Lavande!' he barked, and Frédéric rushed to cut some from the box at the end of the room. Thierry chopped it incredibly fine, so quickly I thought he would lose a finger, then he called for a tiny crystal bottle of lavender essence so potent that as soon as he opened it the entire room was overcome with the scent, like a spring meadow. Delicately, his little finger tilted upwards, he let two ... three drops fall into a basin, whisking all the time with his other hand. The tiny purple flecks of lavender were almost completely hidden as he paced across the room once, twice, three times, his left hand working furiously, his right holding the basin close. Occasionally he would stop, dip a finger, lick and resume, possibly adding a tiny drop more cream, or a little of the dark chocolate from the other vat. Finally he announced himself satisfied and stepped away from the basin. Benoît carried it over to the oven, where it would be shaped and melted and tempered ready for tomorrow.

Then Thierry hollered, 'Moulds!' and immediately Frédéric was there with the fresh batch of chocolate. Thierry poured it expertly into the moulds without spilling a drop, then inserted the tray into the large cooling shelves. Without pausing, he turned around; Benoît had already silently placed a large box of jellies in front of him. Thierry chopped them into the tiniest of diamond shapes, each exactly alike and perfect. By the time he had finished, the chocolate had hardened and he removed them briskly from the fridge, turning the mould upside down so that thirty-two perfect chocolates popped out on to the worktop. He pressed the diamonds of jellied fruit into the tops of the whirls, then, with a mere glance, sent one down to me.

'Tell me what you think,' he said.

I bit into it. The soft, sweet edge of citrus – it must have been cut from the lime plant – mellowed the perfectly balanced chocolate; the entire thing tasted so light it could have been good for you. The flavour didn't fade away in the mouth; its richness intensified, grew stronger. The tiny tart jelly on the top stopped the sweetness from overpowering the rest of the bonbon. It was perfect, exquisite. I smiled in pure happiness.

'That is what I like to see, heh?' Thierry gesticulated to the rest of the room. 'That is the face I like. Always the face I like. Today we will make lavender four hundred piece, rosemary and confiture, mint . . .'

He turned to Alice. 'You want to try?'

She gave him a stony look.

'I joke,' he said to me. 'She does not eat. Like a robot.'

'I do eat,' said Alice frostily. 'I just eat food, not poison.'

The wonderful aftertaste of the chocolate suddenly turned ashy in my mouth and I wanted to cough. Thierry looked at me mischievously and winked broadly, and I smiled back, but I wasn't sure I like that either, being lumped in with the massive fatties.

'It passes?' said Thierry.

'It is sublime,' I said, honestly. Frédéric smiled at me, which gave me the impression that I wasn't doing badly so far.

Thierry snapped his fingers and Benoît handed him an espresso into which he poured copious amounts of sugar. There was silence in the room while he necked it, then he crashed the cup down and announced, 'Finish!'

He and Alice swept out of the workroom, and the men immediately started to move. Frédéric gave me a mop and instructed me to basically wash and polish anything that wasn't tied down. Once they'd got going, they moved with awesome speed, turning out Thierry's creation exactly over and over again in the huge moulds: the lavender, then the rosemary and jam, which sounded very peculiar to me until they let me taste it, at which point I couldn't imagine why anyone would ever eat anything else.

At eleven o'clock, Frédéric took off his dirty apron, swapped it for a more formal clean one with the name of the shop and his own name embroidered on the pocket, and went to open up. The shutters made a loud rattling noise, echoing throughout the street as the other shops, cafés and emporiums started opening up for business too. Even though I'd noticed through the hazy workroom windows that the sun was up, seeing it beam in through the front of the shop made me blink.

My back was already sore from stooping to clean so many nooks and crannies in the workshop, and now Benoît indicated that he wanted me to start on the copper vat, which had a complicated-looking box of harsh-smelling cleaning products attached to it. Claire hadn't been wrong about the hard work.

Before I started, Frédéric beckoned me out for a cigarette break at the front. I didn't smoke, but I kept him company as he waved and bantered with the other shop owners setting out their stalls; the little bookshop was putting out racks of paperbacks, some of them, I noticed, looking a bit dog-eared; there was a print shop with vintage maps of Paris in careful plastic pockets, and some larger touristy work – Monet,

Klimt – on the walls for sale. One shop seemed to sell nothing but different types of tea, all in little metal boxes, brightly coloured, lining the walls in a hundred flavours: mint, cardamom, grapefruit, caramel. That shop smelled dry and refined, of leaves; not the earthy deep scents of Thierry's. But from the friendly way Frédéric hailed the proprietor, a tall, thin, older man who looked as desiccated as the leaves he sold, as if a stiff breeze would blow him away, I imagined they must get on all right, the two things complementing each other. Directly next door to us was a shop selling bits and bobs: brooms and dustpans and mop heads and nails.

Above street level, windows were being opened; the little roads were so narrow here you could see everybody living cheek by jowl. Coffee was being drunk, papers unfurled – *Le Matin*, *Le Figaro* – and everywhere the smooth rattle and chatter of French, reduced to a background melange. I couldn't quite believe it: here I was, hanging out with a true French person, in a road full of professional French people, working in a French place, drinking sticky coffee and watching the world go by. I was slightly delirious with the lack of sleep and on a bit of a sugar rush if I was being perfectly honest, but I couldn't help the huge bubble of excitement boiling up inside me, even though I was, when you got down to it, about to spend the rest of the day scrubbing a gigantic metal vat. You had to be, I was assured, very, very careful not to infect the vat with cleaning products, nor disturb its patina, which was what gave the mixing depth. Benoît had gone on about it till I was cross-eyed. Well, I would deal with that problem in a moment. For now, I was happy just standing outside, smelling Frédéric's heavy Gauloises smoke, watching a perky-looking dog with a newspaper in its mouth prance up the street, and a trio of pigeons spiral up amongst the high roofs, and hearing the chime of bells from across the river.

'He likes you,' said Frédéric. 'Be careful. Alice will not like you.'

'I can handle Alice,' I said, which was sheer bravado and actually a bare-faced lie. People confident enough to be rude always rather impressed me. 'Is she his girlfriend?'

Frédéric snorted. 'Without Alice, Thierry would stay in bed all day every day eating his own work. She is the one who pushes him, who made him famous. She is always worried that someone will steal him.'

But he looks like a gigantic pig, I didn't say. And also, surely, unbelievably glamorous and worldly Alice was hardly going to bother with me.

The first tourists of the day were already heading down the cobbled street, cooing and remarking on the quaintness of everything. One or two were following guides, and when they saw our sign, their faces lit up.

'The hordes descend,' said Frédéric, flicking his cigarette quickly into the gutter and returning to the shop with a large smile pasted on his face. 'Bonjour, messieurs dames!'

♡

From inside the workshop where I was scrubbing, very slowly, the gigantic pan with a toothbrush, like some kind of sadistic punishment, I could see the heads of people in the shop bobbing around. Sometimes Frédéric would put his head through the swing door and bellow at Benoît, who continued, utterly methodically, setting out tray after tray of the fresh chocolates, which sold as quickly, it appeared, as he could put them in the fridge, even though the prices were absolutely startling. I couldn't believe how much they cost. Frédéric explained to me later that yes, it was expensive to make chocolate the way Thierry did it, with the utter best of everything, but even the very finest of herbs didn't cost that much. Alice, however, had decided that unless customers found things eye-wateringly costly, they didn't appreciate them so much; they'd also found that every time they increased their prices the shop got busier and they got profiled in more upmarket magazines. And so it went on, till people came from across the world to visit the famous, the one and only, fresh chocolate shop on the rue de Chanoinesse, and Thierry kept on doing what he did and paid the staff, Frédéric remarked crossly, very little, whilst Alice salted it away and bought Chanel handbags. I wondered how much of this was true and how much just anti-Alice speculation.

At midday promptly, Frédéric shut the door and brought the shutters down. Benoît turned off all the machines and vanished on a wobbly bicycle that looked too small for his big frame.

'Where's he gone?' I asked.

'For a siesta, of course,' said Frédéric. 'And lunch.'

'How long do we get for lunch?' I asked. In the factory we got forty-five minutes – it had been brought down from an hour in a concession round to let us leave a bit earlier – but that was annoying as it wasn't long enough to go into town or shop or meet anyone or anything like that.

Frédéric shrugged. 'We shall open again at three o'clock.'

I looked at him, not sure if he was joking or not. Surely he was.

'Three hours?'

Frédéric didn't seem to find this the least bit surprising.

'Well, yes, you have lunch to do and perhaps a little nap . . .'

Now he mentioned it, a nap didn't seem like a bad idea, I'd been up since the crack of dawn. He smiled gaily and sauntered off, leaving me standing alone. Alice marched out without a goodbye and climbed into a van laden with fresh boxes. Thierry waved her off, then turned and fixed me with a surprisingly humorous eye.

'Lunch?' he said.

Chapter Eight

Apart from the chocolate, I'd had nothing to eat all morning, and I'd been up for such a long time. Thierry offered me his arm – he wasn't a very fast walker – and we crossed the Pont Louis-Philippe and vanished into a maze of streets, mostly filled with tourists, with the occasional local who recognised and nodded a head to Thierry. We passed wide roads with long chains of cafés and restaurants with picture menus outside and optimistic tables set in the street. He ignored these completely, and when we got to the far end of the Marais, he twisted quickly into a tiny cobbled alleyway between two large blocks of apartments with white shutters and washing hanging from the top windows. You wouldn't have noticed it was there if you didn't know exactly where you were headed. At the end of the tiny lane was a little wooden sign with a large pot on it swaying in the breeze. It looked like something out of Diagon Alley and I glanced at Thierry questioningly. He said nothing, but winked at me.

It was, in fact, a restaurant, and when we opened the old brown door, a gust of noise and smells and warm air flooded out. Inside everything was brown and wooden; there were coppers on the wall and it was ferociously hot. Tiny brown wooden tables and benches, built for earlier, thinner generations I would have said, were crammed together higgledy-piggledy on different levels. Everyone appeared to be shouting and I couldn't see a vacant table anywhere. A large woman in a dirty white apron and glasses appeared and kissed Thierry rapidly on both cheeks, gabbling something I couldn't understand then led us both to the back of the room, from where I could see, behind the bar, a huge brick oven roaring away.

We were jammed into two seats cheek by jowl with a pair of men who appeared to be having a furious argument about something but who would abruptly stop every so often and burst out laughing. I had just squeezed in when the old lady returned, cocking an eyebrow. Thierry leant over to me, 'I will order you the duck,' and then, when I agreed, simply nodded to the woman, who immediately sent over a very small, whippet-thin boy with water, bread, napkins, utensils, a vase of deep, fruity-looking wine and two very small glasses, all of which he unfolded on to the table at lightning speed. Thierry poured a tiny glass of wine for me – I thought it was to taste it – and a rather larger one for himself. Then he dipped a piece of bread into a bowl of olive oil, and sat back chewing it contemplatively. He seemed fairly content not to ask me too much about my life or even what I was doing there. I felt very nervous suddenly.

'So,' I said. 'You've always had the shop?'

He shook his head. 'Not always. I was a soldier too.'

'Really?'

I couldn't imagine Thierry as a lean, mean fighting machine.

'Well, I was an army cook. Yes.'

'What was that like?'

He shrugged. 'Horrible. But then I came back to my shop. Then I was much happier.'

'Why is it called Le Chapeau Chocolat?'

He smiled at that, but before he could answer, our food appeared.

I had never eaten duck before, except with pancakes at the Chinese when Cath and I were flush. I had thought it was a small thing. This was a huge breast, like a monster Christmas turkey. On the top was thick crispy skin, like crackling. There was a green salad and small roast potatoes on the side, and a yellow sauce. I watched Thierry as he chopped into his duck right across the middle and dunked it in the sauce. I immediately did the same thing.

The juicy, crunchy skin of the duck exploded in my mouth. The taste was just incredible; hot and salty and tender all at once. I looked up at Thierry. 'This is amazing,' I said. He raised an eyebrow. 'Oh yes, it is good.'

I looked around at the other tables. Almost everyone else

was also eating duck. This was what the place sold; oven-roasted duck. Amazing. I smiled, then wiped away some grease that wanted to run down my chin. The potatoes were hot and salty and the salad was peppery rocket. Everything complemented everything else. It was one of the best meals I had ever had. Everyone else was taking it completely in their stride, chatting, carrying on, pretending this was normal. Perhaps if you lived in Paris it *was* normal.

Thierry launched into explaining to me, excitedly, how they made sure the oven was exactly the right temperature, and how they balanced out the flavours. He was fascinating on where they sourced the animals (who had to live happy lives – a stressed duck was a bad duck apparently), genuinely interesting and animated; completely and utterly wrapped up in the subject, and I stopped noticing his bulk and breathlessness and caught only his hearty laugh and obsession. Maybe I could see what Claire had seen, just a glimpse.

Finally, after waving his knife in the air claiming he could smell that his neighbour's wine was corked, he caught himself and laughed.

'Ah, always I talk too much,' he said. 'I get carried away, you know.'

'It's good, I like it,' I said. He raised his eyebrows ruefully.

'No, no, I don't pay enough attention ... So tell me; you leave your boyfriend in England?'

'I don't have a boyfriend,' I said shortly. Thierry raised his eyebrows.

'But a woman like you ...'

I couldn't work out whether he meant 'a woman as nice as you' or 'a woman as old as you'.

'Uh huh?' I said.

'You look like you should have a boyfriend,' he said.

'Well,' I said. Maybe he meant dumpy, as though I'd settled down and given up. 'Well I don't.'

Thierry returned to his plate, and, on finding it empty, looked sad.

'Well. Do not fall in love with Frédéric, he has nine girlfriends.'

Given that I could probably squash Frédéric in a strong breeze, I felt this to be unlikely. I finished off my meal and did as Thierry had done, running bread around the plate to mop up the juices. Oh, it was so good.

'And what about our friend Claire?'

I realised I hadn't been able to check my email since I'd got here or let her know how I was getting on. Surely Sami would know an internet café somewhere, although he seemed a bit exotic for email, as if he would actually get everything delivered by carrier pigeons wearing bow ties.

I shrugged. 'Was it glamorous, Paris in the seventies?'

'Paris is always glamorous, no?'

I nodded.

He looked distracted for a moment.

'We were good friends, Claire and I,' he said, then stared at my bread and grinned broadly. 'It is very sexy, a woman who eats. You will find a boyfriend in less than five minutes, I am sure. Stay away from the Bourse, they are all bad bad men.'

The Bourse, it turned out, was the stock exchange, and Thierry launched into a very funny attack railing against privileged bankers. Afterwards he sat back in contentment, ordering us both another coffee, which came accompanied by a tiny flute of clear spirit.

'Eau de vie,' said Thierry. 'Essential.'

He swigged it down and I did likewise, only to find out it was a ludicrously strong spirit that made my eyes water. I started to cough. Thierry laughed.

'It is nice to make your acquaintance,' he said.

'Likewise,' I replied, once I'd recovered.

'And now, a nap!'

I had a tiny moment of wondering if this wasn't some kind of ridiculous seduction technique – surely not – but no, Thierry headed back to the shop, and I clambered up the many steps to the tiny apartment – half crawling the last flight – tumbled into bed and fell fast asleep as soon as my head touched the pillow.

♡

Thank goodness for Sami. At about three o'clock he emerged from his bedroom loudly singing an operatic aria that was far too high for him and making coffee hiss on the stove. When I came round, still a little drunk on food and eau de vie, I hadn't the faintest idea where I was.

'Chérie!' said Sami as I emerged, blinking, into the warm afternoon light in the apartment. He glanced at his watch. 'I thought you had a job.'

My heart leapt into my mouth.

'I do!' I said, panicking. 'I did. Shit.'

'Arrêt! Stop!' said Sami. He came over and smoothed down my hair, then wiped under my eyes where, presumably, I was all streaked with mascara. 'Do not worry about it, chérie. You may be a little late.'

'It's my first day!' I moaned. In the factory, you had to clock in and clock out otherwise you got your money docked. Not to mention the fact that it was ridiculously rude. I was an idiot not to set my alarm.

Sami eyed me up carefully. 'It is a siesta,' he declared. 'Not an invitation to become completely unconscious.'

A slender slip of a person hurried out of Sami's room to the little bathroom. I smiled at Sami, who completely ignored me.

'Allons, go,' he said. 'Rush. And do not say you are sorry. British people say they are sorry one thousand times a day. Why? You do not mean it. You are not really sorry. You should save it for when you are actually sorry. Otherwise it is meaningless.'

'Sorry,' I said, without thinking. He gave me a stern look.

'Now. Go. Do not get drunk.'

'I'm not drunk,' I said, offended.

'No, but you're English. So. It can happen at any time without warning. Come home late. I might have some friends here.'

I catapulted down the stairs, deciding to save time by not switching on the lights, which turned out to be a terrible plan, as I jarred my ankle on the bottom step. As I hared out of the block, I heard the first-floor door open and close quickly. Ugh, nosy old woman.

Turning into the rue de Chanoinesse, my heart sank. The shop was open once again, its striped awning rolled out, its subtle frontage glinting in the afternoon sun, a line of happy punters queuing up outside. But worse, Thierry, I saw, was already there, with Alice. Her lip curled when she noticed me. Why was she being so snooty?

'Ah, it's you,' she said, not even bothering to search for my name. 'We thought you'd found the work too hard and gone home.'

'I fell asleep,' I said, feeling my cheeks flare up bright red. With the others I might have managed to laugh it off, but this woman was like a scary headmistress. She looked disapproving.

'Well, I don't think the most successful artisan business in Paris runs particularly well on people being asleep,' she said icily. 'I'm not sure this is going to work out.'

I bit my lip. She couldn't mean to fire me, could she? Not when I'd just started.

'I'm really sorry,' I said. 'It won't happen again.'

Thierry turned round with a huge grin as I scampered in under Alice's gimlet gaze.

'We thought you had escaped! And taken all my secrets to Patrick Roger, huh? He would love to get his eyes on my workshop.'

I shook my head vigorously, tears stinging behind the lids.

Thierry turned to Alice.

'I took her to Le Brulot,' he said, looking mock-sad, like a little boy. 'So you see, it is all my fault.'

'Who paid?' asked Alice immediately. Neither of us answered. I'd never even seen the bill.

'She is a new girl in Paris,' said Thierry. 'She should understand lunch, yes?'

Alice still looked mutinous. His voice softened.

'You were a new girl in Paris once, non?'

'I don't eat lunch,' said Alice. But the aggression had gone out of her and she tutted and shook her head at Thierry, who shot me a glance of secret triumph. I couldn't help but smile.

♡

The afternoon showed the other side of Thierry, away from his perfectionist bent in the workshop at the back. As I tidied, fetched and scrubbed, I watched him with the customers: flirting, cajoling, letting them taste a little bit; giving tiny sips of hot chocolate to the children. He was as much a master out here as he was through the back of the shop, and when he presented the customers with their enormous bills, he would stare them out manfully so they handed over their credit cards without a murmur. It was a class act, I decided. He believed in his product so thoroughly, he couldn't help but transmit his enthusiasm, and the queues outside on to the cobbles were there to see him as much as anything.

At seven promptly the shutters were pulled down and I looked around. The shop was almost entirely empty, like a baker's at the end of the day. Anything not sold was immediately thrown out, and I cleaned like a demon. Eventually Thierry came into the back of the shop, smiling to see me polishing the brass.

'Ça va?' he said.

I nodded frantically, desperate to make it up to him. He glanced behind him. For the first time, I didn't see Alice there.

'How is ...' He went quiet, his natural exuberance suddenly seeming a little stifled. 'How is Claire?'

I carried on polishing so he didn't have to see my face. I knew it would betray the worst. While I had been at home, the recipient of the best physio and rehab the NHS had to offer, Claire had had an argument with her oncologist. She had told him she wanted an end point for chemo, after which she didn't want to do it any more. He had got very cross with her and reminded her that she wasn't that old. She had been very sharp with him, then so crotchety when I saw her that I had suggested immediately I shouldn't go to Paris. That was the only time she got even a little cross with me. What was the point of anything, she said, if I couldn't even do that? She was going to be absolutely fine, if only to spite her bloody oncologist.

I shrugged. 'She's ... she's been better.'

'Tell me more about her,' he said.

'Well, we were in hospital together,' I said. 'So we kind of became friends. She's the one who told me to get away. Well, forced me actually,' I added, remembering. 'She made me do it.'

'Good for her,' said Thierry. 'And is she ... she has a husband, a family?'

I shook my head. 'No. She's divorced.'

Instantly I saw in his eyes a sadness – and something else too, perhaps.

'Truly? Oh, but she was a beautiful girl. A beautiful, beautiful girl.'

I agreed; in our little town, before she got ill, she had shone like a star.

'But she will recover, non? She is not old. Oh, well, we are all old,' he grumbled to himself. 'But she ... she was so beautiful.'

'Who was so beautiful?' came Alice's perfect vowels, her accent retaining a tiny hint of the aristocratic English it must once have been.

'No one, no one, darling,' said Thierry, turning and pasting his beaming grin back on his face. 'Let us leave. Do we have a quiet evening?'

Alice looked at me with her eyes narrowed. Then she said, 'Yes, darling. We must drop in to François's cocktail party, they are expecting you. And the ambassador's. It is all business.'

'It is all ridiculously tedious,' said Thierry irritably. 'People are no fun anymore. In the old days, it was all wonderful and we could dance and smoke and now it is just everyone standing and looking worried and muttering about money, money money.'

'Well, if you didn't eat and drink so much, you might enjoy it more.'

'Non, I have to eat and drink to enjoy it at all.'

They headed off into the warm evening. Frédéric had already zoomed off on his scooter; Benoît was waiting for me to finish, tapping his heavy keys in his hand but not saying a word. I smiled at him in a jolly fashion as I left, but he did not return it.

'Bye then!' I said cheerily in English, but he didn't turn around.

Still weary, and a bit shell-shocked – practising with Claire was one thing; doing nothing but talk French all day long was a bit horrific and exhausting and had done nothing but prove to me how terrible I was at it – I clambered up the stairs. My missing toes were tugging painfully at me. This drove me crazy. Honestly, when I had all my toes, I swear I couldn't tell them apart. Now I'd lost a couple, it was all I could think about. They acted as a bellwether, telling me when I was a bit tired or run down or doing too much – all of which I could have predicted would happen today.

I thought about my toes all the time. No more sandals in the summer; no more lovely pedicures for going on holiday, when your feet get all lovely and brown and you feel summery long after the end of the trip. Now I was stuck in great big clumpy ugly shoes all the time; high heels were kind of difficult too, because anything pointed at the toe twisted my other toes very painfully and my chiropodist had told me to steer well clear. She'd also told me not to worry about it, hardly anybody walked up and down a beach counting other people's toes, and plenty of people had six to a foot and no one ever noticed, and other things like that, and I had smiled and pretended to agree with her, all the while vowing never to show off my feet ever again.

How I would manage if I ever met someone, I put to the back of my mind. I was too busy focusing on convalescence and trying to figure out how to survive for the rest of my life with the only half-decent employer in the district no longer in need of my services and my money from the factory running down. Anyway. No one would get to see my deformity, and that was the end of it.

As I limped up the final flight of stairs, Sami was standing on the landing, waving a green bottle at me. He was wearing a multi-coloured silk bath robe that was far too short for him. I tried not to look upwards as I ascended.

'Alors!' he shouted. 'The evening is beginning.'

'Not for me,' I said quickly. 'I'm exhausted.'

Sami looked hurt.

'You don't want to meet my friends?'

I really, really didn't. For one, my French was finished. The end. Fini. The idea of going out with Sami's doubtless colourful friends to somewhere noisy, then coming over as a total dud, was depressing. Really what I wanted to do was slump in front of the television, but I saw that the TV was already on and remembered – which was stupid, of course; why wouldn't it be – that it was all in French and seemed to consist of four blokes round a table shouting at one another. I sighed. I'd give anything for a dog doing cartwheels on *Britain's Got Talent*, possibly accompanied by pizza. I'd thought at lunchtime I'd eaten enough for the entire day, but my stomach seemed to think otherwise. I should have got some shopping, but I wasn't sure where to go. And there wasn't a thing in the apartment, I could tell. It smelled of exotic shower gel and cigarette smoke and a large sandalwood candle.

Also, apart from meeting Claire, the accident had changed me, it really had. I'd kind of felt up for anything before that, and the realisation that I wasn't, in fact, invulnerable was quite painful. I called it getting better, but actually, it was more like hiding.

Chapter Nine

There was, as I was to discover over the course of many, many evenings, no point whatsoever in trying to avoid a night out with Sami. And also, that a night out with Sami wasn't like a night out with anyone else. When me and Cath went out, for example, we'd tell some other people where we were going, and there'd be lots of texts and messages from people about which bar we'd be in, then we'd always end up at Faces because it had a dance floor and we'd do some dancing, and we'd end the night with a kebab at Pontin Ali's. That's what everybody did. All the nights were roughly the same, some more fun than others. Normally we saw a fight; occasionally Cath got into one.

Sami, however, had the skill – just as he did with his costumes at the opera house – to take the everyday, the bland, the tawdry and with hardly any money, but a bit of imagination, turn it into magic.

He could always find out where an exhibition was on, or a flash mob was going to happen. One evening the great Monaco circus had just arrived in town, and we sat on the tiny roof terrace of a cheap restaurant that served the best bouillabaisse in Paris, at mismatched tables festooned with tiny fairy lights, and watched the elephant and the tigers march out of their smart transporters. Another time he insisted everyone wear the colour blue, then talked us into a private view of a hot young artist as the entertainment, where we drank their wine and conversed loudly and pretentiously about the sculptures until asked to leave. He had an ever-shifting coterie of night-time friends: bar workers, box office staff, butchers and bakers; actresses and guitar players; anyone who worked antisocial hours, who finished when the restaurants and bars were closing up and needed to know someone who knew how to have a good time in the twilight world.

I didn't know any of that that first evening, though. All I knew was that although I was tired, I was eager too: for company; to be with people who didn't know all about me, who wouldn't make tired old jokes week after week about Long John Silver (I had only just stopped using the cane; I kept leaving it everywhere anyway). My long sleep at lunchtime and the adrenalin of all the new experiences had left me energised and overexcited; there was, I realised, no way I was going to sleep if I just went to bed. None at all.

'Go on then.'

I dressed in a very plain black dress that Claire had seen on an online shop and suggested I buy. To me it looked like absolutely nothing; I preferred things a bit more stand-outy, but she'd said this was more how to dress in Paris, so I had huffed, then agreed when it went in the sale. It was weighted down in the hem, so it actually did lie very nicely, and the only – the ONLY – benefit of being so stupidly ill was that I currently weighed less than I had done my entire adult life, so it fitted me smoothly without any of my normal lumps and bumps (usually I had two handfuls of stuff round the bottom of my back I could just kind of lift; well, I supposed a couple of months of working in a chocolatier's would sort that out for me).

Sami came and watched me getting ready.

'Aren't you going to put any make-up on?' he said. I shrugged, then glanced over at him. He was wearing peacock-blue eye shadow that kind of glittered. Oddly, it didn't make him look less masculine; it simply highlighted his luscious dark eyes and gave him a very dangerous look.

'Are you a transvestite?' I asked. One thing about having to get by in another language: I was never able to make space for niceties, or anything other than being very upfront.

Sami laughed. 'No,' he said. 'I just like to be beautiful.' He gazed in the mirror, obviously reassuring himself that he was.

I'd never heard a man speak like that before. He was wearing a tight-fitting black suit that looked incredibly expensive, with a brand-new white shirt, a turquoise tie and a bright turquoise handkerchief in the top pocket that exactly matched his eye shadow.

'You are,' I said, approvingly. To me he was like some exotic bird of paradise. He turned me by the shoulders and put me in front of the mirror.

'You look half-gypsy,' he said approvingly of my pale curly hair that never would settle down. 'Arrêt!'

He vanished and came back with an enormous professional make-up case laden with potions and ointments.

'Stand still.'

I submitted myself to his bidding and closed my eyes. When I opened them again, I was amazed at what I saw.

Sami had drawn a thick line of kohl right across the top of my lashes, fanning it out way past my eyes. It gave them huge, smoky definition, and he'd smudged powder on top of that, and added mascara. LOTS of mascara. Suddenly my eyes looked enormous in my face.

'No lipstick,' he said. 'Better like this. You may look mysterious and like you are wearing black on purpose and not because you are lazy about your clothes.'

'I'm not lazy about my clothes!' I protested. There wasn't much point in buying nice things when (a) I couldn't afford them, and (b) I had to wear a uniform at the chocolate factory so I just tended to sling on jeans and a top underneath. It was quicker and easier and I didn't really have to think about it. Cath and I liked to dress up for going out at the weekends, but that meant I always needed new outfits, so I had to buy the cheapest I could find really, so that I didn't wear the same things all the time. It wasn't a case of being lazy. I told myself. It was a case of being practical.

114

In the slim-fitting black dress, though (I normally chose clothes to disguise the bits I didn't like, especially at the back), with the huge eyes … suddenly I looked like someone completely different. Not the young, who-cares, back-of-the-class Anna. And not the more recent Anna, with the slightly shell-shocked expression, the lines of weariness and wariness around the eyes. No, I looked like someone totally strange and new. I attempted a smile, but it didn't go with my new look, which was more mysterious, less friendly.

Sami laughed. 'Are you pouting?'

'No!' I said, blushing.

'You are! You are loving looking at yourself.'

'NO!'

'That is good!' he said. 'That is exactly right. Now. Come. Martini.'

I followed him out into the darkening city night. The tourists with their colourful backpacks and upside-down maps had retreated now to their hotels, and the large restaurants with pictures on the menus that thronged the Place de la Concorde. The night felt like ours. We jumped on a bus that took us over the bridge and up the steady hill to the north; to Montmartre.

Claire had often spoken about Montmartre; it was her favourite place in the city. She said that on hot days it was often the only place you could get a breath of wind, climbing up the steps and sitting at the top. She said they used to park their little car up there – good luck, I thought,

115

seeing the parking restrictions there now – and picnic at the top of the steps.

Sami hopped off the bus and led me down a side alley and through another. I had not the faintest idea where I was. Occasionally I would hear clinking glasses and snatches of happy conversation, or I would catch the scent of garlic and onions and oil simmering in a kitchen, or the bright warm scent of bread from the all-night bakeries. Finally he came to a stop and indicated a large building that was completely silent. There was a narrow passage and it was up here he led me; to the side was situated a tiny door, behind which shone a bright yellow light.

Sami knocked brightly three times and the door was opened by a young girl dressed like a fifties cigarette girl. A huge blast of heat and light and noise blew out at us and I stepped backwards. She accepted some cash from Sami and ushered us inside.

Down a long flight of stairs we found ourselves underneath the street in a huge crypt. It must have been a cellar, or some kind of storage. At any rate, now it had been transformed into a club. At one end was a makeshift stage, and on it were a group of musicians playing fast and furiously for all they were worth: a trumpeter, a tall man wearing a fedora playing the double bass, a drummer who reminded me of Animal from the Muppets, and a tall woman in a fuchsia dress scatting into the microphone. People were dancing, or sitting at cheap foldaway wooden tables. Many of them were wearing forties-style clothes. I noticed to my horror that most of them were smoking; I knew there was a smoking ban in France too, but nobody seemed to observe it, and down here in this place with its one rickety stairwell and no fire exits as far as I could see, it felt dangerous.

Over in one corner was a hatch serving great pitchers of wine and nothing else; there was also corner seating further away from the band, and Sami immediately saw some people he knew and bounced up to introduce us. A waitress stopped by and asked if we wanted wine, but Sami demanded she make us a proper martini, and after rolling her eyes, she agreed.

I'd never had a martini before. Not a proper one, at any rate, clearly. It tasted like someone had nicked it out of a petrol tank. I spluttered and coughed until I attracted attention, then had to pretend that nothing was wrong.

As soon as we had sat down, people had started to circle our table. Sami, not surprisingly, knew everyone there; people who are very friendly, I have found, tend to be friendly to everyone. I felt a little foolish, in fact, thinking that his eagerness to take me out was to do with anything intrinsically interesting about me; rather it was his typical benevolence towards everyone in the world. As I sipped my martini, I watched him greet everybody with the same effusiveness. Sami, I concluded, was simply one of those people who liked everyone, required an audience and wasn't terribly fussy who it was.

Well, that was all right, I told myself, as no one else even looked at me. I wasn't truly surprised; the girls were all so glamorous, with heavy dark eye shadow that had gone out of fashion in the UK years ago, set against pale skin – no fake tan here – and they were all fashionably skinny. The boys even more so, and they dressed better. They wore heavy-rimmed glasses and nobody except Sami smiled or laughed; they just waved their hands in the air. Eventually one of the skinny boys grabbed one of the skinny girls to take her dancing. She pouted even more than she had been doing previously, which clearly meant yes. I watched them disappear into the sweaty crowd, looking sinuous and elegant and somehow strangely out of time.

I took another sip of my cocktail – in fact, a second cocktail; I appeared to have finished the first – and felt strangely dislocated and dreamy. The odd thing was, although I knew on one level that where I was was glamorous and interesting and different – everything I was meant to be here to discover – I also knew that it wasn't me. I could see, looking around, that I didn't fit in. I wasn't Parisian and sophisticated and skinny and beautifully dressed. I was too old, too parochial. It was an interesting world to observe, to visit, I thought, looking at Sami with his head back, taking part in four conversations at once; downing his martini and smoking a cigarette through a holder. But these easy bohemians . . . I didn't think there was much point in me trying to ingratiate myself, even if I did manage to understand a word anyone said. I glanced at my watch. It was late. I stood up.

'I have to go,' I said to Sami.

He looked up at me, surprised. I didn't think it was just tobacco in his cigarette; the pupils of his eyes were huge.

118

'Go? But we've just arrived! And there's a sky-top party we all simply must go to later . . . in a bit . . .'

'Thanks,' I said. 'But I have work tomorrow.'

'How will you get home?'

'I'll find a cab,' I said boldly. I had no idea how I'd get home.

Sami waved a lazy hand.

'All right, my petite Anglaise who works so hard. Everyone say good night to Anna.'

A man to whom I hadn't been introduced was standing there. He turned to Sami and said something in a low voice.

'Of course she will,' said Sami crossly. 'Darling. More martinis please.'

Then he blinked.

'Of course. You two have to meet.' He grabbed the man, who was tall and slightly thicker-set than most of the good-looking young beau monde around. He had been draped around one of the very skinny model-looking types and looked rather annoyed at being disturbed.

'This is Anna.'

The man looked completely nonplussed by this information. Rather than kiss me on both cheeks, or say 'Enchanté', like most of the other people I'd met, he thrust out a hand rather brusquely without looking me in the eye.

'Well, hello,' I said, taken aback.

He was still talking, crossly, to Sami.

'She'll never find a taxi,' he was saying.

'Of course she will,' said Sami. 'Or a bus, or a friend.'

The man rolled his eyes.

'I'll be fine,' I said. I was tired and a bit drunk and cross from the martinis, and I suddenly wanted very much to be in my bed. I didn't like these strangers discussing me like a piece of furniture. The Métro was probably still running anyway. I smiled shortly.

'Good night.'

♥

As it turned out, the rather grumpy young man had proved to be right. The streets were completely deserted. So much, I thought, for this being a big all-night party town. I'd been to London twice, and as far as I could tell, Soho and Trafalgar Square kept going all night every night. Here, though, it was practically silent.

All the taxis cruising the streets seemed to have lights on but didn't stop. My heart started to jump a bit. Maybe the system was different here. Maybe if you had a light on, that meant you *weren't* free. So I tried hailing a few cars without lights, but that didn't do me any good either, until one unmarked car with a man in it started slowing down a bit close to me and I turned tail and scampered up some steps. I glanced anxiously behind me, wondering exactly how safe Paris was, after all. About ten people had warned me already about pickpockets. What about muggers?

I heard a footfall somewhere behind me. The street lights, utterly charming though they were, wrought iron in the old-fashioned style, gave out picturesque but rather dim circles of light. At the moment, I would have liked full-beam motorway service station blindingness. I could barely see my way ahead and hadn't a clue where I was going. I started walking a little faster. The footsteps behind me sped up.

Oh crap, I thought. Oh God. I was stupid coming out by myself. I was stupid coming out at all, full stop, with a new flatmate I barely knew. I should have stayed inside and eaten packet noodles and, I don't know, had a good cry or something. I moved faster, trying to see a street that led somewhere more wide open with a better chance of company, but all the roads ahead seemed equally tiny and mysterious. Oh bugger.

Straight ahead was the outline of the huge church, the Sacré-Coeur. I decided to head for that, not from some old-fashioned idea about sanctuary, but with the expectation that it would have a nice big courtyard, somewhere with lights – you could see the floodlighting right across the city. I ran up more steps, and behind me the feet got faster too, closer and closer, my heart pounding in my mouth, my hand searching in my bag for something I could use as a weapon. I grasped the big old-fashioned iron key that opened the door of Sami's building and told myself to aim for his eye.

'HÉ!'

The voice was deep and throaty and I could tell by the tread that it was someone heavy. Shit. Right. This was it. The footsteps were closing in. I was in a small cobbled courtyard nowhere near the church, surrounded by boarded-up shops and tightly shuttered flats. Would they open up for me? I doubted it. I took a deep breath.

'AAARRRRGH!!!!!'

I screamed with all my might and leapt on the dark shadowy figure, the key outstretched in my hand, trying to stab it into his face. I caught him off guard and he toppled over hard on the cobblestones, me coming down on top of him, still trying to get at him with the key and screaming the worst obscenities I could think of.

I didn't realise at first that there was an equally terrified screaming coming from underneath me. A pair of extremely strong arms was trying to keep me away from his face. I had reverted to English – extremely Anglo-Saxon – and suddenly he spoke in English too.

'Please, please stop . . . please . . . I don't mean any harm. Please.'

The meaning didn't filter through straight away, and I was so crazy with adrenalin I'm not sure when exactly I would have stopped, if a shutter at the top of the apartment block above us hadn't suddenly opened, and, without warning, a bucket of water poured down on our heads.

That stopped me. Panting, I realised I was sitting on top of the grumpy man from the bar. He was holding my hand in a vicelike grip at arm's length, but I had already managed, I saw, to make a good gash in his forehead. Seeing the blood suddenly made me wobble.

'Oh,' I said, shock and faintness washing over me. I

swayed and nearly collapsed on top of him. He quickly moved his hands to my waist, holding me up.

'What the ... what the HELL did you think you were doing?' I finally managed to gasp, as I clambered up. I was soaking.

'I was shouting at you. Didn't you hear me? I didn't catch your name first time.'

'You don't follow a woman like that!'

'Well you don't march out into a foreign city if you don't know your way home. Sami is fun, but he's always going to choose the party over you.'

I brushed down my dress, as he lumbered to his feet. His English was extremely good, only the merest hint of a French accent.

'So you were ...'

'I came to find you. I was knackered, and I'm heading back your way anyway. I can't keep up with Sami's partying.'

'I can imagine,' I said, which was as close as I could get right then to an apology, with my heart still racing at a million miles an hour. 'Oh God, I've hurt you.'

As if he hadn't realised before, he put a large hand to his face, only to feel the blood trickling down. He pulled his hand away and looked at it.

'Gross,' I said, appalled. I felt in my bag for a tissue, but I didn't have one on me.

'That is awful,' he said, suddenly looking very wobbly himself. 'Have you stabbed me?'

'Of course I haven't stabbed you,' I said defiantly. 'I've keyed you.'

He didn't understand till I showed him the key, then recognition dawned. My already anxious body suddenly pounded with fear that he was going to be furious. Instead, to my enormous, shattering relief, he shook his head, opened his mouth, revealing a white-toothed smile, and started to laugh.

'Come, come with me,' he said, and directed me up a tiny alleyway that looked forbiddingly dark. I had one more second of panic, at which he added, 'Please. I certainly wouldn't attack you now.'

'I have my key,' I said, giggling nervously as the adrenalin finally started to leave my body.

To my total surprise, the narrow alleyway opened out on to a wide, brightly lit thoroughfare that had cars thundering down it, and here and there a café still open. The man led me to a tiny coffee shop, inhabited by several Turkish men using a hookah, and a dark-eyed proprietress with bags under her eyes who raised an eyebrow but nodded brusquely as he asked her for two coffees and a bathroom.

I sat there quietly until he came back, his wound cleaned up somewhat, holding paper towels to his head.

'I'm sorry,' I said again quietly. The coffee arrived. It was hot, black, and about fifty per cent sugar. It was just what I wanted.

He shook his head, then glanced at his watch.

'Argh,' he said.

'Don't show me,' I said. 'I have to be up in a few hours.'

'I know,' he said. I looked at him.

'Who are you?'

He grinned and I caught something then ... saw something in his face.

'I'm Laurent,' he said. 'You're Anna, I remember now. You work for my dad.'

♡

1972

Thierry worked from first thing in the morning, so at noon he made a decision to close the shop for three hours rather than the traditional two. When Benoît, his assistant, suggested that this was commercial suicide, he pointed out that Italian shops closed for four hours, and that people would wait.

Claire would put the children down for their naps, under the cheerful supervision of Inez, the housemaid, and slip out, Madame and Inez swapping meaningful looks.

The two of them would wander across Paris's bridges, each more beautiful than the last. One foggy day, which turned the city black and white, like a Doisneau photograph, they strolled the Pont Neuf, every cobble, it felt to Claire, smoothed by lovers meandering across it for hundreds of years.

Thierry would talk and talk – of flavours and schemes and what he had learned in Innsbruck and Geneva and Bruges – and occasionally he would remember to ask Claire what she thought of things too, but it didn't really matter to her; she was happy to listen to him; to rejoice in her understanding, which improved day by day; to revel in the warmth of his full attention, because when he got back to the shop, he would instantly be surrounded by people who wanted a piece of him: some business, or a word, or an idea, or to congratulate him on his taste or ask him about something in the newspaper. When they were in public, he was everybody's. Tracing out their own circuitous routes around Paris, he was all hers, and she found herself unable to ask for any more.

Never again in Claire's life would time speed away from her so quickly as it did during those walks, those lunches. Three hours felt like the blinking of an eye, and she would float through the afternoon, so light-humoured and good-natured that Arnaud and Claudette would cling to her, happily repeating the English songs she taught them, lisping along to 'Hun-eee, oh! sugerrr, sugerr ...'

Mme Lagarde kept a close eye on her, and when she judged the time to be right, she casually came into Claire's room one night and sat down on the bed.

'Now, chérie,' she asked, kindly. 'Please tell me you know about contraception.'

Of all the shocking and strange things that had happened to Claire on her trip, none was as bizarre as this elegant woman of the world referring to ... well. Matters. Of course she had a rough idea, picked up from her time at Chelsea Girl; she knew what a rubber was, kind of, and the girls spoke casually about being on the pill, although the thought of going to nice old Dr Black, who'd known her since she was a baby, and asking him for pills to have sex was completely beyond her imagination, while the idea of these matters being discussed under the Reverend's roof was simply impossible.

It being in another language helped, of course it did. But Mme

Lagarde's cool, confident manner in discussing sexual hygiene as if it was nothing more nor less important than regular hygiene (which indeed in Madame's eyes it was) was an eye-opener for Claire in more ways than one. Firstly, she declined the offer of prophylactics, but promised to ensure they were used. Secondly, she took Mme Lagarde's matter-of-fact tone and unflustered manner and stored them away somewhere. Years later she was to end up taking all the sex education classes in the school, as most of the other teachers couldn't face it. Statisticians always marked down the lower rate of STDs and teen pregnancies in the Standish ward of Kidinsborough, an otherwise very deprived area, simply as a blip. It was nothing of the sort.

♥

As soon as he said it I realised immediately. Of course he was. The build, the dark brown eyes; he was far more handsome than Thierry could ever have been, but fundamentally they were very similar, down to the long black eyelashes and the spark of mischief in the eyes, now the panicking was over.

'You look ...'

'Please don't say I am like a thin version of my father.' He looked down and patted his small stomach with a weary look. 'Aha, not so thin.'

Actually he wasn't fat at all; just big, with a barrel chest and broad shoulders.

'Well, you can't look that much like him,' I said. 'Otherwise I wouldn't have stabbed you with that key.'

'Well, unless he's really difficult to work for,' said Laurent, downing his coffee. 'Ah. That's better. Am I dry?'

His curly hair stuck up in all directions and he had a lot of dark stubble on his chin.

'Do you have any big meetings today?' I said.

'That bad, huh?' he said. 'Hmm.'

'So why did Sami want to introduce us?' I said.

'Oh, Sami likes to think he knows everyone.' Laurent thought about this and qualified the statement. 'Okay, he does know everyone. He thought it would be funny, introducing us.'

'Why?'

'Well ... because ...'

'What?'

'Because he knows my dad and me ... we don't get on that well.'

It was hard to imagine anyone not getting on with the avuncular Thierry.

'Oh no! Why not?'

Laurent held up his hands.

'Just father–son stuff ... nothing really. How is he?'

'I don't know,' I said wanly. 'He seems pretty happy to me.'

Laurent looked quite fiery. 'Really? That is why he weighs three hundred kilos maybe? This is what a happy man looks like?'

'Well, your mother seems to keep him in line,' I said nervously.

Laurent's expression turned icy.

'That's not my mother.'

I figured I'd probably said enough for one night. Laurent drained his coffee and looked up at me, his smile back, his shortness forgotten.

'Sorry,' he said. 'I don't think I made a very good first impression.'

'Apart from the attempted mugging and the terrible parent issues,' I said, 'you're doing totally fine. Do you want me to pay for the coffee too?'

He looked a little shocked till he saw I was joking.

'No,' he said. 'Are you any good? At chocolate, I mean. Not violence.'

I shrugged. 'My old boss said I had a nose, whatever that is. But your father does things very differently. I'm going to try my best. I ... I owe it to someone,' I said. 'To stay. And do what I'm doing.'

I looked around on to the street, still thronged with night people.

'Even if coming to Paris does seem a bit ...'

'Un peu trop?' said Laurent quietly, in French. A little too much.

'It's been a long day.'

'Come on then,' he said. 'I came to take you home. I will.'

I followed him out on to the street, wondering where his car was. But it wasn't a car. Tucked away under a railway bridge about a hundred metres away was a beautiful shiny powder-blue Vespa.

'Only way in town,' he said, when he saw me looking at it.

'It's cool,' I said.

'It's essential,' he replied, unlocking the seat and handing me a pale blue helmet that matched the bike. His own was a vintage black one with large old-fashioned goggles.

'What is this, the girl's helmet?' I joked, before realizing that it smelt of hairspray. Well of course, he must have a girlfriend. Probably tons. I felt a little odd putting it on.

'You've been on a scooter before?' he said.

'Oh no, I haven't,' I said, the helmet halfway on. 'Is it just like a bike?'

'No,' he said, scratching his head. 'No, it really isn't. Uhm. Just. Okay, move when I move, okay? Like, if I lean over ...'

'Lean the other way, for balance,' I said promptly.

'Uh-oh,' said Laurent.

'No?'

'The opposite. When I lean, you lean.'

'Won't we fall over?'

'Probably,' said Laurent. 'How bouncy are you?'

♥

Driving through the Parisian dark, clutching a large man on a tiny bike (with a man bag over his shoulder – all French men had them, I noticed; they seemed to make perfect sense), I tried to follow his lead as to when to lean. It was hard to predict, as he never signalled, and often didn't wait for lights to change, simply ploughing straight ahead. The first few times I buried my face in his soft leather jacket. After that, finding myself still alive, I attempted to trust him, and began to take some notice of my surroundings.

We roared down the Champs-Elysées, its broad pavements and tall white buildings glowing in the moonlight. Every time we turned slightly towards the left, I would see it there, following us like the moon: the unmistakable form of the Eiffel Tower, lit up with spotlights. I couldn't take my eyes off it, standing there so brazenly. Nothing else around it could lessen its impact.

'What are you doing?' growled the voice on the front of the bike as I twisted my body to get a better look.

'Sightseeing,' I replied, half my answer lost in the wind rushing past us.

'Well stop it. Follow me.'

And he grabbed my right knee quite forcibly and tugged it more tightly round his waist. I clung on and let the sights of Paris come to me as they would: a church here, its square belfry askew; the great windows of the stores glinting in the streetlights; the occasional snatches of west African rap from passing cars; once, on a street corner, a couple slow-dancing to music only they could hear. A crescent moon, a gentle scent of perfume and flowers as we passed the Place des Vosges, the air fresh but not cold against my skin, Laurent in front still travelling at what seemed to me terrifying speeds, the old street lamps flashing past us.

Suddenly, even though I didn't know where I was or what I was doing, not really, and quite possibly with the help of two martinis, I suddenly felt amazing. Nobody, nobody in the world – apart from Laurent, who didn't count, as I'd only just met him – nobody knew where I was, or what I was up to. I didn't know what lay ahead, I didn't know what I was going to do with the rest of my life, whether I was going to succeed or fail, meet someone or stay single, travel or go home.

It sounds so stupid seeing as I was thirty, had no money, eight toes, a garret rental with a socialite giant, and a temporary job. But suddenly, I felt free.

Chapter Ten

1972

'*Spaghetti Bolognese.*'

'*No.*'

'*That is not possible.*'

'*I tried spaghetti hoops,*' said Claire, lying back on the grass.

'*I do not know what that is.*'

'*They're all right.*'

'*All right. All right. Why would you put something in your mouth that is only all right?*'

Claire giggled. They were having a picnic in the *Jardin du Luxembourg.* It felt almost magical to Claire that only weeks before, she had been looking at the young lovers, so smug and contented with their wicker baskets, their casually discarded bicycles and empty wine bottles. They made it look so simple; she had been so envious.

And now here she was too, lying half on a rug, half on the grass under a blazing blue sky. M. and Mme Lagarde had taken the children to Provence for a week. Originally Claire was supposed to go with them. When Mme Lagarde had said she wouldn't be necessary, Claire had immediately panicked and worried she'd done something wrong. Being sent back to the Reverend in disgrace would be more than she could bear.

Madame had laughed at her worried face. She wanted Claire to give her love life a chance; have a little adventure of her own. It hadn't escaped her notice that Claire had come more out of her shell; she was loving and carefree with the children, more willing to speak up. She had roses in her cheeks and a light golden tan; her appetite was good, her eyes were sparkling, her French coming on in leaps and bounds. She was already a long way from the worryingly pale, hopelessly introverted schoolgirl who had arrived on their doorstep two months before. Now, thought Madame, Claire should have a holiday too.

First, she took her shopping.

'As a thank you,' she murmured, brushing off Claire's stammerings that they had already done so, so much for her.

She took her to her own atelier, situated just off the Marais. It was a tiny shop front, with a sole sewing machine in the window and no signage. A woman in an immaculate black knit dress cut starkly to the knee with a starched white collar appeared in front of them.

'Marie-France,' said Mme Lagarde. The ladies kissed, but with no noticeable warmth. Then the dressmaker turned her pale blue eyes on Claire, who felt herself quailing under the weight of such scrutiny.

'Her legs are short,' she barked.

'I know,' said Mme Lagarde, uncharacteristically humble. 'What can you do?'

'But the lower part of the leg should equal the length of the thigh.'

Marie-France harrumphed and indicated to Claire, without saying anything, that she should follow her up the perilously narrow twisted staircase.

The first floor, in complete contrast to the poky shop below, was a large, airy room, lit by enormous windows on both sides. At one end, two seamstresses, both tiny bent ladies, hunched over sewing machines without looking up. Another tiny woman was pinning the most beautiful material – a huge, heavy swathe of pale grey taffeta, that shimmered and reflected the light like running water – on to a dressmaker's dummy, ruching it at the bust, then pulling it in towards the waist, making tiny, invisible darts with a clutch of pins from her mouth so quickly it was almost impossible to see what she was doing. Claire stared at her, utterly fascinated.

'Disrobe,' said Marie-France without emotion. If Mme Lagarde found this in the slightest odd, she didn't let on to Claire with even a twitch of the lips. Claire took off her cheap cotton summer dress and stripped down to her petticoat and bra. Marie-France made it clear with a roll of the eyes that the petticoat also had to come off. Claire felt cross and a bit shaky. Did she really have to be so rude? She'd never taken her clothes off in front of a stranger before. This made her think of Thierry, and blush.

Marie-France watched her impatiently, then whipped off a long tape measure that had been hanging round her neck like a white snake and, at the speed of light, started measuring her up, shouting out measurements – in centimetres, of course, Claire realised, two seconds after wondering if she'd put on lots of weight without noticing – to the woman who had been pinning taffeta, and was now jotting down details in a large, navy blue leather-bound book.

'Nice flat bosom,' she said to Mme Lagarde. Claire had certainly never heard it described like that before. 'And the waist is small. Good.'

She glanced up at Claire and addressed her in perfect English, even though Claire had given every indication that she understood her in French.

'That is what your waist should measure now for the rest of your life. It is in the book.'

Mme Lagarde smiled. Claire glanced at her.

'That's good,' whispered Madame. 'If it goes in the book, that means she approves of it.'

Marie-France snorted. 'I've yet to meet an English girl that could hold on to it.' She looked up. 'The babies come, they think, a-ha, now I shall lie in a field like a large cow and wait to be fed.'

Claire thought of her own mother, with her lovely rounded bosom and strong, capable arms. She had always thought of her mother as beautiful. But it was difficult to believe that she and Mme Lagarde had been school girls at the same time, were the same age. Madame looked closer to her own age.

'Raise your arms ...'

After rapidly jotting everything down, Marie-France gave a nod to her assistant, who led them up another flight of stairs. This room was dark and cramped, lined ceiling to floor and wall to wall with every kind of material imaginable. It was like an Aladdin's cave; there was gold ribbon, and silks in the deepest of hues: turquoise, pink, scarlet. There were many different tones of black, in every possible material, from the finest, softest mohair wool to the lightest, most delicate chiffon; navy, too. Florals large and small, some so loud you couldn't imagine who could wear them, to tiny etched daisies on a heavy sunken cotton so tiny you could barely make them out. There was voile, and large rolls of calico for pattern cutting; stripes of every conceivable variety; and, over in the far corner, protected by a dust sheet, the lace and satin, in white and oyster and cream, for the brides. Claire couldn't help it, she gasped. Marie-France almost let a twitch cross her lips.

'I see you're thinking ahead,' she muttered. Claire coloured again and turned back.

'Now,' said Mme Lagarde, all business. 'Nothing too sombre. She's not French; she'll just look like a clumpy English girl on her way to a funeral.'

Claire was barely listening, she was still studying the colour and feel of the fabrics lining the extraordinary treasure cave of a room. The street noise and traffic of Paris outside had disappeared; she felt as if she was in another world.

Marie-France gave a sniff. 'She cannot be chic.'

'I don't want her to be chic,' fired back Mme Lagarde. 'Chic is for spoilt bobo girls who never work a day in their lives. I want her to be what she is: young and pretty and unspoilt.'

'For how long?' said Marie-France, and Claire wondered how such a rude woman could even get up in the morning without everyone she knew wanting to kill her, but she didn't have much time to think about that, as Madame, with a practised eye, picked out a light cream poplin lined with a navy stripe, and a soft green silk with a border of gentle yellow wild flowers.

Seconds later, to Claire's regret, she was back in the main atelier, where the tiny woman, who didn't say a word through her *mouthful of pins, started draping her at the speed of light, while Marie-France and Mme Lagarde bickered and disputed and lengthened and shortened.*

There was no mirror ahead of her, so Claire let her thoughts wander ... to what Thierry would say when he saw her in her new finery, and beyond, to what she would do ... what she could do ... in a week where she would have the entire house to herself. It made her heart beat terribly fast. Of course Thierry had asked her back to his apartment, and of course she had refused. It didn't seem right.

It wouldn't seem right under her host's roof either, but Madame had been so matter-of-fact, so open about what she thought was a healthy stage of development that ... well, Claire didn't think she would mind. She bit her lip nervously. Would it seem terribly forward? Terribly rude?

But then, the way Thierry made her feel every time he touched her hand, every time he held her elbow to manoeuvre her down the street ... it made her feel hot and cold and completely overwhelmed, unable to concentrate on anything. And now it was August, and in just a few short weeks she would be headed home, back to Kidinsborough, and the Reverend, and school, and then on to secretarial college, or the grim teacher training place they had up the road, not the university her teachers had been so keen to encourage her to.

Did she dare?

'Bon,' said Marie-France, finally, without smiling. 'You can stop. You stood well.'

'She liked you,' said Mme Lagarde, as they stepped out onto the hot pavement. They shared a look, then, an instant later, both of

them dissolved into giggles, for one instant more like friends than employer and au pair. Claire didn't think she'd ever seen Madame laugh like that before. It made her look even younger.

♥

A mere week later, the dresses were ready. Claire went nervously into the shop, where the wordless seamstress was making final adjustments. Marie-France raised an eyebrow and barked a quick bonjour in greeting, then marched her upstairs. This time Claire was grudgingly accepting of the fact that she would be stripping down in public, and had worn her whitest set of underwear. The first dress shimmied over her head like a light silken waterfall. As the silent seamstress zipped up the side zip, Claire could already feel that it fitted her absolutely perfectly. For a tiny second Marie-France and Mme Lagarde regarded her totally silently, until Claire was sure there must be something terribly wrong with it, or it didn't suit her. Then Marie-France sighed, just a touch, and said, very quietly, 'Oh, to be young again,' and with a wave of her hand indicated the seamstress to roll out a long mirror that had been hidden behind the wall. The sun streaming through the back windows, Claire suddenly caught a glimpse of herself. It was not the reflection she was used to in the bathroom mirror: the pinched, pale-faced English girl with the scrubbed-looking nose and slightly doleful expression; the hair colourless, the shoulders thin.

The Parisian summer sun had added a very light golden tan to her skin and brought out tiny freckles all over her nose. The green of the dress brought out the colour of her eyes and gave them an intensity they'd never had before. Her hair had light streaks in it and had

139

grown down past her shoulders, and suddenly her thinness, which had always caused her to be described as peaky-looking, was flattered and emphasised; her tiny waist was cinched in, and curves had been added to her hips by the full skirt – not at all in fashion, but what did it matter when it suited her so well. The line of yellow flowers along the bottom emphasised the pretty leanness of her calves, without drawing attention to the fact that she was still shorter than average.

It was beautiful. Claire Forest, scrawny, shy only child of the fearsome Reverend Forest, had never been praised for her looks in her life – her father thought it vain and rather wicked to be proud of the way you looked – but today, Claire too felt beautiful.

♥

During the next few weeks I started to settle in. The work was extremely hard, and unrelenting, but I liked it and was even starting to get the hang of the husking and the conch. Frédéric was funny and flirtatious (a different girl every week would turn up for him at the shop, all of them pouty and disdainful, which was exactly how he liked them – he liked, he explained, to prostrate himself fully in front of a strong woman who would control everything. It was no surprise our flirtation hadn't exactly progressed). He was also voluble and fiercely purist about every stage of the chocolate-making process. Benoît continued to treat his job like a monastic calling. Alice never lost the look of distaste she put on every day when she saw me turn up, but Thierry was taken with me and liked to chat – and I liked to listen, thankfully – as he pontificated on life, and chocolate, with chocolate being by far the more important, obviously. He would often take me for lunch whilst Alice toiled away, showing me the best croque-madame, or how to eat shellfish properly. After work I would often go out with Sami, who turned out to be the most fun omnisexual Algerian flatmate I'd ever had, when he wasn't complaining about opera singers who got too fat and budgets that got too small. I didn't see Laurent about much after that first evening. Sami said he was quite the boulevardier, always with a different model on his arm. I imagined Thierry had been similar when he'd been younger. Poor Claire.

After two months of this, I found I loved getting up at the crack of dawn, patting Nelson Eddy, the dog who fetched the newspaper for his mistress who lived on our street every morning; seeing the freshly cleaned cobbles come to life, water dribbling down the drains; the tiny funny-looking vans delivering drinks and fresh food; the smells of bread baking everywhere; the running hither and thither of kitchen staff – the sheer number of restaurants in Paris was dizzying, and Thierry seemed intent on visiting all of them; then the glancing up through the roofs and the pigeons to the tiny floating clouds miles above to see if it was going to be another glorious day. That summer, it seemed, every day was a good day. I liked most of all getting dressed and going out on my little terrace first thing. The whole of Paris, laid out in front of me like a huge tray of macaroons, glowed rose pink, and I would think of the boarded-up high street of Kidinsborough with the pound shop and Kash4Gold, and how when it rained the canal would spit old bikes out on the towpath, and feel as far away from home as if I'd landed on the moon. Sami and I often crossed paths at four a.m., he coming in, me getting up for work, and we would stop and take a coffee (with brandy for him; nothing for me, as every time I ran out of milk I had to go down six dark flights to find some and it never seemed worth it, so I just learned to drink it black). Sometimes he was with chaps, sometimes with girls, sometimes alone, sometimes with an entire party. It was very fortunate I didn't work normal hours, it could have been a disaster. The eyrie was absolutely tiny, with no working kitchen beyond coffee, no shower, and a bath you had to sit in with your knees pulled up to your chin.

I loved it.

I knew I was getting into it when Cath and I swapped emails. I think I was just a bit overexcited and needed to tell someone. In retrospect, Cath probably wasn't the right person.

Hi C! I just got back from the most amazing party on a boat in the middle of the Seine. There were fire jugglers (my flatmate took me, everyone he knows does something stupid like that) and they kept setting drinks on fire and people kept trying to leap over them. Then these two chefs came on. One of them is

my boss's son, but they've fallen out
with each other. Anyway, they were
trying to hurl crêpes over the flames in
little pans, but they kept falling out
and it was hysterical and brilliant.
Hope you're good, Anna

♡

Dear Anna,

On Tuesday I put four hours' worth of
extensions in 'Ermine' (she used to be
called Sal, do you remember? Daft bint)
McGuire's head for her *X Factor*
audition. She smoked through the entire
thing. She wanted red, white and blue
and kept on talking about how she was
going to pull Simon Cowell. It took all
afternoon and I had to have the door
blowing open on account of her wanting
to smoke. I think I've got bronchitis.
And I lost one of my new snakeskin nails
in it. I said what was she doing, being
the new Michelle McManus? And she told
me to shut it, but I'd been standing all
bloody day. Then she came in yesterday
her eyes red with crying and said nobody
had even seen her and she'd waited nine
hours in the hosing rain and the colours

had all run and it was my fault and she
wanted her money back. I said she could
go whistle and she said she could go
punch me in the head. I got out the big
scissors.

The police have said they won't press
charges, but I have to give her the hair
back in a box. I said I wouldn't be
touching it, it probably had crabs
already. PC Johnson smiled and said he
got off at nine. So I'm off out.

Come back soon,

Cath

I hadn't meant to gush to Cath, but it was really a proper fun
night. Well, it had started in the morning. Thierry had
marched in huffing something about refrigeration (he was
furious about it; even if we were running horribly late you
couldn't ever put his work in the fridge, because it took away
the highly polished shine). Anyway, we'd had an electricity
bill and Alice was spitting feathers about it and basically
implying we should work in the dark or something, and
Frédéric had mentioned the fridges and Thierry had started
huffing and puffing and getting red in the face, until eventually he'd signalled something to Benoît, who had immediately
run up the street and returned with two dozen eggs.

'Anna! Come with me!' Thierry hollered. He had kind of taken me under his wing a bit. I was happy about this, obviously, in that I wasn't going to get sent home to annoy Claire, but I could always feel Alice's gimlet eyes boring into me.

'Chocolate pots,' said Thierry. 'Seeing as we are paying for all this electricity ...' He glared balefully at the large fridges, then grabbed the eggs and started separating them into two bowls, so quickly and deftly it was fascinating to watch. He showed me how to whisk the whites up at the speed of light, then passed me the bowl.

'Can't we do this in the mixer?' I asked tentatively, my wrist getting tired.

'We can buy them from the supermarket,' he barked back. 'Would you like that? Would that suit you?'

Next, he started to melt some of the day's fresh plain chocolate in a huge bain-marie-style device over boiling water, very carefully, stirring all the time. He added milk powder and cocoa powder, then the whites, even though I raised my eyebrows at him. 'You make it stick together,' he said, 'if you want. Don't question my methods.'

He was smiling, though, so I knew it was all right. He made the whole lot into a kind of paste, then he studied the line at the back of the greenhouse for a long time, humming and hawing. After changing his mind several times and picking up and putting down a large bag of almonds, eventually he settled on half ginger and half lime, sprinkling them in and tasting the two vats. Then, indicating to me to do the other one, he poured the contents of one of the bain-maries into two dozen little ramekin pots. Not taking any chances, I put mine in with a big soup ladle. Then we lined them up on trays and Thierry flung open the doors of the fridge.

'Ta dah!!! Now I shall make use of you, you money-guzzling goddess!' But of course the fridge was actually full of milk and butter, so Benoît dashed to clear some shelf space for us to put in *les petits pots*.

Thierry took himself off for a mid-morning digestif, and by the time he returned, the little pots had set and darkened to a glossy sheen. He moued, muttered something to the fridge, then announced that this was all they were good for, this and eating his money. He took out a tiny silver spoon and let me taste the lime one. It was extraordinary. Lighter than air, whisked into a melting nothingness that left a dark, rich sensation on the tongue and an extraordinary desire to eat more of it; it was hardly like eating at all; more like a dream of flavour.

He priced the pots at something extortionate. We sold out in fifteen minutes. I made him promise to stand over me one more time whilst I made them and he said he didn't have the necessary forty years to teach me where I was going wrong, but I was pleased nonetheless.

When I got back that evening, Sami was cross. He was making costumes for a production called *La Bohème* (he said it in a way that assumed I hadn't heard of it. I hadn't, but nodded my head importantly. I guess to him it would have been like someone saying they'd never heard of Michael Jackson), and he said his bohemians had all gone too far bohemian and he couldn't get them to come to any fittings so he was going to have to track them down at their house, except they were living on a barge.

It was a gorgeous evening; the light in Paris felt like dripping gold.

'I don't suppose,' said Sami with some sarcasm, because he kept asking me to come out in the evenings and I hardly ever said yes, partly because I was shy, and a lot because I was constantly knackered, and embarrassed about my French, 'you're going to come.'

But I was buoyed by Thierry's careful lesson of the day, and how accepted it was making me feel, and for once wasn't too exhausted, so to his total surprise, I said yes.

The houseboat that the singers were living on was full of people enjoying the evening, drinking and juggling and hanging out. I pasted on my best grin as Sami was swallowed up by a hundred of his closest acquaintances, and got myself a glass of champagne (I was quite impressed that they didn't have enough money to rent an apartment but wouldn't dream of stinting on the fizz). By the time I came back up deck from the tiny galley, someone had started up the engines and we were putting out into the Seine. I wasn't entirely sure this was legal, and looked around dubiously as the barge narrowly avoided one of the pleasure boats – the bateaux mouches – that patrolled the waters. We headed upstream under the bridges and past the crowded stone banks. Notre-Dame and the Eiffel Tower bobbed in and out of sight and the party grew wilder. As we moored just off the

Île de la Cité, two men, to huge roars of encouragement, produced what I soon realised were huge torches. At first I was horrified – they were going to set the boat on fire and kill us all. But then I thought, well, I am in a foreign country, having an EXTREMELY foreign experience, and anyway I can't get off the boat, so I may as well just go with it. But I made sure I was as far away from the action as possible.

The two men, stripped to the waist, lit the torches and started juggling with them. The boat was bobbing up and down but they kept their balance perfectly, and it was both funny and frightening at once. People on the banks of the river were gathering to watch. Sami was ringmastering, shouting and gesticulating with his arms.

Suddenly I saw a familiar face, bent low in conversation with a girl, but, it seemed, not really paying attention to what she was saying. His eyes searched the boat. Then they saw me and he smiled, briefly, in recognition and raised his hand. Before I realised what I'd done, I'd smiled too and waved back. It was Laurent, Thierry's son. Instantly I felt rather guilty, as if it was a betrayal of the lovely day I'd had at work with his dad. I bit my lip and he grinned and turned back to the girl, but not before Sami grabbed his arm and started yelling at him. At first Laurent shook his head – no, no, definitely not – but before I knew it, someone had stuck a frying pan in his hand and a white chef's hat on his head and the music had been turned up and everyone was clapping. He lifted his hands in a gesture of surrender and, in the oddest coincidence, started cracking eggs into a bowl, his deft,

strong fingers behaving exactly like his father's. I was hypnotised. Someone brought up flour, too, and milk, and he
whisked it all up – again in the same way as Thierry – then
the jugglers brought their torches down and started throwing
them more gently, as, to my utter astonishment, Laurent
melted some butter in the little pan and started to cook pancakes over the flames. Each new crêpe was flung in the air in
near-perfect timing with the torches themselves, and greeted
with rounds of applause, particularly the one that flew right
off the boat, to be immediately snapped up by an enormous
seagull.

It was stunning to watch. At one point, reaching for a pancake he'd flipped right up out of the pan, Laurent stretched
a long arm over me, lost his footing and landed nearly in my
lap.

'Oof,' he said. 'Bonsoir mam'zelle.'

'Hello, Laurent,' I said. He'd straightened up really
quickly.

'The spy!' he said, but his eyes were twinkling in a way
I'd seen before.

'I'm not a spy! How could I be a spy? What, I'm going to
steal a pancake recipe?'

'You shall tell my father I am a partying good-for-nothing,'
he said, his big dark eyes sparkling at me.

'That very much depends,' I said, 'on whether or not I get
the next pancake.'

He looked at it, all perfectly cooked, then grabbed a
bottle of Grand Marnier from the side of the boat and poured

the orange liqueur over the top of it. As the alcohol burned off, a delicious smell filled the air. Then he picked up a napkin and, in a move that seemed almost like magic, flicked the pancake on to it and in a trice folded it up into an envelope so I could eat it.

'I shall tell him you're a very good boy,' I said. The crêpe was painfully hot, but totally delicious.

Something crossed his face at that moment, something that wasn't just about him being a party boy. Some remembered pain.

'No,' he said quietly. 'No. Don't tell him anything at all.'

I looked straight at him, wondering what these two larger-than-life personalities could possibly have fallen out about that was this bad.

'Come in and see me,' I said, a bit tipsy, not quite realising what I was saying. Then I stopped, horrified.

'I don't mean like that,' I said. 'I mean, come by to see me and you can see your dad. But not like that.'

He smiled, put out a callused hand and suddenly, out of the blue, touched my cheek. I flushed a fiery red.

'Ah, not like that, huh?'

I reminded myself about Frédéric and that this was what French men were like. Incorrigible flirts. Ridiculously flirtatious. Cor, they were good at it, though. I resisted a sudden strong temptation to reach out and touch his stubbled chin; his thick curly hair.

'Laurent! Laurent! More crêpes! Encore!'

The girls were calling for him from the other side of the

boat; the torches still burning high. I checked my watch. It was late; I was up early. Someone moved the boat next to a jetty to allow me to get off and a party of people dressed as Harlequins to get on.

Laurent smiled, as if he knew exactly what was going through my mind, then gave me a quick kiss on either cheek – perfectly normal here, I knew, absolutely standard French behaviour, so there was no reason for it to set my cheeks flaming – and vanished back into the crowd, as I, with a mix of relief and regret, found my way across the gangplank and back to the safe ground of the Île de la Cité. The lights and the fire and the laughter and music from the barge lit up the river all the way home.

Chapter Eleven

It was barely eight o'clock the next morning and I was sweeping up the husks when I heard the ting of the front door bell. Frédéric and Benoît looked at each other, confused. They had been playing the radio loudly. French pop music was, I discovered, very much an acquired taste. Frédéric immediately turned it down and called out, 'Bonjour.'

But standing in the doorway, without Alice, or any of the constant motion and bluster I'd got used to, was Thierry, his large bulk outlined in the still hazy light from the front door, his normal broad grin completely absent.

'Anna,' he said. 'Come, walk with me.'

I did as he said. It was going to be a beautiful day, but there was still a hint of dawn chilliness in the air. There were no tourists about this time in the morning; it was mostly just shopkeepers, the rattling of grates, the sluicing of dirty water from the mop buckets down the drains; everywhere the scent of coffee and fresh baking.

'Let us walk,' he repeated, without saying anything else. I glanced at him quickly, wondering if his knees were up to it. He didn't look like he took any exercise at all. He saw me glancing and smiled, though less ebulliently than usual.

'I used to love to walk,' he said. 'I used to walk everywhere. It was my favourite thing to do. Look!'

He took me down the cobbled lane that led to the Île Saint-Louis and then across the beautiful Pont Neuf, which was lined with the padlocks of lovers. People just leave them there, to signify their love, and the authorities let them stay. They're beautiful. A bateau mouche wended lazily down the river, and a large flock of seagulls took off just in front of us. Ahead was the sombre, riveting wall of the old Bastille.

'Paris changes too much,' he said, even though I was thinking absolutely the opposite. He pointed out a huge field of banners over on the left bank. 'Look, they are having a festival,' he said. 'Food from all around the world.'

'Why don't we take a stall?' I said, not thinking about it. He looked at me.

'Because we do not need to! We are far too good.'

'All right,' I said. 'It was just an idea.'

'Does Chanel take a stall at a market? Does Christian Dior?'

I didn't point out that you could find those brands all over the world, and decided to change the subject.

'Why don't you walk so much anymore?'

'Because I am busy, because Alice does not like to walk, she thinks it is vulgar.'

'How is walking vulgar?' I couldn't stop myself from asking.

'Well, because you cannot wear beautiful shoes, and you look like you cannot afford a car.'

I thought that was possibly the stupidest thing I had ever heard in my life, but I'd already insulted him once this morning, so I decided to keep it to myself.

'I like it,' I ventured instead. 'It's a good way to see a place.'

'It is!' agreed Thierry fervently. We'd reached the other side of the bridge; the morning rush-hour traffic was struggling for places on the roundabout, but we ignored them all. He turned and gestured back at what I'd already come to think of as my home: the Île de la Cité, the familiar square towers of Notre-Dame visible through the gaps.

'Look at it! A perfect city state in miniature. Everything you could possibly want is there.'

Except a supermarket that opens at lunchtime, I thought but didn't say.

'You could live on that island for ever and never leave. People did. It was the first inhabited area of Paris. Right in the heart of the world.'

I smiled at his absolute certainty, then ran to catch him up. He moved surprisingly swiftly for such a large man.

He looked at me.

'I got another letter from Claire. She is very unwell,' he said.

There wasn't any point in prevaricating.

'She is,' I said. I felt immediately guilty. Sami had the oldest laptop in the world, and sometimes we could hook on to our neighbour's wi-fi but I hadn't kept in touch anything like as much as I should have. Claire didn't have a lot to occupy her days, a bit of gossip would have come in very handy. Later she told me she was thrilled I was too busy and happy to write, and she was so convincing I almost believed her. I called Mum and Dad every Sunday and told them about new things I'd tried and new food and they tried to sound interested but I don't think they were really. They told me about the dog (barbed wire in paw) and Joe (new building apprenticeship, fat girlfriend). And Cath texted or emailed from time to time. But my new life felt so immersive. I vowed at the very least to be better at talking to Claire.

'What was wrong with you?' asked Thierry.

'I lost two toes,' I said.

Thierry scrunched up his face in pained sympathy.

'Ah, look.'

He showed me his little finger. It was slightly blunted. He'd obviously sliced the top off.

'This is how I knew I was bound for sweets, non? No more butchering for me. No more cooking for big hungry soldiers in the desert. Ugh.'

I nodded in sympathy.

'So,' he said. 'And she ... she has all her toes?'

'She has cancer,' I said.

'Yes.'

We were walking above the embankment by the river, which was running fast today, a kind of dark blue colour. There were a lot of boats ploughing up and down; goods and coal were coming in.

Thierry stared at the water as if he didn't see it.

'Ah, the cancer,' he said simply. 'It is the sniper at the party. Everyone is happy, then . . . *boum*.'

We kept staring.

'They can do many good things for cancer now,' he said.

I shook my head. 'Maybe. She has it in three places. It is hard to have it in three places. And she is stubborn.'

Thierry glanced at me, then looked away very quickly.

'So it is as bad as that.'

'Maybe.' I shrugged. I didn't want to think about it.

'And her family is kind?'

'Her sons are very good.'

'She has sons?'

'Two.'

'Ah, sons,' he said, and I supposed he was thinking of Laurent.

'They are kind? They look after her?'

'They're wonderful,' I said. He harrumphed.

'Mine would not call the pompiers if I was on fire.'

He bit his lip at this.

'Oh, my little Claire,' he said suddenly, as if I wasn't there. 'My little English bird. My little Claire.'

1972

'You look ... you look beautiful.'

*Claire giggled. She had never seen Thierry lost for words; she
didn't think it was possible. He was as greedy for words, for ideas
and new information and jokes as he was for food, for wine, for
chocolate, for Paris, for her.*

*They were in the garden of the Lagardes' house, deserted since the
family had decamped to Provence, leaving her alone in Paris. It felt
like everyone had left, en masse. The entire city had emptied out,
leaving the heat for the soft breezes and mimosas of the south.
Businesses had closed down, restaurants were no longer serving. The
city was like a ghost town. Or a playground.*

*In a feat of devastating boldness, Claire had left a note at the
shop, in the morning, before he would be in. She had thought about
it many times. She had gone to Papeterie Saint Sabin, the great sta-
tioner's, and spent an enormous amount of her earned cash on the
most exquisite stationery. She had been almost unable to choose; it
was all so beautiful. Finally she had gone for a pale green and yellow
flower, very similar to her new dress. The heavy cream envelope was
lined with pale green and gold stripes. It was absolutely exquisite. Her
heart in her mouth, she had slipped into M. Lagarde's private office,
all leather chairs and heavy furniture, and borrowed one of his fountain pens, trying to make sure not to blot the ink. And she had written,
simply, a time and the address, her hand shaking with excitement.*

*Of course he had come; had found her, as she planned, round the
back. He took off his hat, his face a little pink in the heat, mopping
his brow. The garden was surrounded by fruit trees, to give the area
privacy. On the perfectly straight lawn, Claire had put out a picnic:*

157

the finest Morbier cheese, which she knew he adored; some pâté and heavy sourdough bread from the tiny southern bakery on the corner; grapes, big, shiny and pitted with seeds – he liked to chop them with a tiny knife, nipping out the seeds with extraordinary dexterity in his huge bear-like paws; carved Serrano ham from the terrifying butcher that she had had to pluck up a lot of courage to enter; and, chilling in a bucket of ice, a bottle of Laurent Perrier '68. Madame had told her to help herself to whatever she wanted. This was clearly pushing it, Claire realised. She would make it up to them, she told herself.

The sun fell heavy and huge, rippling through the trees as she sought out some shade. The light felt thick and golden, almost like syrup, as she waited, unable to concentrate, fiddling with her hair, her new dress, the food, the delicate china she had carefully removed from the tall armoire in the dining room, the small jar of fresh flowers that she'd picked from the beds, from behind other plants so hopefully nobody would notice. He made his way round to the door which led on to the little back alleyway between their grand imposing street and the next, knocked, quickly, then entered.

Claire stood up. The sun lit her pale hair; made it shine as if it were gold. The gentle green silk of her dress ran off her like a river; she looked like something conjured from the water, or a dryad from the trees.

'Claire. You look . . . you look beautiful,' he breathed, quietly for once, moved to silence. She stepped towards him, and he pulled her close, then sat her on his lap in the shade of the trees. Nothing was eaten. Words were no longer necessary. Some little time later, the birds started into the bright blue sky.

Thierry led me down to the corner of the street, where there was a tiny, packed boulangerie with a few tables and chairs very close. You could no longer see the river, nor the Île de la Cité, sat in the middle like a great ship. Thierry barked a quick order to the waiter, who came charging back through the middle of everyone with two tiny coffees, each with four sugar lumps placed on the side, and two enormous religieuse buns – two profiteroles, one smaller than the other, covered in chocolate and held together by cream, so they looked like little nuns or priests. Thierry ate his without thinking about it, then held up his hand for another, like a cowboy downing whisky shots at a bar.

Then he paused, watching me eat. The bun was totally delicious.

'It was difficult,' he said. 'Her father … well. We were very young. It was the summer. She had to return, and I got called up for my national service …'

He looked up at me, and suddenly, through his jolly, tubby demeanour, I saw a lot of sadness in his eyes.

'When you are young,' he said, 'you think you will get lots of chances at love. You are careless, you spend your youth and your freedom and your love because you think you will be rich with all these things for ever. But they do not last. You spend it all, then you see if you have spent wisely.'

He took a more reflective bite of his second cake.

'I thought … I thought we would have time, always. That the summer would never end, that things would never have to change … Because I am an old fool, Anna. Don't be like me.'

159

'Things aren't so bad for you,' I said, instantly. He smiled.

'Ha. Thank you. You are kind.' He leaned forward. 'Do you think ... do you think I could talk to Claire?'

I tutted. 'Have you never heard of the telephone? You can talk to her whenever you like.'

'I feel uncomfortable on the telephone,' said Thierry. 'And also I did not know; what if she didn't want to talk to me?'

'You two are worse than teenagers,' I said, remembering how Joe had had a crush on Selma Torrington and sat in his bedroom for a week. My other brother James found a poem he'd written, and we were so taken with the horrible seriousness of it all, we didn't even tease him about it.

'You're grown-ups,' I said. 'Just phone her. Or write back to her.'

His face looked unhappy again.

'I don't ... I am not so good with the letters.'

'Well, you have to do something.'

'Then I shall do that,' he said. 'You think she would be pleased to hear from me?' he asked again, beckoning over the bill.

'Of COURSE!' I said, exasperated, and he smiled.

♡

He positively bounced back along the riverbank with me, sweating slightly and seemingly full of newly inspired energy, pointing out various landmarks and saying did I think Claire would be able to travel, and would she like to come and visit, and pondering how much she might have changed in forty years, and asking questions I couldn't answer, like what her husband was like.

'Oh,' I said. I had been wondering when would be a good time to bring this up, but hadn't seen an opening in the conversation so far. 'I met your son.'

He stopped short and looked at me.

'Why?' he said. 'How did you meet my son?'

I didn't say I had thought he was going to try and attack me and steal my mobile phone.

'Um, just about town,' I said. Thierry narrowed his eyes at this.

'I thought this was your first time in Paris,' he said.

'It is,' I stammered. 'I just have a very sociable flatmate.'

Thierry looked displeased.

'Well. He is a do-nothing.'

'Doesn't he have a job?' I said, a bit shocked. I'd just assumed he did. Maybe that was why he had such a tiny scooter.

'Well, if you call making ridiculous confections for a great big company that is not your father's company and everyone says, oh, I see he does not work with his evil father . . .'

His face went brick red.

'Sorry,' I said. 'I really am. I didn't realise things were quite as bad as that.'

He shook his head.

'He says I was not a good father. He makes Alice smoke too much.'

I thought about Thierry's self-obsession and gadfly enthusiasms, and decided that they were probably not ideally suited to fatherhood.

'Maybe you are very alike,' I ventured.

'We are not at all alike,' he said. 'He doesn't listen.'

'Shall we get back?' I said. I didn't particularly want Benoît to take against me anymore than he already had. They'd be shutting for lunch soon, and I still had pots to clean.

'He never listens to me, his father,' said Thierry, and stepped out into the road. A car screeched and swerved to avoid him, and we both jumped back, frightened.

'Idiot!' shouted Thierry, his face purple, shaking his fist in rage at the disappearing grey Peugeot. 'Bloody monster! You cannot drive! You should not be allowed to drive!'

The lights had changed and I ushered him across the cobbled road, as he continued to shout threats and gesticulate behind him.

'You bloody son of a pig! You do not look where you are going.'

We were one step on to the Pont Neuf when it happened. The pavement was busy, thronged with people going to work in the huge Ministry of Justice building, and ready to visit the cathedral, and several of them found their way blocked as the huge man suddenly stopped short in the middle of the pavement, clutching his chest and his left arm.

Chapter Twelve

1972

The Lagardes returned from Provence in the middle of August, tanned and relaxed. The children had been happy to do little more each day than paddle in the stream at the end of the garden, try and catch snakes in pillowcases and fall asleep in restaurants, little Claudette often under the table, as they met up with friends – the same friends, Madame noted with amusement, that they saw all the time in Paris, dressed a little more casually and discussing the local dishes with some passion. More than once her thoughts had strayed to Claire, and whether she had done the right thing leaving her alone with that bear of a man. She had, she decided. The girl was nearly eighteen years old and had never been allowed an inch of freedom her entire life. She was a sensible child, he was a kind man. This would be good for her.

Her eyes swept the house. It was immaculate, everything placed perfectly, Claire standing there with wide, nervous eyes; she'd obviously been up all night making sure everything was just right. There was a (watery, poor) shepherd's pie in the fridge that she'd made for them, and to Madame's practised eye Claire looked rosy, happy and well and truly in love.

Claire herself felt delirious. Somehow she'd thought that when she and Thierry got together – if they ever did; she hadn't quite been able to believe it would actually happen – it would somehow calm her down, quell the craziness in her breast, the fact that she spent every moment of the day thinking about him. In fact, if anything it had got worse. The softness of his curly hair; the fire and tenderness in his eyes; the bulk of him . . . They spent every moment together they could; eating, talking, making love, all of it done with Thierry's huge appetite for life. She felt as if he had brought her to life; that she had been leading a black-and-white existence and with the arrival of this exuberant Frenchman, everything had burst into colour; the Reverend's house was Kansas, and Paris, to her, was Oz.

Mme Lagarde caught up with her after they'd been home a couple of days. Claire had been beyond conscientious with the children, listening patiently to all their stories of sticklebacks and wading and hammocks and bees, playing and painting with them, and taking them to the new exhibitions. But her soul only awoke at five o'clock, when she would run to the shop and he would drag her into the back room, behind the huge copper vats, kissing her passionately as if he hadn't seen her for months, insisting she try this or that: a new taste, a new flavour, then a restaurant where he would inveigle her into snails, or foie gras, or linguini with tiny clams she had to prise from their shells, or lobster thermidor to a backdrop of wildly kicking girls; then he would take her back to his little set of rooms at the top of Place des Arts, the noise of the street and the street lamps still bright beneath them, the chatter of French at high speed and cars occasionally whooshing past, and they would make love, over and over again, before he would dress and courteously take her home, dropping her before midnight with a kiss, and the certain knowledge that they could do it all again tomorrow.

'My dear,' Madame said quietly as Claire was preparing to go out, this time in the pale cream stripe. Claire's back stiffened, as it always did. There was something inside her, deep down, that didn't feel as if she deserved this; that she was doing something wrong. In her father's eyes, of course, she was. Her polite, stiff weekly letters to her parents, full of the doings of the children and the sights of Paris, gave so little away, her mother worried that she was actually terribly miserable and lonely, though surely if she was so unhappy she'd have found a way to make an international call. Ellen made sure she answered the phone all the time, just in case it was the operator asking them to accept a reverse-charge call and the Reverend said no.

'It's all right,' said Madame to Claire's back. She was fastening in some tiny emerald earrings Thierry had bought her. She had laughed and said he didn't have to buy her anything at all and he had said that really he would like to buy her diamonds like Elizabeth Taylor, but he was just starting out and this was all he could manage. They were very small, like tiny green chips, but they matched her eyes and were beautifully set in a twist of antique silver. She would have loved them anyway, because he had chosen them for her. The fact that they were tasteful too made her hug herself gleefully inside.

'You're not in trouble,' said Mme Lagarde. Claire felt relieved. It was ridiculous to keep panicking like this. Thierry thought she was being hilarious. She was a grown woman. Who could begrudge her her happiness? Claire wasn't so sure. God was always watching. And so much happiness; so much pleasure. It didn't feel right somehow. Somewhere in the back of her head, a tiny voice kept telling her she was wicked.

She turned round.

'You know the children really are wonderful, Mme Lagarde. You've done such a great job with them.'

Madame waved her hand. In her opinion, like that of many Frenchwomen, children flourished better the less their parents interfered.

'I just wanted to say, my dear, that we have grown very fond of you during your stay here.'

Claire felt herself blushing. How could they like her, when she had been . . . when she had been out every night like an alleycat, said her inner voice – that sounded a lot like her father.

'We will be very sad when you have to leave us . . . in two weeks.'

Mme Lagarde was doing her best to be gentle.

'You are going back to school, non? I think that will be right for you. You should continue your studies, you have plenty of brains. University life would suit you.'

'I don't think so,' said Claire, shaking her head miserably. Most of her energy went on not thinking about leaving. Two weeks was for ever. It was a long time. She could worry about it later. 'My father thinks university is a waste of time. He thinks secretarial school. Or teacher training.'

Mme Lagarde frowned. 'Well, you are good with children … but don't you think there are other things you could do? Or other people you might meet?' She was nothing if not practical.

Claire swallowed, all her happiness gone. She stared fixedly at the parquet floor, not trusting herself to speak. Madame gently lifted her head and looked her in the eye.

'I hope you have been happy here,' she said, very clearly and distinctly. 'And that when you go home you will have many happy memories.'

Claire understood, of course she did. She was only a girl. Thierry was barely twenty-two, at the very beginning of his career. What did she think was going to happen? That she was going to stay in Paris and get married?

Of course, on one level, deep down, that was exactly what she thought. She had a silly, girlish vision of Thierry and her, she in something from the special corner of Marie-France's shop, in a beautiful park on the Île de la Cité … not that they could get married in a park, of course, that was ridiculous. And not that she could afford a wedding dress. And they had only known each other a few weeks. The whole thing was impossible, she knew, even if Thierry had mentioned anything beyond August at all. And he had not.

She couldn't imagine Thierry in Kidinsborough, catching the number 19 bus, walking to the Asian shop on the corner to pick up Pot Noodles for supper. She couldn't see him propping up the corner of the Crown, the local pub, drinking a pint and talking seriously about who was going to score on Saturday. He didn't even speak English. How would he choke down her mother's Yorkshires, which shattered like glass, or her vegetables, which generally resembled mush? The first time Claire had eaten glazed carrots at Maxims, she genuinely refused to believe it was the same vegetable they ate at home. He couldn't come over. The idea was ridiculous.

But Arnaud and Claudette would be at school; Claire wasn't needed round here. She had to go back to school herself. And although Thierry could afford to neglect his business in August, when there were no galas, no parties, no social set to cater for, that would change in September; he would have to work harder than ever just to keep afloat. There would be no room for her in all of this. She knew that.

She thought all this in the split second it took to lift her head.

'I will,' she said, returning Mme Lagarde's steady gaze. 'I will have good memories.'

♡

Thierry staggered back, and the passers-by stopped and cleared a space. I grabbed his arm, and thankfully a strong-looking man with a beard helped me lower him to the ground. He was making horrible sounds. I pulled out my phone and stabbed 999 over and over again, but it didn't go through and I felt as if I was in a horrible nightmare. The bearded man took the phone and showed me that I had to dial 112 instead – it hadn't even occurred to me that the emergency number might be different – but when the operator answered in French, I suddenly found myself struck completely dumb. Thankfully he took the phone back off me and barked out our location.

Behind me, a woman who had announced that she was a

nurse had put a scarf under Thierry's head; he now appeared to have lost consciousness. I crouched down and held his hand, whispering in English that everything was going to be all right, even though I didn't know whether it would be at all. Someone came along and shouted, 'Thierry Girard!' – it wasn't till much later that it struck me that only in Paris would someone recognise a chocolate-maker in the street – and many other people stopped after that and looked concerned and murmured to each other. Somebody took a picture on a phone, and the man with the beard growled and called them a filthy name, till they sidled away, head down. Then the nurse, thank God, leant over Thierry and started doing chest compressions, and I swore with everything I had in me that I was going to attend a St John's Ambulance course, just like they'd suggested every year in the factory. The idea of having to give fake mouth-to-mouth to Mr Asten, the first-aider, was so repulsive we had just laughed and scoffed every time the subject had come up. I vowed now that I would take it and make everyone else I knew do it too, just as long as . . . as long as Thierry was all right. He had to be all right.

Minutes later, I heard the ambulance. The nurse had told us that Thierry was breathing and that the guys who were coming would know exactly what to do, but when they jumped out, they looked at Thierry, and then at the stretcher, then they shook their heads and there was some conversation. I wanted to shout at them to get on with it, but it was increasingly clear that they didn't think they could get him on to the stretcher.

Finally, one of the paramedics and the man with the beard called six strongish-looking men out of the crowd. They wheeled the stretcher back into the ambulance and secured it there, then the men carefully lifted Thierry's enormous bulk inside, as I sobbed with relief, at the same time feeling cross that Alice and Laurent between them hadn't done something about curbing Thierry's appetites and his greed. Then I remembered that I myself that morning had watched him eat four cream buns and smoke three cigarettes. I could no more have stopped him than fly to the moon.

The paramedic motioned me inside the ambulance. I was torn. I needed to get back to the shop to tell everyone what had happened and – oh God – contact Laurent. But of course I had to go with Thierry. Someone had to.

♡

The smell of hospitals doesn't seem to change much from country to country. The paramedics had called ahead, and when we got there, they had a much larger stretcher waiting. I trailed along uselessly behind, then got sidelined by an administrator who needed all Thierry's insurance details, none of which, of course, I had. I hadn't even realised the medical system was different here, that you couldn't just turn up. The administrator made it entirely clear that I was a useless chancer who had no business snarling up her morning with my boss's inconvenient heart attack, and I found myself fervently thankful that, despite its faults, the NHS would just fix you without shouting at you for paperwork first. I became terrified that they were going to ask for a credit card, until finally one of the nurses brought in Thierry's wallet, which she went through with practised ease until she found a green card that was obviously what she was looking for. She then gave me the glad eye, as if I'd known all this and had been keeping it from her.

After that there wasn't much to do but go in search of an internet connection or a phone book or anything that could get me in touch with the shop. Except I didn't want to travel too far from Thierry's side in case something happened or he simply needed a hand to hold. From time to time a young doctor would come out and in polite and slow English ask me if I knew Thierry's blood group, or whether he was diabetic, or whether I could sign a consent form. It was horrible. I had no idea of the number for directory enquiries, and after a few stabs at it, I sighed and nearly threw my phone down, as it dropped another bar and came close to running out of charge.

Eventually, there was only one thing left I could think of.

♡

Claire sounded half asleep and groggy when she picked up her home phone. It was a relief, though, firstly that she was there, and secondly that she was obviously getting some sleep. At times during the treatment she couldn't sleep at all.

'Anna!' she said, clearly delighted to hear from me. 'How are things? I've been thinking about you! How are you getting on? How are you settling in?'

'I'll tell you everything,' I said quickly. 'But right now I'm in a bit of a tight spot and I need to ask you something, and then I'll call you back, okay?'

'Well, yes, all right,' she said, sounding a bit taken aback. 'Is everything okay?'

'I'll tell you later,' I said. 'But please, can I ask you – do you know the shop telephone number? Um, I've come out without it. Is there any way you could track it down?'

There wasn't even a moment's pause. Not a second.

'67–89–12–15,' she rattled off.

I couldn't hang up straight away.

'You know it off by heart?' I said.

'Oh yes,' she said, suddenly sounding far away. Then she pulled herself together. 'Well, no mobiles in those days. You had to learn all your phone numbers off by heart.'

'And you still remember ALL your phone numbers?'

There was a little pause.

'Not all of them, no.'

I swallowed. 'I really do have to go,' I said. 'I'll call you back, I promise.'

And I hung up before she could ask any more awkward questions.

♥

The phone in the shop rang for so long that I thought they'd already closed up for the morning. I prayed that they hadn't. And that Frédéric would answer, not Benoît.

Thankfully for once my prayers were answered. I could

hear Frédéric's shock as I explained as well as I could what had happened – my French was all over the place suddenly, like something had shaken loose in my brain and I had completely forgotten how to talk. I realised when he asked me which hospital Thierry was in that I didn't even know, and had to ask the grumpy administrator, who looked at me like I was the biggest idiot ever to walk the face of the earth.

'L'Hotel-Dieu,' I said.

'Fine,' said Frédéric. 'It's close by. I'll shut the shop and let people know ...'

He paused, and his voice cracked a little.

'Is he ... I mean, he's going to be all right, isn't he? They're fixing him.'

'I don't know,' I said honestly. 'I really don't know.'

♡

The doctors invited me in to see him as he was prepped for surgery. It felt absurd, somehow, to care so much for someone I'd known for only a few weeks, but seeing him there, unconscious, the great life force of him flat on the bed like a huge walrus, his moustache flopping sadly, covered by a tube inserted in his nose – I immediately burst into tears.

'We give him bypass,' said the young doctor in English. 'We hope ... we hope it will work. He is a difficult patient.'

'You mean he is too big?' I said.

The doctor nodded. 'He is ... it is difficult for us to do what we need to do.'

I didn't envy her, having to get down through all those layers.

'But,' I found myself saying, 'he has … he has a big heart, you know? It is worth it.'

She nodded again without smiling.

'It's always worth it,' she snapped briskly.

♡

After I'd squeezed his hand once more, watching him go down to theatre in the specially big bed, I sat in the foyer, idly leafing through a magazine I wasn't even slightly interested in, trying to leave my phone alone because it really would run completely out of charge if I even touched it once more. When everyone else came, I would go and call Claire and tell her. Although I worried slightly. Thierry had obviously been a friend of hers for a long time; would it upset her more to know? I could just tell her I'd been lost or something, make some excuse. Though would that be fair? But then again, it was rather odd that she hadn't seen him in such a long time. They couldn't really be such good friends, could they?

I scanned the entrance, waiting for someone, anyone to show up. I didn't think I'd ever felt so lonely in my whole life.

♡

1972

To Thierry, it seemed perfectly simple.

'You are my girl,' he said. 'You come back, huh? When I get

leave? At Christmas? We shall have a wonderful time, Paris is sensational then. They light up the boulevards with a hundred tiny candles and the Tour Eiffel glows red and green. Perhaps it will snow, and I will keep you warm in my little garret, non? And I will make my hot chocolate for you. It is stirred one thousand times and filled with cream so that it melts down your neck like being embraced by a man who loves you, huh, chérie?'

She tried to smile, as she kicked the first of the falling autumn leaves from the path. In four days' time she would be putting on a school uniform she had undoubtedly grown out of since last year. She had filled out, she knew. There was colour in her cheeks. She had come to Paris a girl and now she felt, indubitably, a woman.

'I don't know,' she said. Christmas in Kidinsborough involved a lot of helping the Reverend with his Christmas load: visiting the sick in hospital, giving bibles as gifts to poor families who might, perhaps, have preferred food or toys. And homework, of course. A levels. She groaned. She'd brought a whole pile of textbooks with her, thinking she might get some work done whilst the children were asleep. Of course that had not happened.

She clutched Thierry's big paw tightly as the chill wind breezed through her thin coat, making her shiver. As much as they were trying to pretend the summer wasn't over, they both knew it was.

Thierry looked at her.

'You are freezing, my little bird,' he said. 'I have a new recipe for hot chocolate, and you are going to be my first customer. Come with me.'

She sat on the wooden counter where Thierry had lifted her, while he fussed around her, constantly stirring the huge mixing jug, pouring

175

in more cream, popping in the tiniest bit of rum, letting it smoke off then adding more. He wouldn't let her taste it until he had added tiny pinches of this and that, thought about it, bounced in and out the back of the shop, shouted at Benoît, considered melting another batch of chocolate altogether, finally dribbling in a pinch of salt and at last considering himself satisfied.

As soon as she took one sip, she knew he was right. It spread right through her body, warming every vein, making her curl her toes up in delight. It tasted like something the White Witch of Narnia might have given Edmund to betray his family, and it tasted like it would have worked.

'Thierry,' she said, awestruck.

'I know, I know,' he said distractedly. He was jotting notes on a piece of paper – he never wrote anything down normally – and he had found a small jar with a screw top, into which he was decanting some of the liquid.

'BENOÎT!' he growled through the back, as the burly young man came running out. 'Make this until it tastes like this. Then lock the recipe up in the safe.'

Benoît nodded quickly, and took a sip. He stopped short, gazing at Thierry.

'Chef,' he said, in a tone of wonderment.

'I know,' said Thierry, a brief look of satisfaction crossing his face. 'I know. I've done it.'

Claire smiled at him. He turned to her.

'And you!' he said. 'You are my muse!' He kissed her, licking away the thick stain from her lips. 'Oh, mixed with you it is only more delicious,' he said, kissing her again.

'You see? You must come back. I need you. You have inspired possibly my greatest creation.'

One of the customers in the shop turned round.

'May I try it?'

Thierry looked at him sternly.

'I don't know. Are you a good man? So far this has only been tried by good people.'

'I don't know if I'm a good man,' said the gentleman, who was wearing a homburg hat and a yellow scarf against the encroaching colder weather. 'But I am a journalist at Le Monde.*'*

Thierry filled a huge cup to the brim and handed it to him.

'My friend! Drink and be happy.'

The man did so. And then he took out his notebook.

Thierry gave Claire a fond glance.

'You see? You have made me a genius.'

Laughing with delight, Claire had never been closer to ripping up her return ticket; packing her bag, living in sin. She threw back her head, tossed down some more of the astonishing hot chocolate. She was almost purely happy.

Except she remembered her mother's last letter, asking if she'd grown much, passing on good wishes from friends and relatives, talking excitedly about the new youth club that had opened up adjacent to the church, about having a drinks party, and she knew, a tiny little corner of her knew, that she would have to go back, of course she would.

♥

The door to the waiting room flew open with a crash. I raised my head; I realised I'd been nodding off. It seemed an odd reaction to the stress, but I'd been here for over two hours, the battery on my phone was completely gone and I seemed to have run out of other options.

I'd seen Laurent around from time to time, usually with quite a fast set of loud young chefs and models. Sami preferred artists and musicians so could be a bit snotty about them. Laurent often had a scrawny, pouty-looking girl on his arm – not the same one each time as far as I could tell – and would nod at me, but little more. I dismissed him as irritating and obviously shallow. He didn't look shallow now, though; he looked demented with worry.

His face struck me as more than ever like his father's but without the weight. His skin was a darker olive; he had huge, expressive eyes that now looked alarmed and worried, and a wide, sensual mouth. He still seemed very tall compared to other Frenchmen I'd seen, and with a solid bulk that wasn't fat, just a kind of comforting size. I jumped up, wiping my mouth and wishing I had a stick of gum.

'What's happening? What's going on? Where is he?' shouted Laurent, sounding furious, as if it was my fault.

'He's in theatre,' I said, trying to sound gentle and consolatory. 'They said it might take a while.'

'Why? Why is it taking a while?'

I shrugged. 'I think it's difficult when … when the patient is a bit heavier than normal …'

'Is it because he's so fat? Stupid bastard. He's such a stupid bastard.'

He glared around.

'Where's Alice?'

'Didn't Frédéric ring her?'

'Probably not; he hates her,' said Laurent.

'Not that much, surely.'

He ignored that.

'What was he doing? What were you doing with him?'

'I wasn't doing anything with him,' I said indignantly. I wasn't the one who'd let him eat himself to death. 'He asked me to go for a walk with him, that's all.'

'That's all? Did he stop for brandy?'

'If it was my job to stop him drinking brandy, I think somebody should have made it a bit clearer to me!' I said, almost shouting.

He stopped short.

'Sorry,' he muttered. 'Sorry, that's not fair. I'm just ... I'm just upset.'

'I know,' I said. 'Of course you are. Hopefully they'll let us know soon.'

He looked around frantically.

'He can't ... he can't die ...'

'Anna,' I added, helpfully.

'I knew that,' he said, putting his hands distractedly through his thick brown hair.

'You know, we haven't spoken for months,' he muttered. 'He can't ... it can't ...'

I shook my head. 'He spoke about you this morning,' I said.

'What, to say what an ignoramus I am?'

'Yes,' I said. 'But in a loving way.'

Laurent's face looked grey.

'Christ,' he said, glancing at his watch. 'Where are those doctors?'

I swallowed.

'What else?' he asked suddenly. 'Why was he confiding in you? You've just got here ... some English girl ...'

Then his eyes widened.

'You're not ... You're not connected to ...'

I nodded, slowly. 'Claire sent me.'

He looked so feverishly furious, I thought he was going to spit.

'That woman,' he hissed.

'She didn't do anything wrong,' I said quickly.

'Tell that to my mother,' he said. 'He walked out on her for some scrawny English witch who reminded him of the first one.'

'Alice is nothing like Claire,' I said stoutly.

'Well he found that out a bit late, didn't he?' said Laurent. 'He'd already wrecked our family. Too scared to mess it up again. Thank God they didn't have any children.' He snorted, then stared again at the door, as if gazing at it might make something happen.

When the door did finally swing open, Laurent was halfway to his feet before he realised it was Alice. She looked absolutely white, the black scarf she was wearing a slash against her pale neck, her lips devoid of lipstick and looking naked and thin, stretched in her face. A vein stood out in her throat. For the first time, I thought, she looked old.

'*What have you done?*' was the first thing she said, almost hissed. It wasn't clear which one of us this was directed at.

'What have *you* done?' said Laurent, standing up completely this time. 'You're the one who punted him round so many boring dinners and lunches with your beau monde chums to show him off, where he had nothing to do but get bored and eat and drink too much. You couldn't just leave him alone, could you, doing what he did best – creating and enjoying himself.'

'How would you know?' sneered Alice. 'We never see you. You're too busy "making it on your own", except of course, oh how convenient, you appear to have a very useful last name.'

Laurent looked utterly furious for a second and a half, then turned away.

'Oh yes, we're all so concerned about his welfare now,' spat Alice, two circles of pink appearing high on her cheekbones. 'Bit too late, don't you think?'

I stepped up.

'Um, maybe we should all calm down?' I ventured. 'I don't think Thierry would want us to be squabbling . . . bad karma?'

They both turned on me, and for a second I thought I was going to get it in the neck. Then Laurent held up his hands in resignation.

'Yes, yes, you're right,' he said. He fixed Alice with a hard stare. 'I think we should put aside our differences for Thierry, do you agree?'

Alice gave a shrug so Gallic it was impossible to believe she wasn't French born and bred, and whipped out her mobile phone.

Moments later, the atmosphere was lifted somewhat by Benoît and Frédéric arriving, both of them with their heads down, clearly miserable. Comforting them gave me something to do. They had closed the shop for the afternoon, but worried customers had already been round asking if it were true, and the newspapers had been on the phone. By the sound of it, Alice was dealing with that side of things. She paced up and down, talking on her mobile, as if keeping herself busy would in itself make a difference. I focused hard on the linoleum. Every minute that ticked by made me feel less optimistic.

Suddenly the doctor was standing at the door, removing her mask. Her face was completely unreadable.

♡

Claire clutched the arm of the chair very carefully. She had tried to call Anna back – she knew there was something wrong, there had to be, she could hear it in her voice – but she couldn't get anyone to pick up the phone. She bit her lip. Montserrat, her carer, was fussing about cheerfully in the background, clearing up, lining up her medicine bottles for later, when the community nurse would come round. Montserrat was great, but Claire didn't want to get into a big conversation with her about how she felt and what was up.

It had been her decision, when first diagnosed, not to tell people. She couldn't have explained why. She didn't want to draw lots of attention to herself to begin with; she couldn't bear to see the pity in people's eyes. She never could. Not when her marriage broke up, not when she had flunked her A levels. It felt more painful than the chemo ever could. She knew on some level that it was pride; stupid pride, inherited from her father more likely than not, but it didn't make any difference.

Also, what was Richard, her ex-husband, going to do anyway? Drop everything and rush back and undo their entire lives? And the boys were busy. When it finally got too much and she had to tell them, they had all been wonderful, but she had always attempted to minimise any pain or discomfort so they wouldn't worry so much. She much more enjoyed the stories of what the children were doing and, sometimes, their hand-drawn cards. Anything that took her out of herself, that helped her stop thinking 'cancer cancer cancer'.

Project Anna had been the best thing she'd found to date. She had told herself it was purely about broadening the girl's life experience; showing her a different way of doing things, the same way that once Mme Lagarde had shown her. These days she only had the memories of the lovely girl she had once been (and she could look back now without false modesty; she had indeed been lovely). Now her body was all pale folds, swollen by steroids and strong drugs; changed by child-bearing and age. She felt herself starting to hang loose from her bones, her teeth soften in her head. But then, seventeen and fair-haired and fresh, she could understand why Thierry had been so attracted to her, even if at the time it had seemed completely out of the blue.

When she'd first got the internet (quite late; she'd had the prickling sensation that even though he'd been dead many long years, her father would not have approved of it one bit), she had of course looked Thierry up. And she'd found him too, often in the pages of the French press, or in cookery books and guides to Paris. His heft had surprised her, although she remembered with pleasure his gargantuan appetite for everything – for food, for chocolate, for sex and wine and cigars, and for her. It wasn't entirely surprising, she supposed, that it had caught up with him. On the other hand, she had led a blameless life of teaching and cooking healthy meals for her family and keeping her weight down and not smoking and not drinking to excess, and look where she had ended up: on a ward with tubes sticking out of her, feeling like she was a hundred and ninety years old, so did it matter, really, in the end?

She had wondered idly, many times, what would happen if she wrote him a quick letter – she knew where to find him, after all. But she had always stopped herself. It was ludicrous; a crush from so long ago, a two-month wonder. She doubted he ever thought of her at all; she couldn't imagine anything more embarrassing than someone turning up in your life you'd completely forgotten ever existed. She imagined him searching his memory, trying to be polite; the awful dawning realisation of how much thought she'd given him throughout her entire life; how much time. It was a ghastly idea. Until Anna had given her the perfect excuse.

♥

Claire lay on her bed in her old bedroom, with its ridiculous posters of Davy Jones and ponies. It was the room of a child, utterly stupid to her eyes now, and seeing it only seemed to confirm how much she no longer fitted in in this place.

She had cried all the way back on the train, on the ferry and on the train again, even as she remembered Thierry's fervent words – do not forget me, do not leave, come back, come back. And she had promised, she really had, but she had no money and no hope and no idea of what to do, and she was trapped in a pale blue bedroom with ducks on the mantelpiece and a valance on the bed, and a school uniform hanging up in the cupboard.

Mme Lagarde had held her hands on the last evening, genuinely sad to see her go; Arnaud and Claudette had clung to her legs.

'I hope you have got a lot out of your stay,' Madame said, and Claire, with tears in her eyes, had sworn that she had, that she could never be grateful enough.

'I don't want to be patronising,' said Madame, 'but it is nice to have love affairs when you are young. But there will be many, you understand? One swallow does not make a summer is the English phrase, I know. You are confident now and you have learned many things on your way towards being a grown-up woman, so take these memories but do not cling on to Paris, no? You have your own life, your own way to make. You are far too clever to hang around, waiting for crumbs, relying on other people, you understand me?'

And Claire, struck dumb with misery, had nodded and remembered the words and knew deep down that it was wise advice. But oh, how much she didn't want to hear it. She wanted Mme Lagarde to say, 'We cannot do without you. Forget school, come and stay with us until you marry Thierry.' Even thinking something so ridiculous brought a blush to Claire's cheeks.

Back home, her mother had been so pleased to see her, but Claire felt like a stranger in her arms. How could it only have been two months? She was a new person. A woman of independence, who worked, then spent her evenings as she chose. How could she be expected to concentrate on algebra and verb declensions?

Her father had looked her up and down. He had never particularly enjoyed Claire growing up, even though she had been as respectful and obedient an adolescent as one could find. It was evident even to his unpractised eye that she was moving further away from him than ever. He grunted.

'I hope you haven't picked up any fancy ways in Paree,' he said. 'They're loose over there.'

'She's a good girl,' assured her mother, stroking her hair. 'You look wonderful, dear. So kind of Marie-Noelle to take such good care of you. She wrote to me.'

'Did she?' said Claire, looking startled.

Her mother smiled a secret smile. It was clear to her that Paris had been everything she'd hoped for her gorgeous but too staid daughter.

'Don't worry, nothing bad. Apparently she was a credit to the family, Marcus.'

'Well, I would hope so,' said the Reverend, looking slightly mollified. 'You would hate to be neither use nor ornament, hmm, Claire?'

Claire nodded. It had rained all the way on the train home. After *the heavy golden light of Paris unfolding on to ancient cobblestones, verdant parks and great churches, the bland red brick and corrugated iron of Kidinsborough, the already dripping cement of the new NCP car park, and the shopping centre with its overturned trolleys outside felt worse than ever. She couldn't believe what she was doing back there. She wished she had a best friend to confide in.*

Her mother had made mince and potatoes for her homecoming, once her favourite. 'I'm really not hungry,' Claire said apologetically. 'I might just go to bed. I'm so tired.'

'Your mother has made good food,' said the Reverend. 'It would be a sin to waste it.'

So she had had to sit, in the dowdy travelling clothes she had last worn at the beginning of the summer – now too short in the leg and too tight in the bust – and try and choke down the overboiled carrots and mushy potato, try not to think about melting Camembert that came in its own little wooden basket, baked in the oven with herbs and served on a crisp green salad (the only salad that had hit Kidinsborough in the early seventies was a couple of leaves of damp iceberg lettuce served with tasteless quartered tomatoes and salad cream); or the golden roasted chickens they bought from a man who sold them on a spit, that tasted so hot and salty that they had let the grease run down their chins, and Thierry had licked it off and she had laughed and laughed. They had mopped up the rest of the juices with the most incredible fresh bread, still warm from the oven, and Thierry had shown her how to tell when bread was at its freshest by the crackling noise it made when you broke into it, adding smugly, 'But Pierre would never give me second bread.'

She could barely remember that girl. And as the days grew

shorter, and school started again, she felt like she was trapped, trapped in the body of a child who was expected to do what she was told.

Every day she woke early, terrified she might miss the postman. Her father wouldn't understand Thierry's letters, but her mother would, and her father would get the gist, surely, or just disapprove in general. She watched him like a hawk; she couldn't trust him not to block any incoming post, but he seemed his normal irascible self, grumbling over his newspaper about the terrible state of everything and bemoaning how Britain was going to the dogs and how the union men were 'wicked, wicked'.

He started preaching this, too, from his pulpit, which did not go down at all well with the local population of Kidinsborough, who were hanging on to their steelworks by the skin of their teeth. His congregation dwindled, and men came from the bishopric in the evening, talking to him in low voices.

As the days went by, it seemed stranger and stranger to Claire that she had received no letters. She had returned to school, gazing at the stranger she had become in the mirror – not the carefree girl striding happily down the Bois de Boulogne, but a sullen teenager in a short grey skirt and a too tight shirt, looking just like anyone else.

In class she barely paid attention, except in French, instead writing endless letters to Thierry about how much she missed him and how much she hated Kidinsborough and how next summer she would find another position and come back to Paris and this time they couldn't make her go back, nobody could. She sent them to the shop, although who knew where he was now, where he was posted.

There was no response.

In November, they moved house.

Claire cried. She begged. She pleaded. She couldn't change address. She ran the whole gamut of teenage rebellion; slamming doors, staying out late, sulking, but nothing worked. Complaints against her father were growing; his old-school fire-and-brimstone sermons had fallen out of fashion. 'Hippies,' the Reverend complained. 'They've ruined everything.'

As a result of this, Claire went out and bought a joss stick, which turned him practically apoplectic with rage.

She sent one last letter, telling herself that surely this one would reach him.

Chérl,

Mes parents horribles insistent que nous déménagemons. Je les detestes. Alors, si tu penses de moi du tout, s'il te plaît sauve-moi! Suave-moi! Je suis à 'The Pines, 14 Orchard Grove, Tillensley'.

Si tu ne reponds pas, je comprendrais que tu ne m'aimes pas et je ne te contacterai encore.

Mon couer, mon amour, viens avec vitesse,

Claire

Nothing.

Chapter Thirteen

I do think there is something about the French psyche that can be incredibly useful. That solid practicality – it is very unusual for a French person to be over the top with excitement or laid low with misery; they do not feel it necessary to be cheery or even terribly polite if the occasion doesn't warrant it – means you can get a lot of necessary information in an unemotional way.

Laurent started.

'How is he?'

Alice whipped round and, without saying a word, shut off her phone. The doctor's face was still completely impassive, and I could feel my heart beating a mile a minute, pounding my chest. I suddenly found I wished I could take Laurent's hand, squeeze it. Just to have someone there as we faced the worst. I looked at his large hairy hand, hanging down by his jacket pocket. It was shaking.

'It's far from clear,' said the doctor, her voice impeccable, ringing out in the small dingy room. 'We have operated, inserted stents. But his general condition . . .' The tone of her voice made it very clear that this was a reproach. 'His general condition makes it very difficult to see what the outcome will be.'

'But he's still alive,' said Laurent, his face an animated mixture of hope and terror.

She nodded curtly. 'Bah, oui,' she said. 'He will be unconscious for some time.'

'I want to see him,' said Laurent. She nodded. We all followed the clacking of her heels along the shiny linoleum floor, until she turned round.

'Not too many,' she instructed. Frédéric and Benoît immediately backed off, and I did too. But Laurent, almost without realising what he was doing, tugged at my sleeve.

'You come,' he said quietly. I realised later, of course, that he just didn't want to be alone with her, with Alice, and all the unsaid things that passed between them. But at the time it felt more than that; I felt like I'd been chosen. Although at the same time, I also felt that if he died it would be my fault.

'Of course,' I said, trying not to betray the nerves in my voice.

'Why is she coming?' asked Alice loudly, but Laurent ignored her. I just stayed out of her way.

♥

The recovery room was gloomy, the lights low. Machines bleeped and whirred to themselves; I looked around to make sure I didn't stumble over any essential tubes or wires. Thierry made a huge mound in the bed, like a gigantic Easter egg. They had, to my terrible sadness, shaved his moustache to insert the tubes up his nose. Without it he looked odd, insulted somehow.

His skin was grey, absolutely grey, a horrible muddy colour that you couldn't look at for any length of time. Alice coughed and glanced down. Laurent, though, was just staring at Thierry's great barrel chest, which was moving up and down.

'Papa!' he cried, stepping over to the bed, his arms open wide. He sounded like a child. The doctor made a disapproving clicking noise and he stepped back, not wanting to disrupt anything, but there were tears in his eyes. He turned to the doctor.

'Thank you,' he said.

The doctor shrugged. 'Don't thank me yet,' she said.

After warning us for the fiftieth time not to touch anything, the doctor left, and we three, an odd trio, were alone in the room, with Thierry, like a great beached walrus, lying between us. There was a silence broken only by the bleeping and the hiss of the respirator, which moved up and down like a broken accordion.

'So,' said Alice at last. Laurent wasn't listening; he was sitting forward intently in his chair, staring at his father. 'This is what it takes to get you to visit your dad.'

I really wanted to knock her block off then. It was like

she'd spent the last couple of hours searching for the most unpleasant thing she could possibly say. Laurent must have noticed my horrified face, because he patted me on the arm.

'It's all right, she's always like this,' he said in English, which was clever, because Alice pretended all the time that she'd forgotten how to speak English.

'Actually, it wasn't my dad I was avoiding, it was you,' he said pleasantly. 'Now would you like to smoke in here and make him worse? Or maybe you'd just like to lever him up and wheel him out to one of your soirées.'

Alice went very white again.

'Actually, I'll have to go and organise the business you want no part of,' she said. 'With two halfwits and whatever she is. By myself. Thanks, though.'

I was struck by a bolt of fear. It had never occurred to me that I was going to have to work for Alice now, but of course she was right. Oh goodness. I hardly knew what I was doing yet; now I was going to have to do it under the disapproving eye of this person who clearly despised me.

'Of course you'd ask if you needed help,' said Laurent.

There was a stand-off then, neither of them prepared to give ground.

♥

It also became increasingly clear that neither of them wanted to be the first to leave, in case Thierry woke up. It was warm in the room, and to my horror I realised I was becoming very drowsy. There must be loads of people they needed to contact, but both were obeying the signs that said that no mobile phones were allowed near the equipment. It was like a power struggle between the two of them, and it made me very cross. Eventually I snapped.

'I'm going to get coffee,' I said. 'Does anyone want anything?'

Alice jumped up, obviously cross that she hadn't thought of it.

'No, I'll go,' she said brusquely, her fingers already fumbling in her Hermès bag for her lighter and phone. 'I'll be back in two minutes.'

After she had left the room and vanished down the long corridor, Laurent collapsed back on to his chair and released a long sigh. He let his curly head continue on downwards, until it was level with the bed. Then he let it collapse into the soft sheets. After several moments of witnessing his shoulders shaking, I realised he was crying.

I stood up.

'There, there,' I said, rubbing his back. 'There, there. He's going to be all right, isn't he? Look at him, all alive on the bed and everything.'

I was speaking absolute nonsense, I knew, just crooning reassuring nothings, but it seemed to do the trick. After another moment, without lifting his head, Laurent took my hand and held it.

'Thank you,' he said, his face muffled in the sheets.

I patted him.

'It's all right,' I said again. 'It's going to be all right.'

'It's never all right,' he said indistinctly.

I knelt down beside him.

'Well maybe,' I said, 'maybe this is a really good time to make it up with your dad.'

'What, before he passes his gun to his left?' said Laurent, turning his face towards me and half-smiling. 'Yeah, right. Thanks.'

'Well, lots of people never get a chance to say goodbye,' I said. 'Anyway, you're going to be lucky. Be sure of it.'

'Are you my lucky charm?'

I smiled. I was the unluckiest person in the world, didn't he know?

'If you like.'

Laurent sat up and wiped his eyes, then ran his fingers through his hair. 'Do I look red?' he asked. 'I don't want the wicked witch to know I've been crying.'

'Maybe it'll soften her up,' I said. 'She can see how much you really care.'

'You couldn't soften her up with a marshmallow massage,' said Laurent crossly. 'I really do think she's made out of old leather.'

'She's panicking,' I said. 'People say strange things when they're worried.'

'Then she's permanently worried,' he said.

'I rather think she is,' I agreed.

I patted him again.

'Look,' I said, 'I haven't seen much, but I'm a fast learner, and I bet Frédéric and Benoît can do just about anything. Let's carry on with the shop for a bit until Thierry's better. It will cheer him up, I think, to know we've gone on in his absence.'

'Or completely finish him when he realises that he's replaceable,' said Laurent, with a twisted smile on his face. I noticed that he was holding his father's lifeless-looking hand in his own. Apart from the fact that Thierry's hand was paler and more bloated, they were exactly the same.

'Well, we'll tell him it is obviously not nearly as good without him,' I suggested.

'Oh, you won't have to do that,' said Laurent wryly. 'He thinks everything is worse without him in it.'

'Maybe he's right,' I said.

Just then Alice came back, with three tiny plastic cups of black liquid on a little tray. I squeezed Laurent's shoulder.

'I'll get back to the shop,' I said. 'I'm not much use here.'

Laurent nodded. 'Yes. Do. And answer the phone, do you mind?'

'Not at all,' I said. 'I'll say he's … I'll say he's …'

'Say he is going to be FINE,' said Alice in a voice that brooked no argument. 'Say that he is going to be completely back to normal and that the shop will go on and everything will stay just as it is.'

Laurent would probably have said that this was just Alice seeking to preserve her investment. I didn't see it like that, though. I saw it as Alice keeping Thierry alive simply by saying that he was going to be okay. And even though I didn't want to be, I was slightly impressed.

♥

It felt amazing to me that when I stepped back out of the hospital, it was that same, beautiful summer day. The sky had tiny ribbons of cloud floating across it, and the afternoon sun fell warmly on the backs and necks of shoppers and sightseers, every one of them, I speculated, happy and carefree, without a problem in the world.

I realised I had no idea where I was. I walked a long way, then realised I could see the Tour Eiffel over my left shoulder and that therefore I was on the left bank and needed to cross the river again. I'd been on the Île de la Cité the whole time. If I craned my neck, I could just make out the familiar shape of Notre-Dame, far away to my right. It would have been a lot quicker to take a cab or the Métro – everything in Paris is further away than it looks – but I decided I needed the walk to clear my head. Being particularly careful about traffic, I stepped out, my toes hurting again. Perhaps they responded badly to the smell of hospitals. Or maybe bad weather was coming, though as far as I was concerned, all the bad things were already here. I slowed myself down to a tourist's pace instead of the bustling Parisian march, and headed doggedly onwards, keeping Notre-Dame in my sights.

There was something about the great cathedral. I knew that it had always stood for sanctuary, ever since the city was really no more than the island and its church. It was impossible not to think about the Hunchback, and Esmeralda, or to look at the gargoyles and not shudder to think of a world where people believed in them absolutely; believed that hell was only a blink or a misstep away, that it was pain for all eternity and the monsters carved on the wall were literal and real and there to tear you apart.

We weren't religious in my family, though at secondary school there was a bit of religious education and it was quite fashionable for a while – don't ask me why – to go to church. Perhaps it was seen as quite a clever thing to do, or a way to keep up with the Muslim kids, who prayed properly and were seen as much cooler. Anyway, I toyed with it till I asked Mrs Shawcourt about it. She was the only kind of cool teacher you could ask about stuff like that. Her face went a bit stiff and she just said, 'Oh, I have had a LOT of church, believe me. Quite enough to be getting on with for this lifetime,' and I was a lot less committed after that.

Round Notre-Dame, though, I felt something else. There were queues of people waiting to get in – most of them bored-looking Italian schoolkids larking about, or American students talking really loudly or elderly couples dressed almost exactly alike, ticking things off in their guidebooks. But amongst them were different people; nuns, and people on their own who didn't have a holiday look about them at all, but rather something very serious and grave. And the distinctive twin towers at the front made the place seem different somehow, special.

As I drew nearer, I realised you only had to queue if you wanted a tour or to go up and see the bells and things. If you just wanted to peek in, you could wander straight up. Even though my feet were killing me and I hadn't eaten a thing for hours and I just wanted to lie down and rest, I found myself mounting the steps.

Inside it was huge. It smelled faintly of flowers, and something else that I supposed was that incense stuff my gran says Catholics use, and floor polish. They were playing organ music gently through speakers, which was a bit confusing. The scale of the place was massive. And if I thought it was massive now, living in the days of skyscrapers and jumbo jets and cruise ships, I can't imagine what it must have felt like hundreds of years ago. The huge friezes of the Stations of the Cross covered the walls in intricate detail, and there was a vast rose-coloured stained-glass window.

Dotted on the pews, looking tiny as ants, were people, mostly singly, just sitting, contemplating. I couldn't join them without paying the entrance fee, and I didn't have a God I could talk to, and even if he had, I couldn't imagine any kind of God taking time off from massacres and famines to help out an ageing fat man who I barely knew. But even so, my heart formed a silent plea – please, it said, over and over again. Please. Just, please.

I felt better.

♥

The shop had a sign on it – 'Fermé cause de maladie' – and some concerned people milling around outside who'd obviously made the trip specially. I knocked heavily on the front door. The workshop round the back technically had a fire exit, but I had no idea where it came out, so I kept banging till I heard Frédéric.

'We're shut! Go away!' he shouted.

'It's me!' I yelled.

Immediately the shutters were raised.

'Why didn't you call? Where have you been?' he shouted at me.

'Because my phone is dead,' I explained. 'And I couldn't find a phone in the hospital.'

'Well that's not very helpful,' he grumbled. 'We've been waiting. Any change?'

'No,' I said. 'I don't think so. But no change is good at this point.'

Frédéric snorted. 'I don't know about that.'

I noticed something. There was no noise in the shop.

'Why are the churns switched off?' I asked.

Frédéric shrugged. 'We cannot continue without the chef, chérie. It's not possible.'

'What do you mean, it's not possible? Are you going on strike?'

'No. But without him ...'

'You're telling me you've worked here all these years and you don't know what he's doing?'

Frédéric's little face grew cross.

'Of course we *see* what he is doing. But what he is doing and what we would do . . . For the conch it is not precisely the same. It is the difference between daubs on a wall and an artist's canvas. It could not be.'

I was used to working in a factory, where our industrial processes basically meant that a monkey could turn out the same chocolate day after day as long as he could remember the sequence of buttons to push. It might mean a lot of banana flavour, though.

'Of course it could,' I prodded. 'Benoît has been here man and boy. Surely we can honour Thierry and continue making chocolate.'

'It is impossible,' he said, looking at me as if he was explaining something very simple to a particularly stupid child. 'It cannot be the same.'

'Well I hope it can,' I said. 'Because I think Alice wants us to stay open. If you want to say no to her, go ahead, be my guest.'

Frédéric visibly paled.

'She cannot want that,' he said.

'She does,' I said. 'I heard her at the hospital.'

He shook his head. 'She does not understand.'

I was kind of on Alice's side over this. Wages had to be paid, I assumed, hopefully including mine. People would still come. Thierry was mostly all about the sizzle and the salesmanship at the front of the shop. I was pretty sure Frédéric and Benoît could carry out the workshop duties. And I could help, I thought. I'd watched them all these weeks, hadn't I? I had a good nose for this kind of thing.

Frédéric called to Benoît, and in a deep-seated hundred-mile-per-hour growl, which reminded me once again how much people were modifying the way they spoke to me so I could understand them, started to explain how crazy everyone was being. Benoît as usual did little more than grunt in response, but in a way that seemed to indicate more displeasure than usual.

'Les Anglais,' was the only remark he made eventually, which made me indignant, as he'd obviously lumped me in with Alice's side of everything.

'It's nothing to do with me,' I said, backing away. 'Speak to Alice, okay? Do you need me to clear up?'

Benoît shook his head.

'It's done,' he said ominously. And then, in English: 'It's over.'

Chapter Fourteen

I could hardly climb the stairs. All I wanted was to get into the flat, to get some sleep. Oh God, and I would have to phone Claire, of course I would. I hadn't even thought about that. Well, I would need to charge the phone first, then I could think about it. Maybe after a bath.

Of course Sami was there. Today he was wearing a peacock-blue fringed shawl over his tanned torso, and bright blue eyeliner. He was obviously waiting for me.

'DARLING!' he exclaimed. 'I heard the horrible, horrible news. Look, I have cognac. It's good for shock.'

At that point in time cognac didn't seem like a bad idea, even though I had only the haziest idea what it actually was. Sami just liked to be in on the good gossip.

'It is the talk of Paris! Where will we get our hot chocolate now? You know, the tenor Istoban Emerenovitz will only sing here if he has a constant supply! Now we shall lose him to the New York Met and the world will mourn.'

I wasn't exactly sure that the world would mourn something like that, but I gave a half-smile and said not to worry, everything was going to be all right. It was odd how in the space of a few hours suddenly I had become the fount of information.

'And you were there?' said Sami, kindness fighting with his curiosity. 'Poor little bird. Was it awful?'

For the first time since the nightmarish dash to the hospital and all its memories, I just let myself go and burst into floods of tears.

'Oh, my little bird,' said Sami, giving me a rather oddly scented hug. 'Would you like your uncle Sami to take you to a party? Yes? We shall go to a party and you can tell everyone all about it and feel much better.'

At that precise moment, there was nothing I would rather do less. I explained this to Sami, who got exactly the same confused-dog look about my not wanting to go to a party as Frédéric had had at the idea of imitating Thierry's recipes, but he eventually left me in peace.

I had little doubt that Alice would get her way – she was that kind of person – so I was going to spend the next few weeks very busy indeed. I just hoped I was going to be up to it.

♥

1972
Although completely wrapped up in herself when she got back to school (the same school, alas, they hadn't moved out of the district),

it finally penetrated Claire's haze that something was up with another girl. At first she couldn't put her finger on what was different about Lorraine Hennessy. Then everyone started gossiping and whispering, and poor Lorraine could no longer do her skirt up, and that was that; she had got herself pregnant, some people said to a boy who'd come to Kidinsborough that summer on the carny and whizzed her too hard on the waltzers.

It wasn't quite still the days of sending women off to special homes for fallen ladies, but they weren't that far away. And for Lorraine to have made it all the way to the sixth form ... you get that far and you think everything is plain sailing after that, gossiped the wifies in the covered market. Poor Lorraine had fallen at the last hurdle, for a twinkling-eyed boy with a missing tooth, dirty fingernails and wild long curly hair. She left school at the autumn half-term and most people carried on regardless.

Claire, though, was obsessed. She couldn't help thinking about it, even when the Reverend brought it up at supper, with much tutting and judgement and disapproval. She imagined herself carrying Thierry's baby; a round, chubby, pink-cheeked laughing little cherub. She'd looked carefully every day at her stomach, just in case. Yes, they'd used precautions, but as the Reverend had said in one of his more risqué sermons, contraception was next to useless; the only true protection was chastity and the love of Jesus Christ.

She wished they'd been less careful. When she ran into Lorraine in the high street – her mother, conscious that her father's spies might be around, wanted to hurry her back – Claire stopped and said hello. She couldn't help it; she drank in every feature of Lorraine's full vase shape; her newly rounded pale breasts; the tight, high bump – so unfathomable that inside was another being; the trembling, defiant look in her eye.

'Good luck,' Claire said. In the two minutes they'd been standing there, they'd both already ignored whispers from passers-by.

'Aye,' said Lorraine, whose mother, next to her, seemed to have aged ten years. Lorraine didn't look proud, but her glowing, fruitful body did. Claire was the only girl at Kidinsborough Modern who envied her; who didn't join in the nasty chatter disguised as concern. She would have taken her bump in her arms and gone straight to the ferry and turned up late at night in Thierry's garret, and he would have been delighted to see her – oh, would he even be there, away marching somewhere – and even if he was the possibility that in fact his face would fall as she arrived, confused, that there might, even, be some other girl in his bed; she was under no illusion that he wasn't short of offers. No, he would jump up, that wonderful broad smile on his face, his moustache tickling her belly as he kissed it and kissed it again, and they would sit up all night making plans for their little one and how he would be the bonniest, best-fed baby in all of Paris, until the dawning sun hit the rooftops of the rue de Rivoli and bright pink morning turned the white streets into a sea of roses with the promise of a fresh golden day beyond ...

'You seem distracted.' It was Mrs Carr, the French teacher. She had been unflatteringly surprised at the improvement in Claire's French during the holidays and was pushing her hard to take it to a higher level; Claire was smart, she could go to university, be a translator, travel the world ... Claire's distraction and lack of interest drove her crazy. Years later, Claire tried harder with the dreamy children than almost anything else. Naughty children needed bound-

aries and direction; that was easy. Motivated children, of course, easier still. But it was the ones with their heads in the air, miles away, that were the hardest to get through to. You never knew what was going on with them.

For Mrs Carr, Claire was particularly frustrating. She was the best French speaker they'd ever had in the school, but she didn't bother doing her homework, she skipped class sometimes and she was hardly present even when she did turn up. Mrs Carr tried to impress on her the importance of A levels, but it didn't seem to be doing the least bit of good. She might have suspected a boy – so many promising young girls could fall completely apart at this age; look at Lorraine Hennessy – but Claire had always been such a sensible girl, raised in a religious home ... Oh, who was she kidding, they were always the worst.

Claire had sixty-two pounds in her Post Office account, which was more than enough to get her to France. The problem was how to get it out; she wasn't allowed to withdraw the money on her own until her eighteenth birthday, which was five months away. It might have been five years as far as Claire was concerned; she couldn't imagine it.

The days went by and the weather turned absolutely vicious: grey and windy and wet, the children wearing hooded parkas that came right up over their faces and completely obscured their vision, so they looked like tiny monsters looming out of the gloom.

Claire knew she was failing at school and couldn't bring herself to care. The Reverend shouted at her, and she stood there meekly, taking it and not really listening. This only annoyed him even more, but she'd been listening to him rant and rave from the pulpit long

*enough not to let it bother her. When the form came for university,
her mother quietly filed it away on the sideboard. Claire didn't even
look at it.*

*The weight she'd gained in Paris fell off her, and the tan faded.
The very experience started to feel like a dream she'd had once, or a
story she'd read, or a film. She wasn't that girl who'd skipped down
the Bois de Boulogne; who'd scooped fresh avocado and salsa
together, its slippery tartness making her eyes pop open, Thierry
laughing at her surprise. That Claire had gone, and the one who
remained looked even younger than before; pale and fragile, trying
to keep warm against the darkening evenings, trudging through
Kidinsborough like a ghost.*

*Her friends and contemporaries were living it up; sneaking into
bars, drinking cider at parties round each other's houses, snogging
and more down by the canal. Claire sat in her room and wrote in
her diary. She slipped out one morning and found, right at the back
of the tiny tobacconist's, the same brand of Gauloises in the bright
blue packet that Thierry smoked. Nauseous and faintly horrified, she
went into the wood and lit one. The very smell made her burst into
tears, but she found herself coming back again and again to smoke
them, in the cold and the wind.*

*Later, Claire thought that had it not been the seventies, she would
probably have been picked up by the school counsellor, or indeed at
home. It wasn't exactly unusual, she learned, after many years as a
teacher, to meet a depressed teen. Normally it was just a phase: home
problems and the inability to realise that everyone else felt as nervous and awkward in their adolescent skin and their sexuality. She
was always patient and kind with these kids, their sleeves too long*

for their hands, clutching at the ends, their infuriatingly mumbled responses. She knew what they were going through and how important it felt to them. She also knew the importance of not letting it pull them down. The biggest disappointments of her teaching career were never academic failures but emotional ones.

As it was, everyone just left her to get on with it, and the wet grey world and her sense of being separated from it and every one in it by a piece of gauze began to feel normal. Until she met Richard.

Chapter Fifteen

For a second when I woke the following morning I didn't think anything, except that I felt refreshed from a good night's sleep. Morning light was streaming in through the French window and throwing panes of bright buttercup yellow across my plain white sheets and old-fashioned blue comforter.

Then I remembered, and my heart dropped. Oh God. I jumped out of bed and paced about in a rush, not sure what to do first. Well, I had to talk to Laurent – but, I realised, stupidly, I didn't have his telephone number. Sami might, but Sami wouldn't emerge from his room till mid afternoon. Okay, first things first. Get dressed. Coffee. I pulled on my dressing gown and stumbled out, nearly tripping over the most beautiful guest asleep on the sofa, who appeared to be wearing angel wings. I recovered just in time and fixed myself a tiny cup of espresso, loaded with sugar, and took it to drink on the balcony. I was definitely getting used to it.

I looked out on to the early Paris morning. Far away across the river I saw a group of police horses being led out to exercise. A small group of schoolchildren were already huddled at the stop for the bateau mouche. Across the road, a woman was taking in washing that had been hanging outside her window on a pulley. We smiled at each other. It seemed so strange to me that somewhere out there was Thierry, being held together by beeping machines, kept alive by plastic tubes coming in and out of his heart. I wondered if Laurent was still there, holding his hand, his heavy head drooping from exhaustion. I was sure he would be. Alice, on the other hand . . . I had a feeling I might be seeing Alice today. I groaned, and set about the daily lottery of seeing if there was hot water or not. Then I remembered. I still hadn't called Claire. I could have kicked myself. I glanced at my watch. It was five a.m. in the UK. She'd still be asleep, hopefully. I couldn't disturb her now. I'd call her from the shop.

I had a lukewarm bath, glanced once again at Cupid asleep – Sami often provided random sofas to various young artistes – and let myself out quietly. My toes – no, not my toes. I always forgot. I was supposed to say, the hospital psychologist had said, 'the place my toes used to be', otherwise I would psychologically not manage to get rid of them. Well. That place was aching a little, but it was better than yesterday, which was just as well. I had a feeling I was

211

going to require all my energy today. Nothing could let me down.

Claire sat by the window, staring out, then down at the telephone, then out again. She didn't want to do anything else. She had tried to sleep, but it hadn't come. She had wanted to call Anna, but got too nervous when she picked up the phone. If it was bad news ... could it be? What was it? The tone of Anna's voice had been so panicky. Maybe she'd just been lost, that must have been it. Lost and worried ... but why hadn't she called back to say she was all right? Why not? Where was she? Claire truly felt she couldn't bear it if sending Anna to Paris turned out to be the second great mistake of her life. She breathed heavily and looked around for her oxygen cylinder. She could hear Patsy, her daughter-in-law, marching smartly up the path with the wheelie bin. She was a trouper, Patsy, a real life-saver. Claire couldn't bear being a burden on her children and their families, but what else could she do? Most of all she couldn't bear the look on the faces of her grandchildren. Patsy and Ricky had two daughters, Cadence and Codie, and she felt that at fifty-seven she should be down on her knees playing with them; cutting out paper dollies and dressing up, passing on funny stories and songs and telling them about their daddy when he was a little boy.

Instead, they gazed at her horrible old grey face, and the oxygen machine, in utter horror. She didn't blame them. Then Patsy would crossly nudge them and they would

212

produce the drawings they had done for her and a new scarf for her head, but truly they were too young ever to remember her as anything other than old and sick and witch-like, and it broke Claire's heart.

'Hello, Mum!' said Patsy, opening the door with her own key. Claire didn't like her daughters-in-law calling her Mum, it made her feel about a million years old, but she wouldn't dream of mentioning it. 'I'll just put the kettle on. Montserrat's coming round to give you a bath, isn't she? Great. Can I do anything for you?'

Claire stared at the phone in her lap. Was there anything to be done now? she wondered.

♡

Frédéric and Benoît were looking positively mutinous, and not even smoking. I raised my eyebrows, then comprehension dawned, as I saw the long, thin figure of Alice opening the shutters. The boys raised their hands to me and I waved back, shyly. I wasn't sure if they saw me as the enemy or not.

'How is he?' I said quickly in English to Alice.

She favoured me with a sideways glance.

'The same,' she said. 'Stable.'

'Oh,' I said. 'Oh. Well, at least he's not worse,' I added, lamely.

Stable, though. I didn't really like the sound of it. I'd learned that in hospital. Critical was the worst. It was very bad indeed. Recovering was the ideal state of affairs really. Stable just meant the same as yesterday, which in Thierry's case meant his life hanging in the balance. I didn't like it at all.

'Hmm,' was all Alice said. Then she handed me her phone. 'Take this,' she said. 'It's ringing off the hook and I don't want to deal with it right now.'

I had no idea what she expected me to do with it. I was tempted to throw it in the Seine, but instead I set it to vibrate and put it in my apron pocket, where it started vibrating absolutely non-stop. I ignored it.

Alice pulled up the last shutter and turned to face us.

'Now. The shop will continue as before.'

Frédéric raised his hands.

'Madame, it is just not possible. An orchestra cannot play without its conductor. A kitchen cannot function without its chef. We will be selling substandard goods.'

Alice went pale.

'It is his wish,' she said.

Frédéric and Benoît exchanged a disbelieving look so obvious she couldn't possibly have missed it. She bit her lip furiously.

'Anna, can you conch chocolate?'

Frédéric and Benoît glared at me, but I was too scared of Alice not to answer her. It was a mistake that was to prove fatal.

'Um, well, yes, I can have a shot, but—'

'Fine. You shall do it.'

Benoît took a sharp intake of breath.

'But I think we should wait until—'

214

'Rubbish. Anyone who doesn't want to work here can go home right away. If you think this isn't what Thierry would want, you can take it up with him, but there may not be a job waiting for you at the end of it. I am the co-owner of this establishment. Don't think I am soft like Thierry.'

None of us thought that.

'I would get rid of the lot of you at a moment's notice if I thought it would keep the shop open and our business alive. In a second. So don't push me.'

We all stared at the ground.

'In you go. Open up. Behave as normal. Anna will flavour. DON"T mess it up. I am going to be extraordinarily busy and I do not want to have to worry about you on top of everything else.'

And with that she tossed the keys to Benoît, turned on her heel and clipped off down the alleyway before I had the chance to remind her that I still had her mobile phone.

♥

Not a word was spoken as we entered the dimly lit shop and passed through to the back. The lighting flickered then came on. Benoît set the coffee machine, but only made two cups, for him and Frédéric. I cleared my throat.

'I'm sorry,' I said quietly.

Frédéric looked at me. 'If we don't stand together we are nothing,' he said, crossly.

'I know, I know,' I said. 'But I think ... I think she might

215

be right. I think Thierry would want the shop to continue rather than us all just going off on holiday or something.'

Benoît muttered something totally incomprehensible.

'I mean, we can have a shot,' I added.

'And lose the reputation of the shop for ever? This is what you British do not understand about the French. You think you must work, work, work, work and open on Sundays and make mothers and fathers with families slave in supermarkets at three o'clock in the morning and make people leave their homes and their churches and their children and go shopping on Sundays.'

'Their shops are open on Sundays?' said Benoît in surprise.

'Yes! They make people work on Sundays! And through lunchtimes! But for what? For rubbish from China? For cheap clothes sewed by poor women in Malaysia? For why? So you can go more often to KFC and get full of fried chicken? You would rather have six bars of bad chocolate than one bar of good chocolate. Why? Why are six bad things better than one good thing? I don't understand. We are not the same, you and I.'

'I know that,' I said, feeling suddenly near to tears. 'I know all that. But I still think we should at least try. Try and make something good, with as much love and care as Thierry would do.'

Frédéric and Benoît stared at me.

'Plus,' I added, 'I don't think we have much choice.'

♥

In the end I decided on mint, surely the simplest of flavours. Frédéric and Benoît drank their coffee and watched me blankly as I scrubbed and cleaned all the vats, swept the floor, then started gathering ingredients.

'I'm going to do everything myself?' I asked at one point, red-faced and sweating from the effort, getting crosser and hotter and more resentful with every minute that passed.

'It's your choice,' said Frédéric, which made me very cross. Benoît, however, surprised me. He stood up, went outside and had a cigarette. When he came back, he was carrying all the butter and fresh cream. I nearly burst into tears. After that, Frédéric did bits and pieces too, but very off-handedly, as if he needed to keep reminding us that he was only here under duress. There wouldn't be as much time to spare so we couldn't leave the chocolate to set; it would need to be flash-cooled. This was chocolate-making on the hoof. I smashed and crashed things about, sweated profusely and cried a bit at one stage, when I couldn't get the conch.

It was lumpy and bumpy and messy, but eventually it was in the fridge.

Finally, at about 11.30, half an hour after the shop had been due to open, the first pieces of chocolate emerged from their moulds.

The three of us regarded them carefully. I cut one gently with a knife. The consistency seemed all right; not perfect, a little fudgy maybe.

'Well, here goes nothing,' I said in English to the men,

who were pretending not to be that interested. I picked up a piece, closed my eyes and ate it.

♥

Well. Nobody threw up, I've had worse. Once, for example, some milk powder that had gone off got into the mix at Kidinsborough and we had to bin 20,000 kilos. We were all made to taste it as a way of quality control to try and ensure it never happened again. This chocolate wasn't as bad as that.

But here was what it wasn't: it wasn't heaven. It wasn't the lightly whipped, melting, astonishing delight that Thierry's chocolate was.

What had I done? We'd churned it the right way, conched it, used all the same fresh, fresh ingredients. But watching someone create and actually doing it yourself are two very different things. Something was missing. It was the difference between an Old Master and a painting-by-numbers kit.

I made a face. The boys jumped up. Those bastards, they were pleased! I think they'd been terrified this entire time that I'd turn out to be good at it.

'This is despicable,' said Frédéric, tasting it.

'It's not that bad,' I said.

Benoît simply spat his piece out into a large and grimy cloth handkerchief. I rolled my eyes.

'Come on, you guys. It's my first time!'

'We can't sell this,' said Frédéric.

'It's not that bad!' I said again. He shrugged, as if to say that if I couldn't understand how bad it was, there was no point trying to explain it to me.

The bell tinged in the front and our heads shot up. Oh lord, it was Alice.

She clacked back in. To my total and utter astonishment, she'd obviously been away having her hair done. She held out her hand for the phone, and I felt in my apron pocket. The last number that had called, I saw, was Laurent's. My heart started to beat faster. Did he have news? Was he at the hospital? What was it? Her attention briefly distracted, I quickly forwarded myself the number, for emergencies.

Alice nibbled a tiny corner of the chocolate.

'It's fine,' she said.

'It's NOT,' said Frédéric, but she shot him a warning look.

'Go out and sell,' she said, warningly. 'Or I'm cancelling lunch.'

This seemed to strike scandalised horror into both of them.

'Right. I'm off to the hospital,' said Alice.

'Um, I think Laurent rang.'

Alice looked annoyed, scrolling through her calls. 'But not the hospital. So it can't be that serious.'

'Aren't you going to call him?' I said as she slipped the phone back in her bag. She stared at me blankly.

'Chop chop, open up,' she said in English.

♡

There was even more of a crowd in the shop than usual when we finally opened the doors; Thierry's illness had been mentioned in the press and there were lots of people there who knew his reputation for only the freshest of chocolate and were anxious to see what was going on and suspicious, I was guessing, about quality control. I sighed, full of nerves. They were about to find out.

♡

Nobody said anything, of course, though Frédéric kept giving me meaningful looks across the counter. They would go outside, try a piece, then look at each other. If it was their first time in the shop, they seemed to be saying, wow, I wonder what all the fuss was about, this stuff tastes like any mass-produced supermarket brand.

If they were regulars, it was much, much worse. They would taste a little on the end of their tongue, like policemen in TV dramas tasting cocaine, then nod at each other as if confirming their worst fears, discard the rest and leave quickly. It was awful. And all the time Frédéric was making his smug I Told You So face. During my lunch break I went to seek out a quiet spot – always near impossible on the Île de la Cité – and sobbed my heart out. Then I remembered someone I hadn't called.

'Claire?'

'Oh, thank goodness.' Her voice was frail, but the relief was unmistakable, and I could have kicked myself for not calling her earlier.

'I'm so sorry,' I said. 'My battery died, and then it was late.'

'But you're all right?'

'Ye-es,' I said reluctantly.

'What is it?'

'It's Thierry.'

♥

Claire knew it then. She knew despite all the truisms about how old wounds healed over and people grew up and moved on with their lives, all those things she'd been told and learned from other people and taken to heart and pretended to believe for years and years and years, even as she had raised another man's children and been another man's wife, and another man's divorcee ... Even through all of that, the way the electricity shot through her heart meant it could have been yesterday; the years just fell off her. Nothing had changed, not a tiny thing.

'What about him?' she asked, grasping anxiously at the oxygen cylinder.

'Is everything all right, Mum?' Patsy called cheerfully from the kitchen.

'Fine, thank you.'

'Would you like a cup of tea?'

Claire shook her head in vexation.

'So,' she said. 'What? What is it?'

A painful lump formed in her throat. He couldn't be ... he couldn't be dead. He couldn't be. Mind you, *she* nearly was, she thought to herself bitterly. But not Thierry, with so much life bursting from him.

'He had a heart attack,' I said, as plainly as I could. 'He's in hospital.'

'A heart attack? A serious one?'

'Yes.'

'Oh, all that chocolate, all that butter,' she said. 'Is he . . . is he . . . oh lord . . .'

'I don't know,' I said. 'He's in the hospital. He's had an operation to put in a stent. They don't know if he's going to be all right.'

'But if he's had the operation . . .'

'Yes, but it's difficult . . .'

I wasn't quite sure how to say it.

'He is terribly fat.'

'Oh!' Claire's voice quavered. 'Oh,' she said again. 'But he's still alive?'

'Well, yes, but he's very seriously ill.'

There was a pause, then, 'Oh, I would like to see him so.'

I didn't know what to say to that. How could she get on a plane to Paris? She couldn't walk three steps without running out of breath. It was impossible. I felt so sorry.

'Maybe when he's better he can come and see you?' I said. 'I'll make him.'

'No, don't,' she said. 'Don't. But let me know, won't you? Let me know how he's getting on.'

'Of course,' I said. 'I'll call you.'

'And what about you?' she said suddenly. 'How are you? How are you enjoying Paris?'

I half smiled to myself as I wiped away a black glob of mascara from underneath my eye. I wasn't going to be the bearer of any more bad news.

'It's ... it's eventful,' I said.

'*Tout va bien apart ça?*'

'*Oui, apart ça.*'

♡

I realised as I hung up that I had been hoping that Claire could have been my saviour, that I could have poured my woes out to her – she would understand, surely. She had been a young girl in Paris once. I wasn't much of a young girl, but she'd sent me here.

I hadn't expected her to be quite so affected by the news. I had thought she would be concerned – but from a distance. When I was recuperating, other people's bad news slightly washed over me, I was too selfish and wrapped up in myself to pay it that much attention. But Claire had responded completely differently; as if Thierry was someone she still knew terribly well, intimately, as if this news about someone she hadn't clapped eyes on in forty years was somehow of intense importance to her.

♡

1972

Claire had seen Richard Shawcourt around. He wore brown horn-rimmed glasses that made him look too serious to be a schoolboy, and sometimes he'd carry a music case. He was carrying it that day as he swung through the woods.

Claire was skipping school. Some days she felt sad, some days dreamy. Today, she felt mutinous. She'd snapped repeatedly at her mother over the breakfast table (there was no point in cheeking the Reverend if she ever wanted to leave the house again) and stormed out nastily, barely even bothering to check the post. She'd started out in the direction of school – she had French oral practice that morning, which she was good at – but had got halfway there and seen a huge gaggle of girls, including Rainie Collender, all giggling and screaming at each other and laughing at Looby Mary, a big lummox of a girl in their year who always walked alone and never spoke. They were obviously being viciously mean to her, even though Mary was clearly educationally subnormal, asking her questions about whether she had a lad and which disco she would take him to, and it turned Claire's stomach all of a sudden, the stupid, pointless cruelties of school life. She wondered what Thierry would do. He wouldn't stand for it, she was sure, his benevolent attitude towards the world wouldn't allow it.

She marched up to them.

'What are you guys, eleven?' she said, her voice not even wavering. 'For God's sake, you're leaving school in the summer and you're running around being bullies.'

'Get over yourself,' said Rainie Collender, who dyed her hair already.

'Oh, it's the French madame's pet, oh je t'aime,' said Minnie Evans, who was Rainie's evil sidekick. Everyone started laughing, but Claire just turned round to Looby Mary and said, 'Are you all right?' and Looby Mary looked really confused, like she hadn't properly understood what was happening in the first place, and scuttled off. The group of girls had reconfigured and were now talking loudly in shocked tones along the lines of 'Well, I don't know who she thinks

she is,' and 'I suppose she thinks she's better than everyone,' and Claire sighed, rolled her eyes and marched off to the woods.

'Aw, too scared to come to school?' shouted Rainie. Claire ignored her.

❤

She sat in the bough of her favourite tree in the copse behind the school, lighting one of her precious Gauloises – barely inhaling, just letting the smell of the smoke calm her down to stop her kicking a tree.

The sound of someone coming made her scuttle down and put it out, trying not to be seen.

'Sorry,' said Richard Shawcourt, looking awkward and a bit embarrassed, his trousers already too short, even this early in the school year. 'I didn't mean to startle you. I just wanted to say well done and make sure you were all right. I never dare stand up to bullies, they break my glasses.'

She looked him up and down.

'What's in that music case, then?' she said.

❤

It was worse than I had anticipated. When I got back, Frédéric and Alice were having a full-blown stand-up row in front of the shutters. They were screaming at each other too quickly for me to properly follow them, but it seemed reasonably obvious from the way they looked at me with furious eyes that it had a lot to do with me and my perceived weaknesses. Frédéric was obviously continuing to insist on the closure of the shop. This solution didn't appear to be cutting any ice with Alice at all. They both gazed at me expectantly.

The good thing about our corner of the Île de la Cité was that it contained lots of tiny alleyways that were good for ducking down. I ducked down one now. Then I rang the number that I had purloined from Alice's phone.

The voice that answered spoke low and quickly.

'Allo?'

'Laurent?' I said. 'It's me, it's Anna.'

He exhaled slowly.

'Anna, I'm at the hospital. Just popped out from the ward to get a coffee, but I shouldn't be on the telephone. This isn't a good time.'

'I know, I know, I'm sorry ... How is he doing?'

Laurent sighed. 'Still no change. These bloody machines are making my ears hurt. And I have to get back to work. I mean, I really have to. They can't do without me.'

This was the worst news I could have heard. I needed him, really badly.

I told him so.

'Please,' I said. 'I need you. To help me out with the shop. I can't do it by myself.'

'But I thought you worked in chocolate?'

'Well I do, but I'm hardly going to be as good as your father, am I?'

'No,' he said, a little quickly for my liking.

'I need help. It's all going wrong. Frédéric and Alice are fighting.'

'Alice would fight with a dead dog in a town hall,' said Laurent. I presumed this was some unusual French saying I wasn't familiar with. He sighed and was quiet for a long time. I could hear beeping and the swishy-swashy sound of the respirator in the background.

'Okay,' he said finally. 'I'm going to leave and do my shift then come back to the hospital. Can you meet me at work? A few pointers, that's all, okay?'

I nodded.

'Where do you work?'

'The Pritzer,' he said. I'd never heard of it, but he said it like I ought to have.

'Come in the back entrance. I'll see you at three.'

'What will I tell Alice?'

'Tell Alice you're going to save the shop, and also that she can go pee on scissors.'

My French had a long way to go.

♥

Alice looked down her long nose at me.

'Well, Thierry won't hear of it. He would never let Laurent's concoctions' – she pronounced the word as if it were poisonous – 'near his customers.'

'I realise that,' I said. 'But I think it might be better—'

'What we are making here is CHALK,' burst out Frédéric provocatively. He'd stopped shouting, briefly, when I made my way over to them, but his ears were bright red. Benoît was nowhere to be found. 'It is a travesty! It is a sin!'

'Um, can we not go quite that far?' I said. 'It's not that bad.'

'Not that bad is as good as terrible,' he said. 'In this shop.'

Alice bit her lip and thought about it for a moment.

'The shop must go on,' she said. 'It must. We have bills, and commitments; we cannot possibly close now, it is our busiest season ... Can you sell the rest of this morning's stock?' she asked Frédéric.

He drew himself up to his full height – about five foot six – and said, 'I can, but I will not, madame.'

Alice rolled her eyes.

'All right,' she said to me. 'Go. And next time you'd better do it right or you'll find that French laws protecting jobs don't cover yours.'

Chapter Sixteen

The Pritzer, I found out, was a very posh hotel on the Place de la Concorde, near the Crillon. It was built in beautiful yellow stone and looked like a castle, with small balconies and canopies over every window. Outside were two porters dressed in livery with top hats, each standing next to a large topiary cockerel. A spotless red carpet descended the steps on to the pavement, where a large man wearing sunglasses and a very small woman who looked like she was made out of icing sugar were descending from a huge black car. They were completely ignoring each other. The woman was holding a tiny dog like a baby. The porters leapt to help them.

'Excuse me,' I said when they'd finished. 'Where's the kitchen entrance?'

Behind the hotel, all was very different. The kitchen entrance was off an alleyway filled with dustbins. The back of the building was old white brick, and a grubby fire door was propped open with several staff in white aprons and tall hats crowded round it smoking furiously. I felt nervous, but made my way through them. Just inside the entrance was an old man wearing a peaked hat and a green blazer, sitting at a desk next to a huge row of time stamp cards. That made me feel a bit more at home, it reminded me of the factory. I told him who I was looking for and he made a call.

A long hall stretched out in front of me, lined on one side by huge carts of linen tended by women in black dresses with white pinafores. On the other side were great swinging doors with round panes of glass set in them, obviously leading to the kitchens, and it was from here that Laurent emerged. In his whites he looked commanding and rather impressive, firing a list of instructions behind me as he came, looking none too pleased to see me, for which I couldn't really blame him. I'd caused him nothing but trouble since I'd arrived.

'Hello,' I said in a small voice.

'Yes, follow me,' he said. 'Can't you tie your hair back?'

I retightened the loop of my ponytail, hoping that would be enough. He grunted, thanked the commissionaire and pointed me in the direction of the hand sanitiser mounted on the wall outside the doors.

I'd never been in such a huge kitchen before. I stopped to goggle for a second, I couldn't help it. It was an utter hive of activity, men (and they were nearly all men) marching to and fro very, very quickly. Most of them were wearing white jackets with blue checked trousers and clogs, though some, including Laurent, wore white trousers and had their names embroidered on their jackets. I assumed this meant something important.

The noise levels were unbelievable. People were shouting in a variety of languages; pots and pans were clanked and hurled across the room. In the corner, four younger men in T-shirts were frantically packing and unpacking industrial-sized dishwashers and two had their hands deep inside pots. On my right, a boy who looked to be around sixteen was furiously chopping vegetables. I had never seen anyone chop anything so quickly; his hand was a blur.

To my left, a long line of immaculate salads was laid out, on to which a man was slicing pieces of perfectly cooked pink duck, all exactly the same, at absolutely precise thicknesses. Another, older man came up to him and told him off furiously for not making them all thin enough, and the man, instead of arguing back, stood with his head down until the rant was over, and then recommenced, apologising.

Laurent caught me staring and gave a half-smile.

'Have you never seen a working kitchen before?'

I shook my head; I'd never seen anything remotely like this. It was like a huge airfield; but once you got used to the size and the noise and the number of people bustling about and the occasional gouts of steam, it seemed to make a lot of sense; it was organised, like ants, not the chaos it first appeared.

Laurent led me down to the far end of the room, where two men were kneading bread. They had huge muscular forearms and looked like miners or navvies rather than bakers. An almost comically large man stood opposite them, icing tiny pastries. His size was completely at odds with the task he was undertaking.

Laurent's station was by the window, which looked out on to the Seine. He had a huge copper pot, very much like the ones at his father's shop, bubbling on the stove, the melting chocolate giving off a glorious aroma. But instead of oranges and mint, there was every manner of flavouring littered around his work bench. Tiny chillies is lined up in bright green and red; yellow marjoram and little pumpkin flowers jostled next to pine needles and sea salt.

'This looks like a mad person's laboratory,' I said.

'I'm going to take that as a compliment,' he replied gruffly. 'Is there any more news? You seem to be the first to know about anything.'

'That's not true,' I said quietly. 'But I do need to ask you this favour.'

He checked on one of the smaller pots he was stirring.

'Try this,' he said.

I opened my mouth eagerly, and he smiled.

'You are a proper chocolate girl. Okay, hang on.'

He blew on it to cool it down.

'What is it?'

He shook his head, then popped it in my mouth.

My first instinct was to spit it out. It was horrible, not sweet at all. It was sharp, bitter, and with an odd warm flavour that I couldn't identify. Laurent was holding up his finger strongly, warning me to be patient.

'It's new,' he said. 'You have to give it some time.'

'It tastes like cat food,' I said, but then stopped talking as the warmth of the chocolate gradually hit my tongue and spread round my mouth. It was the most extraordinary, rich sensation and tasted like nothing I'd ever had before. It was also slightly horrible, but as soon as I'd finished it I immediately wanted more.

'Wow, what WAS that?' I said eventually, looking hopefully at his pot.

'Slow-roasted tomato chilli chocolate,' Laurent announced proudly. 'If you don't use the very bitterest of beans, it makes you throw up. It's a hard one to get right.'

'It's not really a sweet at all,' I said.

'It's not,' agreed Laurent. 'Wait till you see what I do to the duck.'

I boggled to think.

'And your dad didn't think this was cool?'

'He just wanted to do things his way.'

'And you don't?'

He shrugged. 'Well, maybe it's better for fathers and sons not to work with each other.'

A small man, quite young, had appeared before him and was now removing trays of quickly hardening chocolate to the enormous fridges. Laurent grimaced and checked his watch.

'Alors, I need to get to the hospital. What is it you need from me?'

I gave him a piece of the chocolate I'd made. He

233

manoeuvred it round his mouth exactly how his father did it. His face fell.

'Oh,' he said.

'The shop needs you to help me,' I said. 'I can't do it.'

'I have been thinking about this,' he said. 'I don't think it's possible. I've changed my mind. No offence, but you worked in a mass-market factory. You don't have the right genes, the right experience.'

'That's nonsense,' I said crossly. 'It's just that I've only been here five minutes.'

'It's pointless,' he said.

He started washing his hands, handing over the stove to another man – this was ridiculous, didn't they have any girls working here at all? – who carried on stirring.

'We need you,' I said. 'I can't do it, not yet. I didn't get to watch him do it often enough. But I'm a quick learner, I promise.'

He looked at me, then gestured round the room. 'Do you know how long it's taken me to work up to this?' he said. 'How many kitchens I've worked in, how many people have shouted at me, how much crap I've taken off everyone, how much bullying I've got for who my father is? How much I've looked and concentrated and learned and observed? And you want me to, what, just give it all up and come back and put mint in milk chocolate? Is that what you want me to do?'

'It's not what *I* want you to do,' I said. 'It's for the shop. It's for your dad.'

Laurent blew his thick fringe out of his eyes.

'Well that's interesting, because the last time we discussed it, he said he didn't want me to cross the threshold ever again and that I was a total failure who'd never learned a thing.'

I put my arm out, but didn't touch him.

'That was before.'

'But if I agree to help, will you let me do my own styles, my own designs? No, of course not. Alice will insist on doing things the old way and I'll be completely trapped again, acting as a slave to my dad, just like he's always wanted his entire life. I will not cook there!'

It was only the general noise and clanging of the kitchen that stopped people turning to look at Laurent shouting. I went pink anyway; I couldn't bear it. I stared at the ground so that he couldn't see how furious I was. But he noticed anyway and didn't give a toss.

'I have to go to the hospital,' he said. 'And I can't lose this job. Not at the moment. There are ... there are no jobs like this. I've worked so long for it, and I'm already being allowed to take more time off than anyone else does, just out of kitchen respect for my father.'

I nodded. 'I understand,' I said, in a flat voice. He was walking me out now, grabbing his scooter helmet from the wall.

'He doesn't want what I have to offer,' said Laurent. 'He's made that totally clear ... I'll be back for evening service,' he told the man at the door, clocking out.

He saw my unhappy face as we stepped out into the bright, hazy afternoon.

'Look,' he said. 'Just . . . try a few more times. It's not difficult, what my father does, believe me. It just takes a bit of
practice.'

'Except I don't have the genes.'

'You don't have the genes to invent it,' he said. 'But a
monkey can copy a recipe eventually.'

I gave him a look.

'I think that just came out ruder than I meant it to,' he
said, a look of apology on his features.

'Well, wouldn't be the first time,' I said.

'Do you need a lift?'

'No thank you,' I said stiffly.

We stood looking at each other, both cross.

'Send my love to your dad,' I said eventually. 'Let us
know how he is. Frédéric is climbing the walls.'

Laurent half smiled. 'Yes, he would be. But Benoît's the
one you have to watch out for.'

I nodded. 'Yeah, well, thanks for all the advice,' I said sarcastically.

And he got on his scooter and sped away.

Chapter Seventeen

The next few nights, with the shop closed over what happily turned out to be a bank holiday weekend, I stopped going home at all. I stayed. I cooked and I stirred and I experimented and I added and took away, and did the bloody conching, over and over and over again. I tried the pistachio – a disaster – and the violet, and the hazelnut. Anything including nuts was a consummate failure.

Eventually, after working until I fell asleep on my feet, I finally got it figured out. If I stuck to just a couple of things – no nougatine, no caramel, no sculpture, no drinking chocolate, or experimenting with dark chocolate, which I simply didn't have the palate for; if I kept it simple – very, very simple – and with the right ingredients, which Benoît had already sorted out – I could do it. Well, I couldn't do it, that wasn't the case at all. But I could produce the two simplest chocolates we did – an orange and a mint – which tasted almost, but not quite, as good as the real thing. Good enough, at any rate, to fool most of the tourists, who were looking for a souvenir rather than a gourmet item.

I melted and mixed and poured, over and over again, leaving the radio on and downing endless amounts of espresso to keep me awake. By Monday night I was as exhausted as I had ever been in my life. At three o'clock in the morning, my phone rang.

'Allo?'

'You live! You are alive! I can call off the fire brigade and Interpol!'

'Sami?' I said, realising that I hadn't spoken to anyone all weekend. 'Is that you? You haven't really called Interpol, have you?'

He chuckled. 'Where are you? Off discovering Paris and your first taste of erotic adventure?'

'Ahem,' I said. 'You're very rude.'

I looked round the workroom.

'What are you doing?'

'We're at the Cirque du Soleil after-party. The gymnasts tend to get a little wild.'

'Oh,' I said. 'You could stop by the shop if you're hungry. I have a lot of taster chocolate left over.'

'Vraiment?'

And that is how, half an hour later, I found myself drinking something entirely suspicious out of a bottle that Sami told me was pastis. It reminded me of Laurent's chocolate in that at first it was horrible, then almost immediately delicious.

It also, given my exhausted and underfed state, got me incredibly drunk very quickly, as I watched beautiful young people whose genders I couldn't exactly ascertain descend on the chocolate with the enthusiasm only people who hang upside down from a roof for four hours a night can manage. By the time the sun started to come up, the chocolate was nearly all gone and the room was clean and tidy, and I realised there was no point trying to get any sleep today either.

♡

The scent of Frédéric's cigarette coming up the rue de Chanoinesse scattered the beautiful golden circus creatures like some kind of dream. He sniffed suspiciously as he entered.

'How long have you been here?' he asked.

I shrugged. 'I wanted to practise over the weekend,' I said.

He glanced around and raised an eyebrow. Then he advanced on the remaining tray in the cooling rack. I stared at him anxiously. Of course the dancers had loved it, but they would love any chocolate at that time of day. Frédéric was the one who really knew.

He took a long pull of water from an Evian bottle to clear his palate, then took a small piece from the baking sheet on the tray. He held it up to the light, then crumbled a little between his fingers to check the consistency. Finally he popped the whole piece into his mouth. I held my breath. I had tried everything I could and this was ... well, if I was totally honest, this was as good as I could do. I waited as he waited, for the chocolate to melt and the full richness of the underlying taste to come through. As we did so, Benoît startled me by turning up silently beside him and watching the process.

Eventually Frédéric turned to me. He wasn't over the moon. I wasn't a hitherto undiscovered genius. But he gave me a tight, trim little nod.

'We can . . . we can manage that,' he said in a quiet voice.

Exhausted though I was, a huge smile spread across my face.

'Merci,' I said, delighted.

Benoît grabbed a piece and popped it in his mouth, then, completely out of the blue and without saying a word, came over and kissed me on both cheeks.

♥

'This is all you have?' said Frédéric.

'Yes,' I said. 'I figured I'd just try and get one or two right.'

'Good idea.'

He checked his phone.

'Alice hasn't called you?'

I shook my head.

'Or Laurent?'

'I don't think Laurent wants anything to do with me,' I said ruefully.

'Well, we're only keeping their business alive,' said Frédéric. 'Why would they want to tell us anything?'

I thought, though, that if Thierry had deteriorated, we would definitely know about it, which was something, I suppose. I went through to the front of the shop to get some fresh morning air and wash my face in the bathroom. There was no sign of Alice.

'Well,' said Frédéric. 'We shall worry about that as it happens. All that matters is that today, we have a shop we can open.'

And when I came back from the bathroom, Benoît had made me a cup of coffee.

♡

Claire looked up at Patsy.

'Patsy, I've decided, I want to take a trip.'

Patsy's face immediately got panicky, as if Claire had suddenly gone mad. Claire wondered if she thought she meant a trip like a long journey into the night, assisted suicide or something. Or just a trip, she also considered. Something very different.

Ricky had got a film out for her called *The Bucket List*. It was absolutely terrible – old men on a cancer ward having a hilarious time – but the concept had stuck with her.

'There is something I want to do. Before … before it's too late.'

'Don't talk like that,' Patsy said, hastily.

♡

1972

Richard Shawcourt's home life was very different to Claire's. He lived in a bought house for starters; not something tied to the church, a nice

241

house, detached. Although now, that didn't intimidate her any more. She knew a little bit about nice houses. Before, she'd barely have given him a second glance, she was so sure of their differences. She'd have laughed at him, in fact. Very few kids like him even went to Kidinsborough Modern, never mind wielding a clarinet. He'd started off very small, she remembered now, just punch bag material, but now, she saw, he'd grown into himself, in the upper sixth, ready to leave for somewhere better, and behind the little wire-rimmed John Lennon spectacles was actually rather handsome, with his wavy dark hair and strong eyebrows. Not that she was interested, of course. He walked her home from the forest that day, asking her about herself, to which she replied in the vaguest of terms, and after that he seemed to pop up everywhere.

Christmas came and went, and a card arrived from Mme Lagarde, full of news about the children, with a fulsome footnote as to how much they missed Claire and hoping that she was (Claire thought, correctly, that this was deliberately pointed) concentrating very hard on her education. There was no mention of Thierry.

So when Richard bought her a large bunch of blood-red roses and a small brooch in the shape of a frog, and took her to the Christmas dance, she let him kiss her up against the back wall of the gym, in amidst all the other snogging, writhing couples, to show the world, and Thierry, and Madame Lagarde and Rainie Collender, how very much she didn't care.

♡

It was Richard who, when she failed all her A levels except for French, comforted her and assured her she could still go into teacher training, and it was Richard – nice, steady Richard, who was going to study engineering science at Leicester – who brought the Reverend round to agreeing to let her leave home. It was Richard with whom she slept in the small modern bedroom in the halls of residence that smelled of Pot Noodle and joss sticks and hash, shocking and exciting him with her prowess; confirming for her that Thierry was a one-off, not like other men. And after dating a few of the long-haired young men on campus, self-conscious in their new flares, talking endlessly about Herman Hesse and Nixon in over-ponderous tones, she gradually realised that Richard was as nice as any man she'd ever met; kind, and sensible, and steady and well-off, and there was no more point in loving your first love than in thinking you were still going to marry Davy Jones.

Much, much later, when they were divorcing – after the initial, earth-shattering devastation, they'd kept it as civilised as possible, waiting for both of the boys to leave home and be nicely settled, very little rancour on either side – Richard, in a rare moment of not being businesslike and distant and organised, had said, 'You never really loved me, did you? It was never really me. I thought you were amazing and different and mysterious, but now it seems to me you were just thinking about someone else the entire time.'

He'd shaken his head in wonderment. 'The thing is, for me, Claire, I got to spend twenty-five years with someone I loved. With someone I really and truly loved. But you ... I don't know what on earth you've wasted your life doing.'

And Claire had smiled stiffly, and signed the papers his lawyer had sent over, and waited until she heard the familiar sound of his Rover turn the corner, and then she sank to her knees and simply disintegrated, becoming unbodied; degenerated into a wavering mass of tears and snot and pouring emotion, soaking the good John Lewis carpet they'd invested in together.

Although she didn't believe, as some did, that cancer was some kind of malignant force or punishment that snuck into you if you were unhappy or upset, she couldn't help thinking that if it was a dark spirit, it would have seen that day – and the nights, the many nights that followed it – as an ideal opportunity to infect a soul that could see nothing but deepest black.

♡

'What do you mean, a trip?' Patsy said when she saw the tight set of Claire's mouth and realised she wasn't in the mood to be dissuaded, and that she wasn't joking either.

Claire stared down at her Hickman line and sighed. This was going to be really complicated and annoying and hard work and dangerous. It was going to upset her children, and quite possibly Anna, whom, she now realised, she'd sent on this mission in a selfish way. It would cause expense and trouble and would perhaps be all for nothing, and she was exactly what she had always been, according to the Reverend and Richard and everyone, it somehow seemed, who'd known her well: a selfish, hard person, with unseemly desires.

She took a deep breath. There was more of the Reverend in her, she sometimes thought, than anyone would ever have suspected.

'I want to see Paris one last time,' she said.

Patsy frowned. 'Are you sure?' she said.

Patsy didn't know anything about Claire's past, because not even Richard knew more than a hint or two. She'd been very careful that they never went to France, even on holiday. She actually made her French accent worse than it was and never joined in a conversation about Paris, even though she was asked about it often. She knew he would guess something in an instant; she knew that the reason he'd initially been so attracted to her was the air of difference she had given off after that summer. So Patsy treated her patronisingly, like it was some kind of whim.

'I am sure,' said Claire. 'I will sort everything out. And I can pay for it.'

She could. Richard had been utterly fair, and her teacher's pension was good, and she had an annuity she hadn't even touched, which, she realised drily, was a great thing for the insurance company and the country as a whole.

'Well, you can take the train now,' said Patsy. 'Ricky and I did it when we were dating. Mind you, I didn't like Paris at all. So rude, everyone always pushing past you and everything so expensive and I didn't even think the food was that good. You couldn't get a decent curry, I'll tell you that. Or a cab.'

Claire suddenly felt exhausted. She loved Patsy, but couldn't possibly explain to her why getting a cab in Paris only ever defeated the point. Or maybe it had all changed. Maybe they'd completely built over it, like the new shopping centre in Kidinsborough, which had turned into a kind of derelict drug run within five years. Or the pedestrian plaza, which was mostly used now as somewhere for people to be sick on a weekend. It was where the ambulances parked up.

Under the Eiffel Tower there'd been an old-fashioned carousel. It didn't move very fast, it creaked a lot, and it made its own music. The children had adored it, they had their favourite horses and they loved the second storey, reached via a child-sized curved wrought-iron staircase, even though it rotated even more slowly than the one underneath it. She wondered if that was still there.

'Well, nonetheless, I want to go.'

'Let me talk to Eurostar. They must have some way of taking sick people.'

'I don't want to take the train,' said Claire, in a moment of sudden realisation. 'I have to go on the ferry.'

'But that will take much longer and be much more dangerous,' said Patsy. 'I mean, if you can afford it, you should go first class.'

Claire saw Montserrat coming up the path and attempted a wave. Somehow just having made the plan was already making her feel better about things.

'No,' she said. 'I shall take the boat. I have friends in Paris. I think they can help.'

Chapter Eighteen

Fortunately, Alice was incredibly grateful for everything. Ha, was she bugger. Honestly, getting a smile out of her would be like getting her to eat something; her entire mouth was a no-fly zone.

'Is it better?' she asked, carelessly.

'Is HE better?' demanded Frédéric, as if he was going to hold all the chocolate hostage until he knew.

Under Alice's enormous sunglasses she looked very drawn.

'He is . . . he is a little better,' she admitted. 'Well, he is no worse. And the stents appear to have taken and, well.'

Her lip curled slightly.

'Every day he loses a little weight. But I wish . . .'

She looked away.

'I wish he would wake up and say something, dammit.'

This sounded not ideal. I knew a little bit myself about waking up in hospital, and I knew, courtesy of Dr Ed, that the quicker you managed to do so, the better it was all round. I was suddenly tempted to ring Dr Ed, find out if that friendly manner was all it had promised to be. But I didn't of course, he wouldn't even have remembered my name.

'What does his doctor say?' I asked.

'Why, are you a professional?' snapped Alice. Every time I gave her a bit of credit for being under stress, she managed to use up every bit of it and eat even further into my meagre reserves of respect.

'No,' I said. 'But I've spent a lot of time in hospital.'

'What's wrong with you?' she asked, bluntly. Everyone was staring at me.

'Nothing, it doesn't matter,' I said quickly. I didn't like people bringing up my hilarious comedy injury. It hadn't been the least bit funny to me.

Alice sighed. 'She says, wait and see, madame, wait and see, as if I have the least option to do anything else. Then she goes off to lunch.'

She glanced around.

'Anyway. As long as you are managing to avoid this being a complete disaster, I suppose it will have to do.'

She stalked off.

'That,' said Frédéric, whose jolly manner was nearly restored and who was almost making up by flirting with female clients what Thierry used to do by charming them, 'was the nicest she's ever been to us.'

I, on the other hand, was utterly at the end of my tether. The fact that Thierry's illness had made the papers just made us busier than ever, and even when Frédéric abruptly told people that today they had a choice of orange or mint or nothing, everyone simply seemed to take that as an acceptably French thing to say.

I scrubbed and cleaned and cooked and mixed – although Benoît helped me immeasurably and silently in the back of the greenhouse – and by seven o'clock felt ready to collapse into bed. If Sami was holding an impromptu masked ball or something, I was going to kill him.

I was the last to leave. I was locking up with the heavy metal key in the large grille – it looked rather like the front of a huge old-fashioned lift – when I heard a scooter roar up the street. I didn't pay it any attention at first – they were ten a penny round here – until it came to a stop right behind me.

'Merde,' came a gravelly voice.

I turned round. Laurent was standing there, looking wild-eyed. I turned back again. I was sick of him, and his stupid feud with a man lying unconscious in a hospital bed.

'Has everyone gone?'

'Yes,' I said, as sarcastically as possible. 'Everyone has gone. Everyone important has gone.'

He blinked a couple of times as I finished closing up.

'Oh,' he said. 'Only ... only ... he's woken up.'

I turned round. Even though I was utterly exhausted, and filthy, and cross at seeing Laurent, I couldn't help it: a huge grin split my face.

'Truly!'

'Truly. He's not saying much, but he's swearing and demanding beignets.'

'Oh! Well. That is brilliant!'

'We're not out of the woods,' he said gravely. 'Well, that's what M. le Medecin keeps saying. But he looks ... he looks a lot less grey, not so much like a dead elephant.'

'Does he know you call him a dead elephant?'

He frowned. 'I don't know. I slipped out before he saw me.'

I threw my hands up in anger.

'You are KIDDING!'

'No,' he said. 'Alice was giving me the feud eyes, and he was telling her he was hungry and she was telling him he was going to have to start getting a whole lot more hungry, and it seemed to be turning into a massive fall-out within about two minutes of him regaining consciousness and I realised why I kept out of their way in the first place.'

He paused. 'I'll see him tomorrow, I promise. Stop looking at me like I'm the big bad wolf.'

He did look a bit like the big bad wolf when I thought about it, with his dark hair and thick brows and bright white teeth.

'You promise?' I said.

He nodded and looked around.

'Also,' he said, 'I wanted to get down here before everyone had left ... I felt bad about the other day.'

'Good,' I said, then used a word I really enjoyed using in French. 'You were unconscionable.'

'I know, I know. That's why I'm here. I just … Everything was getting on top of me, you know? I'd been spending all my nights at the hospital … I was tired.'

'So you came here to apologise?'

'God, no. I came to show you how to make something.'

'Well, maybe I can already make something,' I said.

He grimaced. 'Alice brought some of that mint stuff you did the other day into the hospital. She thought it was all right. It was filthy. None of the staff could believe it.'

That was my first day's efforts.

'You are SO rude,' I said.

'No,' said Laurent. 'I just don't think you realise how bad it was. So, now I am here.'

'Well, you're too late,' I said.

He waggled his eyebrows at me.

'I doubt it.'

I sighed. Even though I was exhausted and had spent the last nineteen hours dreaming of a bath, and what I'd do to Sami if he'd used all the hot water again to take his make-up off, I took the keys out of my apron pocket.

'Come on then,' I said, wearily.

Inside, everything was gloomy in the dusk. Laurent looked round with a practised eye as I fumbled my way through to the greenhouse to switch the lights on there. We couldn't put the lights on at the front of the shop, in case everyone thought we were open and started hammering on the shutters like chocolate-starved zombies.

Laurent wasn't following me. I turned back to look at

him. He was running one of his hands through his thick curly hair.

'I haven't . . . I haven't been in here for . . .'

I raised my eyebrows.

'Well. A long time,' he said. 'Years. Maybe ten.'

Even I was shocked at that.

'You haven't been here in ten years?'

Laurent suddenly looked very unhappy.

'The smell in here,' he said. 'It hasn't changed a bit.'

He ran his hand along the long wooden counter top, worn smooth over the years.

'It hasn't changed a bit,' he repeated wonderingly, shaking his head. 'You know, sometimes down the street I pass someone eating some. I can smell it a mile off. It doesn't smell like the chocolate you get anywhere else. Every time I smell it, or see the bag . . . it's like being punched in the gut.'

I shook my head and put the coffee machine on.

'You know,' I said, 'families fall out for all sorts of reasons. My friend Cath's mother didn't speak to her sister for sixteen years over a purloined Silver Jubilee scarf. But fighting over whether or not you should add spice to chocolate . . .'

I thought about it some more.

'Maybe all family feuds are totally stupid,' I concluded.

Laurent looked as if he was going to disagree, but instead followed me through to the back. He gave an involuntary 'oh' of nostalgia; even I could see that the greenhouse hadn't changed in decades.

'I used to come here sometimes when I was a little boy,' he said, breathing in that wonderful warm scent of plants and cacoa, like a deep chocolate rainforest. 'Benoît used to chase me round the vats.'

'He's still here.'

'I'm not surprised. My dad is very loyal to employees who never answer him back.'

He came over to one of the work benches and swung himself up on to it.

'Come on then,' he said in a challenging way, and I was so tired, so sleepy and woozy with everything that had gone on, that I thought, just for a tiny instant, that he was asking me to get up there with him. He looked so comfortable and at ease, his long legs splayed as he surveyed the place he'd once called home, that I nearly found myself walking across the room; letting him haul me up on to his lap. And after that . . .

Then I realised he was asking me to bring him some of the chocolate I'd made. I flushed bright red, flustered, sure that my face had betrayed me, but he wasn't paying attention. I found some squares of orange that had been badly wrapped earlier and put to one side. Laurent looked at me and smiled.

'Come on, don't look so nervous. Where's your new stuff? You tried your best, and now I'll give you a helping hand, okay?'

He thought I was nervous about the chocolate. I'd almost forgotten about it.

I extended some on a plate. He took a piece and put it in

his mouth. I'd got past Frédéric, but there was no way Laurent was going to be satisfied. Still, I was having a shot.

Laurent closed his eyes. There was total silence in the room, with only the tick of the wall clock and the faint rumble of the Métro far below the cobbled streets. After what seemed like an age (which I used to study him; his long eyelashes casting a shadow on his cheek, his unruly curls, the five o'clock shadow climbing up his long jawline, his lips unusually pronounced for a man), he finally opened his eyes again and looked straight at me. There was something different there from his usual mix of annoyance and amusement. It looked perilously close to respect.

'You did this?'

I nodded.

'Alone?'

I nodded again.

He looked to the side.

'You know it's not . . . I mean, it's not Girard.'

I nodded.

'But . . . I've tasted worse.'

'I've tasted worse? That's not actually a compliment.'

'Oh, it is. It is. You've definitely got . . . you've definitely got something.'

He ate another piece.

'Okay, well here you're missing the black pepper. You need it to bring up the base notes. And a touch less butter, okay? This isn't for children, or Americans. And stir a little less, you've over-churned. It messes up the components.'

I looked around for a piece of paper to write all this down on. He stopped chewing for a second.

'But overall,' he said, 'you've done really well.'

I didn't want to say that it had taken me practically all weekend, but he must have seen my eyelids drooping.

'Look, let's leave it for now, and I'll come and talk mint with you another time, all right? Do you want to go and get something to eat? I am absolutely super-fatigued, and I think you might be too.'

I nodded gratefully – another all-night session in the greenhouse at this point might just have wiped me out – and followed him out of the front door, locking up again, then letting him lead me down a tiny maze of alleys I still hadn't worked out. Three turns, and we were at yet another one of those dark doors that seemed to appear out of the middle of nowhere. I felt for the tourists in the huge outdoor restaurants that lined the Seine or the Bois de Boulogne; they had no idea, could never know about these places. The locals were jealous and selfish with them, had no interest in sharing them. Paris could be pretty tough on the newcomer. This one had nothing but a tiny mushroom over its door to let you know it was even there.

Laurent knocked and was answered by a stooped man with a napkin thrown over his shoulder. For a second he paused and stared. Then he took a step back.

'Laurent?' he said incredulously.

'Yes, Salvatore, it's me,' said Laurent.

The old man, looking close to tears, threw his arms

around Laurent's neck, kissing him three times on each cheek.

'I thought ... God help me, I thought it was your father's ghost standing there. You look so like him.'

'So they say.'

'We haven't seen you in ...' The man shook his head. 'It has been so long. So long.'

'I know,' said Laurent.

'And now. Finally. You are here to run the shop. Your father?'

'He's recovering,' said Laurent firmly. 'I'm just helping out.'

The old man looked closely at me.

'And this is your wife? Your girlfriend?'

Laurent waved his hand. 'Oh no, nothing like that. She works for my father. Hey, Signor, can you get us something to eat?'

'Of course, of course,' said Salvatore, throwing open the old wooden door into a passageway from which emerged the most amazing smells of mushrooms sizzling in garlic and butter, with white pepper and all sorts of other things I couldn't identify.

But I barely noticed the stunning aromas; I was so tired and shaky that suddenly I was furious that Laurent had referred to me in such a dismissive way. I mean, I knew that technically he was right, and that was all I was, but ... after everything we'd bloody been through. Couldn't he at least have said we were friends?

I realised as he ushered me through into a tiny restaurant not much larger than somebody's front room – decorated like someone's front room too, with family photographs and knick-knacks, nearly every table filled with people concentrating furiously on the process of eating, as a tiny old woman ducked and bobbed between the tables carrying piled-high plates as if she was dancing – that actually, if I was being completely honest with myself, I had perhaps seen us as something more than friends. That if I was being completely honest with myself, I did actually fancy him a bit. I suppose it was the high emotional pitch of the circumstances in which we'd been thrown together, and the fact that I'd been alone for so long that had made me fixate on the first available male.

But it was also something about Paris that had re-awoken me. After the accident, after my illness, everything in Kidinsborough had seemed so very cold and grey and lifeless. I'd seen the similarities between myself and Claire, even though she was twice my age. She had noticed them too, and sent me here to bring me back to life. But I'd forgotten how it worked. I'd forgotten how people fancy each other and get together. It's very rarely because one person thinks the other person is responsible for their father having to go to hospital and a really terrible cook. I bit my lip. Oh God, I was such an idiot. I felt so stupid.

'Anna?'

He was asking not what I wanted to drink, but whether I wanted the red wine Salvatore had already brought over. I shrugged and let him pour me a tiny glass.

'We shall have the risotto, of course,' he said. 'Marina, has it changed at all?'

The tiny old woman had much the same reaction to Laurent as Salvatore, except her kisses were even more effusive. She spoke in a rat-tat-tat Italian-accented French that I could barely follow, but I did catch her response.

'No, of course it is exactly the same. We wouldn't change a single thing. If you change a single thing when you have something perfect, it is all wrong! Wrong and terrible and a disaster.'

Laurent cocked an eyebrow at me, but I was too unhappy to flirt back with him. I just nodded, suddenly feeling terribly weary. He attempted to make conversation, but I felt so unsure of myself that I could barely mutter responses. Eventually he too lapsed into silence until the food arrived. Then he closed his eyes and inhaled the steam. It smelled almost impossibly rich and flavoursome, full of onions and cream and stock and good things.

'I ate this as a child. Whenever I came here, I would insist on having it,' he said. 'When there was a good day at the shop. Or a bad day. Or an average day. My dad would just say, everyone to Salvatore's, and we would take the table there' – he pointed to the largest table, which was by the fireplace and had mismatched rickety chairs – 'or if it was hot, on the terrace . . .' He broke off. 'Hé, Salvatore. Do you still have the terrace?'

'Would you like to move?'

'Of course, it's terribly hot in here, isn't it?'

258

Salvatore shrugged – he had obviously lived in this environment all his life – but he lifted the plates and Marina grabbed the glasses before we had a chance to help her and they disappeared through a tiny door at the side that I hadn't noticed before. We followed. I could feel the pain in my toes as we ascended a tiny spiralling staircase three levels above the restaurant, past what was clearly their private apartment. Eventually we came to another door and popped out of the old building like corks.

It was bigger than my little sliver of balcony, and the old building bulged out over the side of the island, so that we were sitting right above the water. Marina had brought a candle, which she put in the middle of the solitary table, and fairy lights decorated the balcony edge, but there was no other light, just the swiftly flowing darkness of the river and the blaze of brightness from the left bank, which felt completely disconnected from us; far away, a different world from the ancient rocks of our old island. Ivy had been roughly trimmed from the side of the building, which gave the feeling of being in a fairy tale. And it would, I thought grimly, have been a fairy tale, if I hadn't been feeling so absolutely rotten about everything.

Salvatore and Marina, with some giggling, left us the bottle of wine and vanished. It was oddly quiet up there, away from the everyday noises of Paris enjoying itself in the summertime. Laurent ignored me for at least five minutes as he plunged his face into his meal, eating at a startling rate, with a huge appetite and evident pleasure. I waited a moment, then, seeing as he was never going to notice me, started in.

I wouldn't have admitted it under torture, but I'd never eaten risotto before. I'd had a Pot Rice, but clearly that wasn't the same thing at all. I think if I'd mentioned it at home, my mum and dad would have stared at me, and Dad would have said, 'Aye, maybe we should try that,' and Mum would have said, 'Oh no, it will be too difficult, I'd get it wrong, it's a bit foreign for me, love,' and quickly made a fish finger sandwich before I could ask again. I could cook a little bit – I could make a roast, and a pie – but this would never have occurred to me. And I knew, the second I had had my first mouthful, that I would never learn to make risotto; that it would be completely and utterly pointless, because it would really require being born into a family who did little else; spending years learning every fine detail about the subtle balance of wine and aged Parmesan and melting translucent onions and mushrooms pre-cooked in a huge furnace with stone floors and walls so they came out perfectly sealed and slightly crisp and absolutely the most meltingly flavoursome thing I'd ever had. In fact, as I would learn later, they were picked fresh and wild in the fields around Versailles every week near grass grazed by the finest of organic cows and an original medieval forest, so in fact you didn't have the faintest chance of even getting your hands on them.

Tasting that exquisite, extraordinary risotto made me understand properly for the first time what Frédéric and Laurent and Thierry felt about their chocolate. That there was a right way and a wrong way and that was that. As someone who had worked for eleven years at Braders, my palate had become used to the substandard. But now, at last, I got it.

'Oh,' I said, after a few mouthfuls. Laurent's plate was already clear.

'How can you eat it like that?' I said, crossly. 'It's all gone!'

'I know,' said Laurent, looking regretfully at his empty plate. 'I just couldn't help myself. God, I've missed it.'

He glanced at mine.

'Don't even think it,' I ordered. 'I am going to eat every morsel and savour every single one and then I am going to lick the plate. And then I am going to lick the plate again.'

He grinned, suddenly, wolfishly, and topped up our glasses. 'You like it?'

'I think it's the nicest thing I've ever put in my mouth.'

His eyebrows went up at that, but I didn't care. I knew what I was to him, so I could ignore him. I could concentrate, from now on, on enjoying what coming back to life had also brought me. Recovering in Kidinsborough, I had eaten my food spicier and spicier to try to make myself feel something, desperately trying to awaken my taste buds into caring about something – anything. There was no new flavour of crisps so stupid that I wouldn't give them a whirl. As a strategy, I now realised, it had been a real failure, adding only inches to my waistline and a sense of slight stupefaction.

I mopped up the juice with some of the wonderful bread set in a tiny basket in front of us. I could barely see what I was eating in the candlelight. A bateau mouche passed below us, and I saw the flashes of cameras going off, taking pictures of the cathedral that would come out, I suspected, a bit blurry and disappointing.

I looked up to see Laurent staring at me.

'What?'

'Nothing,' he said.

'You're not having any.'

'It's not that. It's just … It's nice to see a girl eat. I don't know any girls who eat.'

I chose not to answer him with 'That's because you go out with stick-thin French girls who don't know how to enjoy themselves,' but instead wiped my face with a napkin. I obviously missed a bit; he took the napkin from my hand and rubbed away on the other side of my mouth, looking at me intently.

'I like girls who are hungry,' he said.

I looked out over the water. In any other circumstances, I thought, this would be so sexy. But if Paris was bringing my soul back to life, it was also – albeit belatedly – bringing my instincts back to life too. I wasn't some popsy who worked for his father. Well, I was. But I was more than that, too.

'That,' I said, shaking my head, 'is the corniest line I have ever heard in my entire life. I bet it works all the time, though.'

Laurent raised his hands. 'It wasn't a line!' he protested.

'Oh, I'm sure it would work on those other girls,' I said, airily. 'But now I have to go.'

It felt good, doing this. Not risking my ego for a little bit of comfort; not lending myself to someone whose embarrassed face I could already imagine in the morning, as he headed back to his world of dainty skinny models who didn't unbalance the back of his scooter.

Suddenly he looked at me as if seeing me for the first time, and I knew I'd been right. He really had been after some quick sex. I remembered how I'd never seen him around with the same girl twice.

'It's early,' I said, glancing at my watch. 'Do you want me to text you where Sami is?'

He shook his head.

'No,' he said. 'No, I'm really tired.'

'Me too,' I said, standing up.

♥

When we left, Laurent doused in kisses again as they waived the bill – 'as long as you bring your father back next time' – I stopped to speak to Marina.

'That was . . . that was beautiful,' I said. 'It was one of the loveliest meals I've ever had. Thank you so much.'

Her face smiled politely; of course she must hear this on a nightly basis.

'Will you look after Laurent?' she asked me, in halting English.

'Oh, he's not mine to look after,' I said, trying not to betray the wobble in my voice. She looked at me, shaking her head.

'You know,' she said. 'You're the first girl he's ever brought here.'

Chapter Nineteen

The email arrived the next morning, as I stumbled out of bed. I'd slept ten hours, thankfully, but it either still wasn't enough or it was far too much, as I felt wobbly and bleary. Sami was capering about the kitchen.

'Sami, what are you wearing?'

He glanced down. 'Oh, this?'

'YES, this! I don't want to see it this early!'

Sami was wearing a pair of tiny, tight bright turquoise Speedos. They were unutterably hideous.

'That,' he said severely, posing his lean body in his trunks, 'is because you're not getting enough. I'm off to the lido.'

He had an enormous tattoo of an eagle spreading its wings taking off from his groin. I assumed when he was naked it would look like a nest and a worm.

'I've had my offers,' I lied.

'I'll do you if you like,' said Sami perkily. 'I'm not very fussy.'

'Someone not very fussy is exactly the top of my wish list, thank you, Sami. Consider me utterly entranced.'

He shrugged. 'But you are French now, chérie. Don't you want to live as the French do?'

'By having sex with an omnisexual giant wearing tiny pants?'

'By enjoying yourself. By enjoying sex and not worrying about whether your body is less than perfect.'

'Uh, thanks,' I said, wondering if it were ever possible for an eight-toed person to have sex without worrying about being less than perfect. I still wasn't entirely sure someone wouldn't just throw up all over me.

'You have to get over your British hang-ups, you know? I slept with a British girl last month. Or was it a boy?'

I rolled my eyes. 'Sami, put on some CLOTHES. You have enough of them.'

'Cost me a fortune in fizz just to get him – yes, it was a him, definitely – in the mood. Then he'd had too much and passed out in the cab.'

'See, where I come from, that's called a jolly good night,' I murmured, briefly checking the clock. I needed to get a shimmy on. I glanced at Sami's old wind-up laptop on the table, from which occasionally, if you were lucky, you could steal wi-fi from someone in the building who called themselves 'Francoisguitare'. And there it was, sitting there, an email from Claire. I hadn't even known she could use a computer. Personal letter seemed more her style.

Dear Anna,

I hope this finds you well.

I liked the fact that she was keeping to the general style of a formal letter.

I have made a decision; I would like very much to visit Paris one more time. I hope as I write that Thierry is recovering. I have no wish to see him, but I would like, whilst I am able, to visit my beloved Île de la Cité. I am sure it is much changed, but then so am I, so is everything. Alors, perhaps I shall even eat some chocolate. If you could help me organise this I would be most grateful. Please don't trouble Thierry with this news, I'm sure he wouldn't be terribly interested.

Your parents came to visit me, by the way. It was very kind of them. Your mother told me not to tell you, but she worries about you a lot and how you might be coping. I told her that in my experience you coped with things very well.

With very warmest wishes,

Claire xxxxxxx

I stared at the screen.

'Good news?' said Sami. 'Boyfriend coming over to shag you sideways?'

I cut him a look.

Good news or bad news, I had a funny feeling this was going to mean an enormous amount of work for me. And why had she told me not to tell Thierry? Surely she would only tell me not to tell Thierry if it actually meant something. I should probably tell Thierry. I wanted to visit him anyway.

And all this time I'd thought she was just my boring old French teacher.

♥

Nelson Eddy the dog had a cocky look to him as he marched down the rue de Chanoinesse this morning. It was another stunning, heart-melting day, the sky a shady pink and blue in the cracks between the houses high overhead. I'd thrown on the lightest sundress I had and noticed right away that it was fitting more easily. Apart from the risotto, it occurred to me, I'd hardly eaten a meal in weeks. Maybe I should invent a diet that involved tasting tiny bits of chocolate all day long and nothing else at all. It would probably do quite well now I thought about it. Cath had done that one with the pepper and the maple syrup, up until happy hour cocktailarama at Wenderspoons when she'd fainted and knocked herself out on the bar rail. I had a sudden guilt attack at the amount of fruit and vegetables I wasn't eating and resolved to go down to the market and buy some of those melons, the ripe honeydews. They would put down fresh, ice-cold strips for tasting, and they were heaven. I wondered if there was some kind of a way of getting them into the chocolate. Laurent would know, I thought. Then I grimaced again, thinking of our awkward supper the night before. Well I wasn't some kind of handy comfort object to him during his dad being sick.

Although I thought about what Sami had said too; that here, pleasure was for the taking. Would it have been so bad, I found myself wondering, finishing the rough red wine, letting him lick the last juices of the risotto from my fingers, clutching him to me on the bike as we came home and ...

My reverie was broken, as ever, by the idea of him suddenly shouting 'Oh God, what the HELL is that?' when confronted with my disfigured foot.

'Bonjour, bonjour!' The boys were both very friendly this morning. 'Do you think you can do it again?' said Frédéric.

'I want to stick to the orange,' I said, then recited what Laurent had told me to do the night before. He nodded gravely.

'You know, they will get sick of the orange,' he added. He didn't have to tell me, I would be quite happy if I never went near the stuff again.

But I set it up to churn more gently, and added black pepper, and cut down on the butter, and sure enough whilst to a purist it would never be mistaken for the real thing, it was notably better enough for me not to have to face up to everyone's scathing looks.

There was, though, no Alice. I wondered what this meant; news, I supposed. Good or bad, I couldn't tell.

At lunchtime I announced that I was heading up to the hospital. Frédéric looked at me. 'Are you taking some of your chocolate?'

I shrugged. I had in fact thought I would do that.

Frédéric put his hand on mine.

'I'm not saying you haven't come a long way,' he said. 'But we don't want to shock him back into returning too soon.'

'You actually think he would leap out of his bed in horror and charge back to the shop as soon as he smelled it?' I said, injured.

'Let's just keep on the safe side,' said Frédéric. 'Let me know if he's woken up. I can't ... After I lost my father, I have had some trouble sitting in hospitals.'

'I will,' I said.

♥

In an ideal world I would have avoided running into either Laurent or Alice. And for once, this morning I was in luck. The great white hospital building behind the Place Jean-Paul-II was gleaming and silent as I quietly gave Thierry's name to the receptionist, who directed me along endless passageways until I finally found myself outside a door with 'Girard' scribbled on a white board in marker pen. I glanced around but couldn't see anyone else there, so I knocked. Hearing no answer, I pushed the door open slowly.

This wasn't intensive care anymore, it was obviously still

a high-dependency unit but nothing like as scary. The heart monitor still bleeped, but the form in the bed was no longer connected to an oxygen mask. He seemed to be sleeping. The blinds were open, and I saw that the view from up here on the eighth floor was beautiful in the sunlight, almost dazzling, even though the room itself was air-conditioned and cool. I turned round with the sun behind me, half blinded. The shape on the bed moved.

'Claire?'

I jumped out of my skin.

'Hey,' I said quietly, in English, feeling embarrassed about my pounding heart. Blinking to get the sun out of my eyes, I moved forward.

'Thierry?'

He was looking at me, confused.

'Claire? You have come?'

'I'm not Claire, Thierry. It's Anna, remember? I'm Anna.'

I moved closer. His face still looked confused – and thinner. Even in the five days he'd been in hospital, he seemed to have lost an awful lot of weight.

I patted his hand.

'Anna.'

He indicated the water on the table next to him. I poured him a glass and sat next to him, helping him drink it. After he'd finished, he blinked heavily and seemed to come back to himself.

'How do you feel?' I asked. 'Do you want me to get anyone?'

He looked at me.

'I thought you were Claire.'

'So I see.'

'You're Anna,' he said eventually. 'You're working in the shop.'

I felt a huge sense of relief that he was making sense. I'd suddenly got very worried that he'd had a stroke or something.

'Yes!' I said. 'Yes! That's me.'

He frowned. 'How is the shop?'

'Don't worry about that just now,' I said, politically. 'Listen. I spoke to Claire.'

His big dark eyes – now that he was a little thinner, I could see the resemblance between him and Laurent much more clearly – and long lashes gave him the look of a slightly helpless, very large puppy.

'Oh yes?' he said.

'She wants … she wants to come to Paris.'

His lips suddenly stretched into a wide smile. They were cracked, and I passed him some more water.

'She is coming?'

'What on EARTH happened between you two?' I burst out suddenly, thinking of Laurent's anger and Alice's insistence on being French, and Claire's silence.

With no small difficulty, Thierry shunted himself up a little on the plump white pillows.

'Careful,' I said.

'I know,' he said. 'But I think I am going to get better. Do you know what my doctor said? She said she wants me walking up and down today. Walking up and down!'

'You like walking up and down.'

'I like walking to a café and walking towards an aperitif,' said Thierry. 'I like walking and disputing and setting the world to rights. I like walking over bridges and through parks and along the Champs-Elysées on a Saturday morning to see the pretty ladies and the small dogs. I do not want to walk up and down the corridors of a hospital in a dress where everyone can see my pee-pee.'

I nodded sympathetically.

'I know. I've been there.'

'You have?' He looked at me.

I nodded. Then, even though the situation was distinctly peculiar, I slipped off my sandal.

Thierry squinted at first. Then he did a double-take.

'You only have ... un, deux, trois ...'

'Yup,' I said. 'Then it finishes. They made me walk a lot as well.'

'What happened?' said Thierry.

'Same as what happened to you,' I said. 'Just a thing.'

He liked this and nodded his head.

'Just a thing?'

'Yes.'

'And then you got over it.'

I considered this.

'Mostly,' I said. 'You're not quite the same afterwards. But mostly.'

He nodded again. 'If I do the walking.'

'Yes. If you do the walking.'

He sighed. 'But, you know,' he said, 'I have already lost seven kilos.'

'Good,' I said.

'Well,' he said, smiling. 'I want to look good when I see Claire.'

'Tell me about Claire,' I said again. But at that moment, the door burst open and Alice marched in, holding a very small coffee and a copy of *Paris Match*. She was wearing an immaculate navy jacket teamed with a red printed scarf and very skinny white trousers. She looked like she was entering a 'Who's the Frenchiest?' competition.

When she saw me sitting on the bed, she pulled up short. Oh for Christ's sake, I wanted to say (in English). No, I am not trying to get off with your morbidly obese sixty-year-old partner who's in hospital after suffering a severe heart attack, okay?

'Oh, Anna,' she said, in the way in which one might (and indeed, in Paris, often did) say 'Oh, dog poo on the street.'

'Hi, Alice,' I said. 'I just came up to see how Thierry was doing.'

'Why?' she asked.

I didn't know the answer to that without betraying Claire.

'Frédéric and Benoît want to know,' I said. 'Frédéric's scared of hospitals.'

She sneered at this.

'Well, tell them he's on the mend. How are sales? I hope you're not hanging back.'

273

'Let me try what you're doing,' said Thierry.

'Best not,' I said. 'Plus, you're on a no-chocolate diet.'

I still wasn't entirely sure he wouldn't throw back the blankets and march down to the shop in horror once he tasted what I'd made.

They both looked at me.

'I'd better get back,' I said, feeling awkward.

'Yes, do,' said Alice, fussing around Thierry's bed. Thierry looked at me with a comical pleading expression, and I realised that saying the Claire word in front of Alice was as much of a non-non as I'd expected it to be. I picked up my bag and headed for the door. Just as I did so, I heard Thierry say:

'No news from Laurent?'

'Oh, no,' said Alice.

I stopped short. Did Thierry not know that Laurent had been by his bedside night after night? That he hadn't slept in days? That he'd left his job to come down to the shop to help me out? He must do.

'Of course he's been here,' I said before I left the room.

Alice turned on me, eyes blazing, as Thierry sat bolt upright. 'Oui?'

'Anna, a word,' said Alice in English. She followed me outside.

'Have you no compassion?' she said. 'How dare you interfere in my family? Laurent hasn't been back since Thierry regained consciousness and God knows when we'll see him. Don't be so cruel as to give a sick man false hope. Much better if it's just done and dusted and they're kept apart.'

It seemed to me that that was becoming a bit of a thing, Thierry not seeing the people that he loved.

'I'll tell Laurent to come back,' I said boldly.

'You can tell him what you like, it won't work,' said Alice. 'I think, personally, if you want to hang on to this job, you'd better keep your nose out of our business. I mean that in a friendly way.'

Alice didn't mean anything in a friendly way.

'I'll go,' I said.

'Thank you,' she said. 'I'll tell Thierry you made a mistake. Thank you for coming to the hospital; I doubt it will be necessary again.'

She turned and closed the door on me. I looked down the endless corridor and wondered, not for the first time, if perhaps, at thirty, I just hadn't actually grown up yet; that there was a whole adult world out there that I couldn't make head nor tail of and that was that. Damn confusing to me, though.

♡

Wednesday was early closing and I got a chance to go home. For once, amazingly, the flat was empty. Sami had the big opening night of *La Bohème* coming up, and I'd promised to go, although I wasn't sure I'd get on with opera. It was a bit highfalutin for me. I liked Coldplay.

I made my way up the stairwell, humming. Perhaps a little nap, then I would log on and see if I could sort out some travel details for Claire. I'd spoken to her on my way back to the shop after visiting Thierry, and we'd agreed that I would go home and fetch her back. This bit about her wanting to come by ferry didn't help; going from London by train would be about a million times more convenient than getting her to Dover, but we'd work something out.

♥

'Mum, you have to see it just isn't fair. It's not right.'

Claire looked out of the window again. The nurse had just changed her dressing and given her a mild sedative while she did it, so everything kind of gently washed over her head. Ricky was talking to her – he was so handsome, she thought. It was amazing she and Richard had turned out such nice children after all.

'I can't take the time off – Ian neither – but it's not even that. A journey like this – next year, maybe. Eighteen months. When you're strong enough and well enough. Sitting on a cross-Channel ferry in your condition, it's just ridiculous. We couldn't insure you to go, for starters.'

Ricky worked in insurance, which Richard had thought was a brilliant thing and Claire had, even though he'd got wonderful exam results and gone to a good university and married a lovely girl and been, his entire life, nothing but a credit to them, privately occasionally found a bit of a shame. She adored her sons completely, but they were so very like their father. She would have, perhaps, enjoyed having a mercurial, ambitious, annoying daughter to fight and spar and bond with, or an odd, intense, clever son who ended up at CERN, or designing bizarre things for the internet, or joined

a band and disappeared for months at a time. Ian was a solic-
itor, and a good one. They were such upstanding men,
pillars of their community. In a way it was a shame when
they were born that the Reverend had taken relatively little
interest in them; he would have been proud of them. They
were both very, very sensible.

She looked at him, feeling a little hazy.

'And you're right in the middle of treatment . . . it's not fair
on any of us. You're just not strong enough. You have to
realise that.'

'I'm not strong enough for any of it,' she said.

'Mum, don't talk like that. You're only fifty-seven.'

'I'm fifty-seven with cancer in three different bits of me.
That's not like those hill-climbing marathon-running fifty-
sevens you see on television, all right?'

She hadn't meant to be snappy – detested it, in fact – but
she had spent a year now – no, when she thought about it,
most of a lifetime – allowing herself to do what other people
wanted her to do, gently following their paths, being a good
girl, doing what she was told. And where had that got her?
Stuck in a chair by a window, with her children annoyed at
her, having broken the heart of a perfectly decent man.

'This is what I want to do,' she said carefully, so she didn't
sound drugged. She was aware that she sounded like someone trying to pretend they weren't drugged. 'My friend Anna
is going to help.'

'The one with the chopped-off toes? She was in the
paper,' said Ricky. 'She didn't get anything like the pay-out

277

she should have done. She was crazy. She should have gone for them.'

'I think she just wanted to forget all about it,' said Claire. 'Anyway, that's not important. I shan't impose on you, you don't need to do anything, we'll arrange it all.'

'It's not about the arranging,' said Ricky, his face suddenly white. 'It's not about that, Mum. It's about whether it makes you sicker.'

They didn't know, thought Claire. They couldn't, with their fit bodies and young families and thinking about the new car and the mortgage and where they'd go on holiday next year and the year after that. Even though every single person on earth was living under a death sentence, to actually have one written down on paper ... However much they tried to pretend there'd be new treatments, new ways of fixing her, more chemo, always more chemo, she knew. That there wasn't a lot of sand left in the hourglass, that the time was coming. That if there was anything she wanted to do, she had to do it quickly. They were scared they might lose her – well, they *were* losing her. They just hadn't faced up to it yet. She had.

There was only one thing she wanted to do. And this was it.

Ricky looked at her mutinous face. 'I'm telling Dad,' he said, as if he was talking to Ian and they were nine and seven again.

Claire shrugged. 'There's not much he can do now, I would say.'

She and Richard were always courteous, although she was

aware that she found it easier to be so than he did. She liked Richard's new wife, Anne-Marie, too, liked her a lot, and her daughter. Anne-Marie in her turn was so relieved that Claire wasn't a terrifying nightmare who still phoned Richard every five minutes and turned the boys against her that she had been very kind, sending her magazines about soap stars that didn't make a lot of sense to Claire, though in her darker moments she enjoyed looking at the colourful pictures of peacock dresses and immersing herself in a world where losing or gaining weight meant love break-ups and romance, not chemo and steroids.

'Well then, I'll call that girl.'

Claire raised her eyebrows. Trying to get Anna to do anything she didn't want to do was an interesting challenge at the best of times.

'If you like.'

♥

I figured I'd phone first. They must have someone who could help out. I took the phone on to the balcony. The blank computer voice explained that my call to DownSouthNetRail was important, please could I continue waiting – whilst I explained back that clearly it wasn't otherwise they would hire someone to actually answer the telephones, then remembered that I was speaking to a machine and wondered if anyone listened in on these bits, then assumed that they didn't, then started to get impatient and cross and wondered if I could do this later.

Then I thought about Claire, how thin and weak she had looked the last time I saw her, and Thierry, his big face suddenly transformed by the huge grin on his face the moment I had said her name. It was so strange to me. I'd never had anyone to feel that way about. I mean, Darr was all right, but, you know. I don't think seeing Darr would be the top of anybody's list, unless you needed some really average rendering done. So I sighed and held on.

'Your call is important to us ...'

It was strange, what was important, I thought, looking down on the street, where already people were gathering in the sunshine for early aperitifs. Tiny glasses of Pernod were brought to a small rickety tables outside the bar opposite, along with a jar of olives and a plate of cooked meat; good customers, then. It was a man and a woman, in middle age, engaged in an intense and lively conversation. I wondered what about. How nice, I thought. How nice it would be to get to that age and still be together and still have so much to talk about. Mind you, anyone looking at my mum and dad would think the same thing, except that in actual fact they would be in the middle of a fight to the death as to whether my father should take his extra macintosh to fishing club or not. When it was abroad, it just seemed so much more exotic and interesting to me. Presumably if you were in the conversation it might not seem like that at all.

'Please continue to hold ...'

The great bells of Notre-Dame chimed the hour – three o'clock. I thought of Laurent at work, delicately spraying the chocolate with sealant so that it wouldn't whiten up and would last right to the very final coffees of the evening in the Pritzer's winter garden, each perfect square imprinted with the hotel's signature. Did people even know? I wondered. Did people even know how much care and attention went into the chocolate on their pillow? Maybe in France they did.

I felt anxious and antsy, restless. I know what Sami would have said: get laid. But I didn't want to get laid. In this big and lovely and scary city I wanted to do what Thierry wanted to do, and Alice presumably, and Claire, and everybody else; I wanted to fall in love.

'Hello, love? Sorry for keeping you waiting.'

The voice was a woman's, reassuringly northern and normal; she sounded motherly, and genuinely sorry for a system that I supposed, when you got down to it, wasn't her fault.

'Hello,' I said. 'I wonder if you can help me.'

I explained the situation, and she hummed and hawed on her end of the line.

'Well,' she said, finally. 'She'll have to change at Crewe. Or London.'

'Crewe's probably better, wouldn't you think?'

'But I don't think ... I mean, we don't accept responsibility for sick people on the train.'

'There'll be somebody with her,' I said, a little testily. 'All I'm asking is can a guard meet the train and make sure we get to the second train okay? It's going to be a big stress for her.'

'Wouldn't she be better flying?' asked the woman tentatively. 'They do lots with wheelchairs and so on.'

'You're a train company!' I said, exasperated. 'Do you tell everyone to get a plane?'

'You don't need to shout,' said the woman. 'I'm just saying, we don't normally do this. Health and Safety won't allow it.'

I snorted, in a proper French way.

'You can't do anything? Look,' I said. 'What's your name?'

'Aurelienne.'

It was an incredibly unlikely name to belong to such a normal, comfy-sounding woman. 'Really?'

'Yes,' she said, her voice softening a little. 'My father was French.'

'It's beautiful,' I said.

'Thank you.'

'Well, then, you will understand.'

And I told her the whole story, about Claire and Thierry being in love, and how they'd waited their whole lives and now they were both sick and it was their only wish to meet, one more time, in Paris. I laid it on a bit, I will say. At the end she was silent.

'Well that's nice,' she said.

'It will be,' I said. 'With your help.'

I was all fired up now, sure I could convince her to see the romantic side of it, sure I could stir her latent French heart.

'It'll be in the papers,' I lied.

'I just don't . . .' she said. Then added, 'You know, I've never even been to Paris.'

'You haven't?' I said, shocked. 'You're half French.'

'Oh, my name is all I have really. He left my mother,' she said. 'She hates the French.'

'Oh,' I said.

'Probably the same in this case.'

'No,' I said. 'They just got separated.'

'Hmm,' said Aurelienne.

'And now they want to get back together.'

'Hmm.'

'And you're going to help make it happen.'

There was a long pause.

'You know, I don't know why she doesn't just fly.'

♥

In the end, using Claire's credit card, I booked us both first-class open train tickets, thinking at least the seat would be more comfortable for her, and it might predispose one of the guards to give us a hand going over the bridge at Crewe. For the price of them, they really ought to let us drive the damn thing. Aurelienne was probably right about flying. Maybe Claire would agree to us flying back. I didn't even know if she'd thought that far ahead. I wondered if she had medical insurance. Of course she didn't. Life seemed to get more complicated all the time. Maybe Sami was right. Maybe I did need something a bit simpler.

As if on cue, my phone rang. I picked it up.

'Allo?'

'Where were you? You have been on the phone for ages!'

'Why, what's happened? Is something wrong?'

'No,' said Laurent.

My heart skipped a beat anyway.

♥

Laurent inwardly cursed himself. He had barely noticed the new little shop girl – well, obviously he'd noticed her when she'd come at him in the street, but not properly. He'd been irritated that she seemed to be so close to his father so quickly, but that was all she was, a mere disturbance on his itinerary of work and the hotel and nightclubs and generally having a good time.

Then yesterday, he couldn't help it: he was impressed. Genuinely, truly impressed. First by her dedication to the shop. He knew that a life in gourmet food had to start very young, but she had tried so hard to help out, and help his dad.

Then at dinner last night. Going back there had been a spur-of-the-moment idea, but once they'd got ensconced, he'd looked at her properly in the candlelight and realised how pretty her face was; how soft and kind her features; her round blue eyes, with their strong eyebrows, and her very plump pink lips that made her look younger than she was. And the generous bosom spilling over the top of her pretty floral dress. She was completely unlike the skinny, high-breasted French girls he usually went for, not, he realised, because she was any less attractive, but because she didn't strut, she didn't look down her nose. She didn't give off a vibe of being untouchably beautiful and effortlessly chic, as even the plainer girls of Paris did – and she certainly wasn't chic, that much was clear. But she was luscious and sexy precisely because, he realised, she didn't know just how sexy she was.

Just at the moment when he'd been coming to those conclusions, she'd eyed him up very clearly and stated how much she didn't fancy him and he needn't think he was getting his own way with her.

If anything could make Laurent Girard very, very interested indeed, that was it.

♡

I looked at the phone, surprised. I hadn't thought I'd hear from him again.

'Well, I've been busy,' I said. 'What is it?'

Laurent had to think on his feet. He really had no idea why he was ringing.

'Have you seen my dad?' he asked quickly.

'Um, yeah,' I said, before working out whether it was politic to answer this or not. Alice had warned me off the family. Mind you, was I really scared of Alice? I thought about it and remembered that yes, yes I was. But it was too late.

'Did you?'

'Yes.'

'How was he?'

'Sitting up. Talking. Smiling.'

'Eating?'

'Ha, not yet,' I said. 'But I'm sure it will occur to him sooner or later.'

'It better not,' said Laurent fiercely. 'I'll kill Alice if she lets this happen again.'

There was a pause.

'Aren't you going to go and see him?'

I was expecting him to do his usual furious denial, but instead he went quiet for a little while.

'I should, shouldn't I?' he said.

'YES!' I said.

'What if he gives me a load of grief?'

'Well, you sit there and take it like a good boy, then you thank him once again for giving you the tools to go out and make your own life.'

'Which he doesn't respect.'

'I know,' I said. 'The difference between making artisan world-class hand-made chocolates in a shop and making them in a hotel is unbelievably huge. I can't imagine how either of you can bear it.'

'Are all English girls as sarcastic as you?'

'Are all French men as silly as you?'

Suddenly his voice changed and deepened.

'Do you think I'm silly?'

In the distance, a fire alarm sounded. It chimed so closely with what was going on in my heart, I almost laughed. The sky was changing now, shades of pink and purple stranding in through the blue, and the streets were filling up with excited young people, mopeds, bikes, everyone out for the evening, meeting their friends, chatting and laughing, up for adventure. It was like a river of brightly coloured life below me, and here I was, up in my eyrie, watching other people's lives pass by below me like a bird.

'No,' I said quietly.

His voice was now totally and completely level.

'I could come and show you how serious I am.'

There was no flirting, no messing around. I had never heard a man be so direct in my life.

I glanced around at the tiny flat – just waiting for Sami to burst in, dressed as whatever bird of prey he was going out as that night – full of light and music. He was living his life. Claire was living her life with this ridiculous scheme. I was thirty years old, in the heart of Paris, and an incredibly attractive man had just made me an incredibly attractive offer.

Could I hold out, flirt with him, buy time? I could. I expected he would lose interest pretty fast. But, really, was that so important, when every second since I'd arrived had filled my life with more new experiences and expectations than I had ever imagined? I bit my lip. Then I thought, sod it.

'When?' I said, and there was no trace of a joke in my tone either.

Chapter Twenty

Laurent had to finish his shift, which gave me several hours to pace about, panicking and changing my mind every two seconds. Perhaps I should just go out. This was crazy. Maybe just pop out and turn off my phone and go for a walk or something, and hide for a few hours.

But then he'd just think me an idiot, a child. And anyway, what did I want to happen?

I phoned Cath, even though Cath would probably have recommended I sleep with a tramp on the Bois de Boulogne if she thought it would get me laid. She screamed with excitement.

'He makes chocolate! Oh GOD. So you're going to spend the rest of your life eating chocolate and having sex. In Paris. I HATE my life. An old woman came in today and asked for a purple perm, Ans. A PURPLE PERM.'

'Well, it's not quite that simple,' I said.

'You're telling me! The purple reacts with the perming

lotion! Half of it fell out and she wasn't exactly Beyoncé to start off with.'

'So . . .' I tried to get back to the subject. I was marching up and down the tiny apartment, feeling incredibly anxious. 'Are you saying yes I should?'

Her voice took on a more considering tone.

'Is he an arsehole?'

'I don't think so,' I said. 'He's a bit . . . troubled.'

'Oh,' she said. 'Because, you know, arseholes can be totally amazing in bed, whereas troubled might mean he'll start crying all over you.'

'I'm sure he won't do that,' I said.

'Is he hot?' she said.

'Yes,' I said, without hesitation. 'Very French-looking. But bigger.'

'Hmm,' she said. 'Does he have, like, a really big nose?'

'Yes!'

'Excellent. I like those.'

Her voice turned serious.

'The thing is, Ans, you have to get back on the horse sometime, don't you?'

'Yes,' I said grudgingly.

'I mean, you're not going to go without for ever, are you?'

'I suppose not,' I said.

'Give him a go, then. Plus Darr was sniffing round asking when you were back.'

'You are kidding,' I said. 'What, sick of all the single ladies already?'

'Looks like it.'

Suddenly compared to Darr, Laurent became even more attractive.

'Okay,' I said. 'I'm doing it.'

'Attagirl,' said Cath. 'Save some French totty for me, by the way. I've had every decent-looking man here, and they're all rubbish.'

♥

Sami was even more to the point when he returned with a trunk stacked high with costumes. He really was working hard for a change.

'Well,' he said, sighing. 'THAT'S not going to work.'

'What?' I said. I had changed into a black top and skirt, which wasn't very sexy really but was just about the best I could do from my small suitcase. I was too nervous to go shopping. I would probably buy the first thing I saw, even if it was a rubber miniskirt and thigh-high boots.

'You look like you are going to work at the Bourse,' he said. 'Not like a seductress.'

'I'm not a seductress,' I said. Sami arched a carefully plucked eyebrow.

'Well you're something,' he said. 'I haven't seen Laurent down the Buddha bar in weeks.'

'Perhaps because his DAD'S IN HOSPITAL?'

'Perhaps,' said Sami. He looked me up and down, then dived into his room.

'I'm not wearing the Speedos!' I yelled.

'Be quiet,' he said, muffled. After five minutes he reappeared. As well as an armful of clothes, he was carrying hair curlers and straighteners.

'Now,' he said. 'Let *ton-ton* Sami work.'

'Oh no,' I said. 'Do not make me look like a dog's dinner. If I'm all painted up like a trollop ...'

'Oh, scared little English girl,' said Sami. 'I am doing none of these things. I am simply ensuring that you feel and look your best. I just want you to enjoy yourself.'

'Everyone does,' I said gloomily. 'It makes it very difficult.'

He pulled out a beautiful red gypsy blouse.

'From the attic scene,' he said. 'Do you have a red bra?'

I did, but I hadn't brought it. Or worn it in months, I realised. It was a good one too.

'Well, pink will do,' he said. 'Better, in fact. More sluttish. Now, have you got HAIR?'

I had shaved my legs in the bathroom and wished Cath was there, she'd wax me on the cheap at home. Also, once I'd shaved them, I'd realised how hideously pale they were. In Kidinsborough I'd have gone and had a fake tan, but they didn't seem to do that here, I hadn't seen anywhere advertising it. All the French girls had this perfect olive skin anyway that didn't need anything. Another wave of fear gripped me. Oh God. What if he recoiled in horror at my patchy white bits?

'I think I need a drink,' I said to Sami.

'Non,' he said, to my surprise. 'Do not. You will not enjoy so much.'

'Well I won't enjoy it at all if I can't pluck up the courage.'
His huge black eyes softened.

'Darling,' he said. 'Darling. It is only pleasure. Happiness. Like with chocolate, yes? It is not there to make you feel guilty, or sad, or ashamed. It is there to enjoy. Think of me. The whole world tried to make me ashamed. It could not.'

I looked at him. He was wearing a bright purple boa around his neck, and his familiar bright blue eye shadow. It had never occurred to me before to think that Sami might be brave. I'd only ever thought he was off his head. But now I saw it.

'Okay,' I said.

He put the red blouse on me. It was lovely. Matched with cropped jeans, so I didn't look too overdone (and could get on the back of the scooter), it looked pretty and fresh and unworried.

'I would add a scarf, but . . .' His mouth made a moue.

'Scarves make me feel like a politician,' I said.

'It's true,' he said. 'English girls cannot wear a scarf. Except for your queen. She is magnifique.'

He took out a large, slightly grubby-looking make-up box, sat me down and went to work, putting on my make-up with one hand and jumping up every few seconds to finish the cigarette he'd left smouldering on the balcony.

'You're going to make me smell all smoky,' I complained.

'Little is more sexy to a French man,' he grinned at me.

Finally I was ready, and he let me have a look in the

mirror. I smiled, happily, in surprise. He'd magically coaxed my mad curls into smooth ringlets and fastened it with a large old-fashioned silver clip so that instead of being its usual cloudy mess it looked like a chic twenties style. He'd kept my face very simple, except for my lips, which he'd filled in the exact same red as the blouse.

'Cor,' I said. 'That's a bit full-on.'

'It's gorge,' said Sami absent-mindedly. 'He'll want to kiss it all off immediately.'

I stood up.

'Now,' said Sami, 'shoes. I don't know why you wear those sandals all the time anyway.'

I didn't say anything.

'What have you got?'

'Converses?'

'Hmm. Go on.'

'I've got ballet slippers.'

'Let's see.'

I brought them out for inspection.

They were some of the prettiest things I'd ever bought. I'd found them just before the accident. They were navy blue and flat, with a little bow in a paler blue ribbon and a striped inner lining, and weren't at all the kind of thing you ever saw in Kidinsborough, where everyone wore heels out at all hours, or trainers. I didn't even know what I would wear them for. They'd be useless for clubbing or the pub; they'd get ruined and everyone else would be talking four inches above me. And they weren't a lot of use for walking in; one splash of rain and they'd be totally done for. And I couldn't wear them to work, or to a music festival.

But they were so pretty and so precious, and the woman who sold them to me had put them in a cloth bag before she put them in a box, and wrapped them up in striped tissue paper and stuck it down with a lovely vintage sticker, and I'd taken them home and put them in my old MFI cupboard and thought about the imaginary garden party I'd be invited to one day.

Then I'd had my accident and that was that. I'd never worn them; they didn't give my foot enough protection, and might even slip off.

Sami glanced them over.

'Yes. Them,' he said. 'They're cute. You'll look like a fifties starlet on the Croisette.'

I rolled my eyes.

'I'll just go put them on,' I said.

'Can't you put them on here?' said Sami.

It occurred to me that getting in some practice at showing a man my foot might not be the worst thing ever. So I sighed, then sat down and took off my sandal.

Sami didn't notice at first. Then his eyes went wide.

'Wow,' he said.

'I know,' I said. Would I ever get used to it, the precise diagonal line cutting across where two of my toes used to be, the livid red stubs. 'I know, it's hideous.'

'Darling,' said Sami, patting me on the shoulder. 'My girl.'

'He's going to throw up,' I said.

'Nonsense, he'll barely notice,' said Sami, casting my foot another worried glance. 'As long as he's not one of those fetishists. Well, as long as he's not a foot fetishist. If he's an amputee fetishist, you're quids in ... Oh darling, don't cry.'

I couldn't help it. I was feeling so wound up and emotional, and this was all I needed to set me off.

'Stop it! All your invisible make-up will run and suddenly you'll be a lot more visible!' said Sami as the tears dropped down my cheeks. I'm not what you would call a pretty crier.

'Okay,' said Sami. 'Okay. I shall make you a martini. A very small one.'

His idea of a very small martini was my idea of a swimming pool, but I was grateful. We sat out on the balcony looking at the darkening sky – me with acute trepidation – and he listened very sweetly to the whole story, shaking his head at the right moments.

'Well, you see,' he said eventually, 'it was a good thing, because it got you to Paris.'

I shook my head. 'You're telling me it was worth losing two toes to get here?'

Sami looked thoughtful.

'I lost my entire family,' he said.

'They'd be so proud of you,' I said, meaning it.

He laughed. 'They'd be so proud of a successful accountant in Algiers with wives and many many children and a courtyard of his own, hé? Not this.'

'Well, I'm proud of you,' I said, chinking my glass against his.

'You don't even have the balls to have sex,' he said, but he was joking, and he clinked back, just as the heavy old door-bell rang.

'Oh GOD,' I shouted, leaping up and spilling the rest of my drink all over me. Great, I would smell like I'd been in the bar all afternoon.

'Put your shoes on!' shouted Sami.

'Yes, yes,' I said, grabbing my bag. I couldn't figure out if it was practical or slutty to pack a fresh pair of pants and a tooth-brush, so I'd zipped them away in the bottom compartment.

'J'arrive,' I called into the intercom, then went to the door. I turned back just as I was leaving. Sami was standing sil-houetted on the balcony, finishing up his drink, surveying his Parisian domain as if deciding which arrondissement he would terrorise that evening.

'Thank you,' I said to him.

'De rien,' he said, flashing me his bright grin. 'Now, enjoy yourself or I really will introduce you to an amputee fetishist.'

'I'm gone, I'm gone,' I said.

♥

I felt rather than saw the door on the first landing open, just for a second. It was the old woman who'd got so annoyed when I'd rung her bell by mistake. Didn't she ever go out?

'Bonsoir,' I said boldly, trying to give myself a confidence I didn't feel, but there was no reply and the door closed on me in the dark, leaving me feeling unnerved. I threw off the feeling and headed out on to the street.

Laurent was standing there in a casual but expensive-looking soft worn-in yellow shirt and jeans. He didn't smile when he saw me, but instead looked at me rather appraisingly, as if noticing me for the first time. I tried not to blush under his gaze.

'You look nice,' he said.

'Thank you,' I said, wishing he was as nervous as I was. But he didn't seem to be at all.

'Are you hungry?'

I was not hungry. I would have quite liked to get very quickly pissed, but I knew that wouldn't help. This wasn't giving Dave Hempson a blowie in his mum's Ford Sierra.

I shook my head.

'Then do you fancy a walk? I've been hunched over a stove all day.'

♥

I needn't have worried about the ballerina shoes. They were light, but they fitted me beautifully, even on the toe end of my left foot, and were like walking on air. We crossed the Pont Neuf and headed down to the Louvre. As we did, old wrought-iron lamps came on, pop pop pop over our heads, and the long chains of fairy lights that lined the Seine sprang into life, glowing in the dusk.

'I love this time of night,' said Laurent. 'All the commuters have gone, all the day trippers have vanished back towards ... well, wherever day trippers go, I have no idea.'

It was true. Above the scent of exhaust pipes and hanging

baskets and garlic sizzling in the pans of a thousand restaurant kitchens was a sense of excitement, of the night beginning. Chatting about food, and restaurants, and bits and pieces, I lost my footing and nearly stumbled. Laurent proffered his elbow without even thinking about it, and I took it. We walked under a huge stone arch, and I couldn't help but gasp; even though I knew about it, and had seen it in films, of course, I'd never been here before: we were in the Place du Louvre. The huge glass pyramid – with another slightly further away – was lit up in glittering white and silver, as if it had drifted into the eighteenth century from outer space.

'Isn't it beautiful?' said Laurent. At this time of the evening the museum was long shut, and there were only a few people dotted here and there, taking pictures of the fountains and the amazing building. The huge space felt like it belonged to us. Above us, the stars were popping out.

'It makes me so proud, all of this.'

'You're a proud kind of person, though, aren't you?' I said, teasing him.

He shrugged. 'No.'

'Well, what kind of a person are you?'

'I am dedicated, you know. I care about my work very much. Yes, I am proud of it. I want it to be the best, the best it can possibly be. Otherwise, what's the point, you understand?'

I nodded.

'You feel this too?'

I thought about it. Since I'd arrived here, I did understand the desire for excellence; for living in a way that didn't settle for good enough. But I'd also seen what it cost – father and son not talking, Thierry ill, Alice bitter and driven.

'I only ever wanted to be happy,' I said, quietly. It sounded like a low aspiration sometimes. Laurent shot me a sideways glance.

'Are you?'

I glanced at him, wondering. Then I turned round and looked at the glorious vista spread out in front of us. I advanced towards the pyramid, my arms outstretched.

'I think you can be happy in Paris,' I said.

'Be careful!' shouted Laurent suddenly. 'You'll set off the alarms! They'll think you're here to steal the *Mona Lisa*.'

'Really?' I said, jumping back, slightly panicked.

'Um, no,' he said. 'But I like seeing you startled.'

I turned towards him.

'Your mouth goes like a big O, and your eyes pop open,' he said. 'I like it. I . . .'

Then, as if losing his drift, he covered the few steps towards me, grabbed me in his arms and kissed me fiercely under the floodlights. I felt the torch of a passing security guard quickly skim over us before I gave myself up entirely to his hard, hungry mouth, his hand on the back of my neck forcing me to him, and I stopped thinking about anything at all.

♡

Claire wondered about packing. It was the summer of course, but she felt cold these days, always so cold. Like a child who needed its blanket wherever it went. Ricky and Ian wouldn't help her – they were sulking – and Montserrat was none too keen on the plan either. Anna had emailed some train times, but hadn't indicated when she'd come back to pick her up. She was working, of course; it was a lot to ask.

It was a lot to ask, yes. And she was a stubborn, selfish old woman. But even so.

She carefully got herself up the stairs and opened her cupboard door. It was late, she couldn't sleep. She could never seem to sleep at the right times. During the day she would doze all over the place, but the nights were very long. She'd taken her painkillers, which normally knocked her out, but tonight she felt slightly excited, more mobile than she'd been in quite a while. Privately she thought it might be the prospect of the journey that was giving her extra energy, extra strength. This feeling motivated her onwards. There was no one sleeping in tonight as they did during the chemo. Tonight it was just her. She was supposed to be recuperating, getting ready for new surgery. Instead, she was packing for a holiday. The thought made her tremble in anticipation.

Illness made you so old. Patsy's mother was older than Claire, a bouncy sixty-two. She'd had Botox and teeth whitening and went to aqua aerobics and looked after the children two days a week when Patsy went to work as an HR manager for the prison service. She was, in fact, exactly the kind of granny Claire would have liked to have been, except instead of soft play and cinema and sweets, Claire would have done art galleries and culture and stories and libraries and restaurants, she liked to think. She would have talked to them about politics and their place in the world and never, ever let them think that Kidinsborough was the limit of their horizons. Patsy's mother thought she was the most terrific snob. Claire supposed she was.

There they were, lined up. The cream striped, and the green floral, both of them faded and zipped into plastic bags. If she'd had a daughter, would she have enjoyed these clothes? Claire wondered. So exquisitely made – and vintage was in these days. Although, it suddenly occurred to her, she'd lost so much weight with her illness, she could probably fit into them herself. The very idea made her want to laugh with the blackness of it. Bent over, bowed down, in the clothes of a young girl . . . She blinked, less sure now that she did want to pack. Next to the Paris dresses was her wedding dress. She'd never been able to throw it away. It made her feel dreadfully guilty now to look at it, remembering how impatient she had been with the little Kidinsborough seamstress, who had fussed around her and stuck her with pins and was nothing like Mme Lagarde's efficient ladies.

♥

Claire had let her mother choose the dress. It was ludicrously fussy, with a nylon train and long sleeves and a high ruffled neck, so as not to offend some of the Reverend's older parishioners.

She liked Richard, she really did. He was kind and he drove down on a Friday night from university in his car and impressed her mother and was polite to her father and called him sir, and they would go out to dinner and he'd tell her about his plans for setting up a business and push her to work harder, and she had, she was going to just about scrape through teacher training college, and he was so touchingly pleased and interested in her, and after three years, he asked her, nervously, if she would like to get married, and she was so busy making everything normal around her and forgetting about Paris that she woke up one day and found that it had worked; that the great crevasse had finally healed over, and that actually, marrying Richard and having a nice house and a life and maybe moving out of Kidinsborough would actually be rather fun.

And the weird thing was, to begin with, it was. It was fun. When the boys were small, they would load them up into their Austin Metro and drive down to Cornwall or Devon and spend holidays sheltering from the rain and eating chips on the sea front, and they'd moved into a nice detached house – Richard had set up his business in town, so her leaving Kidinsborough dream had not come true – and the boys had had music lessons and football club and school friends and birthday parties and everything was as nice as it could be, and if Claire ever felt a sense of 'Is this it? Is this really it?', well, a lot of people felt that way, especially women with children in the late seventies, and teachers in the early eighties, and she put it down to normal ennui.

When the boys had gone to college, Richard had had an affair with a girl in his office that racked him so badly with guilt she couldn't believe for a second that he'd got enough enjoyment out of it to be worth the bother. He had been shaking, sodden and drenched with sweat the night he'd come home and told her. She was making corned beef salad with salad cream. She hated corned beef, it had occurred to her. The boys liked it, so she'd served it every third Thursday for about twenty years. Her overwhelming memory of the evening, during which Richard sobbed and begged forgiveness, was a curious sense of relief that she'd never have to eat corned beef again.

It was when he had looked up at her, desperate for her to forgive him; to make it all right, or even to start tearing at his clothes in a fit of deadly jealousy, attacking them with the shearing scissors, that he'd realised. It had gradually dawned on him that his affair didn't really, at the end of the day, matter to her that much, because she wasn't in love with him; not really, hadn't ever been. And that was when he'd got really angry.

♥

Claire fingered the dress. She *had* loved him, in her way, as much as she could. But it just wasn't enough, not in a marriage. She'd felt lucky, though; he had been scrupulously fair in her settlement; always kept the love and attention of his boys. A lot of her friends had not been so lucky. A lot of her friends who had married in the full heat of desperate, undying love, pure soul mates, had then come to hate their partners and turned bitter, living in much worse unhappiness than she and Richard ever had. There was nothing to say that she and Thierry, with all their class and cultural differences, wouldn't have ended up tearing each other apart in despair, ruining their children in the process, whereas Ricky and Ian were as well-adjusted as it was possible to be. The way the world was now, who was to say that level-headed, compatible companionship wasn't the way to run a marriage anyway?

Still, she fingered the dress sadly. Oh, there was never any accounting for the human heart. And no one looking at her now, she thought, would ever see anything other than the wispy bald head, the lack of eyebrows, the weight loss. They wouldn't see the tentative bride, or the joyously happy teenage lover, or the unfulfilled housewife or the middle-aged woman who had rather enjoyed living on her own again, with no boxer shorts to wash and no huge dinners to make.

It was a terrible dress. A daughter would never have wished to wear it. She sighed. She should probably go to her scarf drawers. Her friends had presented her with a succession of jaunty scarves to cover her baldness. She hated them all. She hated having to pretend to be jaunty when all she wanted to do was throw up. But it was so kind of them. It showed that they were thinking of her. And people liked sick people to be jaunty; it made them feel less scared and awkward. So she had better pack a few.

She felt, for the last time, the hem of the green dress with its tiny picked out daisies. Alors, she thought. Whenever she thought about Thierry, it was always in French, as if she was adding a layer of code to her most innermost secrets. It was absurd to think that on some level she was trying to hide her thoughts. From who? From her father? But the Reverend had never spoken any other languages.

Alors. Thierry would get a shock when he saw her. Mind you, from the sound of things, he'd changed a bit too. And did it matter, in the end?

♥

We pulled ourselves away. He smiled at me, completely unselfconsciously. I couldn't help it, there was something very attractive about the fact that he absolutely didn't give a damn about what we were doing or whether anybody saw us. It also made him look a bit wolfish.

'Come with me,' he said.

I smiled. It felt a little late to play the coquette now, given that I had the pink bra on and everything. But my heart was beating painfully, partly from the excitement, partly from the nerves.

'I shouldn't,' I said. 'You're turning me into a double agent.'

He laughed. 'I need a double agent,' he said. 'No. Forget that. I need you.'

He took my hand in his great big one. It was hard to believe that his thick fingers could make such delicacies out of sugar and cacoa and butter.

'Race you back to the bike,' he said.

It was late now, and the streets around the Île de la Cité were nearly deserted as the crowds went to eat in the Marais or further north.

'I can't run,' I said. Truthfully, I hadn't tried.

'Of course you can,' he said, looking at me severely. 'You might jiggle a bit, but I like that.'

I stuck my tongue out at him.

'On your marks ... get set ...'

'No!'

'Go!'

We burst off across the great Place du Louvre, my thin soles crunching against the gravel. It had been so long. The soft evening wind blew in my face, my hair streamed out behind me. Laurent was very fast for such a big man, and looked very young, occasionally turning his head to laugh at me, the wind whipping his curls in his eyes.

'J'ARRIVE!' I yelled, redoubling my efforts. Although I was out of breath, running, properly running at the very limit of my capacity, suddenly felt so liberating. I hadn't realised that I missed it; didn't even remember ever doing it. I had filed running away with summer sandals and my youth. Now, though, I raised my hands in the air with the sheer exhilaration.

As we got to the side of the bridge, I tried to jump a tricky step. I launched into the air, and it flashed through my mind in a heartbeat that I wasn't going to make it. My toes couldn't flex properly and I had no stability on that side. I came down on the stairs heavily, left side first, my legs folding up underneath me, knocking the side of my left foot and the tips of where my toes used to be very hard against the harsh stone.

I crumpled, tears springing to my eyes even though I didn't want them to. It hurt like absolute buggery.

Instantly Laurent turned round, his face full of concern. He leapt to my aid, even as another passer-by stopped to see if I was all right.

I blinked, trying to breathe properly and not burst into sobs like a baby.

'Merde,' I said. 'That really, really hurt.'

Laurent crouched down by my foot, and just at that precise moment I realised that of course the force of the impact had knocked off my beautiful shoe, which was laying half a metre away, spattered with blood.

'MON DIEU!' he shouted. My hand shot to my mouth. Oh God, he thought my fall had somehow knocked my toes off. I glanced down; they were not a pretty sight, all grazed from the cobbles.

'No, no, it's okay,' I muttered, feeling like the world's biggest freak. I started to try to get up on my own; Laurent was struck slightly dumb. Then he remembered his manners and darted forward, but his touch felt tentative as he took my arm.

'It's ... it's just ... I had an accident,' I muttered, my face bright red. I wanted the ground to swallow me up. Everything I had ever feared, everything I had worried about me being a big weirdo, impossible to fancy, seemed to be coming true.

'Of course,' he said, and before he could help himself, his eyes flickered up and down my body, as if calculating which other parts of me might be missing. It felt like a slap in the face.

'I ... I lost my toes,' I added.

The colour came back into his cheeks a little bit.

'Sorry, I just got a bit of a shock.'

'Yes, I know. It's weird,' I muttered. This was every bit as bad as I had thought it would be.

'No, no, it's ... its fine.'

But it wasn't. Suddenly I felt very strongly that I wasn't comfortable; that I couldn't be the kind of carefree European girl I had been trying to be. I had come down to earth with a literal bump.

He smiled at me finally, nervous.

'Uh, do you want to come over and tell me all about it?'

But the extraordinary, breathtaking kiss of just a few minutes ago had evaporated; now he looked awkward, and I was covered in blood and needed cleaning up. I was a bit wobbly and he noticed.

'Are you all right? Can I help you?' He put his arm round me.

'Can you just help me home?' I said, leaning into his reassuringly broad chest. 'I'll be fine, I just ... I have to work tomorrow.'

'Come on then,' he said, propping me up. 'You can't hop the entire way.'

Part of me was absolutely terrified he was going to offer to carry me, but we leaned together like two old drunks, and made silly small talk of the kind you do when you've just kissed someone and then kissing has, for whatever reason (e.g. lack of toes), suddenly fallen off the agenda. He didn't ask me how I'd got the injury, for which I was grateful.

At the door of my building, I tried to get away as quickly as I could. 'May I help you up the stairs?' he said gallantly.

'No, no, I'm fine. Lovely to see you,' I said, suddenly sounding like I was out of *Downton Abbey*.

He blinked. Then, looking as if he'd just made up his

mind about something, he leant forward and kissed me very gently on the lips.

'Perhaps one time you can tell me about it,' he said. Then, without another word he turned and walked away, disappearing into the night. I listened until I heard the scooter fire up with its usual roar, then went inside, finally letting the tears flow.

I didn't even bother putting the lights on as I hobbled up to the sixth floor, sobbing loudly, uncaring of who heard me. At one point I thought I heard a door open, but I didn't turn around.

Sami was in the middle of inspecting himself in the mirror. I suspected he'd done nothing else since I'd left.

'CHÉRIE!' he cried when he saw me. 'Chérie ...'

He caught sight of my stricken face, the tears messing up the beautifully applied make-up he'd done just hours before.

'What happened?'

'He saw my foot and completely freaked out,' I said. 'Can't say I blame him.'

'Didn't you warn him?'

'What, that I'm hideously deformed?'

'Yes!'

'No, I didn't get the chance. I fell over and my shoe came off.'

Sami hit his forehead with the flat of his palm, then disappeared into the tiny kitchenette, reappearing shortly with a bowl of warm-ish water, a soft cloth and a cocktail glass full of clear liquid with three olives in it.

'Dirty martini,' he said. 'It's the only way.'

As he gently lowered my foot into the bowl, I took a gulp from the glass, then nearly choked. It took about five seconds to hit my bloodstream.

'God, that is helpful,' I said, feeling its warmth spreading through my body. 'It's like medicine.'

'It is,' said Sami. 'I'm a doctor.'

I managed a grin, then burst into tears again.

'No one will ever want me with this foot,' I said.

'Don't be stupid,' said Sami. 'You almost scored a really hot bloke. All the girls love Laurent. He has an air of mystery.'

I snorted. 'There's nothing mysterious about him. He's just a bit grumpy. Well, sometimes. Then he lightens up and, well, he's really interesting.'

Sami sighed. 'Yes. Maybe you being unimpressed is why he likes you?'

'No. It's him who's unimpressed by me,' I said, sorrowfully. 'Why can't everyone just fancy me and then I could choose the ones I wanted?'

'Ah yes,' said Sami. 'The great beauties, they have such happy lives. Anyway, you are dressed. Come with me.'

'Where are you going?'

'You will like it. It is a rehearsal.'

'That's what I need. A rehearsal. No, hang on,' I said, the cocktail getting to me. 'Laurent was meant to be my rehearsal, so I could go off and find the real thing. And I stuffed it up.'

'No matter,' said Sami, glancing at himself once more in the mirror to his satisfaction, then putting on a silver waistcoat and a pink scarf to go with his incredibly tight trousers.

'Oh Lord,' I said.

'Darling,' he retorted. 'As if anyone's going to think you are with me.'

♡

I followed him down to the street and he immediately disappeared – did anyone in Paris actually walk down the roads? It was as if there were streets for the tourists and short cuts for everyone else – round the back of our building, where I was surprised to see an overgrown garden, then cut across a major thoroughfare to the Pont Saint-Michel. We went into a large building that appeared to be some kind of radio station, then down some steps by a side door, with a commissionaire peering lazily over his copy of *France Soir* to nod us through, and into what was clearly a recording and theatre space. It had red velvet seating, thick walls, plush carpets and a huge, dimly lit stage. There were about six or seven people down the front, two of them smoking. One raised his arm to Sami, who waved back madly.

'Anna is unlucky in love,' he announced to the throng, who all made sympathetic noises and budged up to let us sit in the middle.

At the front of the stage, an anxious-looking man with long grey hair and a walking stick was talking into a walkie-talkie. Then he hit the stick on the ground quickly, twice, twisted round and shouted to someone in a dimly lit box over our heads. Instantly, lush waltz music started up from a huge sound system. Startled, I jumped. The lights changed on stage, and suddenly it was as if it were lit by millions of flickering candles. Figures started to emerge from the wings; men from the left, women from the right. The men were wearing buttoned jackets, the women were in wide crinolines, their faces pale. They looked like they had come from a different age. To my eyes absolutely seamlessly, the two groups came together, the women slid into the men's arms and they began to dance. It was sublimely beautiful to be so close to them, as they spun and floated across the dance floor with the music, the skirts rustling as the men picked up the tiny women as if they were feathers. The music changed and slowed down, but the dancers, instead, sped up, pirouetting faster and faster. It seemed incredible that none of the couples hit each other moving across the floor, and I was riveted.

'NON NON NON NON NON!'

The grey-haired man was beating his stick on the floor again.

'That is insupportable! Do it again but correct.'

The music stopped and the dancers stood in a row, but they still looked ethereal to me, like something from a dream.

'It's disgusting, do you hear? Like sixteen cows stamping in a meadow.'

'They're amazing,' I whispered to Sami, who shook his head.

'They're from the Ballet Nationale de Paris, so they've been rehearsing for something else all day. Now they're tired. But, you know. They must eat. This will be our ball scene in *La Bohème*.'

'Don't ballet dancers get paid well?' I said, truly surprised. As the music started again and they glided off then back on to the stage, I couldn't help but appreciate every graceful arm extension; every perfectly turned-out leg. I had seen dancers at the pantomime, but never anything like this, so exquisite. The girls were unutterably tiny, like fragile little birds, their delicate bones visible through the skin until I almost felt worried for them. I wondered, as they leapt up on their pointes, if having flat toes might not give me some kind of an advantage.

As I watched them dance again and again, totally hypnotised, I gradually started to see the tiny incremental differences in rhythm that might make them less than perfect, and made the teacher burst into apoplectic shouting. Like cowed army recruits, however, they never talked back or did anything other than meekly follow orders. Finally the music swelled one last time, and even the porter who had let us in and who was now sweeping the back of the room, paused to watch them twist, float, fly in the air in a movement that was glorious together, as if they weren't sixteen separate people, but one spinning circle, with component parts. It struck me that it would also look perfect if seen from above.

Everyone felt it; there was harmony and joy in the room

as they stepped and twirled faster and faster as the music got slower and slower, until the great wide skirts were almost a blur and the men were lifting the women in the air, then passing them between them one after another until you couldn't see who was who. It was ravishing. The grey-haired man let them continue all the way through to the end, whereupon they finished, perfectly, almost silently, and in the next second disappeared off the stage so quickly it looked like a trick.

Although there were only eight of us there, we clapped our hands off. The dancers appeared back on stage, pink and pleased, and clapped each other too. Sami had been right; it was exactly what I needed to take my mind off what had happened.

'Okay! Dinner!' shouted Sami, starting to round everyone up. 'We shall go to the Criterion. They won't mind.'

I glanced at my watch. It was nearly midnight, and I had a busy day ahead.

'I shan't join you,' I said, suddenly distracted by the sight of one of the dancers taking off her shoes, revealing blood on her toes. She was exceptionally beautiful, but her foot was disgusting, covered in weird lumps and bumps and bunions, the toes all misshapen and bunched together. I couldn't take my eyes off them, till I realised that she was aware of me staring at her and wrenched my gaze away.

'I know,' she said, smiling. 'They are disgusting, non?'

'Mine too,' I said, suddenly feeling slightly excited to be in any way included in this otherworldly gang. 'Look.'

314

I showed her. There was still blood on my ballet slippers.

'My God,' said the girl. 'Ah well. Who wants to wear heels anyway, right?'

I smiled at her and she smiled back. She must have been about five foot one.

'Right,' I said.

I went up to Sami and kissed him.

'Good night,' I said. 'Thank you.'

Sami kissed me back on the cheek.

'Don't worry, chérie. It will be all right.'

'Thank you,' I said again.

Chapter Twenty-One

During the next few weeks the queues for the shop definitely fell off a bit. I panicked. Frédéric did try and persuade me that this was normal in August; that Paris emptied out and most of the businesses shut down – in fact, we would be closing ourselves for a fortnight at the end of the month. I had no idea what to do with myself. I supposed I should go home, see Mum and Dad. Or maybe invite them over, although they'd have to book a hotel, and the whole process would worry my mother to bits. If I could get to Thierry, who was being kept in hospital for what seemed to me a very long time – the French, it seemed, did things very differently – then I could nail down the exact date for Claire to come over. It seemed to me that the sooner the better, although I know her periods of feeling better and worse ebbed and flowed. It was difficult to time them exactly.

I called her late one night.

'Hello?'

'Anna!'

I tried to gauge the tone of her voice. It sounded a little breathier, but not much.

'Have you been running?'

'Ha, yes, very amusing. How's your accent coming along?'

I smiled secretly to myself. In fact, people had almost stopped addressing me in English, as they had done to start with – Parisians all seemed to speak wonderful English and take great delight in showing it off to you, thereby thoroughly dissing your French in the process. But the last couple of weeks, as I'd spent more and more time out the front of the shop, that had really started to change. I would never be like Alice; almost pass for French. Everything from my hair to my shoes screamed 'rosbif'. But no longer did everyone scramble into English at the first sight of me; people even forgot to slow down now when they were talking to me. I took it as the greatest of compliments (even though it meant I had to ask them to repeat themselves all the time).

'Super bien merci, madame,' I said cheekily. I could almost hear her smiling down the telephone.

'I have written to Thierry,' she announced out of the blue. 'I have told him I am coming. With you, of course. On the thirtieth of August. As the shop is closed then I hoped that would be OK with you?'

'Perfect,' I said. He must be up and about by then.

'Can he ... Well. I would like him to meet me at Calais.'

I thought privately that Alice would rather let him climb Mount Everest without oxygen, but I didn't say it.

'Okay,' I said guardedly. 'I mean, he's had a major operation. Um ... I'm just a bit worried about you and the bags and everything ... I mean, I'm confident I can help you, but I'm not sure he could get to Calais.'

Claire snorted. 'Ha! No one wants me to go. Not one other person. Everyone thinks you're trying to kill me.'

'I do want you to go! I'm coming to fetch you! I booked the tickets! But I'm not sure I can perform miracles.'

I wondered briefly if everyone else was right, then put the thought out of my mind. If *I* got really ill – well, I suppose we all do one day, there's no way around that. But if I got really, really sick, and there was something I really, really wanted to do, I'd have liked very much for someone to help me, even if everybody did think it was a stupid idea. If you asked me, the stupid idea was cancer. It was a bloody stupid idea, but hardly my fault.

Claire calmed down instantly.

'I'm sorry,' she said. 'I'm just getting agitated. Don't worry. I've left ... well, if anything happens, you'll be totally exonerated.'

'Um, okay,' I said, not entirely sure how I felt about that.

Laurent hadn't been in touch at all, which made me slightly annoyed, then pleased that I hadn't slept with him, as presumably that would have come to the same end and, regardless of Sami's libertarian spirit, that would have made me unhappy.

Given that Alice had also told me to back off, it made it very hard to find out how Thierry was doing and how much he knew about Claire's plan. Alice popped down to the shop every couple of days and hummed crossly when she looked at the cashing up, but was frustratingly tight-lipped on Thierry's progress. All I knew was that he had to still be at the hospital, because, as Frédéric said, if they'd let him out even for a second, he would have been back in the shop before they'd taken out the drip.

Chapter Twenty-Two

Claire was ready. So ready. Everything in the house was immaculately tidy. Her oncologist had been cross at first – like all doctors, Claire surmised, he liked mindless gratitude and obedience. Well, like all people, she supposed. But he'd gradually got used to the idea, postponed her next round of chemo and prescribed her several very strong emergency painkillers just in case. He'd warned her repeatedly that she wouldn't be insured in France and that her E111 wouldn't help her out with her pre-existing condition and that she could get in serious trouble, but she clearly wasn't listening, so in the end he had smiled and wished her all the best and reminisced about a time as a young medical student when he'd snuck into the Folies Bergère and it had been the best night of his life, and she had smiled back. Paris touched so many people.

Her suitcase was packed. Her sons had both come round

and sighed heavily and complained and begged her to change her mind, but of course to no avail. She had more colour in her cheeks than she'd had for over a year.

♥

Taking the train back to the UK was a revelation. I couldn't believe how nervous and anxious I'd been on my way here; how sick I'd still felt, in body and in spirit. How I was convinced it would be such a disaster and I'd be thrown out for being a fraud, or that I would sit in a rented room for three months not talking to anyone because everyone would be so rude to me and I wouldn't be able to speak the language.

Before I got on the train, I would probably have said, on balance, that more bad things than good had happened. Thierry's illness, my non-starter flirtation with Laurent; my very slow learning to make one or two types of chocolate that even now I was only beginning to truly appreciate.

But on the train, as I smelled the awful fake aroma of the hot chocolate dispenser – which had never bothered me before – and watched the brightly dressed bottle blonde British girls getting on, with their big bosoms and ready smiles and little gin and tonics in their hands, I realised that I had changed. That I was more comfortable, more confident – not just than I'd been since the accident, but maybe than ever before. Okay, so I had hardly taken Paris by storm, but I had made friends, and kept my job, and eaten some unbelievable food ... I stroked my plain pale grey Galeries Lafayette dress, that I wouldn't have looked at three months ago but which now I felt suited me very well, and listened to the safety announcements, feeling quite at home in either language, and took out my magazine, and settled my head back and realised how happy I was to be going home, but how happy I would be to come back too.

♡

I hadn't rung Laurent, for lots of reasons, the main one being I was a big fat crazy coward who hated dealing with things straight on, but I had emailed him, telling him when we'd be arriving in Paris, with all the dates, and hoping that Claire would be able to see Thierry. What I meant by this, clearly, was that I hoped Laurent would smooth everything over with Alice, but I didn't put it like that.

Anyway, I was putting stupid thoughts of stupid Laurent out of my head completely. As if in strict defiance of what he or any other French person might think, I marched straight up to the buffet and ordered a large packet of Walker's crisps – cheese and onion – and ate them, straight from the packet, in public, something no French person I had yet met would ever have done. So there, I thought.

♡

Mum burst into tears when she saw me. Which I know should have made me happy, obviously; it's nice to be loved, of course, I know I'm lucky, but, you know, MU-UM. Also, I hated the implication that she was totally sure that I couldn't leave the house on my own without being eaten by crocodiles or kidnapped by white slave traders. It was a bit insulting, to be honest, that she was crying tears of relief that her useless daughter hadn't actually died while travelling to the nearest possible foreign country to Kidinsborough (unless you counted Liverpool. HAHAHA, only joking).

I didn't say any of this, of course, just buried my head in her shoulder, so pleased to be home. Dad patted me lightly on the back in his jolly way.

'Hello, girl,' he said.

'Hi, Dad.'

I found myself choking up a bit, which was ridiculous, as I'd only been away for two months, but I hadn't been like that girl Jules in my class who'd gone away to university miles away then worked in America and travelled all over the place. That wasn't me at all, never had been.

I looked at Kidinsborough critically through the car windows. Another pawn shop had opened. Another little caff had closed down. The people seemed to walk so slowly. I wondered, almost abstractly, if I was turning into a snob, but it wasn't that. If you believed the papers (which I didn't really understand anyway), the UK was doing well, whilst France was pretty much running on fumes, but you wouldn't see it if you compared a street in Kidinsborough with say, the rue de Rivoli.

On the other hand, that was hardly fair. I was sure there were plenty of grim former industrial towns in France, cluttering up the border with rusting railway tracks and thundering lorries. I watched a woman shouting at her pram. She was wearing two vests, both grubby, neither of which reached all the way over the rolls of fat down to her leggings. She was pushing a buggy loaded up with huge thin plastic bags through which the family bags of crisps were clearly visible.

I winced. I was turning into a snob.

♡

'ANNA! Have you turned into a total and utter snob?'

It was Cath on the phone. I was so pleased to hear from her.

'YES!' I screamed back. 'I can't help it! I don't know what to do. I'm kind of horrible now.'

'Everyone in France is horrible,' she said, with all the authority of someone who'd been told off by a ferry operative on a school trip to France in 1995. 'Everyone knows that. They eat dogs and stuff.'

'They don't eat DOGS,' I said crossly. 'Where did you even hear that?'

'Well, dogs or horses or something.'

'Mmm,' I said.

'OH. My. God. It's true. Do they eat horses?'

'Well, if you eat cows, I don't really see the difference . . .'

'Oh my utter God, that is totally rank. Did you eat a horse? Oh man, that mings the mong.'

I started to feel less snobby.

'Get ready,' said Cath. 'We're going out.'

It was good to be home.

♡

Cath let herself into my room, armed with hairdryers and curling tongs. She stopped short when she saw me.

'What?' I said.

'Dunno,' she said, but she didn't look pleased. She had a bright blood-red streak through the top of her hair which made her look like a particularly cheerful vampire. 'You look ... different.'

'That's because I'm not in bed vomiting up blood and crying,' I pointed out.

'No, even after you got sick.'

'Well, I'm not out of work and crying in the morning.'

She shook her head. 'Neh. It's more than that.'

She opened up her hairdressing bag and pulled out two clanking bottles of WKD.

'Um, Cath, we are thirty,' I reminded her. 'You don't need to smuggle drink into the house. Dad would make us a martini bianco if we asked him nicely.'

'It tastes better like this,' she said. 'Can I smoke out the window?'

I rolled my eyes. 'Yes.'

She lit up and climbed on to my bed, regarding me closely.

'You've lost weight,' she said accusingly.

Actually, I'd lost a lot of weight in hospital, then regained it all by staying indoors being depressed and eating extra-spicy KFC. The last few weeks had been so busy, I hadn't even really noticed, which was, I will say, not at all like me. My jeans had certainly felt looser, but I still considered myself fatter than every other person in Paris. The women were so tiny. Maybe I was just falling into line.

'You've gone Frenchy-thin,' she said. 'Hmm. Do you smoke now and eat nothing all day except frogs' legs and dog?'

'It's horse,' I said.

'I knew it!' yelled Cath. Her eyebrows would have arched if she hadn't had that dodgy cheap Botox that she didn't even need.

'It's that man, isn't it?' she said. 'The one who makes chocolate.'

'No,' I said. I took a swig of the blue drink. Had it always been this revolting? I wasn't sure. 'He saw my foot and had a serious freak-out.'

Cath put her bottle down. Her voice was quieter.

'Seriously?'

'It's all right,' I said, taking another gulp. It wasn't much better than the first time, but I persevered. 'It doesn't matter.'

'What a twat,' she said.

'Oh no, it wasn't really his fault . . . My shoe fell off and he thought my toes had fallen off too.'

She was quiet for a second, then suddenly we both burst out laughing.

'What an idiot!' she said when she paused for breath. 'Thank God you didn't brush your hair; he'd have thought your head was falling off.'

The blue drinks must have been getting to us, because we found this very funny too, and suddenly I realised that whilst

326

I might have been learning lots of new things and having new experiences, I hadn't had a bloody good laugh for ages.

We headed out to Faces, and there were loads of people there I hadn't seen for absolutely ages and everyone was dead nice and bought us drinks and congratulated Cath on beating that shoplifting charge, at which Cath assumed a heavenly look and pretended she wasn't in the least bit surprised, and a bunch of lads we went to school with were there and that was so funny, the married ones all fat and tired-looking, the unmarried ones all flash and bragging about their cars, and a few more blue drinks and everything seemed hilarious again, and I even ended up giving Darr a bit of a snog for old times' sake – well, he was there, and I felt like I needed the practice, but he was absolutely, I realised, rubbish compared to Laurent, so I quickly knocked that on the head, then me and Cath marched home arm in arm singing a Robbie Williams song and it was exactly what I needed.

I still felt different, though. Like I was an outsider, looking in. That I was playing at being a Kidinsborough girl rather than actually being one. Even though I was, wasn't I? Of course I was.

♡

It was very kind of Claire not to ring until the afternoon the next day.

Actually, it was better than kind, it was bliss. I sat in front of the gas fire, watching telly – my Mum had taped loads of reality shows; she likes anything where people come to a sticky end – and eating toast (no one could believe it when I told them the French had never really heard of toast and ate this indigestible crunchy pre-burned stuff) with Marmite, and the boys let me have some of their massive supplies of crisps, which was their way of saying they were pleased to see me, and my dad didn't really say anything much, just popped his head round the door every now and again, smiled, then popped out again. I'd forgotten how nice it was at home. I'd also forgotten that by the next day, Mum and I would probably be driving each other up the wall and I'd be down at the discount store begging for a job . . .

And I had promises to keep. The second I saw the wheelchair, I knew this was going to be a bigger task than I'd counted on. It was . . . well, it was huge.

'I know,' Claire said. 'I hate it too.'

'It's just so . . .'

Claire was sitting on the sofa and we were both staring at the ugly, hideous big NHS wheelchair that we both knew so well from trips through hospital corridors to operating theatres and blood testing departments, with jaunty porters who always had a cheery word. But now it was just us.

'Well I'm sure I can fold it up,' I said, not sure at all. I'm only five foot three, and a bit wobbly on the one side.

'And people will be kind,' said Claire firmly.

I looked at her. She'd lost even more weight; the bones in her face made her look like one of those ballet dancers from the opera. Blue veins were visible underneath her skin, except

328

on her arms, where repeated stabbings had caused them all to retreat and hide. The story was that she was off the chemo so she could get well enough to be operated on. She insisted this was the case, but she didn't look better to me. Not at all.

She didn't wear a scarf or a turban in the house, and I inspected her head. It was covered in soft fuzz, like a duckling's.

'I reckon Cath could do something with that,' I said, but she didn't smile. I noticed she didn't like to get too far away from her drip, which usually indicated that she was in pain.

'How are you feeling?' I asked softly, even though I knew it was a question she got asked ninety times every day.

'Well, I'd be a bit better if everyone didn't keep telling me not to go,' she said, almost snappily for Claire, who never snapped, not even over my inability to grasp the subjunctive (a really stupid tense they have in French solely for shouting at people).

'We'll be fine,' I said with renewed vigour. 'We shall charm every porter from here to the Gare du Nord.'

She gave me a slight smile and her hand fluttered a little to her neck.

'He ... he seems pleased I'm coming.'

'Yes, I know,' I said. 'It was the first time I saw him smile after his heart attack.'

I didn't tell her about Alice and Laurent. I would deal with all that later.

I looked at the large suitcase Patsy had packed, under duress. It contained an oxygen cylinder we would have to declare at customs. I was terrified of it and the situation in which I might have to use it. I was terrified full stop. What if they didn't let us go? That might even be better, part of me thought. Then we could say we'd tried our best and that was that, and now they could talk like sensible people, on Skype, and I could go back and work the shop back up for Thierry, and after that ... well, I'd come home, I suppose. Get a flat with Cath, figure something out. I'd worry about that when it happened. But for now ... one thing at a time.

'I only have a small bag,' I said, although my mum had loaded me up with bacon and cheddar cheese and anything else she heard I couldn't get hold of easily. She felt I was fading away. The idea of changing trains in London scared the crap out of me, I didn't know London at all, and it didn't open itself up to walking in it the same way Paris did, but I'd worry about that later too.

We were leaving Tuesday morning. I had Sunday lunch at Mum and Dad's, made conversation with my brothers, saw a lot of Cath and tried to persuade her to come and visit me – I reckoned she and Sami would get on, even if they didn't speak the same language – but she became unusually sheepish.

'Neh,' she said. 'I don't think it's for me.'

We were walking down by the canal on Monday night, looking for something to do. It was warm out, still.

'You'd love it,' I said. 'There's a party every night and champagne everywhere and it's really beautiful and I live right at the top of this spooky old house.'

She turned to me sadly.

'You're dead brave, you are,' she said. 'Everyone thinks you're the quiet one, but it's not like that really.'

'Don't be daft,' I said. 'You're the one that jumped into the canal fully clothed that New Year's. I thought you'd kill yourself.'

Cath shook her head. 'Oh, it's one thing hanging round here,' she said. 'Out there ... neh. You might as well take me to the Amazon jungle. This is where I belong, Anna. Along with the shitty shopping trolley in the canal, and Gav, and me mam and everything really. You're not like that.'

'Course I am,' I said.

'Neh,' she said. 'You're the brave one.'

And we linked arms and walked back home together.

♥

At seven a.m., my dad was running the car outside Claire's house. It had suddenly turned cold and he was sounding very cross. Our train wasn't till twenty past eight, but I had decided better safe than sorry, which was just as well, as we were having a heck of a job trying to fold the wheelchair into the boot of the car, and I was starting to wish I hadn't bothered and wondering whether the very first half-hour was an acceptable time to give up the trip altogether.

Dad got out and helped me, whilst Claire sat in the front seat, the seat belt almost flat against her, so thin was she now. I'd locked up the house – it was immaculate, the fridge empty, which I found slightly off-putting. She'd be back in three days. But I wasn't going to argue with Patsy (again),

Claire watched us in the rear-view mirror swearing and sweating as we tried to manoeuvre the wheelchair in by taking down the back seats, but we still weren't having much luck. We were going to be very tight for the train as it was. And the London train went from the furthest platform. I could feel myself starting to panic.

'Are you sure you know what you're doing, love?' said my dad quietly, to which I could only reply, 'I haven't got a clue, Dad.'

Being my dad, he just patted me on the shoulder, and that was the best thing to do. Even so, it wasn't boding well.

Suddenly, up the deserted street glided a very large, very quiet car. You didn't often see one like that round Kidinsborough, it looked to be one of those enormous Range Rover things, all shiny black. It slowed down next to us and a distinguished-looking man stepped out beside us on the pavement, dressed in a smart tweed jacket.

Claire gasped in the mirror, then, very slowly, opened the front door and, holding herself carefully, got up and out of the car on her own.

'Richard?' she said.

♡

She wouldn't have expected him in a million years. She stared at him, completely *dumbfounded*.

'Richard,' she said again.

It sometimes felt to her like he had hardly changed a bit, was still the awkward boy with the clarinet case and

332

the thick glasses. His glasses were still horn-rimmed, but she'd always liked the style, so he'd never changed them. He still had all his hair, and having a new wife and a stepdaughter had kept him trimmer than he might have been otherwise. She could still remember his admiring tone from so long ago. He'd never taken her off that pedestal. That had been the problem, really. No, she chided herself. *She* had been the problem. She had always been the problem.

'What are you doing here? I am going, you know. It's kind of the boys to worry, but I truly feel this is something I have to—'

'No,' said Richard simply, raising his hand. 'I'm here to help.'

♡

I had no idea who this geezer was – he was handsome for an old bloke, that was for sure – but it became clear pretty quickly. I looked at his huge Range Rover.

'Why don't I drive you in that?' he said. 'Then you won't have to get on and off the train.'

I thought about all the money Claire had spent on first-class rail tickets, but didn't mention it.

'Great,' I said, with massive relief, and I meant it. The folded-up wheelchair fitted into the back of the car with ease, and I helped Claire up the high step. I'd never been in such a fancy car before.

Dad looked on, a bit crestfallen. I felt bad about that.

'Look, it's good that Richard's helping us,' I said.

Dad looked at his old Peugeot.

'I like your car,' I said. 'This is a stupid car. It's going to destroy the planet and kill us all. OOH look, it has a telly in the back seat!'

Dad smiled ruefully. 'You're off again then,' he said.

'Not for long,' I said. After living in pyjamas and one slightly ill-advised neon miniskirt for two days, I'd put my Paris uniform back on.

Dad shook his head. 'Your mother thinks it is for long. She thinks you've left.'

'Don't be daft,' I said, my voice cracking a bit. 'This will always be my home.'

Dad gave me a hug.

'There's always a home for you here,' he said. 'That's not quite the same thing, mind. Anyway, you're thirty, love. About time you got your life started, don't you think?'

♥

I felt like a kid sitting in the back seat, but I didn't mind. There was a stack of DVDs on a little shelf, obviously for the grandchildren, and Richard offered to put one on for me.

Claire hadn't spoken much about her ex in hospital, although the boys were very good at coming to see her, and it was clear they must have resembled him. I understood that it had ended and that they had an amicable relationship, but what had ended it and why, I had no idea. I figured it was best to slip the headphones on and let them get on with it.

♥

Claire glanced briefly at Anna in the back seat, completely engrossed in the film like a child, and smiled to herself. She was in a little pain – her joints felt sore, as if she had flu, and a headache was circling and threatening to descend, but thankfully she wasn't vomiting. For that, small mercies.

Richard had asked her why on earth she wouldn't just take the Eurostar, but she was adamant. She wanted to go on that boat again. She didn't like words like closure, but yes, it was important to her.

She and Richard chatted here and there – mostly about the boys. It was funny how quickly they fell back into their old ways together. She glanced at his hand on the gearstick. He had always been a good driver; took it seriously, got upset if she had a dent, or scratched the side. It had used to matter a lot.

Once they hit the great long stretches of the motorway, empty in between the rush hour and the holiday traffic, he put the cruise control on, sat back in his seat a little. She heard his knees crack. She wasn't the only one getting on a bit.

'So,' he said, quietly. 'Whoever it was – that you thought I never knew about. Is it him?' Claire nodded. Richard shook his head. 'This was a very, very long time to keep a flame burning, Claire.'

'I think ... I mean, it's too late now. I know that.'

She glanced down at her lap. It always seemed easier to talk in cars, when you could stare out of the window, she supposed. And you weren't face to face.

Richard shook his head. 'Do you know what I wish?' he said, his hands steady on the steering wheel. 'I wish that just

335

after we'd met, and you were all dreamy and distant, that I'd called you on it. That I hadn't pretended that it was just because you were some mystical fairy, or been so terrified of losing you. I wish I'd just said, "Who is it?" and then let you go. I bet by the following year the glow would have come off it anyway.'

'Maybe,' said Claire.

'And you could have come back to the UK and then you'd have been pleased to have me.'

'I was always pleased to have you,' said Claire.

He glanced across at her, as if he thought she was being sarcastic. A light squall of rain blew against the windscreen.

'Well,' he grumbled. 'Too late for that now.'

'I know you want me to apologise,' said Claire. 'But I can't. We raised two lovely boys. We spent twenty years together. That's more than a lot of people do. I didn't mean to make you unhappy.'

'I know,' said Richard. 'And I shouldn't have done what I did.'

She shrugged. It was water under the bridge now.

'The boys don't tell me much ... well, I'm not sure how much you tell the boys. You're so damned closed, Claire ...'

His irritation threatened to spill over, but he managed to control it, swinging out to overtake a lorry that was wobbling precariously in the middle lane, water sluicing from its chains.

'I mean ... I mean ...'

'How bad is it?'

Richard nodded, as if he couldn't say the words out loud.

Claire turned to him. She had spent some time living with this, which was why she had spent so much time living in the past.

'Um, it's spread again,' she said quietly, the only sound in the car a slight buzz from Anna's headphones and the swish-swish of the windscreen wipers. 'That's the reason my hair's growing back. I told the boys I'm resting up, but no. We've ... postponed the next round of chemo.'

Richard took a sharp intake of breath.

'Jesus.'

'I know. You wouldn't believe the fight I had to get these.' She opened her palm to reveal a tiny bottle of diamorphine. 'Ssh,' she said, almost smiling.

'But you seem so ... I mean, you're just yourself, except thinner.'

'I would say my days are better and worse,' said Claire. 'At the moment, a little better. I think my body is just so pleased not to have any more chemo. But I don't know how many good days there will be.'

'How long?'

Claire took on her oncologist's ponderous tones.

'Well, Mrs Shawcourt, I wouldn't say months.'

Richard let a hiss of breath escape through his mouth. Then he said the one word Claire had never heard him say in his entire life.

'Fuck.'

Chapter Twenty-Three

Laurent looked at Anna's email and read through it again. This was ridiculous, it didn't make sense. His dad was only just home, he'd heard through the grapevine, but under strict diet and movement controls for at least another three months. Alice would have absolutely nothing to do with it, that much was sure. And he could hardly do it; even if his father would consent to look at him, he still had work to do and the logistics were horrible. All for that woman.

Though she was old now, he knew, old and sick. Well, maybe when she and Anna got to Paris, he'd try and arrange something. Yes, that would be better.

He thought about Anna. It struck him suddenly as a very 'her' thing to do; to go straight away on this wild goose chase to help out an old lady. She wouldn't even think twice, the same way she didn't think twice about visiting his father, or trying to make things right in the shop, or . . .

He cursed himself again for freaking about her foot. He'd hurt her feelings, over something she obviously couldn't help, and he hated that he'd done that. She wasn't like the tough, hard-edged Parisian girls he knew, not at all. She wasn't chic and skinny; she didn't know the right places to go or the right things to wear. She was soft and a bit squishy and . . .

It came to him in a blinding flash. She knew the right thing to do. She just did. And that was what made her different. He didn't; he was a stupid coward who walked away from things the second they got difficult. He needed her.

Suddenly he wanted Anna back in Paris as much as he had ever wanted anything. He stared at her email again. Tomorrow. She would be here tomorrow. He hit *respond* then realised that he didn't know how to say what he wanted to say. He didn't know what he wanted to say or what he was going to do. He stared at the blank page, then shut down the internet window and did what he always did when things got on top of him. He went to work.

♥

I woke up without the faintest idea where I was. It was raining outside. I was stretched out on a back seat so comfortable it felt like a huge leather sofa. I jerked my head up. We were at a petrol station. Claire was asleep in the front seat.

Richard came back to the car. His eyes were red and he was rubbing his nose a little and I didn't want to bother him. Plus, of course, I didn't know him at all. I shushed him as he glanced at Claire, and he went round to the boot, pulled out a blanket – of course they were the kind of people who would have blankets in the car – and very gently put it round her.

I wondered. I mean, Thierry was great and funny and fun and life-enhancing, but I couldn't imagine him for a second putting a blanket round Claire like she was made of porcelain. I could imagine him talking about it, and asking someone else to do it, and suggesting it, and making a joke of it. But not calmly and precisely tucking it in, with the utmost respect for her.

Not wanting to make any noise, I smiled at Richard and he smiled back.

'I got you a sandwich,' he whispered. 'I don't know what you like so I got one of each.'

I grinned. 'Lovely! Can I have the ham and tomato?'

He passed it over with a bottle of fizzy water and a bar of Braders chocolate.

'Sorry,' he said. 'I didn't know if you ate absolutely loads of the stuff or if you were practically allergic.'

He got in and started the car, again very gently.

'I can probably eat it if you don't want it.'

'No,' I said, looking carefully at the familiar mid-brown wrapper.

The factory had sent me (along with numerous official-looking letters absolving themselves from responsibility) a huge basket full of Braders products whilst I was in hospital. I hadn't been able to as much as glance at them in a newsagents ever since.

I picked it up.

'I think it's time,' I said, but Richard was already signalling his way out on to the motorway.

I peeled away a corner of the wrapper and inhaled the smell, carefully and fully, just as Thierry had shown me. Suddenly I was back in the factory with Kyle and Shaz and punching in and Easter overtime and the visit from the Duchess of Cambridge that time that everyone else had got wildly excited over and that made me feel like an underachieving troll.

But, I suddenly realised with excitement, I could smell more than that. I could take it apart in my head. I could smell the vegetable oil; the tiny note of additives that we covered up with more sugar; the grade of the sugar; the weakness of the cacoa beans. It was rather thrilling to realise that if I wanted, I could probably cook up a batch of this at home. I blinked several times. Frédéric would have hurled it from him in utter horror like it was a live snake, of that I had no doubt. Instead, I closed my eyes and took a bite.

Here was the weird thing: even though I knew that it was made as cheaply as possible to sell in large quantities; even though I knew it wasn't anything like the high-end, pure product we made at Le Chapeau Chocolat, that it was meant for bland generic tastes, designed to be unchallenging rather than delicious ... it WAS delicious. It melted at exactly the right moment on my tongue; it filled my mouth; it tasted sweet and creamy even though I knew exactly how much cream was in there (none at all) and it broke off in soft crumbly chunks. It was completely gorgeous. I didn't know what it would taste like if you hadn't been born and raised with it, but to me it was good and British and comforting and reassuring and I wished Richard had brought loads of it to stash under my bed in Paris for when the tasting all got too much.

'Mmm,' I said quietly.

Richard grinned at the wheel.

'It's like having the kids back again,' he said, but not in a mean way.

A road sign showed we were less than one hundred miles from Dover.

♥

I looked at the sky dubiously. How bad did it have to be before they stopped the ferries running? Our tickets were for this evening, and I had been planning on finding a cheap hotel by the terminal the other side, then doing the final leg tomorrow when we were better rested.

Anyway, my plans had all changed now. We had train tickets, but I had no idea what Richard was intending to do. Was he going to drive us to Paris? I didn't want to ask him in case – I could already tell he had impeccable manners – he then felt obliged to take us all the way. He might not even have his passport. I decided just to sit tight and see what happened.

Claire didn't wake up all the way through passport control. I thought customs officials might get suspicious and make us wake her, but they didn't seem too fussed and waved us on through. Richard had hopped out and bought a ferry ticket for the car so quickly and unfussily I had hardly noticed him doing it, and when I tried to thank him and offer him money, he waved me away.

'If Claire pays you back it will be my money anyway,' he pointed out, though not unkindly. We were both getting worried about how soundly she was sleeping. She had absolutely assured me that her doctor was happy for her to control her own medication for three days, but now I wasn't so sure.

'Claire,' said Richard lightly as we drove on to the great clanking ship. It was full of cheerful-looking holidaymakers, their cars piled high with sunhats and inflatable chairs and tents and bicycles and excited children, desperate to start racing all over the boat. The train might be more convenient, I thought, but I doubted it was quite as much fun for the little ones.

Claire nodded and stirred a little, and Richard prodded her again, after we'd been led into position in the lower deck and stopped the engine.

'Claire?'

♡

She had bugged him for ages and he had said, don't be ridiculous, only tourists ever want to go up the Tour Eiffel, and she had said, well I'm a tourist and he had said, you are not a tourist, you are a muse, and that was undoubtedly the most thrilling thing anyone had ever said to her in her entire life and she had jumped on him and locked her legs around his waist until he had laughed his huge booming laugh and agreed, so one very warm lunchtime, when everybody else was off eating properly, like normal people did, he said – he was absolutely rigid about his mealtimes, as was nearly everyone she'd met there – he had led her threading through the new Métro line and right up to the very base of the huge metal structure, queuing in the heat, Thierry mopping his forehead with a large handkerchief.

'I love it,' she said.

'It is for chocolate boxes,' scoffed Thierry.

'It is,' said Claire. 'You should put it on chocolate boxes.'

Thierry had frowned at her as they'd waited for the lift, which shot them up, at an angle of course, like a rocket, and she had trembled in excitement as they went up, the première, deuxième, troisième stage. She would not be happy until they had reached the very top, he noticed, and smiled at her enthusiasm.

Although Paris below was warm and still, up here the wind blew back and forth and there was a chill to it. Thierry immediately took off his jacket and put it on her shoulders, but she didn't want it there; she wanted to feel the breeze, after the heat of the city. Her pale hair streamed back against her shoulders and she turned and smiled at him, and he managed, with rare presence of mind, to take out his Leica and get a quick shot of her, her dark red lips – it was the same colour Mme Lagarde used, and she had taken it on board – pulled back in a huge, laughing smile as she tried to hold her large straw hat on her head. As they had gone round the other side, looking out over the river and the flatlands beyond, the wind had finally got the better of them and it had gone, blown off, dancing on the thermals just out of reach.

'Noooo!' Claire had yelled, reaching for it, then had turned to him, once more buckling with laughter.

'Little hat! Little hat! I will save you!' Thierry had shouted, pretending to climb up the iron balustrades until a guard came along and told him sternly to stop what he was doing immediately.

'I shall buy you hats,' Thierry boasted, as they finally made their way back down, having exhausted every view and examined the instruments of M. Eiffel himself. 'I shall buy you every single hat in Galeries Lafayette and you shall keep the ones you like and as for the others, we shall return here and let them fly away. And I hope that whoever finds your hat will be as happy as you and I.'

And she had kissed him all the way down in the elevator, as the lift operator averted his eyes. Le Tour Eiffel often did that to people.

Gift boxes from Le Chapeau Chocolat had carried a tiny, discreet hat mark in the corner ever since.

♥

'Claire!' Claire felt the hand on her shoulder and looked up to see Richard and Anna staring at her anxiously.

'Phew,' said Richard.

'It's all right,' said Claire. Her mouth was very dry; a side effect of the drugs, she knew. Fortunately Anna was already holding out the bottle. What a dear girl she was. She took it and tried to smile, but her lips cracked painfully.

'Just napping.'

She tried to swallow. Some of the water ran down her neck. She realised that sleeping in the car had made her terribly stiff. She didn't know whether she could actually move at all. Everything hurt. Anna wiped away the water, and helped tilt the bottle. It was one of those sports ones with the teats like a baby's bottle. Claire wondered dimly why it was called a sports bottle when it was clearly designed for babies and invalids.

Suddenly the great engine of the ferry sprang to life. The deck, which had already been swaying, started to move and tremble. Claire glanced around. She remembered the *Herald of Free Enterprise* suddenly, and how frightening it must have been. A voice came over the tannoy announcing in English and French that conditions weren't ideal and advising passengers to leave the car decks but to stay inside the boat as some choppy water had been forecast. Claire suddenly realised where she was.

'I want to go up on deck,' she announced.

'There's a lounge,' Richard said, looking worried. There was a wheelchair lift, but the boat was moving so much he wasn't even sure about getting the chair out of the back of the car without it swinging about wildly. All the other passengers had left, climbing up the coloured stairwells into the body of the ship.

Claire shook her head. 'No. Up. I want to get up.'

She saw Richard and Anna share a look and nearly cried with frustration. Her stupid, stupid, wretched body that wouldn't do a single thing she wanted it to.

♥

Claire looked awful. She could hardly even drink out of a bottle. We had to get upstairs but I didn't have a clue how we were going to manage it. I went round to the back of the gigantic Range Rover; I could hardly reach up to open it, swaying with the boat as it seemed to reverse itself. I hadn't been on a ferry since I was thirteen with Cath, but we'd been too busy singing Oasis songs to notice.

As I was trying to figure out the lock, I felt Richard's eyes on me. I glanced up at him and he shrugged, then reached into Claire's side of the car, undid her seat belt and gently, as if she was a child – she was as light as a child, I could see – lifted her up in his arms. I grabbed the blanket.

'Richard!' Claire protested, and I could hear the pain in her voice, but I think we all knew there wasn't a better way. Carefully, Richard mounted the narrow stairwell. 'All right there, sir?' we heard a cheery sailor say, and Richard muttered something about not wanting to bring the wheelchair out, and the sailor said, 'Let me know if you need a hand then,' in a way that made me want to travel with that ferry company and no one else for the rest of my life.

The top of the ferry was bright and bustling, like an old airport terminal. There were shops and bars and a duty-free and an amusement arcade already full of children screaming and stabbing at the flashing lights and bells. I could smell chips, and glanced into the large lounge, full of seats, the reclining ones already taken by the frequent travellers, who clearly knew what they were doing. We attracted a few curious glances, but we simply ignored them and forced our way through to the quietest corner of the lounge we could find, where Richard settled Claire gently, then pretended not to be out of breath.

'Why don't I get us all a nice cup of coffee?' I said.

♡

Alice was standing in the doorway of their house when Laurent arrived, her arms folded. Behind her he could see expensive-looking private nurses moving silently over the highly polished parquet. Fresh orchids sat in the corner.

'He's not here,' she said.

'Don't be ridiculous,' said Laurent. 'Look, he doesn't need to talk to me. But he needs to have the choice.'

'No,' said Alice. 'And he doesn't want to talk to you.'

'Fine,' said Laurent. 'I'll drive and not talk.'

'No,' said Alice.

'Yes,' said Thierry, stepping out from the anteroom, where a fire was blazing despite the warmth of the afternoon. He was wearing an enormous smoking jacket. If Laurent hadn't been so wound up, he might have smiled.

Alice looked at them both, her fingers tightening and her high cheekbones stretching taut and pink.

Suddenly, Alice and Laurent's eyes both flickered to the dish for keys that stayed by the door. Without thinking, Laurent reached out a long arm and snatched them. Alice grasped in horror. Laurent, equally horrified by what he'd just done, backed away towards the van. Thierry followed him.

'No!' shouted Alice, but it was too late. She could do nothing but stand and watch the van drive away. Then she swore under her breath. In English.

♥

When I got back with the coffees, I could see that Richard and Claire were in the middle of an argument. Claire, I noticed, still hadn't moved. I rummaged in her medical bag for the Tiger Balm – I remembered how much she'd enjoyed it in hospital – and quietly started to rub it into her shoulders. There was nothing to her, I felt. Just knotted bits of muscle, struggling on alone. Her tufts of bird hair – the scarf had slipped off again – made me want to cry.

'I'm not taking you up there,' said Richard. We could see out of the porthole windows the waves bouncing up and down; there was a slight tang of vomit in the air, as if it had already affected some of the passengers. The sea looked an odd mixture of green and black, and spray and rain bounced against the windows. Even though this was only a tiny section of water to cross – people swam it, for goodness' sake – it didn't feel like that. It felt like we were out in the middle of the ocean.

'I need the fresh air,' pleaded Claire, her voice quiet now. I glanced at her medicine. She had taken a little more, but she seemed to be entirely compos mentis. I wondered how powerfully it could fight the pain of the hideous viper; the tumour growing inside her, spreading, filling her with blackness, hollowing her out. Her face was still composed; still beautiful even.

'It's not right,' said Richard. 'Don't you want to see the boys again? And Cadence and Codie?'

Claire looked away.

'Of course I do,' she said. 'There are ... there are a few things I want to see again, yes.' Her jaw looked stern.

'You'll catch pneumonia.'

'I've had worse,' she said. 'I have worse.'

Richard put his fingers on the bridge of his nose and rubbed, fiercely.

'You didn't have to come,' she added, pressing home her advantage. 'I didn't ask you too. Anna and I would have been all right on our own.'

I tried to appear inconspicuous and not point out the obvious, i.e. that Richard had made it all about a million zillion times easier than it might have been, and if it hadn't been for him we'd probably still have been at Crewe station, or more likely back at home.

Richard glanced at his watch.

'Okay,' he said. 'When we're coming in to Calais. And not before. Okay?'

Claire nodded weakly, and Richard pulled out his phone and stormed off before she could badger him anymore.

I carefully did Claire's elbows and wrist joints.

'Is it very bad?' I asked quietly, feeling her wince.

'It isn't important,' she replied, and I wondered if she felt as I did: fearful, regretful that we'd undertaken this at all.

Three quarters of an hour later, after I'd taken Claire to the bathroom and we'd done what we could in the swaying cubicles, Richard reappeared, again with food, that none of us felt like. The storm hadn't abated, and even the happy, screaming holiday children had quietened down.

'Are you still set on doing this?' he said gruffly.

'Yes,' said Claire, with dignity. 'And I think I can walk now.'

Her muscles had slackened up with the drugs and the

massage; very carefully and precariously she made her way up out of her chair, and Richard and I took an arm each and we started to move, very slowly, out of the salon and towards the steps at the back of the boat.

There was a sailor standing there too, but we explained that we really wanted to go up top, and he looked at us and told us to be careful but he wasn't stopping anyone, just kids, he explained.

Through the swing doors at the top, the wind caught us straight away and nearly sent us staggering right to the side. It was extremely strong, the clouds above us black. Seagulls screamed through the air, desperately searching behind the boat for discarded chips and other excellent human morsels. The wake churned up the already foamy waves in a long line.

Then we turned round to face the front, and Richard let out a low whistle.

Straight ahead of us, where the beaches and cliffs of Calais were spread out in front of us, the little old section of the town on top of the hill, the weather had cleared. It was as if someone had drawn a line down the middle of the sky between the UK and France. Calais had hardly any cloud and the late afternoon sun was piercing down to illuminate it.

'You did this on purpose,' muttered Richard, but Claire wasn't listening. She was walking forward, on her own, hand on the railing but otherwise steadily. The deck was deserted. She skirted round the lifeboats and buoys until she was right up at the prow.

'Ma belle France,' she muttered under her breath as I ran to keep up with her.

We both stood as far forward as we could, as the wind slowed and the rain died off, and gradually things came into focus and the ferry port came closer and closer; and right at the very tip of the furthest dock we saw two figures, one standing, one slouched in his own wheelchair. My better eyesight caught them first.

'Look,' I said to Claire, taking her hand to point in the same direction, as if she was a child. 'Look over there.'

Chapter Twenty-Four

As the tannoy came alive again, instructing everyone to return to their vehicles, Richard held the lounge door open for us.

'You go this way,' he said, indicating a line of foot passengers lining up with bicycles and rucksacks.

'What do you mean?' I said.

He shook his head. 'I've come … I've come as far as I possibly can.'

I realised then that he'd seen the figures on the dock.

'It's all right,' he said, seeing my face. 'They know I'm coming straight back.'

In such a short space of time, I realised, I'd come to rely on him as being the grown-up.

The boat was sloshing about, manoeuvring itself up to the dock.

'I'll get the chair and your bags,' he said. 'You're going to be fine.'

His face was grave and full of sadness as he disappeared down the stairs. I watched as a long ramp, to let pedestrian passengers off, extended to the quayside. There was a passport box with a hot, grumpy-looking man in it – I still couldn't believe the change in the weather. It was as if a great dotted line, like on a map had separated the UK from the rest of the Continent. People were blinking in the sunlight. The smell of fried breakfasts and sprayed perfume and damp carpet from the ferry receded as we breathed in the fresh air.

'Oh,' said Claire. 'I think I need to sit down.'

♡

Claire still couldn't believe that Richard had done all this for her. He set the chair down as if he'd been handling wheelchairs all his life, instead of designing load-bearing joints.

'Thank you,' she said, feeling both weak and terribly nervous. She hadn't been able to eat a thing, which she knew wasn't good for her, but she dreaded vomiting and being unable to clean herself up; she couldn't face it. Cancer was such a disgusting disease on top of everything else. Sometimes she wished she had something at least a bit romantic, like consumption, maybe, like in *La Bohème*, where she could lie on a sofa, cough into a handkerchief for a bit, then die in an elegant fashion, without the vomit and the diarrhoea and the baldness and the bollocks of it all.

Her heart, though, fluttered. Her eyesight wasn't what it was, and she hadn't recognised the figures on the pier at all, even though Anna had jumped and shouted and clapped her hands in excitement. She would just have to take her word for it. Maybe Thierry was half-blind too. That might be useful. She tried to stare out from the ferry, now rapidly emptying, but it was hard to focus in the bright sunshine.

Suddenly Richard was crouching next to her. He made a slight noise getting down there. Now he was face to face with her. That was one good thing about her eyesight, she thought. He didn't look massively different to her now than he had at school, his tufty hair, his thick glasses. She smiled. He didn't smile back. He took her hand.

'This is as far as I go,' he said quietly.

She nodded her head. She understood.

'Thank you,' she said, from the bottom of her heart.

He shook his head. 'Oh, it was nothing.'

She was cross that he didn't understand what she was saying.

'No,' she said. 'Thank you. Thank you for everything. Thank you for making me go to teacher training college, and for taking me away from the Reverend and for marrying me even though you knew I didn't really ... and for the wonderful boys, and for making me secure.'

'I'd rather have made you happy,' said Richard, tears glistening in his eyes suddenly. She hadn't seen him cry since that awful night so long ago when he'd confessed his affair.

She shook her head. 'I don't ... I think I was too stupid to realise it. But I think I was happy. Silly, daft, head full of nonsense ...'

They smiled at each other, a smile of long understanding,

355

then both of them looked out at the French shoreline. Claire had a sudden memory ... The boys must have been very little and they were on a huge beach, first thing, almost no one else around except some dog-walkers, but Ian had always been up at the crack of dawn, even on holiday. The boys had been in their bathing costumes already and they had charged headlong into the water, then squealed like tiny baby pigs when they realised how freezing it was. And instead of laughing at them, or ignoring them, Richard had seen their predicament and gone tearing in too, straight into the perishing water, picking up a boy under each arm and throwing them around until they'd got used to the water and could splash at each other and laugh and laugh and laugh. They'd come out blue and chattering, and she had wrapped them all in towels and poured Richard hot coffee out of their Thermos and he had declared it the best drink of his life.

How could she have forgotten all of that?

'But it has been a happy life. Full of happy things. It has. I just wish I had appreciated it more at the time ...'

Richard pulled her tufted head into his shoulder and she smelled a scent she hadn't smelled in years.

'Sssh, my love. Sssh,' he said, stroking her scalp, and she realised then what he was really saying, and that it was goodbye, and she pressed her cheek against his, already marked with five o'clock shadow, and they stayed that way until the crewmen started to come up with apologetic looks on their faces, and Anna was staring at them, she realised, with a worried look on her face too, but that didn't really matter now, and she clasped Richard's hand very tightly and said she would see him soon, and he grimaced and didn't reply. One of the nice young sailors helped push the chair down the ramp, and Anna pulled the wheelie suitcase behind them, and Claire tried to turn her head, but her neck was stiff, and the sun was so bright she didn't think she could have looked into the dark of the great ship anyhow. And she knew Richard. He wouldn't have waited, he wasn't that kind of man. Then they were being whisked through passport control and Anna had taken control of the wheelchair and there were two figures waiting, right by the dockhouse, and Claire's heart started to pound faster than she knew her oncologist would have liked.

♥

Claire was quite wrong about Richard. He stayed watching until they disappeared behind the barbed-wire gates of the ferry terminal. He watched as all the happy, sunburned holidaymakers filed on to the ferry. He watched as they cast the lines and the great ship revved itself up again, and he stayed watching up on deck as the coast of France retreated further and further behind him into the darkness of the onsetting night.

He drove home through the rainy night, arriving at two o'clock in the morning, smiling when he saw the roast beef and mustard sandwiches Anne-Marie had made and left out for him. Then he sat in his front room and got drunk for one of the very few times in his life.

Chapter Twenty-Five

At first Claire thought with a terrible start that Thierry was standing right in front of her. He was exactly the same: the thick curly hair, the twinkling eyes. No moustache, but ...

Then she realised that this must be Laurent, whom Anna had told her about. He was incredibly attractive. She wanted to glance at Anna and see her expression, but she knew, she knew ... she must look at the person sitting straight opposite her. She focused.

She tried not to wince. It was Thierry, of course it was, but he looked ... he looked so unwell. She knew this was ironic under the circumstances, but even so. His face was grey, and his skin looked rumpled and ill-fitting. He had an oxygen cylinder attached to his wheelchair.

But the moustache was growing back, and under the heavy brows, his black eyes were the same.

He gazed and gazed at her for a long time, equally, Claire realised with a sinking heart, horrified at what she had become. Reaching out, she clasped Anna's hand, hard.

All of a sudden, Thierry burst out laughing. In that instant, Claire remembered the flashing eyes, the infectious noise of it, and she smiled. It was impossible not to.

'Look at us!' he shouted. 'Look at us! We are the very last donkeys in the knacker's yard, Claire! The worst!!'

With great difficulty, and his son giving him his arm with a dubious expression, he stood up on slightly wobbly legs. He was wearing, Claire noticed, smart pale linen trousers and a light pink shirt. Always stylish.

Not to be outdone, she gave Anna her arm, and rose painfully to her feet. She went to him, and he took her in his arms.

'My little bird!' he exclaimed. 'You are even smaller than you were!'

'You aren't,' said Claire, her voice muffled in his shirt. Suddenly she felt the pressure on her arm disappear. She drew back, and turned to see Anna rush towards Laurent, throw her arms around his neck and kiss him.

Thierry looked at her, raising the eyebrows she knew so well.

'Aha, life goes on,' he said in his booming voice, and Claire was so startled and pleased that she laughed and sat down in her chair with a thump.

♥

I couldn't help it. Not when I saw him. I'd thought he was being petulant with his father, difficult. I had underestimated him; not understanding that of course he would do it, could change and shift all his plans, deal with Alice – God, Alice, I would worry about her later – and the fearsome French doctors. It was basically a kidnap. I was truly overwhelmed. And emotional, too, I told myself afterwards. I couldn't believe Richard and Claire had bothered getting divorced. If I had a nice-looking, decent man who looked after me like that … well, I didn't, so there was no point in thinking like that.

Apart from that, Laurent's handsome face, that full, kissable mouth, that mop of curly hair … I had to admit it. He wasn't a little fling, as Sami had imagined. He wasn't a holiday romance, a story to laugh about with Cath down Faces. He gave me a look, a half-smile that said, as clear as a letter would have done, that he was sorry, and that this was his make-up offering … and in that instant, in the evening sunshine, I forgot all about Claire and Thierry, forgot all about anything except how much I wanted to kiss him.

When I finally came to my senses and stood back, pink and a little breathless, he gave me that broad smile.

'Well,' he said. 'I am pleased to see you too.'

Then I cuddled Thierry and told him to cover his neck in the sun and asked him how it was to see Claire again, and he beamed and said she was still beautiful, and Claire blushed like a girl and said no she wasn't and Thierry said well she was doing better than him and Claire laughed and said, yes, yes she was, and I said did Laurent kidnap you and he sniffed and said yes and that we must stay out of the way of the police, and Laurent looked a bit awkward.

Then I suggested that if we were going to get back to Paris tonight we would probably have to get a move on – the sun was setting – but Thierry pshawed that idea and said, well of course we had to eat first and he knew just the place, and I laughed at the fact that both Thierry and Laurent were utterly horrified at the idea of missing dinner.

Calais wasn't very glamorous, full of hypermarkets selling cheap fags and booze, and travellers' hotels that offered weekly rates, but Laurent led us to the white Chapeau Chocolat van and put Thierry and Claire carefully in the front (I rode shotgun perched in the back) and spun us off the auto route and into a network of country roads and flat green fields till we arrived at a tiny farmhouse that barely seemed to be a restaurant at all.

Laurent marched in confidently and a fat man came out, muttering in a harsh northern accent I found difficult to understand, but I quickly realised that Laurent had basically pulled a 'don't you know who I am' on him and was insisting that they feed the famous chocolatier, the way a footballer or a rock star might have behaved in England. When Laurent lifted Claire down, she made a little 'oh' sound, as if she recognised the place.

The man fussed and worried around his elderly visitors. I was worried about Claire, she seemed so frail and she'd hardly eaten all day, but in the tiny restaurant – which was absolutely full, the waiter had pulled up and washed down fresh tables and chairs himself and put us outside under a shady chestnut tree – I ordered her a beautiful lobster bisque and took off her shoes so she could let her bare feet touch the grass. The meadow nearest us had cows wandering back from pasture, the grass full of the poppies unavoidable in northern France and Belgium, bees humming wistfully around us, reminding us that autumn was just around the corner. Thierry ordered snails and seemed on the point of asking for a second starter, but Laurent gave him a very sharp look and he didn't and had the fish instead. Everyone had one small medicinal glass of red wine.

At first conversation was difficult; where did you begin after forty years? But Claire made a good fist of her soup – I had it too, it was utterly sensational, followed by a side of bream I would never have dared order just a few months ago, with locally gathered mushrooms. I wasn't surprised this place was so busy.

'So,' she said finally, putting down her spoon. 'Where did you go? I wrote to you at the shop but you never replied.'

Thierry stopped mopping up the garlicky butter of his snails. Alice was going to have her work cut out with this one.

'Beirut,' he said, as if it was the most obvious thing in the world.

'Beirut? But I thought . . . I thought you were just going to march around the Place de la Concorde a few times. You got called up?'

'Of course I got called up,' said Thierry crossly. 'Everyone got called up.'

Claire's hand went to her mouth. 'In Beirut?'

'Of course. There was an insurgency,' said Thierry. 'Didn't they report it in your papers?'

Claire had spent that entire year mooning about and focusing entirely on herself. Of course she hadn't read the papers.

'I didn't realise,' she said. 'I thought you were in Paris.'

'I had the papers in my pocket when I waved you off,' said Thierry.

'We came here on the way,' said Claire faintly, playing with the grass with her toes.

'Yes, we did.'

'You made me try the hake.'

'I'll make you try it again in a minute.'

She smiled, weakly.

'But . . . letters . . .'

'Of course, I'm bad at paperwork . . . But Madame Lagarde had your address . . . I wrote from the desert. She did not forward me to you?'

Claire's hand flew to her mouth. She remembered the elegant woman again: *Take these memories but do not cling on to Paris.*

'I thought it was my dad,' she whispered.

'I thought you had gone back to England . . . got married . . . had children.'

'And I thought you had met someone else,' said Claire.

Suddenly everyone looked at Laurent, furiously doing arithmetic. Laurent muttered under his breath and excused himself from the table.

I was worried about Claire getting overtired and agitated.

I'd much rather she was asleep in bed right now, but she was a determined so-and-so.

'Oh,' said Claire quietly.

'Oui,' said Thierry.

I nearly swore out loud. No wonder Laurent was so cross with his father ... and his skin so olive.

'I did ... I could not stay,' said Thierry. 'I was a soldier. Then I was not a soldier. And I was so young, and I had a business to run.'

We were both looking at him. I felt for him; so young, and a local girl, pregnant and shamed ...

'But I sent for him,' said Thierry quickly.

'You did not send for me,' said Claire, softly and sadly, nodding to herself.

'Has he forgiven you for that?' I asked.

'I don't think so,' said Thierry.

We were suddenly interrupted. The proprietor had come over and cleared the plates away, the hake had been and gone, and coffee and eau de vie had appeared from nowhere. I was trying to explain that we hadn't ordered it when the little man put down a plate full of Chapeau chocolates.

We all gasped, amazed.

'Where did you get these?' said Thierry. The cost of sending away for them was astronomical, Alice saw to that, and Thierry was reluctant to fulfil private orders. He preferred everything to be eaten on the day. To keep longer they needed less cream and a touch of preservative, which he hated using.

'I keep them,' said the man. 'For my most special customers. Which you undoubtedly are.'

And then he insisted on getting his photograph taken with Thierry, and some other customers came to have a look at what was going on, and when they realised who it was, they were also effusive in their compliments until the proprietor had to open the entire box and Thierry had to promise to send him another one, and sign the photograph.

When the hubbub finally died down, Thierry turned his kind, ruined face to Claire.

'Chocolat,' he said. 'It's all I'm good for, really. You see what I am saying?'

Claire nodded, and moved a hand to his arm.

'You,' she said softly. 'It's you I was only ever good for. It didn't do me a lot of favours either.'

Thierry put his huge hand on her tiny bruised one and held it there, as the crickets started to make noises into the night and the huge bright stars overhead popped out one by one.

♥

I crept off to find Laurent. He was finishing up a slim black cigarillo by the trees. They were loud with insects.

'Sorry,' he said when he saw me. 'Filthy habit. Very rare.'

'I don't mind,' I said, and I didn't really. The smoke smelled exotic on the warm summer evening. 'I quite like it.'

There was a silence.

'So now you know,' he said.

365

'He was very young,' I said.

'So was my mother,' said Laurent.

He glanced back towards the table.

'Claire,' he said. 'She is very, very sick.'

I jumped, guilty at being away.

'She is,' I said. 'I'd better go check on her.'

Gently Laurent ran his hand down my face.

'You like to fix things,' he said softly. 'Can you fix me, Anna Tron?'

Chapter Twenty-Six

I would have preferred us to stay the night, but Thierry had promised to come home and Laurent was anxious to be off. I was more concerned about Claire. Her breath sounded thready and ragged, and she had had a very long day. Thierry was exhausted too. Laurent and I exchanged worried glances as we got into the van, propping them up as best we could against each other. Claire helped herself to another dose of the morphine, which I watched surreptitiously, trying to figure out how much was too much, before shaking my head at the craziness of it all. As Laurent barrelled down the road at top speed, Thierry and Claire leant against one another, her head nestling under his arm, as if they'd slept that way every night for forty years.

We didn't speak. I felt as if anything I might say would be wrong. Laurent drove furiously fast, all his concentration on the road. I looked at him, wondering why he still couldn't talk to his father. But I put that out of my head.

I would just try and enjoy, instead, the very fact that they'd come for us; Claire's look on the dockside; the kiss we had shared. I touched my mouth briefly. He was a very good kisser. Those lips. But why hadn't I noticed ...? He probably, I realised, had a strange accent I simply hadn't picked up on because my French wasn't good enough, like Americans being completely unable to distinguish between Scottish people and Irish people. Sami, now I came to think of it, probably spoke very differently too. How odd that I had simply never noticed, lumping everything I had come across in Paris as simply terribly foreign, without considering how foreign, exactly.

I watched his head of shining black curls in the dim light from the dashboard as we sped along the dark motorway, incredibly fast. He was focusing entirely on driving and I felt myself in such safe hands that I, too, must have drifted off to sleep.

The suburban lights of Paris woke me up as they flitted against the windscreen, and I stretched uncomfortably. I had booked Claire into a very nice hotel not far from the apartment, and we practically carried her into it. I made sure she was settled and breathing, but she barely stirred. I would have to stay. The room was small, and I sat down on a chair by her side. She tilted her head.

'It's all right,' she breathed.

'It is,' I said. 'Everything's going to be all right.'

I patted her hand. With difficulty, she shook her head.

'No,' she said. 'You don't have to stay. You've done enough. Go get some sleep.'

'No chance,' I said.

She smiled. 'Oh for goodness' sake, Anna. I promise not to die tonight. Is that enough? Now do what your teacher says and go and get some rest. I have a lot I want to do in the next few days and it won't help if you're buzzing over me like an annoying bee.'

'I'm not an annoying bee,' I said.

'Shoo!'

I stood, hovering, not quite sure what to do, until I heard her breathing slow into sleep, and it sounded better; like normal sleep. I looked at her for a while until I heard the faintest of voices, 'Stop staring at me,' and then I backed out of the room. I'd come back first thing.

♡

Alice was waiting outside the shop, in the middle of the road, looking absolutely and completely furious. Laurent and I hopped out of the van, both bone tired, and she climbed in without a word to either of us, fired up the engine and disappeared.

'She'll get over it,' muttered Laurent.

'Did you *steal* the van?'

'I sent her a text apologising for the snatching. I'm sure it'll be all right.'

'Hmm.'

We wandered over the deserted cobbles round the corner. Up in the tiny apartment, I could see lights flashing. Oh God, Sami must be having a party. Of all the things I didn't feel like, that was definitely right at the top of my list. My face fell.

'Well, good night then,' I said to Laurent, wondering if I might manage to sleep through it.

'Good night,' he said, and made to walk away, then, suddenly, stopped himself. The street was in total silence, apart from some calypso music I guessed was coming from the flat.

'No,' he said, almost to himself, then strode back towards me. 'No, no, no, no, no.' He took me in his arms and kissed me again, deeply and thoroughly, until I felt, like magic, my tiredness evaporate, and a heady, sensual longing overtake my limbs.

'Come back with me,' he said. 'Please. I don't want to be alone tonight. Come with me.'

'I have to be back,' I said, half laughing. It was stupidly late. 'I have to check on Claire, and I have to go to work tomorrow.'

'Well there's no point sleeping now,' he teased in a challenging tone. This was more like the Laurent I knew. I found myself blushing. I couldn't help thinking that the last people to see me naked had been about one hundred and fifty student doctors, a score of agency nurses, my mum and, on one awkward occasion during my convalescence, my dad. It had been a long time for me.

'Hop on,' said Laurent, firing up the scooter.

♡

This journey felt different from the first time he had taken me home, when I had been so lost and confused. It went quickly, as we flashed past the holidaymakers drinking in the Place de la Concorde, the lights of the great hotels making them as brilliant as ocean liners in the night; snatches of orchestral music issuing from their windows open against the warmth of the evening. I snuggled in close and smelled Laurent through his shirt; the warm heavy scent of him. It was better than any perfume I'd ever known. We headed north once more, back to Montmartre, where we'd first met, the great thoroughfares thinning out as the roads became quieter and narrower until finally the scooter was bumping over cobbles and I had to hold on just to avoid losing my balance on the corners I now knew to lean over for.

My heart now was thumping hard, and the feel of him filled my senses. Occasionally he would take his hand off the handlebars in order to caress my knee in a reassuring way, and each time he did so I felt a thrill go through me. I tried not to panic. It was only sex. I used to do it all the time. Okay, I used to do it with Darr, after I'd drunk a few shandies, but this was different. Now, although we'd had a couple of glasses of wine, I was stone-cold sober, certainly more sober than I'd ever been when I'd slept with someone for the first time before, and I hadn't fancied any of them as much as I fancied Laurent. My brain was in turmoil; I barely saw the fun fair we passed, lit up still, and the rows of hanging lights between the old-fashioned lamp posts.

If Laurent knew what was going through my mind, he didn't mention it. We drew up in a tiny back street that wasn't a thoroughfare at all, but rather a little three-sided square situated around a bench. The buildings weren't the traditionally grand arrondissement apartments; they were older, and made of grey stone, which matched the colour of the cobbles beneath them. They looked like they had been transplanted from some other part of France altogether. Many of them had ivy growing up them, with balconies only on the top floor. He led me to one of these, a large door, painted bright red, slap bang in the middle of it.

'This isn't an apartment,' I said, suspicious. 'Where are we?'

He looked a bit awkward, and pulled out a large set of old keys.

'I never bring anyone here,' he said. 'Welcome, I suppose, my shy English mademoiselle.'

Then he winked at me to show me he wasn't really that nervous, turned the old-fashioned door handle and waved me inside.

I stepped into a formal hallway opening into a huge reception room with panelling that wouldn't have looked out of place at Hampton Court. A large, abstract candelabra with random candles dotted in it added to the illusion. The room was at the back of the house, away from the little square, and the entire back wall was glass. Outside was a spotlit garden on several different levels, immaculately raked in squares and rows of herbs and vegetables, with gravel paths running between them. Looking through the glass, I could see to the right another glass wall which obviously housed the kitchen, a shining stainless-steel affair, very professional-looking.

'WOW!' I said, unable to say anything else.

From the hallway, there were floating steps leading upstairs, presumably to the other levels. Bookshelves lined one side of the huge panelled room, and on another was an enormous fireplace, currently with a large glass bowl of limes sitting in the unused hearth.

'Why do you never come here?' I said, my voice echoing in the room. 'If I lived here, I would never ever leave it, ever.'

Laurent looked a bit shamefaced.

'Mm,' he said. 'It's ... it's my thing.'

'What do you mean? You drive a really rackety old scooter.'

'I know ... I don't spend much money really. So it all goes on the house.'

I glanced at him, a half-smile playing on my lips.

'Your dad didn't buy it for you?'

He looked fierce. 'As if I'd take a penny.'

'Well, it's lovely.'

'Would you take a house from your parents?'

I thought about it.

'I can't imagine anything making my dad happier than being able to buy me a house.'

Laurent winced.

'He did offer ...'

'Aha!' I said in triumph. 'So he's not totally evil?'

'I was so proud,' he said, miles away, staring out at the little garden. 'I wanted to show him I could do it as well ... do it better.'

I patted him on the shoulder.

'You're going to hate me for saying this,' I said, 'but you are quite alike.'

Laurent half smiled and led me through to the kitchen. Unusually – in my experience, for a man – the fridge was full of butter and cheese and eggs and vegetables. I was impressed and made a mental note never to invite him round to dinner at Sami's. He pulled out a bottle of champagne. I perked up immediately.

'When my dad moved to Paris from Lot et Garonne, he lived in a single room in an attic with no hot water or heating,' said Laurent. 'He slept in every item of clothing he had in the wintertime. And he worked his way up. I've heard the story a million times . . . normally from Alice.' He snorted.

'So of course you had to do the same?'

He nodded. Then he grinned.

'Do I sound like an idiot?'

I shrugged. 'It is,' I said, 'a very nice house.'

His face lit up.

'Thank you!'

Standing there lit by the fridge, which was still open, with the spotlights in the garden highlighting his curls and the shadow of his long eyelashes against his cheeks, I thought he was the most gorgeous thing I'd ever seen in my life.

I moved forward and kissed him, and he kissed me back, with none of the amused nonchalance he'd shown before, but with a total, committed fervour. It was fierce and it was fantastic.

'Now can we stop talking about your dad?' I said, when we finally came up for air.

He put the champagne bottle down on the counter.

'I will sweep you upstairs,' he said, grabbing me round the waist. My eyes strayed to the bottle he'd put down.

'Oh, my little English girl,' he laughed. 'Do you think you need to get drunk to enjoy yourself with me?'

I wriggled, red in the face .

'Not drunk exactly,' I muttered. 'But a bit of Dutch courage wouldn't go amiss.'

Laurent took my hands in his strong grip and stared into my eyes intently.

'You, my gorgeous Anna, are going to come upstairs with me. And we are going to make love, if that is what you want, and you will be perfectly sober, and you will enjoy every second. Oui or non?'

Oh lord.

♥

The sun was coming up. It shone through the pale gauzy curtains and on to the bed, where I lay in Laurent's arms. He was asleep but I had not slept at all, and I felt that light, dreamy way when you're not sure what is real and what's a dream. I turned and kissed his hair. He had, in the end, lightly caressed my toes. He had lightly caressed every bit of me. Then we had become less gentle. A lot less gentle.

'Oh, Anna,' mumbled his snoozing form.

'I have to go,' I whispered.

'Don't.'

A huge hairy arm came over and trapped me.

'I have to,' I said, 'I have to work.'

'Oh Christ,' he said, shooting bolt upright and searching for his watch. 'So do I. I said I'd take the early shift.'

'Surely not this early?'

'You've never worked in a hotel, have you?'

'No,' I admitted. He smiled at me and kissed me.

'You are even more luscious in the morning,' he said. 'Oh, my love. Stay awhile.'

'I thought you were going to work?' I said. 'Anyway, no. I'm worried about Claire. I shouldn't have left her last night.'

'She was happy and sleeping,' argued Laurent. 'Anyway,' he smiled, 'didn't you enjoy what we did instead.'

I smiled back, feeling myself flush again. He cupped his hand to my cheek. 'I like it when you turn red,' he said.

'Shut up,' I said.

I grabbed my clothes – it felt odd to think I had put them on in Kidinsborough. I desperately needed a bath – and went to leave. I didn't want to. I felt like I was coasting along on a sea of happiness.

'Oh God, I don't know how I'm going to get through today,' I giggled. 'It'll be even worse than normal.'

'Just concentrate, you'll be fine.'

'Okay,' I said.

I looked at him.

'One thing you haven't told me about,' I said.

'There are a million things I haven't told you about,' he said, smiling. 'Now I think we will have time to get to know each other.'

I smiled. 'Yes please. But Laurent, what about your mum? Wouldn't she like to know about Thierry? Wouldn't she like to see him?'

I knew the second it came out of my mouth what a dreadful mistake I had made; the shutters dropped down almost immediately.

'I'm sorry,' I whispered. 'Another time?'

'This is . . .'

I thought of the Laurent I'd seen around town, handsome, charming, keeping everything light.

'Am I moving too fast?' I said. He said immediately non, non, non, but I left anyway. After I let myself out, as I passed his scooter, I wanted to kick it.

Chapter Twenty-Seven

Claire was dreaming. She was dreaming that she was in Paris and the light reflecting off the white stone buildings on to her face was the one that only came when she was there. She felt lighter than air; in her dreams she could move as freely as she liked. Why had she thought she was sick? She wasn't sick at all, she was fine, the doctors had got it all wrong. Silly doctors, she was so fine she could fly, look.

Suddenly, even in her dream, she realised that of course she couldn't fly, and little by little she started to float, her disappointment as bitter as ashes in her mouth, to the surface, still caught, still trapped in her body riddled with blackness, useless and shaming. All her mornings felt like this; beached from dreams into the harshness of another daily struggle through reality.

She blinked twice. One thing was different, though. It was that light. With a burst of pure happiness she remembered. She was in Paris. They had made it. She was here.

There was a knock at the door, and Anna entered, carrying two small cups of coffee she'd brought up from the lobby, and a bag of fresh, flaky, still-warm croissants between her teeth. She made a smiling grimace – she looked exhausted, Claire noted, but rather well – and went over to the window, where she pulled open the thick curtain to reveal a window box filled with white roses, and a view all the way to the Eiffel Tower. It was enchanting.

'Not bad, eh?' she said, putting the coffee down and kissing Claire on the cheek. 'Good morning. How are you feeling?'

Claire shrugged. 'Actually,' she said, sounding surprised, 'I didn't have a bad night.'

Normally she woke three or four times, often feeling as if she would choke.

Anna helped her to the toilet and got her dressed, apologised for being so early but said she didn't know when Claire would wake and had erred on the safe side, and then disappeared to the shop. Claire watched her go with a smile on her face. She was dedicated, that girl. She'd been right about her. She'd do well.

Then she sat back with the complimentary copy of *Paris Match*, by the window Anna had opened, and listened, for the first time in forty years, to the noises of Paris waking itself up, as she sipped the strong sweet coffee and nibbled at a croissant and felt the sun warm her aching bones.

It was the first day back after the break and I was earlier than Frédéric or Benoît this morning, which was a first. Mind you, they'd probably got some sleep, which was better going than me. I hovered around on my own – Frédéric had the keys – wishing I had something to do with my hands, like smoke.

The van pulled up first. My heart sank and I cursed. Now I was going to have to deal with Alice all by myself.

Alice almost fell out of the driver's seat. For once, her face wasn't immaculately painted. She was wearing yesterday's clothes, and her hair was scraped back in a ponytail. She looked nothing like herself at all; I barely recognised her.

'Alice?' I said.

She looked up at me. Yesterday's mascara was running down her face. She was in a terrible state.

'Are you all right?' I asked in alarm.

For the first time in our acquaintance she answered me in English.

'No-o-o,' she said in a long shudder, launching herself across the cobbles and sitting down on the step. Then she burst into huge sobs.

'What's the matter?' I said, fear gripping me. 'Is Thierry all right? Was the trip too much for him?'

Unable to speak, she shook her head.

'No, it's not that . . . He's better,' she said, bitterly, almost spitting the words out.

She looked up at me with undisguised hatred.

380

'How can you ... how can you take him away from me?' she said, then burst into fresh floods of tears.

'What do you mean?' I said, genuinely confused. She couldn't be talking about Laurent, could she? No, surely not. No, that would be absurd. Nonetheless, I found a blush covering my face. Oh God, that div, I hated the effect he had on me.

'My Thierry,' she said, as if I was a total idiot. 'You take MY man, MY partner, and you set him up with some fantasy from his past, as if I don't even bloody exist ... I mean, how the FUCK am I supposed to compete with that?'

She sounded funny in English, not nearly so posh, more Essex if anything. She rubbed fiercely at her eyes.

'Well, thanks very fucking much. I'm only the one that's kept everything going, kept the books, kept the suppliers happy, kept everyone away from him so he could concentrate on doing what he does best ... and this is the thanks I get.'

I blinked several times. It was true, she was completely right. I hadn't given her feelings a second thought, except to try and stay out of her way. But of course I wasn't trying to usurp her. I was trying to help someone else. I didn't know how to explain it.

'I'm sorry,' I said, unsure whether this would work or not. 'That's not what I meant ...'

I knelt down.

'You know how ill she is?'

Alice glanced up. 'Thierry said she was sick, but he's so happy to see her, he's like a little boy. He's been doing his physiotherapy exercises, after he'd told his doctor he absolutely wouldn't do them. He's been eating veg and making plans and ... I haven't seen him so alive in a long time.'

She looked up at me.

'He's going to leave me.'

'Of course he's not going to leave you,' I said, thinking privately that if he was, her bad temper would have driven him to do it a long time ago.

'Listen to me,' I said, sitting down next to her on the kerb. 'You know and I know that Thierry is an optimist, yes?'

She laughed, a tiny bit. 'You could say that.'

'Doesn't really like facing life's difficulties.'

'He does not,' she said. 'Like his own blasted belly.'

I smiled at that.

'You have to know,' I said. 'Claire is really sick. Really, really sick. She shouldn't be here. She should be in a hospital.'

The reality hit me.

'No,' I said slowly. Claire hadn't said anything; the true state of her health was between her and her doctor. But gradually I realised that what I was saying was true; took in the full enormity of it.

'No,' I repeated. 'She shouldn't be in a hospital. She should be in a hospice.'

I looked at Alice to make sure she realised the significance of what I was saying, although it was for myself as much as her.

'Alice, coming here ... this is the last thing Claire is ever going to do. Do you realise that? She's going to go back to the UK, and then ...'

I bit my lip.

'And then she is going to die,' I said.

Alice's eyes went wide.

'Really?'

'Yes,' I said.

'Oh God,' said Alice. 'Oh God.'

She fell silent, obviously thinking about how recently she had nearly lost Thierry.

'He never told me,' she said.

'He may not know, she's keeping it quiet,' I said.

'Even if he did, he would pretend it wasn't happening,' said Alice, and we both smiled.

We sat a while longer, watching Benoît lump up over the arch of the street.

'So,' I said eventually.

'So just let them get on with it,' she said ungraciously. 'Is that what you're trying to say? Butt out, Alice?'

I thought about it.

'Yes,' I said. 'But not for long. He is yours, I think. Don't you?'

She half smiled. 'I doubt anyone else would put up with him.'

I smiled at that as she headed back to the van.

'That goes double for his son, by the way,' she shouted, but I pretended not to hear her.

Frédéric arrived too, kicking away his cigarette and petting Nelson Eddy the dog.

'Bonjour,' he said. 'Ready for a full day's work?'

I watched as the grille rattled up.

'Sure,' I said.

Chapter Twenty-Eight

By eight o'clock I was completely hazy with tiredness, and we'd already had to throw away two full trays of orange chocolate because I'd over-creamed it and it tasted like chocolate yoghurt. Benoît was muttering and Frédéric was looking very agitated and asking me what Alice had said, which of course I didn't repeat. For some reason I had promised to gen up on hazelnuts over the holiday. Of course I'd done nothing of the sort, and with le tout Paris aware that we were re-opening today, it was a bit late to start. I half-heartedly started roasting the nuts, Frédéric reaching fussily over my shoulder to pull out the green ones. Then I turned round too quickly when he startled me and knocked the second copper vat so it spluttered and started spitting out chocolate all over the floor, which I then skidded on, getting a flashback so vivid I burst into tears. Frédéric did his best to be sympathetic, but I could tell it was only making him more agitated, and Benoît was muttering something to himself along the lines of how he'd never had a woman in the kitchen before and this was absolutely why, when suddenly I heard a noise on the roof of the greenhouse.

All three of us jumped. Someone was crouching on the roof! The shadow was plain above us, a sinister mass over our heads.

'Merde,' said Frédéric, dashing to the sink and grabbing the huge knife that we used to chop the herbs.

'Who's there?' I shouted, my voice quivering. There was no response. I was glad the boys were there. We moved towards the window. A large dark shape hung there ominously, then suddenly, with an enormous thump, it jumped down into the courtyard beyond. In a second Benoît had opened the back door and we'd all piled out on top of the crouching figure.

'AARGH! AARGH! STOP IT! GERROF!' it shouted, and I realised it was Laurent.

'Stop it, stop it, everyone,' I said, standing back.

'I can't believe you're attacking me again,' said Laurent, shaking himself off.

'Try to avoid breaking and entering into our workshop then,' I said, breathless and annoyed. 'What the hell were you doing up there?'

'Nobody would answer the front door. What the hell were you doing in here?'

Fortunately, neither of the boys grassed me up for my noisy boo-hooing. Laurent looked at me, then glanced at the floor.

'Um,' he said. 'I'm sorry. I'm sorry, after last night. I clammed up. It was rude.'

'I'm used to you being weird,' I said, unhappily.

'I know.' He sighed, then suddenly switched to English. 'This is hard ... I am trying, Anna.'

'*I'm* trying to get done for GBH,' I said, but the joke was lost on him.

'Frédéric, can you get us two coffees?' he said. Frédéric, amazingly, went and did it without complaining. Benoît, muttering, went back to mop up the workshop. I shivered a little; it was chilly out here in the little courtyard, which got no sun. We accepted Frédéric's coffee with thanks. I glanced at the clock, a little worried.

'I grew up in Beirut,' Lauren said, slowly. 'My father was sent because they were expecting trouble. They got it.'

'Oh no,' I said sympathetically.

'Actually,' he retorted, rather snippily, 'Beirut is a beautiful place. Beaches, skiing, the food ... oh, the food.'

I stared ahead and decided to let him do all the talking.

'Dad was stationed there during the conflict. It ... Life there was very hard.'

He lost his thread.

'Your mother?'

He shook his head. 'Can you imagine how she was treated when her family found out she was pregnant by a French soldier?'

'No,' I said.

'My grandmother used to steal round. In the middle of

387

the night, you understand? In case anyone saw her? To bring us food.'

'So they didn't . . .'

'Did he offer to marry her, you mean?' He shook his head. 'Oh no, he had different ideas about this. He even told her about Claire.'

I bit my lip. That seemed so thoughtless, even for him.

'What about when you came along?'

'He sent money,' allowed Laurent. 'And when I was seven, he brought us over for a while. He'd met Alice by then.'

'Was she kind to you?'

He snorted. 'My mother was far more beautiful than she was. Alice was insecure from the get-go. Pretended I was some little slum boy that didn't exist.'

'Why didn't they have children?' I wondered.

Laurent shrugged. 'Because she's a witch?'

'She's all right,' I said. I was learning more and more about how difficult it must have been for Alice to hold on to this strong-willed, selfish man.

'What was it like?' I asked.

'Paris? Amazing,' said Laurent. 'Oh my goodness, it was so clean and airy and cool! The huge houses and the streets . . . and no one looked twice at my mother, once she took her headscarf off! It was like she was free again, not like Dahiyeh, where everyone knew about her shame.'

'She sounds amazing,' I said.

He nodded sharply. 'She was. She did a fucking good job on her own.'

'Did you want to stay?'

'We couldn't. They weren't married. Mum couldn't just settle here. Anyway, even though being at home was pretty horrible, it was still home. Her mum was there.'

'What did you think of Thierry?'

'When he was interested in me, it was great. Being the focus of his attention, you just felt you lit up his world. And he showed me all about his work and I was interested ... very interested, you know.'

I nodded.

'He liked that, so I was his funny little dolly for a while. Then, you know, we went back and it was as if he'd forgotten all about us again.'

'He's not a great letter-writer,' I said.

'Men like Thierry ...' said Laurent. 'They are the sun, yes? Everyone else just has to orbit around. It is the same with any great chef; with conductors; with tennis players. They are the light.'

There wasn't, I thought, any bitterness in his voice. I looked up at him. It was as if he'd seen his father for what he was, and accepted it. He caught sight of me.

'Have you been crying?' he said. I nodded. 'Did I make you cry?' I nodded again, not wanting to say it was my eye. Anyway, yes, he did make me want to cry.

'Oh GOD,' he said. 'I am the worst, most selfish man in the world. I don't want to be like him, Anna.'

He pulled me into his arms and held me, close and tight, my head burrowed in his shoulder.

'I never want to make you cry again,' he whispered in my ear. 'Never again.'

'Too late,' I said, making a funny snorting noise and holding on to him like I would never let him go till he was kissing me again. There was a stern knock on the window. Frédéric was looking anxious. Benoît, I was amazed to notice, appeared to be smiling.

'CUSTOMERS!' Frédéric was saying.

'YES!' said Laurent, leaping to his feet. 'Let us cook!'

'Hang on,' I said. 'Just . . . Your mum.'

'Brain tumour,' said Laurent, shortly. 'When I was fifteen. Dad paid all the hospital bills. Wanted her to come to Paris, but she didn't want to intrude. Then he brought me here, got me an apprenticeship, set me cooking. It's been all I've wanted to do ever since.'

'But not in the way he wanted?'

'No,' said Laurent. 'He felt guilty, and I was fifteen and needed someone to blame. He offered to set me up in a house; he never did that for Mum. She lived in that crappy apartment block all her life.'

'That's why you wouldn't take his money?'

There was a long pause.

'You know,' I said, 'I bet you didn't ruin her life. I bet you made her very happy.'

'That's what she said,' said Laurent. 'Doesn't stop me hating fucking hospitals, though. But I think I've just about forgiven Dad.'

He held me by my hips and looked straight at me.

'I don't know what it is about you, Anna Tron,' he said. 'You seem to make me calm and happy when you're about and miserable when you're not. I don't know why that is.'

I paused. I was thirty years old and I had said the words, but never in a way that I meant as truly and as sincerely as I did now; not to Darr, God bless his spotty soul.

'It's because I love you,' I said. I wouldn't normally have said it first, but oh, I was so exhausted, punch-drunk, emotional. And, I realised, I loved him so very terribly much, even when he was petulant, even when he was grumpy, even when he was teasing me. I thought I might have been in love with him from the second he'd given me a lift on his scooter.

'Oh,' said Laurent, his mouth opening. 'Yes. Yes, that must be it. I must love you. We must be in love. Of course. Of COURSE!' He banged his hand comically on his head. 'I can't believe I didn't think of it.'

Then he gathered me up into himself as Frédéric shouted 'CUSTOMERS!!!' repeatedly at the window of the greenhouse, and Laurent only stopped kissing me for long enough to shout, 'But we are IN LOVE,' back at him.

And then I realised something else. It was like someone turning off a radio I hadn't even known was still playing. Suddenly the itching, the fuss, the pain, the twinges; all the sense in my missing toes that weren't really there simply vanished. And I felt completely whole.

Thierry was fastening his tie in the mirror. For the first time in a very long time he seemed to have space in the collar. Alice came up behind him and smoothed down the shoulders of his shirt.

'Ah, don't fuss me.'

'No,' she said, and glanced away. 'I shan't fuss you.'

He looked at her. He had slept so well and woken up feeling better than he had in years. He found it annoying on a very deep level that less wine and pastries were making him feel this much better.

'Alice,' he said, his voice softening. 'You know in my life I have loved three women. One of them is dead, one of them is dying and one of them is you. So please, do not be cross with me today.'

Alice came back up behind him and ran her hands through his still thick hair. She burrowed her face in it.

'I can't lose you,' she said.

'You won't,' said Thierry. 'You won't. I promise.'

He twisted himself round, carefully, to face her. She could see the scar, still angry-looking, through his unbuttoned shirt.

'I have done so many ... well, no. I have not done many things in my life. I have made chocolate and thought that that was enough.'

Alice blinked hard.

'I have not looked after my toys like a good boy,' he said, smiling ruefully. 'Can I make it up to you now?'

Alice thought of the years she had spent loving him, even

when he was old and fat; even when she had shelved her plans for children, knowing they were too busy, seeing how he was with his own little boy, who hero-worshipped him so painfully. Some people always sacrificed more, she knew.

'Yes,' she said, kissing his forehead.

'But I must also . . .'

'Do this. Yes. I know.'

She drove him to the hotel as he requested, to see the woman he had never forgotten; the slender Englishwoman who had shaped his taste so very much . . . but she did not stay.

♥

I had seen him in the kitchens at his hotel, but not here. I knew my place; I sat at the back out of the way, my arms around myself, as if I was hugging a secret too good to hold. He knew his way around, though, of course he did, probably better than anywhere; he'd played here as a boy. He looked at the plants along the back wall as he set the vats churning in motion, husked faster than anyone I'd ever seen, did the conch like an artist, his arms moving with the same graceful flow as his father's: taking yesterday's batch, adding cream and testing, adding some more. He went to the store cupboard and found the large pepper grinder, then to the lemon tree, stripping it completely of all its lemons. We'd never used them; Frédéric said they were only for nougatine. Laurent chopped them roughly, then stood over the churn, squeezing and tasting again.

'This is the only way,' he said. Well, I suppose it was for him. I wouldn't know what I was tasting for. Until I learned, I supposed. He added more lemon juice, then lifted the plant pot of coriander.

'M'sieur!' protested Benoît, but it was too late. Laurent rubbed the leaves into nothing into the chocolate mix.

'That,' I stated, 'looks like it's going to be disgusting.'

'We will make a gourmet of you yet,' said Laurent, grinning.

He tasted a little more and made a face.

'Yes, you're right. It is disgusting. You have to balance. Without balance, it is just horrible. With balance, you can do anything.'

He looked at me.

'When you lost your toes, could you balance?'

'No,' I said.

'But now you can do anything, right? You compensated and made it better?'

I shrugged. 'Yes, I suppose so.'

'Well. Just like that, I will hold up this chocolate.'

'I'm not sure this metaphor is really hanging together,' I said, smiling, but he hushed me and kept on working feverishly.

Finally, he tried one last time then immediately stopped the paddles from turning.

I opened my mouth obediently.

'That's what I like to see,' said Laurent. He let a drop cool, then rest on my tongue.

I'd expected it to be awful, just weird, but it wasn't. The depths of the chocolate base were deepened by the pepper, giving it a dark edge, but then shot through with a sublime light sharpness. It was clean, delicious and utterly moreish.

'Oh my God,' I said. 'I have to eat more of that.'

'Yes!' said Laurent. 'That's right.'

He tried some himself.

'Yes, exactly. Perfect. I am a genius.'

'Can you teach me how to make it?'

He looked me up and down.

'Two months ago I would have said no. Now, I think you can do anything.'

Frédéric interrupted us kissing to say that there was going to be a riot in the queue lining up outside and did we want him just to call the Bastille now? Everyone left in Paris knew that we reopened today and there was a rumour that Thierry was on the mend and would be here too – I knew the hotel was going to call a taxi for him and Claire, but I wasn't sure when. I felt a momentary stab of concern, before remembering Claire chiding me to get on with things. They would be all right.

Frédéric set the chocolate on the cool shelves double quick as Laurent twirled off to start another batch of mint and bitterest aniseed. I started to clean up, then out of interest went to see what happened when the lemon went on sale.

The first person to try some was M. Beausier, one of our regulars. He was small and slight, considering the amount of our chocolate he put away. Perhaps it was his staple diet. He took one bite and his eyes popped open.

'Mon Dieu,' he said. 'Is Thierry back in the kitchen?'

He turned round to the queue and started handing out little squares for people to taste.

'Try this, try this,' he was saying excitedly. 'I must have some more!' he called over to Frédéric, who raised his eyebrows and sighed in a dramatic way. The people in the crowd who'd tried it started muttering enthusiastically and placing large orders.

I turned back to Laurent.

'I think there's going to be a riot out there,' I said.

He straightened up. His face looked nervous and exhilarated at once.

'What do you mean? They're hating it?'

'Nooo,' I said. 'They're loving it.'

'Really?'

'Of course really! Come on, my love, you know you can cook.'

'But in my father's kitchen . . .' he muttered, pushing his hair out of his eyes.

'Yes,' I said. 'In your father's kitchen. You are also wonderful.'

He smiled, and I felt in that instant both immense love for him and a sudden rush of love for my own father, who would love me no matter what, whatever I did and how. He wasn't famous or a brilliant genius or world-renowned. Except to me.

'Now, get on and make some more,' I said, but Laurent couldn't; he had to come and see for himself.

The crowd was still standing around in the shop, unable to disperse, telling each other how amazing the chocolate was. And of course because there were lots of people, other people had come up behind to see what was going on and were watching and adding themselves to the queue, and the entire stock had nearly sold out.

M. Beausier, who had known Thierry a long time, gasped when he saw Laurent. But everyone else's attention was diverted by a long car pulling up outside.

♡

Thierry seemed stronger already than when she had seen him yesterday, thought Claire. He was very smartly dressed and carrying a large bunch of flowers when he arrived at her door. This was how it would be, she supposed. He would get better and better and recover as she got worse and worse. She had had a very bad coughing fit in the bathroom that morning that, she knew, would have made her oncologist order her straight back to the hospital. For a moment she nearly weakened, thinking suddenly how nice it would be to call an ambulance and let the professionals take over; slip into a drugged sleep and let them clear her lungs and drain what they needed to drain to make her more comfortable . . .

But she knew, more clearly than anything, that the next time she went into hospital she wouldn't be coming out again. She had one chance, only one chance, to do this. Plucking up all her courage, her hand shaking, she managed to insert the tiny chips of emerald in her ears.

She didn't want to take too much morphine either; it helped, but it blurred the edges, made her feel as if she was walking through a cotton-wool dream, where nothing really mattered. This did matter; it mattered to her a lot. And it was only one more day. So she wanted to stay clear for it, even if she felt at any moment that her bones might shatter, or her whole body might simply curl up and immolate, like in a film she had once seen about nuclear war.

She had drunk some more water and done her best with her face. She could not, she found, walk across the bathroom to get back to the bedroom.

Cursing roundly in a way that would have surprised many of her ex-pupils, Claire crawled, very slowly, across the floor.

♡

'How are you?' he said, covering her emphatically with kisses. 'I have been ordered to walk about and take exercise, so I walked to the lift to see you.'

Claire smiled.

'Can you take a walk with me?'

'No,' said Claire. 'Not today.'

'Well, that is a shame,' said Thierry. 'I always enjoyed our walks.'

'So did I,' said Claire. 'But I have ordered tea. Now tell me everything.'

'And you too,' insisted Thierry. 'Then I shall take you to the shop.'

'I would like that,' said Claire. 'I would like that very much.'

♥

I realised later that the taxi hadn't had space for a wheelchair, and the hotel had had to order a bigger car. But it did look a bit like a limo had drawn up, as Thierry stepped out of the big black car.

The crowd, instantly, burst into applause. Thierry looked incredibly jolly and better already than he had the day before, never mind those awful days in hospital, and acknowledged their applause with his hand. Someone started taking photographs.

Then father and son caught sight of one another. Thierry stood stock still for an instant. I saw a look of fear and nerves and defiant pride pass over Laurent's features as clear as day; I could already read him so well. Someone handed Thierry a piece of the chocolate. Slowly, very slowly, he placed it on his tongue and held it there, closing his mouth. There was absolute silence on the rue de Chanoinesse. All the other shopkeepers had come out to see what was going on.

Thierry chewed, meditatively and carefully. Then he stopped and gave a short, sharp nod.

'Mon fils,' he said simply, and he opened his arms. Laurent ran into them like a little boy.

♥

I helped Claire out of the car into her chair, which barely fitted in the narrow shop, and through into the greenhouse beyond. Laurent went back to making his new chocolate, and another batch of the lemon. Thierry, keeping a beady eye on him, remarked, as Laurent wielded the pepper grinder, that he was going to give him another heart attack, but mostly stayed out of the way. Claire sat comfortably by the plants and I took a couple of photos. It was funny to think she'd been here before. Had it changed?

'Not at all,' she said. 'Benoît, I remember you here as a young man.'

Benoît merely grunted.

'That's what he was like then too,' she confided.

Thierry went over to the sink and washed his hands.

'I am going to make you some medicine,' he said to Claire, who smiled.

'I would like that very much.'

I watched, fascinated, as he picked up a tiny whisk, that looked absurdly small in his huge hands, and a little metal poêle, and started working over a low heat, adding brandy and vanilla in tiny drops, tasting as he went. I spotted Laurent watching him whilst pretending not to.

Eventually it was made and warmed and poured into a huge clay cup, slightly chipped. Thierry took a tiny knife and carved perfect scrolls of chocolate from a large plain bar to decorate the froth on the top. Then it was taken over to be presented to Claire as if it was on a silver salver.

'It's the same cup!' she exclaimed with pleasure.

'I kept everything that reminded me of you,' said Thierry simply. 'When I returned from the army … ah, I had changed.

Life had changed. It made everything more complicated and less free and … well. I liked to keep some things to remember.'

I watched as Claire drank. She closed her eyes briefly. We didn't serve hot chocolate in the summertime, but I knew how legendary it was because people kept telling me about it.

'Oh,' she said, and this will sound fanciful, but she really did look slightly restored after she drank it; more colour in her cheeks, and a sparkle in her eyes. And she drank the whole cup with obvious pleasure, the first time I had seen her eat or drink with real appetite in nearly a year.

'Did you come all this way for a cup of hot chocolate?' I asked, and she smiled slightly.

'Well, mostly.'

Thierry followed the exchange and burst into a huge grin.

'I still have it,' he said smugly.

'Of course.'

He poured the last dregs into her cup and she finished them regretfully.

'I shall make you another.'

'You can make me one tomorrow, before I go,' she said.

I looked at Thierry, who had nodded without trying to insist that she stay longer. She had obviously told him everything, then.

'Now, Anna,' said Claire, turning her attention to me. 'I want to see where you live.'

'Do you?' I said. I wondered who Sami would have staying over today from the demi-monde. 'No, don't. It's up loads of steps, and it's just a tiny apartment, a box room really.'

'I've come here to visit you and I'd like to see it,' said Claire, in a 'do your homework' voice, so I wheeled her round the corner over the cobbles, leaving the boys behind to deal with the lengthening line of excited customers.

♥

It didn't take long, even though manoeuvring the wheelchair on and off kerbs was a tedious business. Paris is not a city built for wheelchairs. As usual, the hallway was in total darkness. Claire scanned the faded list of bells.

'I haven't put my name on it,' I said. 'I'm only here temporarily.'

She looked at me with that penetrating gaze of hers.

'Are you?' she said. I squirmed and looked down.

'Um, I'm not sure.'

'Well, be careful of those Girard boys,' she said.

I pushed open the heavy door. She could walk if she held my arm.

'I wish . . . I wish I'd held on to mine,' she added.

I found the light and squeezed it hard, then we progressed, very slowly. Upstairs I heard the mysterious door on the first landing open again. My heart sank. Oh no. That scary old woman. The last thing I needed now was for her to march out onto the landing and start having a go at me because Sami's chums kept leaving the door on the latch and played music at unlikely times of day.

We ascended the stairs at a glacial pace, as the door creaked itself wide apart. Claire stopped still on the landing. I blinked.

Just before the light went out, I saw the other woman standing there too. She was incredibly old, her hair white, her figure bent.

'Claire?' she breathed.

♡

Madame Lagarde's apartment still contained much of the old furniture from the days when her family had owned the entire house. It was grand and baroque, but a little much for the space. It was, however, impeccably tidy and luxurious, a thick Persian rug in the spacious front room. There was even a maid, who sat us down and went off and brought back cups of lemon tea in bone-china cups.

The two women were gazing at each other.

'I didn't know,' said the older woman.

Claire shook her head. 'Why would you? Thierry mentioned the address.'

'Yes, I . . . I always wanted to help him.'

She finally turned round to introduce me.

'Anna, this is Marie-Noelle Lagarde. I lived here too when I first came to Paris.'

'Upstairs?'

'Yes, upstairs, but it was all one house then.'

'Before the socialists,' grimaced Mme Lagarde. 'Of course we divorced. It was quite fashionable back then.'

'What about Arnaud and Claudette?'

'Both well. Claudette lives near here and comes round often; her children are wonderfully good to me. Arnaud is in Perpignan, getting a suntan.'

Claire smiled. 'They were dear children.'

'They are,' said Mme Lagarde. 'And they were very fond of you.'

A silence fell between them.

'With ... with Thierry ...'

Mme Lagarde lowered her head.

'I apologise. I am sorry. I thought it was a summer fling that would fizzle out and you would both be better for it. So did your mother.'

'My MOTHER?'

Mme Lagarde nodded. 'I miss her very much, you know. We were pen pals our whole lives.'

'My *mother* said you could take the letters?'

'I was Thierry's poste restante when he was away in the army, yes. We both thought it was the right thing to do. And you know, the divorce; I had very little time for romance in my life just then.'

'And all that time I blamed my dad.'

Mme Lagarde smiled. 'Never underestimate the power of a woman. I am sorry. I thought it was right.'

Claire shook her head.

'I was so sad.'

'He was too,' said Mme Lagarde. 'And when he got back from Beirut ... Oh, Claire. You would not have known him. He was not the same man. Even chef corps see things they should not see. He put on a happy face once more, but he was not happy, not anymore.'

Claire nodded. 'I see.'

'And then of course you got married and your mother was so happy ... She liked Richard a lot, you know.'

'I do know. He really spoiled her, was always taking her out for tea and buying her presents.' She smiled at the memory. 'I thought he was being a suck-up. Now that I think about it, he was being terribly polite and kind. He's a very good man.'

'That's what she said.'

We finished our tea and the two women embraced.

'You are not well,' observed Mme Lagarde. She seemed, I thought, a very straightforward kind of a person. I liked her.

'No,' said Claire.

'And I am very old.'

'Yes.'

'When do you leave?'

'Tomorrow.'

They paused at the door.

'So,' said Mme Lagarde. 'In another life.'

'I hope so,' said Claire, and the two women embraced again and I stood back a little.

♡

Claire wasn't sure she could make it to the top floor. Madame had invited her to see the hideous garages that had been built when they'd sold off the garden – a heartbreak she clearly wasn't over – and she'd had enough trouble managing that. But she didn't want to let Anna down, or to worry her. Tomorrow Thierry wanted to take her back up the Eiffel Tower one last time. She would think about that when she got there. Now all she wanted to do was take enough morphine in the bathroom to get her through the next half-hour. Then the next. And the next.

'GREETINGS!'

The entire apartment was covered in draped material and Sami had a manic look in his eye and a mouthful of pins. A short, fat, grumpy-looking young man was standing with a large cummerbund swathed around his middle.

'It'll be ready! It'll be ready!'

The man glanced at his watch.

'Five hours till the dress.'

'Oh SHIT,' said Sami. 'Darling, have you got any Dexedrine?'

'Yes, Sami,' I said. 'Of course I have Dexedrine.'

He was so caught up in what he was doing that he missed my being sarcastic for a couple of seconds, then remembered his manners and apologised to Claire.

'Forgive me, we are on tonight. The grand dress rehearsal. It will all be FINE.'

'Ow,' said the man, as Sami pricked him with a pin.

'And you are all coming?'

'Um,' I said.

'You are coming! Of course! To the opera house!'

'Oh, I'm not sure . . .'

'You are not sure?' said Sami. 'These performances have

406

been sold out for months. They will be attended by the President, by the Prince of Monaco, by everyone who is anyone in le tout Paris, and you are being offered a sneak preview for free.'

Claire spoke up.

'Which opera is it?'

'*La Bohème*,' said the young man. 'And I am playing Marcello, and I should be warming up my voice right now.'

'Oh!' said Claire, then glanced at me. 'I love that opera.'

I'd never been to an opera in my life, all I knew was that song from the football. Suddenly the man, who was the most unprepossing individual I'd ever seen, opened his mouth.

Even Sami stopped moving. The sound that came from him was as thick and rich as Thierry's chocolate. It was melting and dreamy. He sang just a fragment – I couldn't even understand the words – but the swoop of his voice filled the house to the rafters. An expression of calm began to spread over Claire's features.

'Okay,' I said quickly. 'We'll come.'

I turned to Claire.

'If you're up to it?'

'If you could take me back to the hotel now for a little nap,' said Claire, 'I can't think of anything I'd like more.'

Chapter Twenty-Nine

Thierry and Laurent met us in the lobby, both wearing dinner jackets and bow ties, Thierry's looking rather baggy round the neck, Laurent's looking very hired and utterly gorgeous. 'It's only a rehearsal,' I said, but I was delighted nonetheless. Claire was wearing a very simple grey wrap that did its best to make her terrible weight loss look chic. I was wearing a present from Claire. It had been a total surprise. She'd looked a bit nervous back in the hotel room, but said she thought it might fit me now (I must have lost weight, I could tell by the way she said it), and it was old, but it might pass for vintage, but if I didn't like it not to worry, she didn't know much about style these days.

But when I saw the dress, I loved it straight away; it was a beautiful soft green and had little daisies round the hem, and though I had thought it might be a bit young for me – I was no spring chicken, after all – in fact the cut and the shape of it was so sophisticated it worked perfectly and showed off my light summer tan. It was the nicest dress I'd ever worn and I could tell by Claire's face when I put it on that she thought it suited me too.

♥

Claire hadn't even understood why she'd brought the dress in the end, until she saw Anna's eager face, flushed and clearly in love and so happy. If she had been prone to thinking a lot of herself, Claire would have been proud that she'd sent her here.

The nap had helped, a little, but not much. She could no longer hold down food; she'd pretended to eat lunch while Anna was out of the room. She hadn't needed to go to the bathroom all day either. 'If you can't go,' her doctor had said, 'that's a sign. Hospital. Double quick. No messing.'

'Yes, Doctor,' she'd said.

And now she was running on fumes, she knew. It was odd; as if her body was giving up like an old boiler, or a car, one bit at a time, just gently shutting down.

She turned her face to Anna, who suited the dress well, but whose face was so brimming with happiness and excitement that she would have looked lovely in a sack. She *was* lovely.

♥

I made up Claire's face for her – some mascara on the two baby lashes she had growing, and some pale pink lipstick – and we looked at each other in the mirror and she said, 'Well,

I guess this is as good as it's going to get,' and we quickly hugged each other.

Laurent's face lit up when he saw me, and Thierry took a sharp intake of breath and glanced at Claire in a way that made me think he might have seen the dress before. I got one of the hotel staff to take a picture on my phone, and Laurent was holding Claire up out of her wheelchair, and tickling me, and as he held us we burst out giggling at the exact same moment as the flash went off.

♥

There were absolutely loads of people there for the dress rehearsal and all of them were studiously dressed down in a way that said 'we are totally music professionals who only care about the art of it and not the silly fripperies', but we didn't mind. Sami had arranged good seats for us in the middle of the stalls by dint of putting a huge roll of turquoise cloth over the top of them, and Thierry insisted on bringing a box of sandwiches and a bottle of champagne in a cool bag. I tutted at him and said Alice would kill him and he smiled and said it was a very special one-off and popped the cork as the tuning-up finished and the lights started to fade.

I thought, I will be totally bored by this. I won't get it and it will be obvious to everyone that I'm just dumb Anna Trent from Kidinsborough, average student, speaks French like a Spanish cow, likes Coldplay.

But then the conductor marched on, without ceremony –

nobody clapped; this was a rehearsal after all – and raised his hands, and all these musicians I could see, hardly any distance away from me . . . they just started to play these strings, running up and down their violins, and it was just totally amazing. It wasn't weird or boring at all, it was beautiful. Then the curtain went up and I gasped. Two men – including the little shortarse I'd met at the flat – were in a bare, cold-looking garret just like mine. It too had a view over Paris, full of twinkling lights and smoking chimneys, and through the window, although I had absolutely no idea how they did it, snow was falling. It was exquisite. Then the men began to sing and I was transported. Sami had told me the story one night when he was hemming, but I didn't really need to know it as I watched the cold, starving men burn their books, then the other man – who was taller and more handsome – met the beautiful Mimi, who wore a dress that was patched and faded but still fitted her absolutely perfectly, as she showed how poor and helpless she was in a voice that reached the very heights of the rafters.

Laurent didn't take his hand off my leg the entire time, as I leant forward, more and more transfixed. I glanced at Claire. Her eyes were half open, her head leaning against Thierry's shoulder. He had her arm around her. She looked awful. I felt a sudden lump in my throat.

'Are you all right?' I whispered.

She nodded. 'Yes, my love.'

'I'll take you home tomorrow,' I said. 'Richard will meet you and take you back to the boys.'

She nodded again. 'Yes,' she said. 'I am so lucky,' and she squeezed my hand. Thierry whispered something in her ear.

Claire could barely make out the figures on the stage. The two boys ... her boys ... oh where were her boys now? She wanted to see them so much. She missed them terribly: the fresh smell of their hair; the way they slept, arms thrown out, spread-eagled on their bunk beds; their little arms around her neck ... Thierry whispered in her ear, 'Don't go,' and she smiled. 'I must,' she said. 'I must go home to my boys ... and to someone I should have loved better.'

Thierry kissed her bald head gently.

'You couldn't have loved me any better.'

'No, I couldn't,' she said.

There was no interval, no pause, as the singers carried on with their scenes. But I preferred that, I didn't want anything to break the spell. Even though these people were singing, I was with them, at the dance, which was perfect; with the street sellers; and finally, as Rodolfo laid Mimi down gently on the couch, kissing her repeatedly, the tears slipped steadily from my eyes. Laurent whispered the name of the aria he was singing – 'Your Tiny Hand is Frozen' – and my heart jumped and stuttered with panic, and I turned, and straight away, even before the orchestra fell silent and the cast stared at us open-mouthed and Sami came charging full pelt right from backstage across the footlights towards us, his long turquoise scarf fluttering behind him, and the ambulance and the lights and the noise, I knew, I just knew, we all knew.

Epilogue

The elderly gentleman, clearly once very handsome, now slightly heavier, but with his bushy moustache as luxuriant as ever, pushed his way to the front of the queue with his cane. He was tall and beautifully dressed and as most of the visitors were foreigners, not French, they let him march through with his air of authority to buy his ticket to the top.

In the lift he stood with his hands clasped behind him. It had been a beautiful autumn. The leaves after the hot summer were burnished bright red and gold, and everyone had returned to the city rejuvenated after their summer break and wildly excited to hear that the great Thierry Girard had gone into partnership – with his son no less – and was no longer relying on past glories but was turning out cutting-edge work and taste surprises. Laurent's oyster chocolate had been talked about for weeks. And with Laurent working shoulder to shoulder with Anna, who had turned out to be such a find – they looked so happy together, bickering affectionately over flavourings, forcing each other to taste some new concoction – Theirry didn't feel the need to go in to the shop nearly as often, and had much more time to walk, to be with Alice, who was less frenetic now the financial future seemed secure but still watched his diet like a hawk; to reflect on how close he had come to losing everything, everything good about his life. Well, he had years now, barring accidents, years Claire had never had. He owed it to her to enjoy them, he felt.

Up at the very top, he turned left out of the lift – most people would turn right, he knew – and went round to the east side, from where you could see the towers of Notre-Dame, their little island, their little haven in the centre of the world. From up here, the movement and traffic and noise felt like nothing, all the tiny business of the human world, scattering around, each carrying inside them a multitude of happiness and sorrow, all those loves lost and found.

The wind was blowing, an autumnal chill in it. He was glad he was wearing the pink scarf Alice had bought him.

He opened up the Galeries Lafayette box. He had wanted so much to give it to her, had meant to, up here. But they had not had time. They hadn't had time to . . . Well. He was not going to dwell on it now.

Thierry took the brand-new straw hat out of its white box, lifted it high in the air over the fencing, and – *pouf!* – let the wind carry it away, watching it dance and fly in the air, high above the chimney pots and cathedral bells and steeples; watching it twist, its ribbon flapping, until it flew up and up, into the blue sky and out of sight.

Acknowledgements

Grateful thanks to Ali Gunn, Rebecca Saunders, Manpreet Grewal, Hannah Green, Emma Williams, Charlie King, Jo Wickham, David Shelley, Ursula Mackenzie, Daniel Mallory, Sarah McFadden, Jo Dickinson, the design team, the sales team and absolutely everyone at Little,Brown and Gunn Media who have worked so hard on these books. I know I'm very, very lucky.

Special thanks to Sarah Tonner and Alison Lake who, through the magic power of twitter, helped talk me through the physical and psychological implications of an injury like Anna's. Thanks to Patisserie Zambetti, who basically let me rent office space for the price of a coffee and pain au raisin. Please continue your wonderful policy of not having Wi-Fi. And thanks to Headline and John Whaite himself (winner of *The Great British Bake Off 2012*! How I love that show.) for permission to use his recipe. It's from his book, *John Whaite*

Bakes ... Recipes for Every Day and Every Mood, which is out in April.

Thanks to Moyes, Manby and Jewell, wonderful Paris companions and of course to the board; to my friends and family, thank you as ever for being there and eating my experiments, failed and otherwise. Special thanks to my beloved Mr B, particularly for the numerous complicated Wednesdays. And to Wallace, Michael-Francis and Tiny Little James Bond, because I know you like to read your names in books. And also because you are everything.

Finally, thanks to the many readers who have dropped me a line, baked a cake, sent me a funny pic on Facebook or a smiley face on twitter. You have no idea how wonderful it is to hear from you and how much it makes my day (my husband: 'makes you insufferable.'). You can always find me on www.facebook.com/thatwriterjennycolgan, or @jennycolgan. But not my website, as I am rubbish at that.

Bon appetit! Ooh, I have ALWAYS wanted to get that in a book. Hurrah!

DON'T MISS THE NEXT IRRESISTIBLE
NOVEL FROM

Jenny
COLGAN

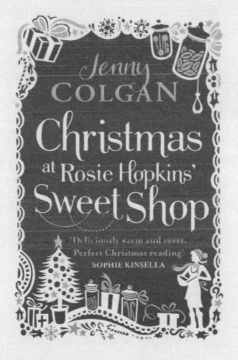

Christmas at Rosie Hopkins' Sweetshop

Coming in October 2013

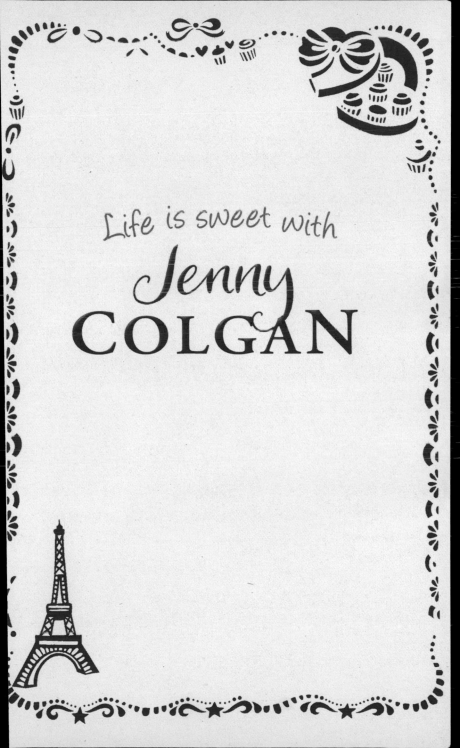

Life is sweet with

Jenny
COLGAN

Author's note

All the recipes in this book, with the exception of the pecan and chocolate plait, (but I can't wait to try it!) have been tested and checked by me.

JC xx

Here are some of my favourite chocolate recipes. They start from *very, very simple* and go up to a pecan and chocolate plait.

CHOCOLATE KRISPIE CAKE

♡

Seriously, we all have to start somewhere, and this is perfect for kids and as yummy as I remember it.

- 100 g melted chocolate – dark or milk, depending on preference
- 60 g butter
- 3 tspn golden syrup
- 90 g Rice Krispies

Melt the chocolate, slowly – although one is meant to use a bain-marie, I normally do it extremely slowly in the microwave, 10 seconds at a time, stirring all along – then add the butter and make sure that is all melted in too. Add the syrup and the Rice Krispies to the mix. You can also add tiny marshmallows and, if you're weird, raisins (seriously, there is a time and a place for raisins, but I feel very strongly that this is not it).

Spoon into paper cases, allow to cool.

NEVER FAIL CHOCOLATE CAKE

♥

This is absolutely the easiest chocolate cake in the world.
You will look at the recipe and sniff and think, hmm,
vegetable oil, but I promise, it makes it all moist and
delicious. You can decide to make it at short notice, always
very useful, and the ingredients don't even need to be
exact.

4 eggs
200 g caster sugar
40 g cocoa powder
120 ml vegetable oil
250 g flour
4 tsp baking powder
½ tsp salt
1 cup strong coffee (espresso or just very strong)
zest of 1 or 2 oranges
1 tsp vanilla extract

Preheat oven to 180°C/Gas Mark 4. Line baking tin – I use
a loaf tin for this, makes it nice and tidy.

Beat together eggs, sugar, coffee and cocoa powder, and
add the oil gradually; then stir in the flour, baking powder
and salt. Finally add the zest and vanilla extract. Pour into
baking tin, then cook for 40 minutes, but do check it – it
can be very runny. Mine had to go back in for a bit longer.
Ice with nutella. Delish!

CHOCOLATE BISCUIT CAKE

♥

My friend Jim first made this, and I got totally addicted to it. I really, really love this cake. Thanks Jim. (NB Please invoice him for the slimming classes afterwards, not me!)

200 g unsalted butter
150 ml golden syrup (2 very generous tbsp)
225 g good-quality chocolate
200 g digestive biscuits, roughly crushed
200 g Rich Tea biscuits, roughly crushed
125 g mixed nuts (walnuts, brazils, almonds), optional
125 g mixed fruit (sultanas, apricots, cherries), optional
1 Cadbury's Crunchie.

Line a 15 cm/6 in round cake tin or a 2 lb loaf tin with a double layer of greaseproof paper. I used a silicone loaf mould. There is no need to line the silicone mould.

Melt the butter, syrup and chocolate very slowly in a pan over a low heat. Make sure that the pan is large enough to take all the crushed biscuits, etc. Add the biscuits, fruit, nuts and Crunchie. Stir well.

Transfer to prepared tin. Level the top and press down well to avoid air gaps. Allow to get cold and hard. It needs about 2 hours in the fridge or about 45 minutes in the freezer. The longer the better. It tastes even better the next day. Wrap completely in greaseproof paper and store in a fridge.

BROWNIES WITH COFFEE AND CHOCOLATE CHIPS

♡

Of course we have to have a brownie recipe, and this one is just the ticket.

450 g plain flour
1 tsp salt
1 tsp baking powder
¼ tsp baking soda
60 g ground coffee
220 g butter
450 g dark brown sugar
220 g chocolate chips
3 eggs, lightly beaten

Preheat oven to 180°C/Gas Mark 4.

In a medium bowl, mix together the flour, salt, baking powder, baking soda and coffee. In a bain-marie or carefully in a microwave melt the butter, brown sugar and half of the chocolate chips, stirring to combine well. Allow to cool slightly, then stir the dry mixture into it. Stir in the eggs. Pour into an ungreased pan. Sprinkle the remaining half of the chocolate chips on top.

Bake in the middle of the oven until the cake has shrunk from the sides of the pan, 25 to 30 minutes. Allow to cool, then refrigerate until completely chilled. Remove and cut into squares. Eat cold or at room temperature. Makes 24 brownies.

BEST EVER HOT CHOCOLATE

♡

This works well on freezing days for tired children. I don't think I can specify how many marshmallows you may need. Just assume twice as many as you first thought.

    125 g double cream
    125 g milk
    100 g excellent-quality dark chocolate
    pinch cinnamon
    marshmallows

Gently heat the cream and milk together – do not allow to boil! Or get a skin! So very, very, very gently! Melt the dark chocolate, carefully, and add it slowly to the cream and milk. Serve with a pinch of cinammon on the top and marshmallows. If you're a grown-up, and were visiting us, you'd get a slug of either Drambuie or Lagavulin in yours too.

MUM'S CHEESECAKE

♥

Here is my friend Lauren's mum's amazing chocolate cheesecake.

50 g butter
10–12 digestive biscuits
1 tbsp honey or golden syrup
5–6 eggs at room temperature
320 g caster sugar
500 g Philadelphia chocolate cream cheese
2 tbsp plain flour
1–2 tsp vanilla extract
500 g cherries in syrup
2 tbsp cornflour

Preheat oven to 150°C/Gas Mark 2.

Melt butter in medium saucepan. Whizz biscuits in a food processor to fine crumbs, stir into butter with honey or golden syrup. Grease a high tin and press the mixture evenly over the bottom. Bake for 10 minutes, then cool.

Separate eggs. Whisk yolks till thick and pale. Gradually beat in 220 g of the sugar, then the cheese, flour and vanilla extract, till smooth. Whisk whites till stiff but not dry, fold into yolk mixture with a metal spoon, pour over biscuit base and bake for 70 minutes. Turn off the oven and leave the cheesecake in for another hour. Chill.

Drain cherries, reserving juice. Add water to juice to make up to 120 ml. Combine with sugar and cornflour in a pan and heat, whisking constantly, till thickened. Boil for 1 minute. Remove from heat, add cherries, cool. Spoon on to top of cheesecake and chill.

CHOCOLATE MERINGUE CAKE

♡

OOH, I do love this, and it is flour-free which is good for people with intolerances to things. It's lovely and crunchy on the top/bottom depending on how you like to turn it out, and gooey in the middle.

    1 shot espresso/coffee made very strong
    2–3 tbsp brandy/liqueur of your choice (gin is amazing
        with chocolate)
    350 g good dark chocolate
    4 large eggs, separated
    100 g unsalted butter, at room temperature, broken up
        into small cubes
    pinch salt (chocolate always benefits from salt)
    200 g caster sugar
    more chocolate for grating over the top, if you like that
        sort of thing

Preheat oven to 180°C/Gas Mark 4. Grease a 20 cm springform tin and line the bottom with baking parchment.

Pour coffee and brandy over the top of your chocolate, broken up in a heatproof bowl, and melt the lot together, either in the microwave or over a pan of simmering water, until it's smooth and glossy. Set aside to cool.

Beat the egg yolks and the butter together until they're creamy, then add the cooled chocolate mix and beat again. In another, *very clean* bowl, whisk the egg whites and salt to soft peaks, then add the sugar, bit by bit, beating with each addition, until it makes a lovely glossy meringue.

Fold the meringue, about a third at a time, into the chocolate mix, then spoon it all into the springform tin and level it out. Bake for about 40 minutes. What you want is a crispy, slightly cracked top, and a middle that's still soft but not actually liquid.

Turn the oven off and leave the cake inside to finish cooking in the diminishing heat. It should be done in about an hour. Take out and leave to cool completely, then turn out by running a knife round the side of the tin, taking off the walls. Either turn it upside-down on to a plate if you like a crunchy bottom, or slide it on to one if you like a crunchy top. Grate chocolate over the top if you think it needs more decoration, but I never bother.

CHOCOLATE CHIP COOKIES

So easy, so delish.

    250 g unsifted flour
    1 tsp baking soda
    pinch salt
    125 g softened butter
    90 g granulated sugar
    90 g firmly packed brown sugar
    1 tsp vanilla extract
    2 eggs
    150 g semi-sweet chocolate chips
    125 g chopped nuts

Preheat the oven to 190°C/Gas Mark 5. In a small bowl, combine flour, baking soda and salt; set aside. In a large bowl, combine butter, sugars and vanilla; beat until creamy. Beat in eggs. Gradually add flour mixture; mix well. Stir in chocolate chips and nuts. Chill the mix for an hour or so if you have the time, then form into little cookies on a baking sheet. Bake for 8 to 10 minutes.

CHOCOLATE MOUSSE

♡

I am unashamed to relate that the first time I made this and it came out perfectly I was INCREDIBLY excited. I had a guest over who's a wonderful cook so I had to pretend I totally knew it was going to be fine all along. Anyway, I have made it a few times since and it seems pretty failsafe and impressive; you just need a little time. You can also add flavouring to it if you like – Grand Marnier is delicious.

25 g butter
200 g chocolate, half milk, half dark
240 ml water
3 egg yolks
25 g caster sugar
200 g whipped cream

Melt the butter and chocolate with 60ml of water (I do this *very slowly and carefully* in the microwave, checking every 10 seconds, but you can use a bain-marie if you'd rather). Whisk the egg yolks, sugar and the rest of the water over a low heat, and whip the cream if it isn't already. Combine all the ingredients and chill for 3–4 hours in fridge.

CHERRY RIPE

♡

My husband is from New Zealand, where this is a national treasure of a chocolate bar, so I re-created it for Anzac Day and it worked very well. Well, I think it worked well; the entire tray was gone by the time I turned round ... This kind of treat that chops up into pieces is great for parties/school fetes etc.

175 g self-raising flour
2 tsp cocoa powder
100 g caster sugar
½ tsp baking powder
100 g butter
50 ml milk
600 g glacé cherries
125 g condensed milk
150 g desiccated coconut
1 tsp vanilla extract
150 g dark chocolate

Preheat oven to 180°C/Gas Mark 4. Butter and line square pan.

Mix together flour, cocoa, sugar, baking powder, butter and milk, and bake for 15–20 minutes. Whiz together cherries, condensed milk, coconut and vanilla, and spread on cooled base. Top with melted dark chocolate, leave to set *if possible*.

MALTESER CAKE

♡

The great thing about this really simple cake is that it
looks much more beautiful and finished than it actually is.
It is a BIG cake, I shall tell you now, for big occasions, and
works very well for birthdays.

250 g sifted self-raising flour
150 g sifted caster sugar
150 g softened butter
4 eggs
50 g cocoa powder
125 ml sour cream
tsp baking powder
pinch salt
½ tsp vanilla essence

For the icing:

500 g caster sugar
100 g cocoa powder
250 g butter
½ tsp vanilla essence
milk if the mixture gets too stiff, to water it down.
Maltesers, to decorate

Preheat oven to 180°C/Gas Mark 4. Grease and line two
(same-sized) cake tins.

Mix cake ingredients till nice and smooth. Bake for
20–30 minutes, or till a toothpick comes out dry.

Beat together the icing ingredients. Ice the cooled cake between the sandwich layers and all over the top.

Then take four bags of Maltesers (actually, scratch that, buy five, just in case you eat one), and start decorating. Even a total klutz like me can make lovely straight lines from Maltesers, and once it's done it looks like something out of a fancy patisserie shop window. Hurrah!

PECAN AND CHOCOLATE PLAIT

♡

I am so thrilled that John Whaite, the winner of *The Great British Bake Off 2012* (although frankly they were all terrific – I dressed my five-year-old up as James Morton for Halloween), has granted us permission to use this recipe – it's from his cookbook called *John Whaite Bakes ... Recipes for Every Day and Every Mood* (25th April 2013, Headline Publishing Group). *The Great British Bake Off* is a show I love dearly and watch religiously. I do bake some of their things from it (the ones that aren't too tricky – I'm scared of the heaven and hell cake), and like any right-thinking person, I worship Mary Berry as the queen she so clearly is.

This plait is splendid, delicious and slightly unusual, so just the thing for something different.

Makes 1 x 14inch Plait

500g puff pastry, shop bought, all butter puff
Flour for dusting
3 slices thick white bread
200g pecans
75g unsalted butter
150g light muscovado sugar
75g milk chocolate chips
1 egg for glazing
1tbsp icing sugar for dusting

Equipment
Food processor

Preheat the oven to 200°C/gas mark 6. Flour the workstation and roll the pastry out into a rectangle of 10x14 inches. Place the pastry onto a baking sheet, lined with a piece of baking paper – this will make it easier to plait the pastry later, without having to then transfer it onto the baking sheet. Set aside for later.

To make the filling, first blitz the bread in the food processor until you have fine breadcrumbs. Place these into a large mixing bowl, and then place the pecans into the processor, and blitz until they too are finely chopped. Place these into the bowl with the breadcrumbs.

Put the butter and sugar into the processor and blitz together until the butter is evenly dispersed into the sugar. Add the breadcrumbs, pecans and milk, and process into a sticky mass. It should have the consistency of a thick pudding batter.

Place the pastry in front of you, still sitting on the baking sheet. Have the pastry so that one of the shorter edges is facing you – so the pastry sheet is portrait rather than landscape. Take the filling and place it in a sausage down the very centre of the pastry. You must leave about 4 inches of uncovered pastry on either side of the sausage. When you have placed all of the filling onto the pastry, sprinkle the chocolate chips onto the filling, and gently press them into it, trying not to spread the filling out though.

Take a sharp knife or pizza wheel, and slice the pastry at either side of the filling into 1cm flaps, cutting away from the filling. So you should see before you a line of filling, with lots of little pastry flaps coming out of it. Rather like a centipede, though a very tasty centipede.

Beat the egg and glaze the edges of the flaps with it, either using a pastry brush or your finger. To make the plait, take the first flap from one side – the first being the flap furthest away from you – and fold it over the filling on a very slight diagonal so that it meets the second flap on the other side. You may need to stretch the flap ever so slightly to get it over the filling. Press the flap gently into position so that it doesn't spring back. Repeat this with the first flap on the other side, and then repeat with the second flaps, third flaps, fourth flaps etc, until all the flaps of pastry are tightly plaited around the filling. The ends of the plait will be open and you will be able to see the filling, so what I do, is take a teaspoon and scrape a little of the filling out and then squeeze the ends of the pastry together to seal it. This just ensures that the filling doesn't leak out and make a right old mess whilst cooking.

Glaze the whole plait with the remaining egg and then place into the oven. Bake for 30–35 minutes, or until the plait is puffed and golden. Remove from the oven and sift over a tablespoon of icing sugar. Serve hot or cold.

MEET ME AT THE CUPCAKE CAFÉ

Jenny Colgan

Come and meet Issy Randall, proud owner of The Cupcake Café.

Issy Randall can bake. No, more than that – Issy can create
stunning, mouth-wateringly divine cakes. After a childhood spent
in her beloved Grampa Joe's bakery, she has undoubtedly
inherited his talent.

When she's made redundant from her safe but dull City job, Issy
decides to seize the moment. Armed with recipes from Grampa,
and with her best friends and local bank manager fighting her
corner, The Cupcake Café opens its doors. But Issy has absolutely
no idea what she's let herself in for. It will take all her courage –
and confectionery – to avert disaster . . .

'Sheer indulgence from start to finish'
Sophie Kinsella

978-0-7515-4449-7

CHRISTMAS AT THE CUPCAKE CAFÉ

Jenny Colgan

Join Issy, Austin, Pearl and Caroline as they prepare for a
very special Christmas . . .

Issy Randall, proud owner of the Cupcake Café, is in love
and couldn't be happier. Her new business is thriving and she
is surrounded by close friends, even if her cupcake colleagues
Pearl and Caroline don't seem quite as upbeat about the upcoming
season of snow and merriment. But when her boyfriend Austin is
scouted for a possible move to New York, Issy is forced to face
up to the prospect of a long-distance romance. And when the
Christmas rush at the café – with its increased demand for
her delectable creations – begins to take its toll,
Issy has to decide what she holds most dear.

This December, Issy will have to rely on all her reserves
of courage, good nature and cinnamon to make
sure everyone has a merry Christmas,
one way or another . . .

'Light and fun read for the sweet-toothed, with a
clutch of recipes as the icing on top'
Choice

978-0-7515-4922-5

WELCOME TO ROSIE HOPKINS' SWEETSHOP OF DREAMS

Jenny Colgan

Were you a sherbet lemon or chocolate lime fan? Penny chews or
hard-boiled sweeties (you do get more for your money that way)?
The jangle of your pocket money ... the rustle of the
pink and green striped paper bag ...

Rosie Hopkins thinks leaving her busy London life, and her
boyfriend Gerard, to sort out her elderly Aunt Lilian's
sweetshop in a small country village is going
to be dull. Boy, is she wrong.

Lilian Hopkins has spent her life running Lipton's sweetshop,
through wartime and family feuds. As she struggles with the
idea that it might finally be the time to settle up, she also
wrestles with the secret history hidden behind the
jars of beautifully coloured sweets.

'This funny, sweet story is Jenny Colgan at her
absolute best'
Heat

978-0-7515-4454-1

WEST END GIRLS

Jenny Colgan

The streets of London are paved with gold ... allegedly.

They may be twin sisters, but Lizzie and Penny Berry are complete opposites – Penny is blonde, thin and outrageous; Lizzie quiet, thoughtful and definitely not thin. The one trait they do share is a desire to DO something with their lives and, as far as they're concerned, the place to get noticed is London.

Out of the blue they discover they have a grandmother living in Chelsea – and when she has to go into hospital, they find themselves flat-sitting on the King's Road. But, as they discover, it's not as easy to become It Girls as they'd imagined, and West End Boys aren't at all like Hugh Grant ...

'A brilliant novel from the mistress of chick-lit'
Eve

978-0-7515-4332-2

OPERATION SUNSHINE

Jenny Colgan

Evie needs a good holiday. Not just because she's been working all hours in her job, but also because every holiday she has ever been on has involved sunburn, arguments and projectile vomiting – sometimes all three at once. Why can't she have a normal holiday, like other people seem to have – some sun, sand, sea and (hopefully) sex?

So when her employers invite her to attend a conference with them in the South of France, she can't believe her luck. It's certainly going to be the holiday of a lifetime – but not quite in the way Evie imagines!

'Colgan at her warm, down-to-earth best'
Cosmopolitan

978-0-7515-3762-8

DIAMONDS ARE A GIRL'S BEST FRIEND

Jenny Colgan

Sophie Chesterton has been living the high life of glamorous
parties, men and new clothes, never thinking about tomorrow.
But after one shocking evening, she comes back down to earth with
the cruellest of bumps. Facing up to life in the real world for the
first time, Sophie quickly realises that when you've hit
rock bottom, the only way is up.

Join her as she starts life all over again: from cleaning toilets
for a living to the joys of bring-your-own-booze parties;
from squeezing out that last piece of lip gloss from
the tube to bargaining with bus drivers.

For anyone who's ever been scared of losing it all, this book is here
to show you money can't buy you love, and best friends are so
much more fun than diamonds ...

'Jenny Colgan always writes an unputdownable,
page-turning bestseller – she's the
queen of modern chick-lit'
Louise Bagshawe

978-0-7515-4031-4

THE GOOD, THE BAD AND THE DUMPED

Jenny Colgan

Now, you obviously, would never, ever look up your exes on
Facebook. Nooo. And even if you did, you most certainly
wouldn't run off trying to track them down, risking
your job, family and happiness in the process.
Posy Fairweather, on the other hand . . .

Posy is delighted when Matt proposes – on top of a mountain,
in a gale, in full-on romantic mode. But a few days later disaster
strikes: he backs out of the engagement. Crushed and humiliated,
Posy starts thinking. Why has her love life always ended
in total disaster? Determined to discover how she got to
this point, Posy resolves to get online and track
down her exes. Can she learn from past mistakes?
And what if she has let Mr Right slip through
her fingers on the way?

'A Jenny Colgan novel is as essential for a week in
the sun as Alka Seltzer, aftersun and far too
many pairs of sandals'
Heat

978 0-7515-4030-7

Keep in touch with

Jenny

www.jennycolgan.com

For more information on all Jenny's books, latest news and mouth-watering recipes

 Search 'Jenny Colgan Books'

@jennycolgan

LOVE TO READ?

Sign up for early sneak peeks of our
hot new books, exclusive competitions and more
www.littlebrownbooks.net/newsletters